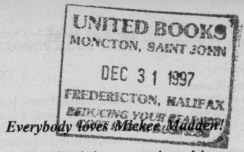
Everybody loves Mickee Madden!

Everlastin' *was a triumph!*

Mickee Madden's *Everlastin'* blazed a trail across America's bestseller lists. Readers everywhere thrilled to the story of Lachlan Baird and Beth Staples, and a house where dreams can come true! Now, Mickee Madden is back, and so are Lachlan and Beth, in a triumphant story of magic, miracles, and love!

Dusk Before Dawn *is even better!*

When Scotsman Roan Ingliss came to Baird house, he had a score to settle with its owner—a 150-year-old ghost. He never expected to be stranded there. And he certainly never expected to play knight in shining armor to a thoroughly modern American woman and her three completely out-of-control young nephews. It was the answer to some of his fondest dreams—and some of his crazier nightmares. Roan had once given up all hope of love, and any expectation of happiness. But sometimes fate takes a hand even when a man's not ready, life hits hardest where a man is least expecting it—and sometimes dreams do come true.

*Turn the page and let Mickee Madden
show you ...*

PUT SOME FANTASY IN YOUR LIFE—
FANTASTIC ROMANCES FROM PINNACLE

HE'D NEVER FELT
ANYTHING LIKE THIS . . .

"I have a question. You used a word this morning that I can't get out of my head," Laura asked.

"Wha' word?" Roan pulled two cups from the cabinet and started making tea.

"You said 'pree'd' I was asking to be pree'd. What does that word mean?"

Warmth spread across Roan's face as he struggled not to grin. He put the teapot down and closed the short distance between them. "Define it, eh? Hmmm. I guess showin' beats the bloody hell out o' tellin'."

Laura had no idea what was coming. Swiftly, as if to completely take her unawares, he lowered his head and lightly kissed her. A spasm of shock rooted her in place, then she jumped back and stared at his amused expression as if he'd lost his mind.

"That's a verra wee pree," he said. "When a Scotsmon put's his blood's worth inta it, the word takes on all kinds o' definitions."

She could only stare at him.

Roan released a thready breath. Gripping her arms, he hesitantly drew her against him. Immediately he felt her warmth radiate into him.

"There's something better than tea ta take the chill out o' a mon," he said.

"Is there?" she breathed.

Releasing her, he said, "Scotch. Would you mind fetchin' a bottle?"

"Good night, Roan Ingliss." Laura stalked out of the kitchen.

Roan laughed. Then laughed again. He looked at the door she'd passed through. One kiss, and the chill of the day had completely left him. He was almost afraid to imagine what making love to the woman could do for him . . .

MICKEE MADDEN

DUSK BEFORE DAWN

PINNACLE BOOKS
KENSINGTON PUBLISHING CORP.

PINNACLE BOOKS are published by

Kensington Publishing Corp.
850 Third Avenue
New York, NY 10022

Pinnacle and the P logo Reg. U.S. Pat. & TM Off.

First Pinnacle Printing: March, 1996

Printed in the United States of America

10 9 8 7 6 5 4 3 2 1

Dedicated to my husband, Steve; my brother Matt and his wife Grace; their boys, Eric, Kahl, and Albie; Danny duCille; Cindy, Eugenia, and Denise.

Special thanks to James Crawford, whose marvelous hospitality at Culgruff House in Crossmichael, made Scotland a wee mair magical!

Glossary

'afore/before
a'/at
abou'/about
ain/own
an'/and
aneuch/enough
aught/anything
auld/old
brither/brother
cauld/cold
claith/cloth
deil/devil
didna/didn't
dinna/don't
doon/down
e'er/ever
e'ery/every
efter/after
faither/father
gae/go
guid/good

haud/hold
het/hot
hoor/hour
i'/it
ither/other
ma/my
mair/more
mairrit/married
maist/most
mak/make
mither/mother
mon/man
na/no
no'/not
nocht/nothing
o'/of
o'er/over
oop/up
oor/our
ou'/out
sa/so

sarry/sorry
shartly/shortly
sud/should
ta/to
tae/too
tak/take
teuk/took
tha'/that
thegither/together
thin'/thing
tis/it's
verra/very
wad/would
wadna/wouldn't
wark/work
warld/world
weel/well
whan/when
wi'/with
winna/won't
yer/your

One

Beyond the fogged windshield of the Volvo, thick, downy snowflakes mocked the wipers' efforts to brush them aside. Not a star shone in the pale gray awning of the night sky. The glistening land was vast and empty, feeding Laura Bennett's desperate need to find shelter. Despite the three young boys carrying on in the back seat, never had she been so cold, or so lonely. The storm was just another obstacle. One more hardship, and she wasn't sure how much more she could endure.

Her fingers gripped the steering wheel more tightly as she leaned and squinted to see beyond the clouded windshield. A tension headache thundered at her temples and painfully tightened the skin across her brow. An invisible vise squeezed the back of her neck. Every sound, every jostling movement of the car, seemed a personal assault on her raw nerves.

"Boys, *please!*" she groaned.

To her further dismay, her entreaty increased the noise. Three-year-old Alby's whining rose a full octave. His sneakered feet repeatedly kicked at the back of her seat. The argument between his five- and seven-year-old brothers also escalated, their voices slicing through her sensitized skull.

Her teeth clenched. She testily rubbed the side of her

hand on the windshield, but the cleared spot began to fog up almost immediately.

"Damn," she muttered, rolling her side window down another two inches.

"Hey! I'm cold!" Kevin shouted.

"It can't be helped." Laura tried unsuccessfully to force herself to relax. "I can't see anything in front of us."

"Can't drive, park it."

"Kevin . . ." Laura took a moment to calm her anger. In the past three days, she'd learned that the boys weren't intimidated by adults. In fact, much to her chagrin, nothing fazed her nephews. Her inexperience with children was in part to blame.

"You're not setting a very good example for your brothers," she went on, hoping to tap into Kevin's conscience. "Now, please settle down. My nerves are shot."

Folding his arms across the back of the front seat, the seven-year-old demanded, "Roll up the window."

Laura glanced in the rear-view mirror to see Kevin smugly staring back at her. "The defroster isn't wor—"

"Roll it up!"

Alby released a wail. Covering his ears, five-year-old Kahl slammed the soles of his cowboy boots against the back of the tattered, red-vinyl front seat.

"Stop it!" Laura warned, her patience a long-forgotten thing. "Sit back and stop—"

"You're on the wrong side, you dummy!" Kevin cried. "Get over!"

Seemingly from out of nowhere, bright headlights bore down on the Volvo. Instinctively, Laura yanked the steering wheel to the right. Kevin released a shrill, "No!" and she swerved to the left. The boys cried out, then became silent momentarily when the tires skidded on ruts of iced-over

snow. By some miracle, the other car passed them unevent-
fully. Laura's stomach heaved. Gulping back a rise of burning liquid, she ground the stick shift into second and tapped
the brake.

"You idiot!"

Laura winced, but decided it wasn't worth scolding Kahl
for his harsh outburst. How could she expect the boys to
respect her decisions, when each one had landed them in
one predicament after another? As she slowed the car to a
crawl, she fought back a sudden urge to cry. All she needed
now was to break down in front of the little hellions and
let them know just how much they were getting to her!

She knew *nothing* about children. The thought of having
her own child had never intruded upon her neatly organized
life.

Rolling down the right rear passenger window, Kevin
poked out his head.

"Kevin!"

He grimaced, but ignored his aunt.

"Dammit, Kevin!" Laura gripped the steering wheel so
tightly, pain shot through her wrists. "If I stop this car, I
swear I'm going to throttle you! *Roll up that window!*"

"I see a *biiig* house." He pointed. "Up on that hill. See
it?"

Laura couldn't see anything but a hazy stretch of road.

"Up there!" Kevin said impatiently, glowering at his
aunt. "Maybe they got a phone."

"I gotta take a slash," Kahl announced.

Distracted, she asked, "What?"

"A slash! I gotta *peeee!*"

Laura glanced down at the dimly lit gauges on the front
of the dashboard. The fuel needle was leaning close to the
E, and the engine light was blinking.

"Are we gonna stop or what?" Kahl grumbled. "I'm hungry."

"Turn right!" Kevin ordered. *"Now!"*

Exhaustion and sheer frustration prompted her to turn the wheel sharply. For several maddening seconds, the vehicle bounced and skidded over iced ruts. Then the tires began to spin on a sudden incline.

Numbly, Laura shifted into first gear. Her green eyes strained to see more clearly what lay ahead within the terrible pale grayness. The world had somehow vanished. Tears brimmed her eyes. One tear escaped down her pale cheek.

"I can't see a damn thing," she said in a barely audible voice.

From the corner of her left eye, she spied a soft, green luminance. She turned her head. Disbelief wrapped its icy fingers about her heart and squeezed.

Up on the hill, green mist bathed an enormous structure, lending it a surreal appearance. For several seconds, she thought she saw the house glide—*rush*—toward her. She felt herself tunneled in darkness, unable to focus on anything but the looming house. Fear threatened to overwhelm her until, suddenly, she could see nothing but the wintery landscape.

The incline got steeper.

Thrown back into the reality of her situation, Laura feared the Volvo would lose all power. Panicked at the prospect of the car rolling backward, she depressed the gas pedal and popped the clutch, hoping for nothing more than to crest the hill. The car surged forward. Cries rang out behind her as the vehicle slid to one side. Grinding the stick shift out of first and into neutral, she slammed on the brake, but it was too late to stop the car from nose-diving into a ravine.

Impact with a tall oak pitched her into the steering wheel. Pain erupted through every part of her body. From seemingly far away, she could hear her nephews' whimpers, but she was steadily withdrawing from consciousness.

"Hold on."

Laura's vanishing consciousness locked onto an omnipresent female voice.

Help had arrived.

The left rear door opened and slammed shut. Laura struggled to fully revive herself. The boys were screaming. Their diminishing voices indicated that they were moving away from the vehicle.

"Boys," she croaked, trying to push away from the wheel and sit up.

"Lachlan's with them. Try to remain still. Help is coming. I promise, everything will be all right."

Help was coming.

Laura felt a compelling need to cry, but she was too disoriented to risk weakening herself with such release.

Jolting movement intensified her pain, tempting her to relax into a void of unconsciousness. She wanted to let go of the pain, of the long days of frustration, and her unwanted new responsibilities. Let it *all* go.

Another voice, harsh and impatient, and marked by a thick Scottish burr, sliced through the riotous agony in her skull.

"The boys," she whispered.

Then blessed, forgiving darkness embraced her.

"Wha' the bloody hell is wrong wi' you!"

The strident tone forced her up from oblivion. Everything hurt. She didn't want to open her eyes. Her lids were so heavy, she knew it would be agony to lift them.

"Leave him alone!"

Kevin's shrill voice jerked her to full consciousness.

"I'll paddle his backside till he can't walk! Give me those, you little bugger!"

Despite the pain racking her body, she managed to draw herself up into a sitting position. She became aware that she was in a large bed, in a bedroom lit only by a fire in a hearth, halfway across the room. A short distance away from the fireplace, a man was unsuccessfully trying to take something from Alby's clenched hands.

"Leave him alone!" Kevin shouted, again slugging the crouching man in the arm.

Fighting back a strong desire to lie back down and close her eyes, Laura got onto her hands and knees and weakly crawled to the foot of the bed. Her stomach churned in warning. She remained perfectly still, watching in dazed bewilderment as the oldest boy pummeled the stranger with his fists.

"Dammi', laddie!"

"What are you doing to them?"

Although her words had emerged at little more than a whisper, they had the impact of a boom. Four pairs of eyes turned in her direction. Then the man swooped up Alby beneath an arm, hauled him to the bed, and dropped him alongside Laura.

"I'll thank you ta tak the matches away from him," he growled down at her, an accusing finger aimed at the boy who was kicking fiercely up at him. "He's already tried ta set two fires in this room!"

Laura winced. Combined with her lightheadedness was the burgeoning threat of her stomach heaving.

"Please," she whimpered.

"Get him away!" shouted Kahl, stalking toward the stranger with fists drawn. "He's been picking on us!"

"Pickin' on *you!*" the man laughed without mirth.

"Give me the matches," Laura said to Alby, a shaky hand held out.

"No!"

"Alby . . ."

Impatiently, the stranger pried the wooden matches from Alby's fingers. "A fine pyromaniac you have here," he said to Laura, his broad chest heaving in anger as he straightened and scowled down at her.

Forcing herself to leave the bed, Laura held onto the brass arch at the foot, and looked to where the two older boys stood an arm's length away. "Kevin, I'm asking you to *please* watch your brothers while I talk to this . . . man."

"He lies," Kevin clipped, the firelight casting one half of his features in stark relief. "Don't listen ta him."

"I-I won't. I . . . just need to talk to him." She gulped back a rise of burning liquid in her throat. "Can I-I trust you to watch after your brothers for a little while?"

Petulantly, Kevin shrugged. "Yeah. We're sleepy, anyway."

"Thank you."

At the same instant she turned to face the stranger, the contents of her stomach won the fight for liberation. It happened so quickly, her hand didn't make it up in time to stop the flow. A moment later, swaying on her feet, she could only gape at the mess on the front of the man's sweater. No thoughts intruded upon her stupor for several seconds, not until she registered the shocked incredulity enlarging his eyes.

I don't believe this, she thought, shriveling within herself.

"Weel . . . leave i' ta me ta be standin' in the wrong place a' the wrong time, eh?"

Laura timorously met his gaze again. Although she was staring into his face, she was oblivious to everything but the glint in his eyes. The pale grayness of total unconsciousness would have been welcome right about now. The darkness. A hole in the ground in which she could hide away and pretend she'd never set foot on this earth. But it was becoming ever more apparent that fate wasn't yet through testing her ability to endure.

Donning a guarded expression, he abruptly took her by the arm and marched her across the room. Stopping at an open door, he looked back at the boys and scowled a silent warning, then ushered her into a dark room. She stood passively waiting, inwardly questioning her lack of fear in trusting this stranger.

A light came on to her right. With calm she could not begin to rationalize, she watched as he adjusted a brass key on a gas fixture alongside an oval mirror above a sink.

"You've a nasty crack on yer head, but na concussion as far as I can tell." Easing his sweater off over his head, he tossed it into a claw-foot tub. "Yer're mair rattled than anythin', I think."

He looked down at her. The soft lighting lent his light brown irises an amber hue. "But then I'm no' a doctor, am I?"

"I wouldn't know," she murmured, her gaze taking in the powerful width of his naked barrel chest and bulging biceps. Suddenly, she found herself overwhelmed by his towering height. The top of her head barely reached his dimpled chin. If she were forced to defend herself, she was afraid the best she could do was bruise his ego.

Even that was questionable.

"Are you goin' ta toss yer innards again?"

Crimson stained her cheeks. "I'm sorry. I-I'll wash your sweater."

"I'd worry abou' maself if I were you. Are you feelin' jaggy?"

Unbidden, her gaze riveted on his sensuous mouth. A cottony sensuality blanketed her brain "Wh-what?"

"Light in the head."

"No. Just a little wobbly."

A skeptical gleam softened his eyes, and he arched a thick eyebrow. "Wobbly, eh? I'll go doonstairs an' fix you somethin' ta—"

"No food!" she gasped, swaying on her feet.

"Aye, na food." Roan scowled, his gaze raking her from head to toe. "A cup o' tea, then?"

"Thank you."

"Whan yer're through cleanin' oop, gae left in the hall an' doon the stairs. I'll be waitin' in the room across the foyer ta the right. The door'll be open."

"Thank you, Mr. . . ."

"Roan. Roan Ingliss."

"Laura . . . Bennett."

"I'll be waitin', Laura."

He was about to cross the threshold when her cold tone arrested him.

"It's Ms. Bennett."

His head turned. The look of dark annoyance he delivered sent a chill along Laura's spine.

"There's an unwritten practice here . . . *Miss* Bennett, tha' whan a womon spews on a mon, he can call her anythin' the hell he pleases."

Laura stiffened. For an indefinite time, they stared at

each other, in some sort of visual war. Then he disappeared into the bedroom, leaving her to brace her hands against the sink, and gingerly lower her head.

God give me strength, she mutely whimpered.

Whatever the man's faults, however provoking his attitude, she had to hold back her temper. He was the only likely candidate to help her and the boys get to Edinburgh.

Glancing into the bathtub, she grimaced.

Roan Ingliss obviously wasn't thrilled about his uninvited guests. If there was ever a time when she needed to utilize her looks—it was now. Appeal to the man's compassionate side—if he had one. Find the right chord to ring his heartstrings. Men seemed to respond protectively to tiny, green-eyed blondes—maybe Roan was susceptible.

She released a sigh of disgust as she went down on her knees in front of the tub. Draping her arms over the rounded porcelain edge, she laid her brow against the cold smooth surface.

Never in her life had she resorted to feminine wiles to obtain anything she'd wanted. Not in her personal or professional existence. But then, she'd never been stuck in a foreign land before, and with dubious custody of three wild boys.

"Desperate measures for desperate times," she murmured, turning on the taps to a desired temperature. With unsteady movements, she began to rinse off the matter clinging to Roan's plain, dark green sweater. She refused to think about regurgitating on her grudging host. Unfortunate for Mr. Ingliss, but she felt immensely better for having unburdened her stomach. It had been just another example of her having lost control since landing in London earlier in the week.

Now, if only the headache would go away. Was that asking too damn much?

A breeze moved through the bathroom and passed through her. Laura gasped. The cold, which had touched her for but a moment, branded itself in her memory.

Her eyes opened as wide as saucers. She glanced about the suddenly too-close quarters and wondered if she were losing her mind, for she was positive she could feel a presence in the room with her. Then it dawned on her that the headache had mysteriously vanished.

"Hello?"

A nervous chuckle rattled in her dry and scratchy throat.

"I must be hallucinating."

The presence melted away from her awareness. A shudder coursed through her as she stood poised, with air trapped in her lungs while she waited for something more to happen. After seconds ticked by and nothing occurred, she sank to her buttocks and braced her back against the side of the tub.

Tears welled up in her eyes.

Laura Bennett, senior designer for Holly Coe Cosmetics, Inc., was not one to easily lose touch with reality. And yet, the past five days had badly shaken her convictions about herself. If she could convince herself a good cry would lessen her misery, she would weep a river.

Ha!

All she would likely get, was another headache.

"Sa where the bloody hell are you, Lannie, you swineheart!"

Roan continued to pace beneath a circular array of swords mounted on one parlor wall.

"I didn't bargain for this, I can tell you! Where are you? Laughin' off yer fool head, na doubt!"

He sharply looked over his shoulder. His heated gaze targeted a large portrait hanging over a Victorian marble mantel. A snort escaped him, then, turning on a heel, he walked to the stoked hearth and glowered at the heart-shaped face of the woman in the painting.

"Beth, give me a hand, here. I know yer're still around. You brought me here ta help. Weel, I did. Now, dammi', I wad like ta return ta Aggie, if you *please*."

A sigh of frustration heaved his powerful chest. "The wind's pickin' oop. I wasn't plannin' on gettin' stuck here. No' even for you."

Hooking his thumbs onto the waistband of his trousers, he deeply sighed. "Beth, lass, I don't want the responsibility o' a *spunkie* Yank an' her laddies. I've no' the patience ta put maself ou' for strangers. I've ma ain life ta worry abou'."

Something compelled him to look to his right. His heart rose into his throat when he found himself staring into a sea of fiery green eyes. An invisible fist slammed into his gut. The skin on his arms and nape tingled uncomfortably.

"How long have you been standin' there?"

Laura released the crystal doorknob and advanced into the room. Pale, her eyes seeming too large for her gamin features, she stopped within an arm's length of her host.

"Long enough." She spared the portrait a glance before spearing Roan's eyes with a look of unquestionable hostility. Then her gaze swept over him, and her right eyebrow haughtily arched. Snug, dark brown trousers accentuated his narrow hips and muscular thighs. Dingy white wool socks covered his feet. In place of the sweater she'd soiled, a dark purple and blue plaid lap blanket lay draped over his otherwise bare shoulders.

Placing his balled hands on his hips, he further exposed

the pale, curly blond hair matting his chest to his collarbones.

A pulse drummed at Laura's temples. Her skin twitched. "For the record, Mr. Ingliss, I didn't deliberately drive onto this property to have a wreck. I lost control of the car . . . which, considering the condition of the roads, is quite understandable. At least it would be *understandable* to a *reasonable* person!"

"Save yer temper for the laird o' this . . ." Roan offered a snide, lopsided grin. ". . . house."

"You're not the owner?"

Shaking his head, he folded his arms across his chest. "There's na consanguinity between an Ingliss an' a Baird."

The news took her aback, but she nonetheless kept her spine stiff. "When do you expect the owner to return?"

"He's somewhere abou'," he replied, casting the room a scornful glower.

Somewhere about? Laura narrowed a fuming look on him. He talked to a damn portrait more kindly than he spoke to her! "Look . . . I'm grateful for what you've done—"

"Na!" Roan exclaimed with a flag of a hand. Turning, he went to a pink and gold embroidered settee positioned upon an enormous red and blue Persian rug, and seated himself. "I don't want gratitude, *Miss* Bennett. I responded ta the heat o' the moment. Nothin' mair."

"Have you always been such an ass, or is this little performance being staged strictly for *my* benefit?"

Roan was at first shocked by her words, then threw back his head and released a booming laugh. When he looked at her again, his bearish countenance had softened. A gleam of mischief brightened his eyes beneath the arched precipices of his eyebrows. " 'Tis been a long day, *Miss* Bennett. Forgive ma ill mood."

"Don't talk to me about long days, *Mr.* Ingliss," Laura said through clenched teeth. "My first and *last* visit to Great Britain has been nothing short of a nightmare. So, please . . ." She affected a sickeningly sweet smile. ". . . *please* forgive *my* ill mood."

"Tea, *Miss* Bennett?"

"No thank you, *Mr.* Ingliss. What I really need is a telephone."

Raking a slow, measuring look over her, Roan gave a shake of his head. "Na phone. Na electricity."

Laura crossed half the distance to the marble coffee table in front of the settee. "You can't be serious!"

"Aye, lass." His gaze lifted to the portrait. "No' long ago, a Yank abou' yer ain age came ta this bloody place. She died here. Whan the house is verra, verra still, you can feel her presence—"

"Oh, shut up! I don't believe in ghosts."

His unsettling gaze searched her features. "Yer caur's beyond repair. An' if the howlin' o' the wind is any indication, the storm's worsenin'. I wad say a guid part o' yer vacation is goin' ta be spent wi'in these walls."

"Why are you trying to frighten me?"

"I doubt the boogie mon could frighten you, *Miss* Bennett. But you see, I know this house, an' the powers tha' control i'. Auld Lannie is undoubtedly derivin' some perverse pleasure in burdenin' me wi' you an' the laddies."

"Burdening *you!*"

Laura hastened to the side of the settee, her hands balled at her sides. Bright splotches of red stained her cheeks. The wild disarray of her short, curly hair, lent her a look of almost comical madness. "I need to get to Edinburgh."

Roan's eyes rolled up to cast her an amused look. "Be serious. I'm no' abou' ta risk ma life ou' in this storm."

"Then who can I contact who *would* be willing to help me?"

Shifting his gaze to the coffee table, he ran his hands up and down his face. "I've na idea."

"I don't believe you."

Releasing a short burst of breath, he got to his feet and faced her. His eyebrows drew down in an angry scowl as he explained, "Believe this, lass: if i' were in ma power ta send you an' yer sons on yer way, you'd've been gone hoors ago."

"They're my *nephews*."

"Ma condolences," he said. Seating himself, he propped his feet atop the coffee table, one ankle crossing the other. Despite his determination to ignore the twitching of his skin, he crossed his arms against his chest and rubbed the irritating sensation moving along his flesh.

Laura gulped past the tightness in her throat. It was obvious the direct approach wasn't going to work. Taking a deep, fortifying breath, she said in her most beguiling tone, "I need help. Please, Mr. Ingliss, you *must* help me."

His eyes closed and he lowered his head. Laura stared down at him, using all her willpower not to succumb to the tears pressing at the back of her eyes. This arrogant stranger had no idea how hard it was for her to ask help of anyone. But she was frightened, not of the woman who supposedly haunted this house, but of what to do about the three lively spirits asleep on the second floor.

This man kept his heartstrings well secreted from outsiders, but she had to find them, even if it meant groveling.

"My sister-in-law died giving birth to Alby," she blurted, and rushed on, "Jack, my brother, remarried a little over a year ago; a nineteen-year-old British girl named Carrie Wilks. Eleven months ago, Jack suffered a stroke and died within a few days."

Dipping her head to one side, she looked to see if she'd spurred the slightest reaction in him. Nothing.

"He was thirty-seven," she added, but to her chagrin, it came out sounding like a cold-hearted afterthought.

Her heart slowly rose into her throat. His silence was a blaring indication that he wasn't going to make this easy.

"We weren't a close family," she went on, a genuine tremor in her tone. "I . . . didn't even come to England to attend his funeral. Neither did my parents. They couldn't bring themselves to interrupt their Hawaiian vacation, and I was . . . engrossed in a project at work."

Ahh. His shoulders jerked. He was actually listening.

"Two weeks ago, Carrie called. I'd never spoken to her before that day. She was crying, pleading with me to come for a visit. She claimed the boys were having a rough time without their father, and said she believed a visit from their aunt would make a world of difference. For the first time, I realized I knew nothing about the boys."

What was he thinking? she wondered, moistening her lower lip with the tip of her tongue.

"Jack had never sent pictures. All I'd ever gotten was a call after each of them was born."

A dispassionate, "Charmin'," was all Roan said.

Me or Jack? Is it just my imagination, or is he taking this all out of context?

An edge of perplexity entered her tone, as she continued, "I arrived in London six days ago. Carrie and the boys were there to greet me. I remember thinking she didn't look old enough to be married, let alone to pass for a stepmother to three children.

"The first couple of days went relatively well. Oh, the boys proved to be royal hellions, but then I've never really been around children. I just kept telling myself that these were Jack's boys, and that I only had a few days left to be with them. Little did I know at the time, I was psyching myself up to fall into Carrie's trap."

When she fell silent for a time, Roan turned his head and narrowly eyed her. "Wha' kind o' trap?" he asked gruffly, as if driven to satisfy his curiosity.

A tremulous smile quirked at one corner of Laura's pouty lips. At long last he was responding. "She suggested I take the boys out for the day. A picnic at the playground. She even packed our lunch. What a disaster that turned out to be. Kahl took a dive in a brook. Alby vanished for nearly two hours and, while I was searching for him, Kevin heavily peppered all the food. They fought me every inch of the way when I dragged them back to the house. Carrie wasn't there. I just figured she went shopping or visiting."

With a nod of his head, Roan straightened his gaze to the hearth. A muscle ticked along his well-defined jawline.

Laura swallowed a moment's disappointment. Was she losing him again?

"When she didn't return that night, I really began to worry. The following morning, Kevin informed me that she'd packed up her things, and had told the boys that they were going to return to the States with me. I went into shock. Kevin handed me a letter she'd instructed him to give me after she'd left. Basically, it said she refused to raise the boys. She was off with her new boyfriend, and it would be useless for me to try to find her."

"Charmin'."

One more "charmin' " out of him, and I swear I'll . . . I'll . . .

"Things became really complicated when I couldn't find the boys' birth certificates. I took the house apart and couldn't find a one. Then that evening, a large burly man showed up at the door, informing me the house was supposed to have been vacated two days prior. He wouldn't listen to a word of reason. Two men were waiting in his van. The three of them stormed into the house and barely gave me enough time to pack up two bags of clothes for the boys. Then they rudely ushered us out onto the street."

Laura cranked her head to one side to observe Roan's reaction. A flutter of nervous tension moved within her abdomen at the sight of his grimly set mouth.

"Carrie had at least left her car, and the keys in the ignition." She moved to the back of the settee. "What else could I do? It didn't seem very important at the time that I hadn't touched a stick shift in ten years, or that I hadn't a clue how to drive on British roads."

She returned to her former position, absently wringing her hands at his continued silence.

"The sidewalks roll up in St. Ives after five o'clock. I had no idea where I was going. I drove until dusk, then the boys and I slept in the car that night. In the morning, I found a small cafe and checked the phone directory for the closest American Consulate. A waitress was kind enough to highlight the shortest route to Edinburgh on the map I'd purchased. After that, I went to a gas station across the street, and we started out."

Damn you, Ingliss! Do you even have a heart?

"The storm began shortly after we entered Scotland. I located a B & B last night, but when I went to prepay for our rooms, I discovered I didn't have my purse. My money, passport, and return ticket . . . all gone. The last place I remember seeing my purse was at the station, and I don't have the foggiest recollection of which town that was in."

Roan continued to stare across the room. Frustration gnawed unmercifully on Laura's nerves. Her gaze lifted to study a circular display on the far wall, of ancient swords, whose points met in a tight center. The sharp, shining metal of the blades winked at her. For a fleeting moment, she visualized holding one of the razor-sharp edges to his broad throat. Let him squirm—

A feeling of absolute loathing swelled inside her, turning her blood to ice. Shivering, she seated herself on the coffee table alongside his right foot. His disquieting gaze shifted to her face. There was something in his eyes she could not fathom, but it filled her with a sense of foreboding. A shiver of primitive awareness swept through her mind, an instinctual awareness, as yet, she didn't understand. He'd done nothing to her to warrant the gloom moving like a mist through her system. She wasn't afraid of him, but definitely chary, and even that was not the normal wariness she experienced when in a man's company. Something deep inside her craved to touch upon his soul. For a reason totally obscure to her consciousness, she had a burgeoning suspicion that to comprehend the components of his personality, would lead her to understand herself.

Nothing that had happened to her since arriving in Great Britain, had made much sense.

There was no denying he was the most handsome, virile man she'd ever met, but she was level-headed enough to know that a cover—however well designed—was nothing but a means by which to entice aesthetic proclivity.

Leaning to, she braced her forearms on her knees. "Mr. Ingliss, I'm practically desperate. No. I *am* desperate. Help us to get to Edinburgh. *Please.*"

For what seemed an eternity, they stared into each other's eyes. Somewhere in the house, a clock gave forth three chimes. Then all became silent, an encompassing silence, further stoking her unease.

What would he say if he knew what an uncharacteristic impact his build and rugged countenance had made on her? Would he bend over backward to send her on her way? Or would he take advantage of her inexplicable weakness?

His features completely occupied her vision. Excellent, defined cheekbones. A thicker, sensual lower lip. Straight nose. But his eyes were his best feature. Surrounded by pale, thick lashes, the soft brown color of his irises cried out to be noticed. A woman could easily get lost in those eyes. A woman could easily fall victim to their spell, and fail to consider the real man residing behind them.

Her gaze lowered to the downy hair on his chest. The underparts of her hands began to itch. Fighting back a fierce desire to comb her fingers across the sea of masculine planes, she said almost in a monotone, "I washed out your sweater. It's laid out over a towel on the side of the tub."

He eyed her skeptically, then reached up and raked his fingers through the thick, longish hair capping his head. After a short time, he placed his feet on the floor, leaned forward, and boldly rested his brow to hers.

Excitement quivered through her. What was wrong with her? She knew that he was testing her courage not to shrink away. What would he think if he knew that it was all she could do not to throw herself into his arms?

"Despite all yer woes, you thought o' ma sweater, eh?"

Her heart flip-flopped behind her breasts. She wanted to laugh at the ridiculousness of what she was feeling. He was a *stranger!* And a rude, crude, infuriating one at that!

The skin of his wide brow was hot. The tip of his nose met hers, and she swallowed reflexly. His musky scent filled her nostrils. She wanted him—

"You know, lass . . ." A slow, tormenting smile strained across his mouth. ". . . you nearly roped me in."

In a barely audible voice, she asked, "Beg your pardon?"

Leaning back against the settee, he mockingly bobbed his head, the devilish gleam brightening his eyes, sorely unsettling her. "All tha' is missin' from yer sad . . . *sad* stary, is a wee dog givin' his life for the sake o' you an' the laddies."

Several seconds later, his words sank in. As if wrenched from the spell she'd been under, she sprang to her feet, hissing, "You heartless bastard!" Without thought, she swung out a hand, and dealt him a stinging slap to the side of his face. The satisfaction she experienced was brief. With a swiftness that left her breathless, his large hands caught her by the waist and swung her down on his lap. He growled deep within his throat as he twisted around and effortlessly lowered her shoulder blades to the embroidered upholstery. Her hand swung up again, but he caught her wrists and pinned them to the material above her head.

The massive, naked breadth of his chest and shoulders filled her vision, mentally disarming her. Fear wedged in her throat. Not because he had effortlessly overpowered her, but because she found his actions inexplicably exciting.

"Let me up," she sobbed.

"The last time I fell for a womon's soft tone, I lost somethin' verra precious ta me."

"Everything I've told you is true!"

"Maybe, maybe no'. As far as I'm concerned, yer're Lannie's problem."

"All right, I'm . . . Lannie's problem! Now, please let me up!"

He retained his hold, his thumb lazily massaging the inside of her left wrist. Pleasurable sensations frolicked down her arms, rippling to the core of her heart. When she could no longer tolerate the havoc his touch wreaked on her skin, she stammered, "W-when can I t-talk to him?"

"Whan i' suits him, na doubt."

She gulped. The one thing she feared most, was fear itself. Too many men had tried to master her, to take care of and dominate her, during the past twelve of her thirty years. Small build. Youthful features. They were a curse. She'd fought hard for independence, but had never before quite found herself in such an uncompromising position.

It wasn't as though she could walk away from this situation. Where would she go? The American Consulate, yes, but how, and how soon?

Bluntness and groveling had miserably failed. What was left? If she screamed at the top of her lungs, would anyone but the boys hear her?

Roan again scowled, but there was a softness behind it that further confused her.

"Perish the thought. I've ne'er forced maself on a womon."

"Forced—" Heat suffused every part of her body. Oddly enough, she hadn't considered the possibility of rape. Her fear had stemmed from her doubting her ability not to *seduce him!* It was several seconds before she could continue, "I never—"

Grimacing, he cut in, "Tha' explains i'." Misunderstanding what she'd intended to say, he drew her back up onto his lap. To prevent her from turning away from him, he threaded the fingers of one hand through the pale, soft hair at her nape. "How auld are you?"

The emerald eyes flashed. "Old enough."

"Auld enough, eh?"

"Look, it never crossed my mind that you would try to—"

"Molest you?"

"Y-yes."

A cynical grin spread across his mouth, then he sobered. After a moment of looking deeply into her eyes, he shuddered, then brusquely ushered her off his lap, and rose to his feet. The blanket lay forgotten, haphazardly draped on the back of the settee.

"Lannie'll mak arrangements for you ta be taken ta Edinburgh. He's guid a' takin' charge, tha' one."

"Why are you so hateful?" Laura asked in a tone lacking emotion.

"Life, *Miss* Bennett. Contrary ta belief, tis no' for e'eryone." He abruptly headed toward the door to the foyer. "I've na great expectations—but ta mind ma ain till I leave this bloody warld."

He was nearly across the threshold when Laura's voice arrested him.

"You're an impossible, *pathetic* man."

After a pause, he turned and delivered her a look of utter boredom. "Aye, sa I've been told." He pointed to the door on the opposite wall. "Go through the dinin' room an' you'll find the kitchen. Help yerself ta wha'e'er you want."

"You're so kind."

Her icy tone prompted a genuine smile on his lips. "Guid night, *Miss* Bennett."

"Mr. Ingliss?"

Roan turned again to look at her.

"Where will you be sleeping?"

He frowned. "I guess in one o' the bedrooms on the second floor. Why do you ask?"

"No particular reason."

"Yer virtue's safe. Besides, yer're a sight. Put some cauld water on those bruises."

Laura haughtily stiffened. "Good night, *Mr.* Ingliss."

Roan stared at her for a moment longer, then walked into the foyer.

Suddenly emotionally drained, she watched him ascend the staircase. Now that she no longer felt desire-heated by his proximity, she puzzled about his psychological makeup. His temper possessed a short fuse. And yet, during their brief encounters, she'd more than once gotten the impression that his past harbored a great deal of pain. It was possible she'd only imagined sensing a conflict warring within him.

If he were a man on the edge, how safe were she and the boys? "Whoever hurt you Roan Ingliss, left some very deep scars," she murmured.

She glanced about the Victorian room and deeply sighed. "This beats sleeping in the car." Her voice took on a sarcastic edge. "But isn't it comforting to know my knight in tarnished armor is sleeping under the same roof?"

Her gaze happened on the portrait above the mantel. An inexplicable sadness surged within her heart as she wondered if that woman was the one Roan Ingliss had said had died in this house.

Had she been the one responsible for his bitterness?

Laura studied the carefree depiction of the woman and gave a bewildered shake of her head.

Why should she care what spurred Roan's sour disposition?

There were enough complications already in her life.

As quietly as he was able, Roan stoked the hearth in the boys' bedroom. For a time, he remained crouched in front of the fire. His troubled thoughts seemed etched deeply across his brow. He hated being in Baird House. And he resented the laird's convenient absence concerning the Yank and her nephews.

Standing, he went into the bathroom. He removed the towel and dripping sweater, then brought them into the bedroom and draped them over the back of a chair he'd earlier positioned close to the hearth. Approaching the foot of the bed, he stared at the young boys who were spooned together in the center of the large feather mattress.

A burning sensation rose in his throat. He looked away. A nagging suspicion continued to goad him, to darken his mood. He didn't like Laura Bennett, and it wasn't all because she resembled his deceased wife. Granted, if her story contained even a bit of truth, she was understandably stressed, but she struck him as being—

And there it was, the suspicion fully surfaced.

The woman was distant. Shallow, detached, and distant.

So it wasn't just her physical resemblance to Adaina that annoyed him. Their basic characters were alike, as well.

She'd confessed she hadn't bothered to attend her own brother's funeral.

Did she resent being saddled with the nephews?

For a time longer, he watched the boys. Emotions he thought to have been long lost, surfaced. The emptiness of his loss reawakened, as painful as ever.

"Damn me, I miss you, Jamey," he choked, tears stinging his eyes.

The presence of the boys was bringing it all home to him. Angry that it should still hurt so unbearably, he headed out of the room. He jogged down the staircase, stopping briefly at the landing to pull himself together, then entered the parlor to find Laura staring pensively at Beth's portrait.

A fierce wind of despondency passed through his heart.

For a fleeting moment, he experienced a chilling sense

of rightness. Rightness? That didn't make sense. She no more belonged in this house, than did he.

His mood further soured.

"Aren't you cold?" she asked, not sparing him a glance. After a short silence, she looked askance at his bare upper torso. "Don't you own another sweater—or *something* to cover yourself?"

Ignoring her testiness, he stood alongside her and looked up at the portrait. "That's Beth Staples."

Laura peered up at him, fatigue clouding her eyes. "The American woman who died here?"

He nodded. A muscle ticked along his bold jawline.

Silence ensued while Laura more carefully studied the portrait. "She was very lovely."

"Still is," Roan said without thinking. When her questioning gaze cut up to him, heat rushed into his face. Clearing his throat, he ventured, "You don't want the boys, do you?"

She paled despite her outer calm. "That's a helluva thing to ask."

"Wha' do you do, Miss Bennett?"

Confused, she murmured, "What do I do? About what?"

"Yer career."

"I design perfume and cologne bottles for a cosmetic firm."

"Mmmm. You live alone, do you?"

Laura frowned up at him. "I know what you're getting at, but I can't understand why it's any concern of yours."

"Humor me."

Throwing her hands up, she stated, "I've been on my own since I was eighteen, Mr. Ingliss, and I live in a studio apartment."

"In ither words, there's na place for the lads in yer life."

"Do you have a grumpy identical twin running around this place, or what?" she asked with exasperation.

A weary smile turned up the corners of his mouth. "Grumpy?"

"Well, you haven't exactly made us feel welcomed here, *Mr.* Ingliss! Look . . . I know nothing about children. I've never given a thought about sharing my life with one, let alone three. But they are my family, and I will do whatever is right for them."

Roan's gaze slowly caressed the contours of her face. "You've na heart for children."

An abrupt laugh burst from her. "If I recall, *you* were the one threatening to spank Alby when I came to!"

"Aye."

"So where do *you* get off lecturing *me?*"

With a quarter turn, he rested a forearm upon the mantel and cocked his head to one side. "Fire kills. Tis tha' simple. But I did o'erreact, an' for tha', I'm sarry. Howe'er, *I'm* fond o' children, Miss Bennett—even little deils like yer nephews. I'm curious as ta what's goin' ta happen ta them once you return ta the States."

"I'm beginning to wonder if I've stepped into the Twilight Zone!" She backed up two paces, crimson flooding her face. "I'm sorry I-I intruded upon your damn privacy, mister. *Damn* sorry! Frankly, I've never met a ruder, more insufferable . . . inconsiderate . . . *oaf* in my life! I hate this whole situation, and I hate—" Her voiced dropped low. "*—you.*"

"Careful, lass," he crooned, a sardonic gleam in his mesmerizing eyes as he straightened away from the mantel. "You could be sendin' me the wrong signals."

"What the *hell* are you talking about?"

"Love an' hate are fast companions."

"Maybe in your dismal little brain," she flung scathingly. "One way or the other, the boys and I are leaving come daylight."

Rolling his eyes heavenward, he considered her statement. Then his enigmatic gaze lowered to her face, and deliberately lingered on her mouth for excruciating seconds longer. "Maybe. Maybe no'."

Beyond caring about his size, she whacked him in the midriff with the back of a hand. "Try to stop me!" she said, and ran past him into the foyer.

Minutes later, Roan remained poised in front of the diminishing fire. Fatigue weighed upon his eyelids. He felt physically and mentally drained, and out of touch with reality.

I hate you hate you hate you . . .

Another woman's voice echoed the words inside his skull. A voice from another time, another existence.

Adaina.

Had he known back then that those were to be the best of times, things might have turned out differently. Perhaps he would still have his son.

The terrible void he'd carried for the past three years, unmercifully yawned behind his breast. It threatened to swallow him up, but not to carry him off to oblivion as he'd prayed for on countless nights. Life was the worst of all punishments. Guilt would ride on his broad shoulders for as long as a breath remained in his body.

"Treasure them, Laura," he whispered achingly into the shadows.

Burdened with despair, he shuffled out of the room.

Two

Laura leaned over the bathroom sink to have a closer look at herself in the ornately framed mirror. A rainbow-shaped, black and purple bruise covered most of her chin; a smaller discoloration marred the outer corner of her left eye. The bright morning light coming through two curtain-less windows accentuated the shadows underscoring her eyes.

She hadn't slept a wink since leaving Roan in the parlor. Sometime during the night, the storm had stopped. She was more determined than ever to continue on her way to Edinburgh. From a mental list of plans, she'd chosen the simplest: find a telephone and call the American Consulate. Surely they would cover her cab fare until she got to a bank and replaced her lost traveler's checks.

"Gimme!"

Kahl's shrill demand made her wince.

"Mine!" Alby cried.

Going to the doorway to the adjoining bedroom, Laura ordered in a stage whisper, "Knock it off! We'll be leaving in a minute."

"I want breakfast," Kevin declared from his sitting position on the foot of the bed.

"Fine. I'll get you something on the way out. Just quiet down, okay?"

"Kahl mean," Alby whimpered. He lifted a hand and threatened to bring it down on his brother's leg.

"Boys . . ." Laura entered the room. Her gaze locked on the two youngest brothers, sitting across from one another in front of the hearth. "We don't want to wake Mr. Ingliss, do—"

She stopped in her tracks, her eyes widening in horror.

"Oh, no. Oh . . . nooo," she moaned, looking aghast at the yarn clutched in Kahl's hands. "Please tell me that's not *his* sweater! Oh . . . boys . . ."

Kneeling, she coaxed the ragged bundle from Kahl and held it out in both hands. "Why?" she asked him, her voice raspy with incredulity.

"We're bored."

"Real bored," Kevin put in, folding his arms against his chest.

"Why didn't you stop them?" she asked.

He shrugged. "I'm not the adult around here."

Closing her eyes, Laura buried her face into the remains of the sweater.

"Don't cry," Alby said in a small voice, patting his aunt's thigh.

Laura lifted her head. "I'm not crying. I'm upset. I simply don't relish another confrontation—"

"Burgers."

Blankly, she looked at Kahl.

"Mustard, ketchup, and relish." He grinned and patted his stomach. "I'm hungry."

"Okay, we're outta here," she said, standing. "Our suitcases are still in the trunk of the car. We'll have to take some extra sweaters and socks . . ." She looked around the room as if uncertain about what to do first. "Shoes on?"

After a quick inspection, she helped the boys into their

coats, then went to a birch wardrobe and removed her own coat. Slipping into it, she watched the boys group in front of her.

"Now we have to be very quiet. We don't want to awaken Mr. Ingliss."

"Where's the ghost?"

Kahl's question took her aback. "While I was . . . sleeping yesterday, did Mr. Ingliss tell you a ghost story?"

"Naw. We seen him."

She looked at Kevin with a frown. "You saw a ghost?"

"Yep," Alby pouted. "He sca-wed me."

"Big *ugly* sucker," Kevin said with a feigned shudder. "Roan said he would have the ghost kill us if we didn't be good."

"Yeah," Kahl affirmed, glancing at his brothers. "Kill us. And he meant it, too."

Angrier than she'd ever been, Laura took Alby's hand and headed toward the door to the hall. "Stay close behind me. And not a sound. Understand?"

"We're not dumb, you know," Kevin snipped.

"You're also not the most obedient children on the planet," she retorted as she drew Alby into the hall.

Kevin slammed the bedroom door behind him, causing Laura's nerves to jump. Delivering all three boys a scolding look, she began to tiptoe down the hall. It wasn't until they reached the top of the stairs that she noticed something dangling from beneath Kahl's down-filled coat.

"Why didn't you leave this behind?" she asked in a whisper as she reached up under the coat and withdrew the tangled yarn.

"I want it!"

"Shhh!" She peered down the staircase, then frowned at the boys. "Quiet. Stay behind me."

During the cautious descent, Kevin imitated a monkey. Hands clasped over their mouths, his brothers tried not to laugh aloud. When Laura reached the first-floor landing and turned in time to witness Kevin's actions, she reached out, took a firm hold on his arm, and drew him to her side.

"Knock it off," she warned in a whisper.

"What about breakfast, huh?" he asked in a hushed tone.

Casting the closed parlor door a worried look, she reluctantly nodded her head. "Okay, okay. But be very, *very* quiet."

Not knowing the secondary hall also led to the kitchen, she ushered the boys through the parlor. Midway across the dining room, an appetizing aroma stopped her cold.

"I smell eggs," Kahl beamed.

Laura grimaced. She was about to turn back in the direction of the hall when the kitchen door swung open. Roan ambled into the room, a plate of steaming food carried in each hand. He offered the motionless group an abrupt nod of greeting, placed the dishes on the table, and headed back into the kitchen.

"Me first!" Kevin laughed, running to one of the high-backed chairs.

"Naw, you piglet!" Kahl cried, beelining for the chair in front of the second plate.

Numbly, Laura lifted Alby and positioned him on her left hip. She remained perfectly still when Roan returned with two more plates and set them on the table. Then he abruptly walked toward her, his hands held out. Without the slightest idea of what prompted her action, she twisted to one side, drawing Alby from Roan's immediate reach.

Roan stopped and placed his hands on his hips. His brows drew down in a scowl.

Laura couldn't help looking over his attire.

Same slacks. Same dingy socks. A plain white half-apron ridiculously hiked up beneath his armpits.

"Do you mean ta starve him?" he asked, impatiently tugging the youngest boy from her arms. He carried Alby to a chair, where he'd earlier stacked two throw pillows. Laura remained in a stupor when he went into the kitchen again, returning with three glasses of milk.

"Do you prefer tea or coffee?" he asked her, the scowl seeming a permanent fixture on his face.

Giving herself a mental shake, Laura jabbed a thumb toward the kitchen door. "I would prefer a private conversation."

Roan took a moment to look at each boy. "Eat oop, laddies. An' spare the china, if you please."

He walked into the kitchen, Laura trailing him. When he turned to face her, she closed the wide door and crossed her arms against the front of her coat.

"Guid mornin', darlin'," he drawled flippantly. "Don't you look smashin' this fine day."

"Drop the sarcasm."

Arching an eyebrow, he crossed his arms against his chest. "Yer breakfast's gettin' cauld."

"Is the owner around?"

Roan glanced about the kitchen. "Doesn't seem so, does i'?"

"The boys told me something appalling this morning."

A chuckle escaped him. "Why aren't I surprised, eh?"

Laura walked up to him and jabbed him in the chest with an accusing finger. "Did you, or did you not, tell the boys a ghost would kill them if they didn't behave?"

Pursing his lips, Roan released a low whistle. "Those weren't exactly ma words."

"Just what the hell *were* your exact words?" she asked

heatedly, the green of her eyes seeming to hold flames behind them.

"Weel . . . now . . . Ah! I believe I said somethin' abou' a foul breath o' death." Roan grinned sourly. "I had ma hands full wi' carryin' *you*. The lads weren't exactly cooperatin'."

"You don't frighten children with—"

A booming, shrill cry cut Laura off, frightening her so that she threw herself into Roan's arms and buried her face in the apron. Another rang out. Quaking, fiercely gripping the cotton fabric, she gasped, "What is that?"

"Those bloody peacocks," Roan murmured, overly conscious of his instinctual action to enclose her slender frame within his hold. Easing his arms to his sides, he absently stated, "You'll get used ta them."

Laura's head shot up. "What? Oh, no. Oooooooh, no!" She backed up to the dining room door. "I don't plan to be here long enough to get used to *you!*"

Reaching out, Roan gripped her arm and drew her toward him. The retort about to spring past his lips, died when he noticed a dark green strand of yarn hanging beneath the hemline of her coat. Without moving her head, Laura dropped her gaze. His scowl returned as he unfastened the lower buttons and removed the wadded remains of his sweater. When he looked incredulously into her face, he was quick to note how pale she'd become.

"Yer handiwark?"

"Don't be ridiculous."

"Ah. The nephews." He held up the yarn to within an inch of her face. "Bored, were they?"

She offered a feeble shrug.

Turning abruptly, Roan deposited the wad in a waste can by the back door. "Ma favorite sweater." He stood in front of her and crossed his arms again. "But, hey. We can't have the wee lads bored now, can we?"

Laura's troubled gaze rose slowly to meet his eyes. "I'll gladly replace the damn thing when I can get to a bank."

"Ma Aunt Aggie made i' for me last Christmas."

Laura rolled her eyes. "Well don't expect *me* to knit you one."

"Perish the thought."

"Perish this," she said angrily, then paled. She looked over her shoulder, murmuring, "They're awfully quiet." Whirling toward the door, she entered the dining room, and jerked to a stop. Her hands went up to cover her face. Roan stepped up behind her then, with a Scottish expletive, rushed past her to the table.

"The little buggers!" he exclaimed, his horrified gaze sweeping over the disaster.

Lowering her hands, Laura forced her leaden legs to carry her closer.

Food was splattered in every direction, staining the Irish lace tablecloth, the Oriental carpet beneath the table, and the east and west walls. Sickened by the scene, she slowly made her way around the table.

"How could they have made such a mess in such a short time?"

Roan shook his head, then ran a hand down his face.

"Oh, no," Laura whimpered, glancing in the direction of a sideboard along the east wall. Walking to it, she crouched and began to pick up the pieces of a porcelain, Oriental figurine.

"Leave i'," Roan ordered, coming to her side. "We've got ta find them 'fore they get inta any mair mischief."

Standing, Laura dishearteningly placed the remains atop the sideboard. "Please tell me it isn't an antique."

"Everthin' here is as auld as dirt," Roan grumbled. Taking her by the arm, he added, "Come wi' me."

They no sooner entered the foyer, than Kevin's voice rang out, "Hey! Look what I found!"

"The library," Roan said, dragging Laura along by the hand. Passing through the open sliding doors, they entered the room to find the oldest boy standing in front of an opening between two tall bookcases.

"I didn't do nothing," Kevin sputtered, gaping at the exposed passageway. "It just opened. No lie! Just . . . *opened!*"

Laura stood numbly at the threshold while Roan rushed to the opening and peered into the semidarkness beyond. Looking at Kevin, he asked brusquely, "Kahl or Alby venture in there?"

"Nope."

"Where are they?" Laura weakly probed.

Kevin shrugged. "What's in there, huh? Can we check it out?"

Roan turned to face the boy, an angry scowl darkening his features. "Where's yer brithers, lad?"

Kevin passed Laura a bewildered look. "What's *brithers?*"

"Alby and Kahl!" Roan snapped.

"I dunno. They took off."

Pulling the panel shut, Roan gave it a push to reassure himself that it would remain closed.

He walked tip to Kevin. "Off where? Ou'side?"

"Naw. I heard them running up the stairs."

"Don't let him ou' o' yer sight," Roan growled at Laura, then stormed out of the room.

With Kevin's hand tightly clasped within her own, Laura silently followed Roan. Every time he shouted one of the boys' names, or slammed a door shut to a room he'd finished searching, she winced. Tugging Kevin behind her, she ascended the staircase with lessening enthusiasm. Roan dashed down the hall to their right, while she remained posted at the top of the landing.

"Kahl! Alby! Come ou', you little buggers!"

A second, a third door slammed home. " 'Tis no' funny, you little monsters! Come ou'!"

From off to Laura's left, she heard low whimpering. Angling her head as though to keen her hearing, she waited a moment longer then went to one of the doors and pressed an ear to it.

She tried the knob. Locked.

"Alby? Alby, are you in there?"

Loud sobs came in response.

"Roan! He's locked in this room!"

While Roan ran toward her, she repeatedly tried to twist the knob.

"Here, let me," he said gruffly.

When he also couldn't get it to unlatch, he plowed a shoulder against the heavy wood. "Dammi'! Lannie, do somethin'!"

Laura became lightheaded when the door silently opened.

"Wow," Kevin breathed in awe.

Alby charged out of the room and squealed in protest when Roan scooped him up into his arms. "Yer're makin' an auld mon ou' o' me, lad," he chided. "Now where's the ither one?"

Squirming, his arms held out to Laura, Alby screeched at the top of his lungs. Before either adult could regain their wits, Kahl ran from behind a heavy velvet drape at the end of the hall.

"Guess what I found—" Halting in midstride at the sight of Laura and Roan, he added a solemn, "Uh-oh."

"Come here," Laura said sternly to Kahl, taking Alby into her arms. She waited until the third boy was in front of her, and went on, "The three of you are going to clean up the mess you made in the dining room."

"The ghost did it!" Kevin exclaimed, eagerly looking to his brothers for support.

"Yeah. Stuff started flying around—"

"The hell i' did," Roan intervened, his expression livid. "Ain oop ta yer deeds."

Kevin petulantly lowered his head for a moment. When he looked up, his tearful, angelic expression nearly doused Roan and Laura's frustration. "Alby did it all."

"Yep," Kahl put in, nodding his head vigorously. "Alby did it *all.*"

"That's i'," Roan growled, taking both boys by the nape and marching them to the stairs. "'Tis one thin' ta do mischief," he continued, urging them into a descent, "anither ta lie abou' i'."

"I found a tower," Kahl squeaked, his thin shoulders trying to shuck off Roan's hold. "Did people live there, huh? Anybody die there? Huh? Did they?"

"It was a place for wee buggers—" Cutting himself off, Roan passed a harried looked over his shoulder at Laura. Although he dearly wanted to rattle the boys as much as they had rattled him, their aunt was definitely not in the mood for one of his fabrications. An immature reaction, he knew, but it was no worse than his deepening urges to throw himself onto the floor and pitch a full-blown tantrum. If nothing else, it could possibly prompt the laird to make an appearance. . . .

By the time he stepped onto the first-floor landing, his

adrenaline had slowed, and his temper had waned beneath a swell of weariness.

Surely Lachlan had to appear before the end of the day. Friends they would never be, but a blind man would have recognized the raw concern Roan'd seen on the ghost's face last night at the scene of the accident.

Unless the Yank and the boys were the laird's way of getting even with this particular Ingliss . . .

Grimacing at the thought, Roan turned to face Laura when she stepped down onto the landing.

"Are you all right?"

The question damn near knocked the wind from him.

Concern, from her?

Searching her eyes, he felt himself inwardly shrinking back. He was acutely aware of the boys' unnatural silence and stillness. He could feel their eyes on him. On their aunt. Back and forth, waiting for some kind of reaction from the adults.

"Mr. Ingliss?"

Releasing the boys, he folded his arms against his chest. "What's ta be done wi' the dinin' room, eh?"

"The boys and I will clean it, of course," she replied icily.

But there was a wounded look in her eyes that bothered Roan. He could not recall ever seeing such a look in Adaina's eyes. "O' course," he murmured, then inhaled deeply through his nostrils. "How kind o' you ta postpone yer hare-brain plans ta trot off inta the unknown," he added, gesturing with his head toward the front door.

"Don't start," Laura warned in a low tone. "C'mon, boys." Her eyes flashed Roan a dirty look. "Let's show this *kind* man how well we can clean up the mess."

"Alby did it," Kevin grumbled.

Kahl gave a snort. "The ghost *made* Alby do it."

Despite himself, a grin cracked Roan's attempt to look stern.

"Never mind," Laura sighed, aiming the boys toward the dining room. "The sooner we clean up, the sooner we can start our new journey."

"I'm all ashiver," Roan mocked, walking behind her.

"And the sooner we can tell Mr. Ingliss where he can go," Laura went on, cutting him a wry grin over her shoulder.

Kevin dashed ahead and entered the parlor. The brothers would have followed but for Laura's hold on the back of their coats. Halfway across the room, she released them, smiling a bit warily when they ran after Kevin.

"There's na guarantee we won't get hit wi' anither storm 'fore the morn's done," Roan said as he fell into stride next to Laura.

Keeping her eyes on the boys entering the next room, she tilted up her chin and retorted, "I'm more concerned about the storm going on within these walls, Mr. Ingliss."

Roan arched a brow. "Me?"

Coming to an abrupt halt—Roan following suit—she faced him and testily looked him in the eye. "You've made it perfectly clear, you don't want us around."

"'Tis no' tha'—"

"Then what is it?" she asked bitterly. "How would you feel if our positions were reversed? Don't you think you'd be just a little unnerved at the prospect of having to rely on strangers?"

Roan released a breath. "Aye."

"You're an ass."

She started to turn away when his large hand took a firm

hold on her upper arm. Jerking her against him, he leveled a dark, brooding look on her upturned face.

"Yer're the maist stubborn womon I've e'er had the misfortune ta know! I may no' like this situation, but I've mair sense than ta let you lead the laddies ou' inta this weather!"

"Let me?" she gasped, her face reddening.

"Aye, *let* you," he growled, lowering his face to within inches of hers. "Use yer brain, you fool! A day or two here won't shatter yer life!"

On tiptoe, Laura brought the tips of their noses together. "Oh, won't it? A day or two more in *your* company, and I'll be on trial for murder!"

Roan straightened up, a dark flush in his cheeks. "Yer're beggin' ta be pree'd," he said through clenched teeth.

Lowering her heels to the floor, she arched a questioning brow. "I'm what?"

Abruptly, he looked toward the dining room door. "Ach! The nickums are tae quiet." As if the devil were at his heels, he ran to the room.

Laura followed at a slower pace, her mind struggling to define the word "pree'd." Nickums she automatically assumed was an endearment . . . of sorts. But pree'd? The way he'd said it had sent shivers along her spine.

She entered the dining room, immediately spying the boys huddled around Roan. The sight struck her as curiously humorous, considering his impatience with them. Then, as she approached, she realized their youthful eyes were filled with awe and disbelief. Slowing her pace, she glanced about her—stopped short, and felt the blood plummet in her body.

Suddenly lightheaded, she unknowingly reached out and gripped the front of Roan's apron.

The room was spotless. The table cleared.

"The ghost," Kevin chimed, looking up at his aunt. "Told ya he's around, didn't I?"

Laura's legs threatened to buckle beneath her. The tightness in her throat refused to release the air trapped in her lungs. Her eyes as wide as saucers, she strained to detect even the slightest sign of what had earlier taken place. Finally, forcing her legs to move, she went to the table and inspected the lace tablecloth. Panic heated her insides. There wasn't so much as a stain to indicate that *anyone* had ever eaten atop the Irish lace.

"Let i' go," Roan said huskily, coming to her side and placing a hand on her trembling shoulder.

Laura could only shake her head in disbelief.

"There are things in this house tha' can't be easily explained."

Closing her eyes and leaning against the edge of the table for support, she willed her reasoning to resurface. She became aware of Roan's hand massaging the back of her neck, but it would take far more than his touch to relax the knotted muscles and tendons.

"Who else is in this house?" she managed.

"Only the five o' us."

She looked up at him. Her eyes misted green pools in her ashen face. "Don't lie to me. Someone—"

"I swear, lass, there's no' anither *livin'* soul in this place."

Tears rolled down her cheeks. "Why are you doing this to us? What kind of game are you playing?"

A wounded look softened Roan's expressive eyes. "I haven't the sense o' humor ta play useless mind games."

"Boys, come here," she ordered, glaring mistily into the masculine face. When they complied, she protectively kept them close to her as she backed away from Roan. "We're leaving. Right now. I swear if you try to do anything to stop us, I'll hurt you."

"Yer're doin' a fine job a' i' now," he grumbled, his shoulders stiffly drawn back.

Her eyes never wavering from Roan's, she ordered, "Kevin, take your brothers into the foyer."

"Huh?"

"The hall," she said irritably, pointing toward the parlor door. "Get going. I'll be along in a minute."

"Do we hafta go?" Kahl moaned.

Kevin looked from one adult to the other, his brows drawn down in a frown. "Yeah, c'mon guys." Taking them by the arms, he pulled them across the room.

Roan watched the boys disappear into the next room before searching Laura's features again. It was on the tip of his tongue to try to explain about Lachlan Baird, but she whirled away. Three paces later, she froze in midstride. Roan stared at the back of her head, nurturing a hope that she'd decided to listen to him rather than sail on the tides of her pride. A moment passed before he noticed that she was violently trembling, and that her head was turned in the direction of the sideboard. He glanced that way and saw nothing unusual.

Weightiness materialized in his chest. "Laura, what's wrong?"

Silence mantled the room. Suffocating silence that completely unnerved him.

Laura's head began to shake. Then she stiltedly walked to the sideboard, her body blocking Roan's view from what had captured her attention. He waited for what seemed an eternity before approaching her. Standing close behind her, he craned his neck to see over her shoulder.

"Explain this," she said throatily, turning to face him.

A tickling sensation moved along his arms as he stared down at the Oriental statue clutched in her hands. When his gaze rose and looked into her clouded eyes, he inhaled deeply and slowly released it.

"Lannie protects what's his."

"The owner," she said dully.

"Aye. He's been dead for o'er a century."

For a long time, Laura stared into his eyes. She was bereft of emotions at this point; physically and emotionally devoid of any feeling. A roar similar to that of waves crashing on a shore, filled her ears. The statue felt unnaturally heavy in her hands, as if vying for her full attention.

"Lannie asked me ta help you efter you hit the oak. He'd spent his energies, an' couldn't solidify ta pull you ou' o' the caur."

With the speed of lightning, Laura threw a punch at the side of his face. Seemingly unaffected by the blow he'd just dodged, he went on, "He'll return—"

She nearly tried to hit him again.

"—in a day or two."

Her hand rose a third time, but he caught her wrist and pinned it to his chest. "You asked for the truth!"

Laura merely stared at him, the fear in her eyes intensifying with each passing moment. The fingers of her left hand tightened on the statue until her knuckles were deathly white.

"I'll go inta town an' call the consulate."

Her head moved in a stilted denial.

"Wha'? You don't trust me?" He scowled, his nostrils flaring. "You'd rather drag the laddies off inta the cauld?"

"Yes," she whispered, giving a weak tug on her arm in a demand for him to release her.

"Damn yer callous hide, Laura Bennett!" Thrusting her

away from him, he stepped back and made a valiant bid to tighten the reins on his temper. "You best *reck* this warnin', girl! If you take the boys ou' inta this cursed weather, you'll be next ignorin' *their* funerals!"

He pointed an isolated finger at her face. "Stay put! If I get back an' I find you gone, I swear I'll track you ta hell!"

"Don't threaten me," she choked.

Rage accentuated the angles of his face. "Think o' the lads, this once. They lost their mither an' their faither, an' have ta rely on *you* ta tak care o' them. *Tha'* scares *me*. Can't imagine how *they* feel bein' dependent on an unemotional, self-centered womon, who has no' the sense o' a church mouse ta stay ou' o' the cauld!"

"Who the hell do you think you are?" Laura shrilled.

"Leave this house 'fore ma return, Laura Bennett, an' I swear I'll have ya brought oop on charges for child endangerment."

Wrenching the statue from her hand, he placed it on the sideboard and stormed out of the room.

Long after she'd heard a door slamming shut in the house, Laura remained perfectly still. Tears streamed down her cheeks in abandon. She was too numb to think. Too numb to do anything but try to will away the echoing of his harsh words in her skull.

He was right. She was being stubborn. What was it about Roan Ingliss that brought out the worst in her? Ordinarily, she walked away from a confrontation. An argument of any kind had never been worth her time or energy. Yet now, she felt compelled to needle Roan.

As she sank to the floor, with her legs folded beneath her, she surveyed the room through a new mist of tears.

Of course she didn't want to haul the boys out into the

cold. Perhaps she *knew* Roan wouldn't let her leave the house under unfavorable conditions. But wouldn't that mean that she *wanted* him—anyone—to take charge of her life?

No!

Somewhere inside her, the real Laura Bennett was hiding. Why, she didn't know, but she wanted her back.

She looked toward the hall door to see the boys coming toward her. A smile strained past her despair. Alby climbed onto her lap and laid his head to her chest. Kevin sat cross-legged on the floor to her left; Kahl to her right, his legs folded beneath him. They passed questioning looks among themselves, waiting for her to say something to assuage their curiosity. They knew something was wrong, but Laura didn't know what to tell them.

The silence took its toll on Alby. He began to whimper as he nestled his chubby face to the folds of her coat. Tears sprang into Kahl's eyes. Kevin fought harder not to give in to the emotions swelling inside him.

"It'll be okay," Laura said softly, encircling Kevin and Kahl's shoulders with her arms and drawing them closer to her. "Mr. Ingliss . . . is going to call the consulate."

"Are we staying?" Kahl sniffed.

"For a while longer," she replied. Despite her efforts, her tone sounded hollow.

"Laura, I gotta take a slash."

A chuckle rattled deep within her throat, and she kissed the top of Alby's head. "Take a *slash,* huh?" Her mood brightening, she smiled in earnest. "While we're waiting for Mr. Ingliss to return, how about if we explore your tower, Kahl?"

His eyes gleaming with anticipation, he sprang to his

feet. "Yeah. It's cool. Maybe we'll find a skeleton, huh? Do you think? Huh?"

"One could only hope," she said wearily, getting to her feet.

The laughter and conversation in Shortby's wound down when a gust of wind and a snow-clad, half-frozen Roan came through the door. Shutting it with more force than necessary, he crossed to the bar, peeling off his gloves along the way.

"Roan, ma boy!" one elderly patron laughed. "Join me for a pint!"

"Later," Roan grumbled as he climbed onto a stool and testily beckoned for the bartender. "Yer phone workin'?"

"On an' off," Silas MacCormick said, eyeing Roan sympathetically from above wire-rimmed glasses perched on the end of his narrow nose.

"Ma tab still guid?"

Silas nodded.

"Have me a bitter ready," Roan ordered, placing his gloves on the counter and sliding off the stool. He went to a black telephone at the end of the bar and lifted the handset to a red-rimmed ear. "Damn," he swore at the silence that greeted him, then slammed the handset home and returned to the stool. Silas's dark eyes twinkled beneath bushy white eyebrows as he placed a handled glass in front of Roan.

"Where you been, lately?"

"Kist House," Roan replied with a grimace.

"Na say. Borgie was by last eve. Left here, staggerin'."

"He's an ass, tae."

"Tae?"

Roan gestured that it wasn't worth an explanation. "Ma

bloody car skidded inta Kastor's dyke." He downed half the warm, dark ale before adding, "Course, he wasn't home so I could use his phone."

"You walked from Kastor's?" With a roll of his eyes, Silas feigned a theatrical shiver. "The wind has a cruel cut ta i'."

Turning halfway on the stool, Roan looked over the dozen other men occupying the establishment. "Taylor been in today?"

"His wife's abou' ta give birth. Me thinks she's got the leash tight around his neck, these days. Can't say as I blame her. He wasn't around whan the ither five popped ou' now, was he?" With a laugh, he pulled a bar towel from his shoulder and gave a swipe over the spotless counter. "Six. Can you imagine six wailin' kids under yer feet?"

A shadow passed over Roan's features but for a moment. "Na, can't imagine i', Silas. Damn, I need ta mak a call."

"Ta Aggie?"

"Na. The American Consulate in Edinburgh."

Silas's eyebrows quirked upward. "Wha' for?"

"'Tis a long stary—"

"Hey, lad," boomed a familiar voice, a beefy hand clapping Roan on the back. William Shaw parked his broad buttocks on the stool to Roan's left. "Oop ta a game o' darts?" His broadening grin exposed a missing upper front tooth. "I'm in ma cups, but feelin' lucky as hell," he added, gleefully rubbing his hands together.

Roan glanced off to his right, to the dart board mounted on the wall of a raised platform area. Looking at William, he gave a solemn shake of his head. "No' today."

"Why no'? I'll spot you a—"

"No' today," Roan scowled into his face.

Lifting his hands in a placating manner, William Shaw

left the stool and returned to his three drinking buddies across the room.

"What's eatin' you, Roan?"

Silas's soft tone elicited a sigh from Roan. "Wha' isn't, these days?"

"Hmm. If I didn't know better, I'd bet ma life you were a mon ainin' o' a lot o' womon trouble. But yer're Roan Ingliss, aren't you. Folks round here know you ta be a loner."

Despite his mood, a gleam of laughter brightened Roan's eyes. "A loner I may prefer to be, ma friend, but tis a womon all right who has me in knots."

Silas rested his bony elbows on the counter, his upturned palms supporting his chin. "Go on," he grinned.

"Nothin' really ta tell. Damn me, I need a bloody phone."

"A Yank, eh? I mean, you did mention the American Consulate, didn't you?"

"Aye . . . on both accounts. She drove smack inta an oak on Baird's land. Her an' the laddies—"

"Laddies?"

"Her three nephews."

"How auld are they?"

Roan shrugged. "Young."

"An' the womon . . . pretty?"

Roan scowled, finished off his lager, then slapped the bottom of the glass down. "You ask tae many questions."

"Ah." Straightening, Silas chuckled. "Yer defensiveness says i' all, ma boy."

"It does, eh?" Arching a haughty brow, Roan wagged a finger at the man. "Ya don't know a thin', auld mon. Trust me."

An air of superiority gave flight to Silas's outgoing personality. "Don't know a thin', you say? I'll bet a day's wage she's young, pretty as a day is long, an' built ta shackle a mon's reasonin'.'"

Flustered, Roan slid off the stool. "I've got ta get back. I'll probably return in the morn ta use the phone." Digging into his right pocket, he extracted some coins, picked through them, and flipped a pound on the counter. "If Taylor, Borgie, or Archie come in, ask them ta come oop ta Kist House. At least, I need ta know if there's a coach goin' ta Edinburgh anytime soon."

"No' likely you'll see the white o' their eyes oop there."

"Just ask."

"Aye," Silas grinned, and winked suggestively. "But I'll tell them no' ta bother you tae long efter dark, eh? Lest you be warmin' yer bones—"

"Yer dentures are tae large," Roan clipped, retrieving his gloves into one hand. "They mak yer head look all shrunk oop."

Silas heartily laughed and offered Roan a jaunty salute. "I'll be damned! Roan Ingliss is smitten wi' a Yank!"

The pub fell silent once again. Roan was conscious that all eyes were on him. Shrugging deeper into his coat, he turned on a heel and beelined for the door. Shouts from a few of the customers made a bid to stall him, but inwardly seething that perhaps the old man's words held some truth, he exited the pub. Icy wind claimed him again. Leaning into its bite, he plowed across the small parking lot, toward Crossmichael's main road. More than half the day'd been wasted trying to locate a working telephone. He knew Laura Bennett wouldn't appreciate his efforts. *If* she were still at the house.

His threat had been rash, and if there was one thing he knew about Laura, it was that she didn't like to feel out of control. But what was a man to do when a woman's stubbornness exceeded the bounds of tolerance? He *did* care what happened to them. He wasn't about to subject himself to sleepless nights wondering if they'd arrived safe in Edinburgh.

Lannie's energies had to replenish soon. If not . . .

Roan didn't want to dwell any longer on the volatile emotions the woman's presence provoked. It wasn't her fault that she resembled Adaina, or that Adaina and Jamey had so tragically died. And it wasn't her fault that he found her so maddeningly attractive.

Dusk was settling in over the land when he trudged up the driveway to Kist House. Ice particles weighed down his thick lashes. He gazed over the facade of the Victorian mansion as he approached the massive, double front doors. Every part of him ached from the cold, especially his feet, which felt as if embedded with fiery needles. He entered the small greenhouse, stomped his boots to shake off the snow caked onto them, and reached for the left knob on the second set of double doors.

The door swung open. Laura Bennett's small frame stood in the opening.

Their eye contact was brief. Brushing past her, Roan entered the hall, shucked out of his coat and hung it on a rack to his left, then began to rub his bare arms with his palms.

"I thought you might need this," Laura said demurely, lifting a blanket she'd earlier placed by the rack.

Without looking into her face, he eagerly shook the blue and purple plaid blanket open, and swung it over his bare shoulders.

"I couldn't figure out how to work the stove, so I didn't put on any water for tea. You look . . ."

Roan met her nervous gaze and frowned.

"Frozen," she completed in a small voice.

"Where are the laddies?"

"Sleeping. Did you . . . Were you able to get to a telephone?"

Roan drew the blanket tighter about him. "Aye, but the lines are doon. I'll try again in the morn."

She stared into his eyes for what seemed a long time before lowering her gaze to the floor between them. "I was worried you wouldn't come back."

Her words took him aback. When she looked up again, he closed one eye and leaned closer.

"All right, hit me wi' the punchline an' get i' o'er wi'."

Laura gave a bewildered shake of her head. "I *was* worried. The wind picked up shortly after you left— What happened to your car?"

He started walking toward the secondary hall. Laura fell into step alongside him. "I slid inta a dyke. Helluva mess."

"A dyke?"

He stopped just past the barroom and looked down at her. "A dividin' wall."

"The car's totaled?"

He arched an inquiring eyebrow.

"It's wrecked?"

"Aye, but *I'm* in one piece," he returned sarcastically.

Her gaze swept appreciatively down his tall frame. "I can see that." She met his brooding gaze, guarding her concern for him. "How far did you have to walk?"

"Far enough," he grumbled.

Clasping her hands to the small of her back, she followed him into the kitchen. Silence accompanied them for a time while he filled a kettle and placed it on a gas burner atop the antiquated stove. He lit one of the wooden matches kept on a wrought-iron rack above the appliance, turned one of the knobs, and lit the unit. Turning and eyeing Laura, he blew out the match.

"There's a question in yer eyes," he said matter-of-factly.

"Not a question." Laura squared her shoulders. "I'm sorry if I don't always understand what you're saying."

Again, he looked at her inquiringly.

"You didn't have to take my head off because I didn't know what you meant by a 'dyke.' "

He smiled mockingly. "An' here I thought I was bein' civil—especially in light o' the fact I'm half frozen an' as frustrated as hell."

"You're forgiven," she said airily, refusing to let him goad her. "Actually, I do have a question." She waited while he pulled two mugs from a cupboard and placed them next to the stove. "You used a word this morning that I can't get out of my head."

He slanted her a look while lowering tea bags into the cups. "Wha' word?"

"This morning, you said, 'pree'd.' I was asking to be pree'd."

Edging two paces closer, her hands still clasped at the small of her back, she dipped her head to one side. "What does the word mean?"

Warmth spread across Roan's chest as he struggled not to crack another grin. Feigning a pensive frown, he closed the short distance between them. "Define i', eh? Hmmm. I guess showin' beats the bloody hell ou' o' tellin'."

Laura had no idea what was coming. Swiftly, as if to completely take her unawares, he lowered his head and lightly kissed her. A spasm of shock first rooted her, then she jumped back and stared up at his amused expression as if he'd lost his mind.

"That's a verra wee pree," he said. "Whan a Scotsmon

puts his blood's worth inta i', lass, the word taks on all kinds o' definitions."

Dumbfounded, she could only stare at him.

Roan released a thready breath. Gripping her arms, he hesitantly drew her against him. Immediately, he felt the warmth of her body radiate through the blanket.

"There's somethin' better than tea ta tak the chill ou' o' a mon."

Mesmerized by his closeness, and the mischievous glow in his alluring pale brown eyes, she breathed, "Is there?"

Releasing her, he quipped, "Scotch. Wad you mind fetchin' me a bottle?"

With the deliverance of the dead, Laura bade, "Good night, Mr. Ingliss," and left the kitchen by way of the dining room.

Roan laughed. Then laughed again.

"Guid night, lass," he beamed, feeling more lighthearted than he had in years. But then he sobered, and brushed the back of a hand across his tingling lips.

An inexplicable ache thrummed within his heart. An ache akin to excitement.

The whistle of the teakettle gave him a start.

Without thinking, he poured steaming water into both cups, then grinned wryly at his absentmindedness.

He looked to the door she'd passed through moments ago. One wee kiss, and the chill had completely left him. He was almost afraid to imagine what making love to the woman could do for him. . . .

Three

Bitter cold winds buffeted the exterior walls of the toasty kitchen. Roan could not block out the wind's mournful whistling as he forced down the bland brose he'd earlier concocted. He also could not shut down his awareness of Laura's silence, or her deep disappointment with his failure that morning to locate a working telephone in town.

She'd awakened at the crack of dawn in a foul mood. Not coffee, or breakfast, or his attempts to cheer her up, had made the slightest difference. He'd even donned one of Lachlan's ridiculous full-sleeved shirts to appease her indignant airs over his state of undress. The woman simply expected more of him than he could deliver.

And it irked him.

So the brose was lumpy. He'd never professed to be much of a cook, although how he could have screwed up something as simple as oatmeal mixed with boiling water, butter and salt, was beyond him. Regardless, a thank-you from the woman would have been appreciated.

Peering at her from his lowered head, he found himself counting the number of times she lifted her spoon to her mouth. Deliberate small portions, as if to prolong the agony of finishing the meal. And her gaze never left the bowl. Too bad. Whatever her mood, her green eyes always fascinated him. Clear. Vibrant. Sexy—

Clearing his throat, he straightened in the wooden chair and pushed his bowl aside. The next time—*if* there was a next time—he decided they would eat at the long dining room table, and not crowd five around a table built to seat two comfortably. The other table would also place them farther apart, which, during his intermittent urges to throttle her, would require him to leave his chair and hopefully regain his reasoning by the time he got to her.

To dispel his mental wanderings, he asked, "Can I get anyone anythin' else?"

Shaking his head, Kahl reached for another oatcake.

"Naw," Kevin said through a mouthful of food.

"No, thank you," Laura corrected him, then looked coolly at Roan and repeated the words.

Roan's gaze clashed with hers. Rising from his chair, he refilled his cup with dark, strong coffee, and sat again.

Kahl giggled. With impish blue eyes he was staring askance at Roan.

"What's sa funny?"

"You look like a girl," Kahl grinned, staring at the ruffled cuff of the shirt Roan wore.

A flush worked its way into Roan's cheeks, and he grinned. "Aye, sa I do. Hard ta believe grown men willingly wore these things, eh?" His gaze cut to the woman across the table from him. She stared through him before looking down at her bowl once again. "Tis the owner's shirt. I braved damnation ta enter his grand suite an' take a loan o' one o' his possessions."

Scrinching up his face, Kevin grunted, "Huh?"

Taking a sip of coffee, Roan winked at the boy. "Lannie's verra possessive o' his belongings."

"That's enough," Laura warned, her eyes flashing at Roan through a darkening expression.

Roan arched a brow. "Beg yer pardon, but wha' *can* I talk abou' wi'ou' insultin' yer sensibilities?" Pushing an ear forward with an isolated finger, he probed, "Eh?"

"Knock it off."

A look of spleen brought ruddy color to Roan's face. "I tell you wha', *Miss* Bennett, mak me a bloody list. An' don't be shy abou' sparin' ma feelings."

"Here we go again," Kahl sighed, his gaze darting between the adults.

Laura cast the boy a heated glance, then rose from her chair and carried her bowl and cup to the sink across the room. Roan watched her, her every stiff movement further fueling his temper.

"I'm neither responsible for yer predicament *nor* the storm."

"I never said you were," she responded, standing at the deep porcelain sink, her back to him.

Turning sideways in his chair, Roan began to drum the fingertips of his right hand upon the table. "Then spare me the dirty looks. I'm doin' the best I can. Yer're simply expectin' miracles where there's none ta be found."

"Naw," Kevin piped in, popping a chunk of oatcake into his mouth. "She's pissed, all right."

"Kevin!" Laura gasped, issuing him a visual scolding.

"Pissed?" Roan rose to his feet, his brow drawn down in a scowl. "Wha' have you been dippin' inta?"

"What?"

"Whiskey?"

"What are you talking about?" Laura asked, visibly rattled.

"Pissed. Drunk."

After a moment, her confusion fled. "No, Mr. Ingliss, I

do not drink. The *pissed* Kevin referred to, means . . . upset."

"Angry," Kevin lightheartedly corrected.

"I think we've heard enough from you," Laura told the boy.

"We're outta bog rolls," Kahl said to Roan.

"Out of what?" Laura asked him.

With a grin, Roan explained, "Toilet paper."

Laura grimaced. Bog roll? Once she got them back to the States, she was going to have to work with the boys on their language.

She was about to turn back to the sink when her gaze happened on Alby, whose brow lay on the table. Frowning, she walked up behind him and leaned over. "Alby? Hon, are you asleep?"

Roan quickly went to Laura's side and placed a hand on the back of the boy's neck. "He's burnin' oop," he gritted out. In a swift, parental movement, he lifted Alby's unconscious form into his arms and carried him to the sink.

"There's a clean claith under the sink," he instructed Laura. He turned on the cold water tap. "Soak i' guid an' lay i' across his brow."

"He seemed fine this morning," Laura murmured tremulously, doing as Roan had instructed. Her face as white as a sheet, she inspected the boy's parched lips, then glanced at the brothers at the table. "Did you notice anything wrong with Alby?"

"He puked next to my side of the bed, last night," Kevin said.

"Why didn't you tell me?"

Kevin shrugged. "Carrie never wanted to hear that kind of stuff."

"Well, I'm not Carrie, am I?"

"Laura."

Roan's soft tone brought her gaze to meet his. "Calm doon."

Tears instantly sprang to her eyes. "I don't know what to do," she admitted in a small voice choked with emotion.

Roan wetted the cloth again and gently dabbed it over Alby's red face. "Ma son had his share o' fevers."

"You have a son?"

Pain radiated from Roan's eyes when he glanced at her. "He died a few years ago."

"From a fever?"

Looking down into Alby's face, Roan gave a solemn shake of his head. "Boys, help yer aunt ta draw a cool bath in yer room," he said over his shoulder.

Kahl and Kevin sprang from their chairs, but only the younger of the two approached the adults.

"I'll clean up the kitchen," Kevin said as he started to gather the bowls.

"No' on yer life!" Roan snapped.

"I did dishes all the time," the boy protested, suddenly seeming far older than his seven years.

Laura caught Roan's glance and nodded.

"All right. We'll be oopstairs," Roan said to Kevin as he turned toward the dining room door. "Join us whan yer're done."

"Yeah, yeah."

The day drew on with excruciating slowness. For the most part, Laura felt completely helpless as she shadowed Roan—until at one point he told her to try to relax and keep Kahl and Kevin entertained. She read to them in the library until they could no longer sit quietly. She took them to the tower, absently listening to the gruesome stories the place visited upon Kevin's fertile imagination. Hours later, at Roan's request, she heated a can of chicken soup for Alby, who refused to take even a sip of the broth. She could barely stand to hear the child's moaning and sobs, while Roan, to her utter bewilderment, seemed quite naturally in his element taking care of the boy. Between baths in cool water, Roan rocked him in an antique chair by the window, humming lullabies to ease his delirium. Laura's tolerance lasted but a matter of minutes before she herded the older boys out of the room to look for something else to keep them occupied.

Late that night, after hacking a smoked ham into uneven slices, she made sandwiches for all but Alby. Roan devoured his while cradling Alby on the rocking chair. Laura and the boys ate theirs in silence in the kitchen. After prodding them to wash their faces and hands at the kitchen sink, she led them back to the bedroom. Uncharacteristically cooperative for once, they climbed atop the feather mattress, removed their shoes and socks, and lay quietly while their aunt covered them with the quilts.

"Don't wake Alby or Mr. Ingliss," she cautioned, planting a kiss on each of their brows.

"Alby still sick?"

"I don't know, Kevin. He needs his rest." She tucked the quilts beneath their chins. "So do both of you. Now close your eyes."

She wasn't sure how long it took the boys to fall asleep. Her body was numb, her mind burdened with recriminations. Glancing in Roan's direction, she felt tears mist her eyes. How easily he slept holding Alby in his arms, as though he'd done it countless times. *He* was proving to be the kind of guardian her nephews needed. Firm, yet attentive. Not like a certain aunt who panicked at the sight of a runny nose.

Caught up in a mantle of self-pity, she rose from the bed and walked into the hall.

Roan's eyelids lifted when Laura left the room, and he stared at the empty doorway for a long time. Then his gaze lowered to the moonlit-kissed face of the boy in his arms.

A smile of immeasurable warmth played across his mouth.

How many times had he rocked Jamey during those three years of his life?

He looked to the doorway again. The smile faded.

Easing himself onto his feet, he carried Alby to the bed and gently laid him toward the center, to Kevin's right. How angelic and peaceful they appeared when sleeping, he thought, and he smiled wryly as he brushed the back of his fingers over each of their brows.

Exhaustion settled over him. Walking into the hall, he was half tempted to go to bed himself, but he was concerned for Laura's state of mind. He hadn't meant to exclude her from taking care of Alby—at least not intentionally. She'd been so pale since the fever in the boy had been discovered . . .

Believing she'd gone downstairs for a cup of something hot, he headed for the staircase. He was about to descend when a draft drew his attention to the opposite end of the hall. The heavy drape covering the tower entry was flapping back.

Frowning at the warmth of the draft, he entered the tower and began to climb the stone, spiral staircase that hugged the rock of the outer walls. Stories he'd heard all his life of Baird's remains being found in this part of the mansion, had long doused his interest in exploring it. He paid no attention to the sparse furnishings of the bygone servant quarters as he ascended. On the fourth landing, at the top of a steep set of wooden steps, he discovered the ceiling hatch open. The instant his head breached the opening, he spied Laura standing by a four-foot tall, crenelated circular wall.

He climbed onto the flat roof, and for a time was content to watch her. She was more than simply attractive, he realized, admiring her slender form, accentuated by the snug dark slacks and brightly colored sweater she wore. Her face, lifted to the silver illumination of the night, showed to advantage the delicate angles of her jawline. Long, graceful fingers lay anchored on the opposite upper arms.

"The fever broke. He'll be fine."

At the first sound of Roan's husky voice, Laura gave a start.

"Thank you."

"It was ma pleasure." Roan stepped to her side and gazed out in the direction of the shadowed waters of Loch Ken. "Tis quite a view from oop here."

Laura nodded.

"Spill i', girl."

Green eyes swung up to regard his profile.

"Somethin' is eatin' a' you. Get i' off yer chest."

"It's been a long day, that's all."

Roan offered her a lopsided grin. "Liar."

"I'm not in the mood for another confrontation," she sighed. She started to turn away when his hand clasped her arm and stayed her.

"And I'm *not* in the mood for another lesson in preeing, thank you," she delivered icily.

"In yer dreams," he chuckled, releasing her arm and lifting his hands in a placating gesture. "I'm here ta talk."

"I can't think of anything we have to talk about."

Roan gave an exasperated roll of his eyes. "Ye're a stubborn womon if I've e'er met one."

Stiffening, Laura countered, "I'm sure you've had your fair share."

"O' women or just plain *stubborn* women?"

The laughter in his eyes crumbled her attempts to appear stern. "Fine. You want to talk?"

"Aye."

"Then tell me . . . how did your son die?"

A shadow of pain clouded his expression. "Tis no' a subject I care ta discuss."

"Are you still married?"

"Na."

"I see," she murmured, staring sullenly out across the glistening land. "The subject you *will* discuss is me, right?"

"Tell me abou' yer family," he urged in a soft, seductive tone.

She eyed him warily, her heart thudding behind her breasts. "Whatever for?"

"I'm curious." Bracing his buttocks to the wall, he folded his arms against his chest and looked down into her defiantly strained features. "Behind all yer spit an' polish, I sometimes see a verra lonely womon."

"Ha," she gasped flippantly with a toss of her head.

"I'm curious, you see, because ma family is close. We're scattered from here ta the west coast, but we keep in touch. We Inglisses have an understandin', we do. Family comes first, whate'er the price."

Laura looked away. She didn't like the feeling of being beneath the scope of his practiced eye. His curiosity was too personal, and she was already having enough of a struggle keeping herself emotionally distant from him.

"Had a brither o' mine died, Laura Bennett—whate'er the differences between us—I wad have done anythin' ta have the chance ta say ma final guidbye ta him," he went on, his tone as painfully probing as a needle in a raw wound. "No' sa wi' yer clan."

A shiver passed through her as she murmured, "Different strokes . . . for different folks."

"Why are you workin' sa hard ta have me believe you've na heart?"

Her anger-brightened gaze cut to his face. "Why do you care if I have heart or not . . . *eh?*" She emphasized the latter with a sneer, then felt instantly contrite and looked out across the scenery.

Roan heaved a whimsical sigh. "I, tae, don't like feelin' helpless, lass." Hearing a sob catch in her throat, he leaned his head back to see more than just her profile. "But yer brither . . . How could you no' come ta say yer guidbyes ta him? I don't understand."

Gulping past the tightness in her throat, Laura unconsciously gripped the rough edge of the wall. "My brother was seven years older than me. We were both passed off to every neighbor, friend, and family member who would take us, while my parents pursued their dream of traveling the globe. We simply got used to them not being around."

Her voice grew huskier as she continued, "Steven resented having to watch over me as much as he had to. When he turned eighteen, he enlisted in the Air Force. I was twenty-two before I heard from him again, and he'd only written to tell me how much he loved England, and his plans to spend the rest of his life here. I got the distinct impression he blamed the morals of all Americans on his hang-ups. He wanted his children to have the kind of family life he'd been denied.

"It was a two-page, bitter . . . *bitter* letter, and at the time, I was angry that he'd sent it to me. I showed it to my parents." A dry laugh caressed her throat. "They shrugged it off, so I tossed it away without a further thought about him."

She paused to will back a threat of tears.

"Then . . . as I told you . . . he called after each of his sons were born. Nothing but a brief gloating message of his ability to procreate."

Shrugging, she ran her fingers through her pale hair. "How ironic that I should now have his sons." She lowered her hands to the wall. "Steven would hate the fact I'm taking the boys to the States, and he would hate the fact that I'm all they have in this miserable world." Her voice cracked when she added, "Justifiably so."

"Have you ne'er been in love?"

She tried to focus on the loch in the distance, but could not. "Love is for dreamers, Mr. Ingliss. I've never believed in dreams, or in magic, or in anything I couldn't see and touch."

An invisible fist closed around Roan's heart. To guard his dismay at her disclosure, he shifted behind her. Placing his hands atop the wall, he caged her within his muscular arms. He was aware of her indignant stiffening, but chose to ignore it while he deeply inhaled the gentle floral scent of her hair. "An' here you are, lass, in the heart o' magicland."

"Am I?" she asked coldly.

"Look around you," he laughed softly. "Wha' do yer eyes tell you? Wha' do you feel against yer skin?"

Laura could not stop a shudder from coursing through

her. "Back off, Roan," she rasped, folding her arms against her.

A smile played across his mouth as he contentedly gazed about the landscape. "All ma life, I've hated this house an' all i' stood for," he began, unwittingly pressing himself closer against her and grazing the top of her head with the underpart of his chin. "An' I've hated Lannie wi' a passion tha' has just abou' eaten away ma innards like a cancer. But sa much has changed ma way o' thinkin' the past couple o' days. His cursed magic has finally opened ma eyes."

Whirling to face him, Laura furiously glared into his face. "So we're back to the ghost stories again? You *ass!*"

Closing one eye for but a moment, Roan winced. "Ye're no' payin' attention, lass. Get yer mind off ma anatomy an' look around you."

Briefly, Laura considered throwing herself from the roof of the tower, or, less dramatic, ducking beneath the berth of his corralling arms and running like hell to the relative safety of her bedroom. But the laughter in his tone challenged her, and she remained rooted. Her shoulders haughtily thrust back, her chin lifted in a show of defiance, she looked into his smiling eyes with as much bravado as she could muster.

"I'm not going to allow you to provoke me any more."

"Ahh, is tha' sa? Weel—" He chuckled and teasingly planted a quick kiss on her brow. "—wha' else but magic wad whisk you from the clutches o' a loomin' oak?"

"I don't find you particularly amusing."

"Na? But then, yer sense o' humor is a wee wabbit—"

"What?"

"Eh?"

"Wab—what?" she frowned.

"Wabbit? Tired . . . ill."

Lowering her head, Laura pressed her fingertips to her temples. "I'm going to check on the boys." A moment later, when he made no move, she wearily peered up into his face. "I'm exhausted. Can't we put this off until the morning?"

"Ye're no' leavin' till you open yer eyes," he grinned with devilish glee, straightening back and folding his arms across his chest. "An' no' till I get a weel-deserved apology for you doubtin' ma word."

"Your word?" Her temper resurfacing, she asked, "Your word regarding what?"

"Lannie."

Laura smacked him on the chest. "When hell freezes!"

"Explain the dinin' room, then. An' the statue . . . ?"

"It never happened," she returned smugly.

"Ach! Ye're sayin' then, we shared the same hallucination?" he asked incredulously.

"Makes perfect sense to me."

"Are we hallucinatin' now?"

A warning light went off in her brain at his coy tone. "Possibly. It's a delightful notion that you're nothing more than a figment of my imagination."

"You just insulted me."

Laura gave an airy shrug.

Scratching his head, Roan walked to the flagpole by the opened hatch and linked an arm around the cool metal. "Tis a warm night, eh?" He waited until he saw a pensive frown crease her brow, then went on, "An' tis strange tha' snow falls ten feet ou' all around us, yet this roof is as dry as a summer's drought."

Awareness slowly seeped into Laura's brain. Turning, she realized that it was snowing—very hard—everywhere as far as the eye could see, except over the tower. Her gaze lifted to see a hole in the clouds directly overhead. A black velvet sky, jeweled with stars, crowned the tower, and only the tower.

The roof was dry, the air warm. And yet, the other roofs to the mansion bore blankets of the white stuff.

"Lannie's doin'," Roan informed, a smug grin turning up one corner of his mouth.

Laura stared at him for a long time before forcing her legs to carry her to the hatch. She was in no frame of mind to try to rationalize the phenomena. "Good night, Mr. Ingliss," she said in a strained voice, then cautiously descended the steps.

For a time, Roan remained hugging the flagpole, his eyebrows drawn down in a scowl. He'd wanted her to face the truth about the house; he'd succeeded in scaring the wits out of her.

Fatigue revisited him unexpectedly. In two days, he'd only dozed off occasionally.

A gasp burst from his lungs when the air became bitter cold, and snow began to fall on him. He quickly descended, closing the hatch behind him.

"You bleedin' cleg," he muttered testily, storming into the second floor hall. "I'll throttle you, Lannie, I swear!"

He was about to enter the room he'd been using when he glanced down the hall. His scowl darkened out of impatience. Laura had implied she was going to bed, but he knew he wouldn't sleep a wink until he saw for himself that she was asleep, and with the boys. Grumbling beneath his breath, he strutted down the dimly lit hall, a palm rubbing the stubble on his jawline. The bedroom door was open when he arrived. He was about to step past the threshold when his bleary vision zoomed in on a tall figure standing by the bed. After a moment, Lachlan Baird followed Roan into the hall, closing the bedroom door behind him.

"Guid o' you ta mak an appearance," Roan grumbled, running a hand through his thick, disheveled hair. His bloodshot, soft brown eyes narrowed. "It wad have been nice ta have had a wee help wi' those little monsters in there," he added in a hushed tone.

"I returned as soon as I could," Lachlan said calmly. "Suppose you fill me in o'er some scotch."

Roan's expression went deadpan. "Scotch?"

"Aye."

An icy cold, internal caress snapped open Laura's eyes. For what seemed a long time, she lay perfectly still, staring into the darkness. She couldn't fathom what had awakened her, or why gooseflesh covered her arms, despite the fact they were tucked beneath several quilts. At first the house seemed unnaturally quiet and still, but an inner sense warned her that something was amiss. Somewhere within the walls of this bizarre mansion, there was physical movement. It was not something she could hear or see, but she knew without doubt that something was happening.

Her stomach in knots, she eased out of the bed so to not awaken her nephews, then tiptoed barefoot in the direction of the door. She groped in the darkness until she found the doorknob, then cautiously stepped into the dim grayness of the hall.

Two gas wall lamps were all that provided light. Remaining on tiptoe, she slowly made her way toward Roan's room, casting fearful looks at the sideboards and antique tables she passed, as if expecting something hideous to spring out from them and grab her.

Then a feminine voice stopped her in her tracks.

"You weigh a ton, you big ox."

A warble of a laugh followed. "Tis ma heart-filled joy ta have you back, weighin' me doon."

"Cut the blarney," the woman said on a sigh.

Laura lit into a run, but stopped again when she reached the staircase. Her heart rose into her throat. A woman's white gown, and a pair of man's black boots, were all that she could see ascending to the third floor.

"Wait—" she called out, then was given a jolt when a piteous groan caught her attention. She looked up to see that the couple was no longer in sight. Another groan beckoned her from somewhere below, and the thought of Roan in some kind of distress, lanced her through the heart.

Moving in swift descent, she stifled a cry at the sight of him sprawled on the floor at the bottom of the staircase.

"Roan! *Roan!*" she gasped, turning him onto his back. Her trembling hands framed his ashen face. "Roan, what happened? Are you hurt . . . or ill—"

He belched, and she unwittingly caught a whiff of his breath.

Amid a stomach-churning odor of eggs was a distinct vapor of whiskey.

Her head reeled from the fumes, but she stared down into his face for a long moment.

He moaned again. Laura smacked him on the chest.

"You're *drunk!*" Taking him by the shoulders, she tried in vain to draw him into a sitting position. "Roan, wake up! You'll catch your death if you stay like this in this drafty hall! Damn you, Roan—" She slapped him twice on the cheek. "—wake up!"

Anger heightened the color in her cheeks as she looked up the staircase. Part of her wanted to leave him as he was and let him pay the price later, but she couldn't bring herself to abandon him. However, she was damned if she was going to sit beside him while he slept off a drinking spree.

She ran to the kitchen and returned a minute later with something clutched in one hand. Kneeling beside him, she took a moment to search his face. A fluttering sensation swirled around her heart. Never had she met a man so utterly masculine, and it was more than his rugged visage and muscular build. There was something about him she couldn't quite put her finger on, something in the way he took charge that gratified a primitive need in her. She'd never allowed a man to try to dominate her in the past. She thought, prior to this Scotland experience, that she'd never allow herself to give up even a small portion of her independence. So why did she, in her heart of hearts, gladden whenever he blocked her threats to leave? Was it because she had subconsciously known she was being irrational, or was the actual reason that she didn't want to leave before *really* getting to know him?

Uncurling her fingers, she took a pinch of the dark ground substance, but stared down into his face for a time longer.

Had she not been in such a state—or so damned proud!— she would have enjoyed further exploration of his *preeing*.

She focused on his sensuous lower lip, and sighed.

Such a wonderful, beckoning mouth. She knew in her heart, she would never work up the nerve to tell him how devastatingly charming was his burr. Part of her initiating their confrontations was to listen to him, although it caused her to inwardly ache to hear the enchanting lilts his tongue created out of the simplest words.

"I've got to purge my system of you," she said in a solemn, low tone. Her gaze was drinking in every detail of his features.

Heaving a throbbing breath, she sprinkled the black substance beneath his nostrils, then clamped the same hand over his mouth. Anxiety began to work its strangulating fibers through her conscience when long moments passed.

Then he sneezed. His hands clumsily tried to pry hers from his mouth.

Laura scooted back as a sneezing fit fully snatched him from unconsciousness. Rolling over and getting onto his hands and knees, he gave in to the paroxysms until they finally began to wane.

Pain sliced through his head with each movement. Numbness tingled through his limbs. His stomach heaved, settled, then heaved again before he began to gulp in draughts of air.

"Are you all right?"

His head slowly turned, and his bloodshot eyes strained to focus on her. "Wha' did you do ta me?" he rasped.

"I couldn't revive you," she replied nervously, scooting back further until her spine met with the bottom step.

Roan gingerly turned on his hands and knees to face her. "Wha' did you—" He sneezed again, groaned, grimaced, and narrowed his eyes on her. "—do ta me?"

She held out a trembling fist, then uncurled the fingers and exposed what lay on her palm and smooth fingertips.

Closing one eye, Roan stared at the substance. "Pepper? You made me snort *pepper?*"

The wounded, incredulous look in his eyes racked her with guilt. "It worked, didn't it?" she asked in a small voice.

Crawling to the newel post and hoisting himself onto his feet, he issued a guttural, "I'm feelin' a wee wabbit."

Laura sprang to her feet, a look of horror masking her face. "Are you going to throw up?"

His eyes narrowed on her as he strained to steady the tottering of his large frame. "Wad be fair play, eh?" He sneezed and nearly keeled over.

"Don't fall, *please!*" Laura pleaded, wrapping an arm about his middle. "The owners have returned. I'll get them to help—"

"Leave 'em be," he growled, placing his brow on the rounded post in front of him. "They're probably makin' love."

Laura's cheeks reddened as she peered up the staircase.

"They've i' comin', lass," Roan murmured, looking up as well. "Lannie's okay. No' the deil I thought him ta be."

"The two of you got drunk. By any chance, did you talk about my predicament?"

As if to move was excruciating, Roan placed an arm about her shoulders and stared down at her upturned face. "Aye, we talked abou' you an' the laddies."

"What did he say?"

Roan scrinched up his face. "Can't i' wait till the morn?"

Taking a fortifying breath, she nodded. "All right. I've waited this long."

"Can you help me oop the stairs?"

"I'll do my best," she replied with an edge of skepticism.

The ascent was slow and tedious. Roan's legs threatened to buckle beneath him about every other step. By the time they reached the second-floor landing, Laura was winded, and her shoulders ached from the strain of trying to support him. She led him into the bedroom he'd been using, through the dark, to the bed, and helped him to sit on the edge of the mattress.

"I'm going to get you a cold cloth. Don't move."

A grunt was his response.

Frustration unnerved her as she stumbled around the room in search of a bathroom. When it finally occurred to her that this room did not have a private bath, she went into the hall and ran to her room. She stopped only long enough to assure herself the boys were still asleep. Then by memory alone, she went into the dark bathroom. Something strewn across the floor nearly caused her to trip. Ignoring it, she removed a towel from the rack, and soaked it beneath the tap in the sink. Careful of her footfalls this time, she exited the bathroom.

After closing the bedroom door behind her, she ran back to Roan's room, saying as she passed the threshhold, "Good, you have a light on— Where are you?"

Panic settled in her brain as she ran to the far side of the large, decorative oak bed. Her breaths roared in her ears when she saw that he was not on the floor as she'd thought. Trying to reason where he could have gone, she cast a wild look about the spacious room.

The towel in her hand dripped on her bare feet, drawing her attention. Feeling lightheaded, she pressed the cold wetness to her face and held it there for a time.

"Somethin' crawled inside ma brain an' died," came a guttural voice.

Laura looked up in the direction of the door. An instantaneous stupor wrapped about her at the sight of Roan staggering into the room, an index finger inserted into his mouth, rubbing a blue substance on his teeth and tongue. Perhaps at another time she would have thought the scene comical, but his nakedness completely shocked her. He staggeringly padded across the room. Lifting a hand over her pounding heart, she watched him with wide wandering eyes.

His utterly masculine physique caused her mouth to go dry. Never had the sight of a man affected her so poignantly—not that she'd seen many in the nude. Still, she couldn't imagine another man having this same effect on her sexual awareness.

He spared her a disgruntled look as he made his way toward the bed. A shiver coursed through him. Damn the drafty house! And damn the scotch clouding his mind! By the time he reached his destination, the thundering in his head had worsened.

"I'm dyin'," he groaned, crashing face down atop the quilt covering the feather mattress.

Barely able to breathe past the tightening in her throat, Laura again buried her face in the towel.

If she didn't get away from this man soon, she was positive she was going to get involved in something she would later regret. Just what she needed. Another complication.

Wasn't it enough that she had the boys to worry about?

What good could possibly come of her succumbing to a whim to make love with this crude, dour Scot?

Silently groaning, she lowered the towel just enough to peer down at him.

Thank God he was too drunk to test her willpower!

Four

Laura had never thought of herself as a prude until this moment. She resented his unabashed display of his nudity, resented her weakness to stop herself from gawking at him. Incendiary sensations moved over her skin, and coiled within the pit of her stomach. Sparks of desire ricocheted inside her skull. Though the lighting in the room was soft, the image of his physique would always remain clearly branded in her memory. Clothing did not make the man in Roan's case.

She was thirty years old, and unable to cope with the sight of a naked heinie!

No . . . not just any naked heinie. Roan Ingliss's, in all its raw glory. He'd strutted toward the bed as if she hadn't been in the room. But he had spared her a brief glance, telling her that this scene had been a deliberate move on his part to rattle her again.

The thought stimulated her pride, and she slowly lowered the towel. Rigid, she languidly ran her gaze down the length of him, then dwelled on the firm curvature of his buttocks. Most of the men she'd known couldn't fill the seat of a pair of jeans two sizes too small. Not Roan, damn him. Muscular thighs and calves. His back and shoulders . . . and biceps. He either vigorously worked out in a gym, or owned the most incredible genes. . . .

Laura gulped. Her gaze went traveling over him once again. The underside of her hands itched. It had been—what?—more than a year since she'd made love. Actually, love had had nothing to do with it. She'd known Dan Faradey for four years. They'd been working at her place late one rainy, damp night, and for the first time in a long time, she'd found herself needing physical comfort. She'd approached the idea with the same directness she used in all her business relationships. Dan had been divorced a little less than a year. Obviously lonely. It seemed natural at the time.

His idea of making love had soured her needs after that night. Dan had been crudely oblivious to satisfying her, and later had left her feeling completely empty, little more than a vehicle in which he'd used to grunt his way to a climax.

Tears misted her eyes as she unexpectedly became angry with Roan. Without a thought as to the consequence, she whipped the towel up, and lashed a corner portion of it across his back.

His gasp rang out amid a blur of motion. Stunned, Laura felt something cinch her wrist and yank her downward onto the mattress. She found herself pinned beneath Roan, staring into his anger-darkened face. Cursing in Gaelic, he planted his elbows to each side of her upper arms, and leveled himself threateningly above her.

"Wha' the bloody *hell* is wrong wi' you?" he asked harshly.

Dazed, she pondered the scent of toothpaste on his breath. Her brand of toothpaste.

"Answer me, womon! Have you na sense than ta bugger a mon in his cups?"

"You're drunk," she accused, a telltale quaver in her tone.

"No' *tha'* drunk!"

She became aware of his cool, muscular, inner thighs pressing against the outer sides of her knees. "I-I dropped the towel."

"You did, eh?" he growled. "Weel, i' had a mean sting ta i', Laura-lass."

"I'm sorry. Get off me."

His bloodshot eyes narrowed suspiciously. "Don't want you ta catch a chill."

"I'm warm enough, thank you."

A sardonic grin ticked at one corner of his mouth. "Aye. I'm feelin' a bit warm maself. Wha' could be the reason, I wonder?"

"Get off me!"

To her immense relief, he rolled onto his side and allowed her to scramble from the bed.

"There is nothing more disgusting than a drunk!" she flung, trembling as she glared down at him.

"Aye, there is," he glowered. "A womon caulder than a winter's night."

"Cold? *Cold!*"

"I tak tha' back." The sardonic grin returned. *"Frigid* best describes you!"

"Pathetic best describes you! *You* leave me cold!"

Roan appeared to sober, a wounded look in his eyes. "Wha' are you afraid o', Laura?"

She stormed several paces toward the door, then turned, her fists clenched at her sides, and glared at him through tear-glazed eyes.

"Certainly not *you!* When I accused you of being 'pathetic,' I was being kind! You're a blustering, ill-tempered *drunk!"*

"Am I, now?" he murmured. Unsteadily sitting up, he

ran a hand down his face. Pain drummed against his temples. His skin felt hot, despite the chill in the room. "Come ta bed, Laura."

Shock swept through her, stiffening her posture.

"We'll talk. Nothin' mair."

Crimson flooded her face. Anger brightened her eyes. "I've no doubt you're incapable of anything *but* talk," she jeered, raking a condemning look over him.

Blinded by fresh tears, she ran into the hall and headed in the direction of her room. An inner voice lashed out at her mind with harsh recriminations. She shouldn't have attacked him with the towel. But then, he had no right to accuse her of being frigid, either!

Sobs caught in her throat.

Did he really expect her to fall into his arms like a love-starved schoolgirl?

Men. Their pursuit of pleasure guided their every waking moment. Yet when a woman desired physical contact, any given number of derogatory names branded her.

Talk!

That was a new one.

Damn him. *Damn him!*

From the moment she'd laid eyes on him, he'd been making her crazy!

A breath of freezing air unexpectedly passed through her. Dazed by the deathlike kiss of it over her skin, she staggered to a halt, bracing herself against a wall with a straightened arm. Her breaths came in gasps as she inwardly struggled to understand what had just occurred. It had been by no means a mere draft, and yet she couldn't begin to speculate what else it could have been.

Taking a moment to gather her wits, she placed a hand

over her heart. She closed her eyes just long enough to miss a flicker of blue light glow beneath the hand.

A tide of calm washed over her. The anger, stress, and frustration she'd been juggling the past two days, melted away beneath a blanketing state of euphoria. She didn't want to question what was going on, not when she felt so lighthearted and free of spirit.

A spring came to her gait now, and she went on.

She would apologize to Roan in the morning. It wasn't fair to chastise him for drinking, not when it was actually her father's alcoholism problem that spurred her resentment of libations taken in excess. Were she to be fair, Roan had bent over backward to make her and the boys as comfortable as possible. She had to remember that he was also under a great deal of stress—

She was nearly to the bedroom when something grabbed her by the arm, swung her around, and pinned her against the wall. Through rapidly blinking eyelids, she focused on Roan's scowling face looming in front of her.

"I'm no' a *drunk,* womon!" he said harshly.

"Then . . . stop acting like one."

Anger emanated from his every pore. His eyes bore into her own, condemning her challenge. At that moment, Laura feared him. Feared his ability to check his dark mood while in his inebriated state. Labored breaths pumped through her weighty lungs. She was about to offer an apology when she saw a blue aura appear on the center of his massive chest. Her gaze flitted up to study the bewilderment in his soft brown eyes. She realized he wasn't aware of the phenomenon. Before she could draw his attention to it, the glow retreated. Trembling in awe, she stared into his expressive eyes.

"Laura," he murmured, "I feel . . . verra strange all o' a sudden."

She nodded, although she didn't understand what was going on, either. He was an attractive man. She'd been aware of that from the beginning. But now she was so vitally aware of the chemistry between them, it was almost frightening. Their hearts were being pulled together as if by a powerful magnetic force. And somehow, she knew he was aware of it, too.

"You are . . . sa lovely," he said, as though amazed at his courage to say the words aloud.

Laura's chest and throat painfully filled with psychological tears. What was wrong with her? She'd never been this out of control! At least in her fantasies he would always be a wonderful lover, attentive, gentle, raising her to fulfillment as no actual man had ever done. She wanted him, but she knew when it was over, she'd have nothing but regrets. The wake of emptiness hurt too much, far more than the occasional awakenings of her physical needs.

"Don't be afraid," he whispered, his hands lighting upon the outer bare thighs beneath her short, cotton nightgown.

"No," she choked, his scorching touch awakening fiercer stirrings low in her abdomen. *"Please, no. . . ."*

His hands stopped at the elastic leg bands of her underpants. After a moment, he pressed himself against her, and she bewilderedly peered up into the hypnotic depths of his eyes. The silence between them gave birth to a span of introspection. Laura, despite her will to try, could not recall ever feeling so lost to desire. It wasn't lust. She was perfectly rational now. Too rational for her liking. And she wasn't feeling lonely or in need of an emotional fix to verify her feminine existence.

It was simply *Roan.*

An instinctual, primal yearning to share the ultimate intimacy with him, unmercifully felled her inhibitions.

Roan, meanwhile, was thinking back on the early years of his marriage to Adaina. It baffled him that he'd never felt breathless at the prospect of making love to her. His hands had never felt afire to touch her. How had he ever considered Laura a clone of her? The features in front of him bespoke of an innocence that he'd never seen in Adaina's face. And Adaina had never possessed the—though it could be outright frustrating at times—fiery spirit of this woman.

"Do you really want me ta stop?" he asked in a low, husky tone, his gaze sweeping over every contour of her face.

She focused on the blue toothpaste visible at the corners of his mouth, then her attention was drawn to his full lower lip.

His mouth made her crazy. Sensual. Sometimes brooding, and sometimes teasing. Lips designed to weaken a woman's control.

She swallowed once, then again when a haze of undeniable desire yawned within her brain. Straining on tiptoe, she pressed her lips to one corner of his mouth. He remained perfectly still while she ran the tip of her tongue over the sweetened spot.

A shudder passed through him, and he lifted his anguish-filled gaze to the heavens.

"Laura . . ."

His erection pressed against her abdomen, prompting her to graze the tip of her tongue to the other corner of his mouth. With seductive determination, she used the inner lining of her lower lip to melt away the rest of the toothpaste.

Roan groaned deep within his chest.

His arms encircled her shoulders. He drew her slender body flush against the rock-hard wall of his. His gaze searched her features as he slowly lowered his head. The instant his mouth closed over her lips, he shut his eyes and lost himself within the sensations building to an inferno behind his chest and within his groin. He became aware of her fingers pressing into the small of his back, urging him closer, as if that were possible.

He deepened his kiss, caressing the soft inner lining of her lower lip with the tip of his tongue. She moaned. Internal fires seized his genitals, causing a shudder to course through him once again. In a bid to rein in his control, he lifted his head and pressed his pursed lips to the soft skin between her eyes.

"Roan," she breathed unsteadily.

"Come ta ma room." He kissed a trail down her cheek, lingered at one corner of her mouth, then lifted his head and looked deeply, longingly into her eyes. "I want you, Laura. Sa much sa, ma brain's on fire."

She lifted her hands and smoothed them over the soft mat of hair on his chest. Desire tinted her cheeks a rosy pink, and brightened the deep green of her eyes. It had occurred to her when he'd first begun kissing her, that the guesstimated amount of whiskey he'd consumed—enough to render him unconscious—would have made the possibility of lovemaking very slim. But the evidence of his attraction, the vertical hardness pressed against her abdomen and thigh, dispelled any doubts she had as to his ability to consummate a union between them.

He began to nibble her left earlobe, his hands cupping and squeezing her rounded backside. "You smell sa guid." His teeth nipped the lobe, then he trailed kisses along her temple. "You taste sa guid." He kissed her mouth long and hard, weakening her knees. "Damn me, lass, you *feel* sa bloody guid!" he added, his inordinately deep tone sending chills of delight through her.

"Why are we . . ." Laura swallowed hard to quell her breathlessness. "Roan, why are we still in the hall?"

Lifting his head, he stared into her passion-glazed eyes and grinned almost shyly. "I'm afraid if I move, all this will vanish 'fore ma eyes. Can you feel ma heart, Laura?" Taking her hand, he laid her palm over the center of his chest. "Tis pumpin' wild."

"Yes . . . yes . . . it is."

"Tis been a long time, Laura-lass." He brushed the back of the fingers of his right hand along her cheek. "I'm a *wee* nervous. I don't want you disappointed, come morn."

A look of utter elation glowed on Laura's face. "No one's ever really cared how I felt about anything." Trembling with happiness, she lightly kissed the dimple on his chin. *Thank you. Oh God, thank you!* "Make love to me, Roan."

A tremor passed through him. His gaze languidly searched her face, and a sad smile played on his lips. "Yer're sa bruised, lass." Gingerly, he touched the discolorations on her features. "Do they hurt?"

"Not really. I forgot about them." She lowered her gaze. "I must look terrible."

"Na." He chuckled deep within his chest. "Bruises an' all, yer're the prettiest womon I've e'er laid these sarry eyes on."

"Gotta pee," came a whimper from close by.

Laura and Roan guiltily cut their gazes toward the boys' room. Kahl stood unsteadily on spread feet, rubbing one eye with a fist, the other hand clutching the front of his underwear.

"Gotta pee *bad.*"

Ducking beneath Roan's arm, Laura deliberately blocked the boy's view of the man's state of undress. "Go back in the room, hon. I'll be right in."

After a moment's pause, Kahl shuffled into the bedroom.

Laura quickly turned to face Roan, crimson staining her cheeks. "Go!" she urged in a stage whisper, giving him a shove in the arm. *"Please!"*

Left at odds by the turn of events, Roan ambled back to his room and closed the door behind him. Shivering with cold, he whipped the top quilt from the bed and haphazardly draped it over his shoulders, then lethargically went to the fireplace and prepared the iron grate with quartered wood stacked to the left of the white marble facing. He rose, took a box of wooden matches from the mantel, hunkered again, crumpled two sheets of 1848 newspaper stacked in a low crate in front of the wood, and built a fire. When the flames had risen to his satisfaction, he lowered his bottom to the cold stone hearth and numbly stared into them.

Kahl's untimely intrusion had broken the spell.

"What's wi' you, mon?" he asked himself aloud in a monotone. "Two days. Two days an' yer're ready ta bed her?"

He gave a solemn shake of his head, then ran the back of a hand beneath his chin stubble.

"Yer're smarter than tha', Roan Ingliss. Tis the house— or tis Lannie settin' you oop for a fall.

"Ooh, I know he shared his bloody whiskey wi' you, but one night o' camaraderie, does no' a friend mak.

"Damn me, I'm tired." He scowled into the flames. The pounding of his heart sounded hollow in his ears. "Whan did you last sleep, eh? No' nod off, mon. *Sleep!*"

Rubbing his hands down his face, he lifted a bent knee and rested his chin atop it. After a while, his eyelids lowered, and his pulse rate slowed, but still he could not sleep. A fluttering reminder of his earlier desire taunted him.

"Where's yer stamina, mon?" he murmured, his eyes remaining shut. "You've got ta banish her from yer mind. Think o' somethin' ither than—"

An inexplicable sibilation passed through his skull. The hearth, the flames, wavered in front of him, became grainy and distorted, then once again sharply defined. Ice flowed through his blood. Lodged in his heart. The air surrounding him shifted, again and again, until suddenly, he felt himself caught up in a passage of movement. His heart thundered. Terror swelled within his brain. Adrenaline flooded his veins, boiling his blood.

He experienced a sensation akin to coming to an abrupt halt. Words bombarded his mind, compelling him to voice them.

> *Ta you, let snow an' roses*
> *An' golden locks belong.*
> *These are the warld's enslavers,*
> *Let these delight the throng.*
> *For her o' duskier lustre*
> *Whose favour still I . . . wear,*
> *The snow be in her kirtle,*
> *The rose be in her . . . hair!"*

The compulsion intensifying, he went on:

> *The hue o' highland rivers*
> *Careerin', full an' cool,*
> *From sable on ta golden,—*

"How did i' go . . . ? From . . . from—

> *From rapid on ta pool*
> *The hue o' heather honey,*
> *The hue . . .o' honey bees,*
> *Shall tinge . . .*
> *Shall tinge her golden shoulders,*
> *Shall gild her tawny knees.*

Roan sagged in exhaustion, and wearily stared into the dancing flames.

"Robert Louis Stevenson's, 'To You, Let Snow and Roses,' " came a breathless voice.

His head shot up, and his heart skipped several beats at the sight of Laura standing by the open door. A breath caught in his throat as his gaze scanned the length of her, from her tousled blond head, to the shapely pale legs visible beneath her thigh-length, simple-cut nightgown.

"So you're a poet at heart, too?" she smiled, easing the door shut. Barefoot, she crossed the distance and leaned against the fireplace wall, facing him. "Had my Lit. professor had your accent, I might have taken poetry more seriously. What else should I know about you, Roan Ingliss?"

"Perhaps the whys an' the wherefores," he said softly, his gaze sweeping her from head to toe, and up once again.

Crouching, she studied his strong features for a time. "Tell me," she urged finally.

Shifting his gaze to the flames, he frowned. "The whys: 'cause yer're here, I suppose. An' lovely—desirable. The wherefores . . . for wha' I'm no' sure. Perhaps for the sake o' a night's pleasure; for a wee time o' escapin' the shadows o' the past."

His eyes, amber in the fire's glow, locked with hers. "Tell me *yer* whys an' wherefores."

Laura didn't hesitate. "The whys are because you're here, I suppose." She smiled a bit shyly. "Not because you're just an attractive man, but because you're *you*, Roan. Does that make sense?"

"Aye . . . I think."

"And the wherefores . . ." She looked down at her folded hands atop her lap and lightly shrugged. "I like to believe I'm an independent, modern woman, but the truth is, I'm not always sure—at least about the modern part." She lifted her gaze to meet his questioning expression. "The last time I, umm, initiated making love with a man, it left me feeling very confused and . . . empty. I-I guess the act made me realize that my mind's longing for physical love could not be satisfied by a random night's fling. Am I shocking you?"

Roan grinned and flexed his shoulders. "Na. Tis nice ta hear a womon speak openly o' such matters. Tae eften, people fail ta communicate. Kahl back ta sleep?"

Laura nodded, then grimaced. "He had a slight accident in the bathroom, though."

Roan arched a brow.

"He, umm, missed the toilet. You, ah, left your clothes on the bathroom floor."

"Ma claes—ma *trousers!*"

Again Laura nodded, a twinkle in her eyes. "I rinsed them in the tub and laid them out over a chair. I doubt, though, if they'll dry by morning."

Roan stared into the fire for a time, then shook his head and chuckled. "Damn me if I squeeze maself inta *Lannie's* trousers."

He sobered the instant their gazes locked. For an indeterminable time, silence bathed the room. Then Roan frowned and cut his gaze to the fire.

"What's wrong?"

He shrugged and drew the quilt tighter about his shoulders. "I don't know. There's a strange buzzin' in ma ears."

"It's probably all the whiskey you consumed."

Roan looked at her. "Na. Tis weird, I know, but I feel fine in tha' respect. Tis you . . ." With a shake of his head, he stared again into the hearth's source of warmth.

"Are you sorry you kissed me? Is that it?"

"Are *you* sarry?" he asked, scowling at her through a pained expression.

Laura took a moment to think over her reply. "You know, it's weird, Roan, but it felt very . . . right . . . as if I'd waited for that moment all my life." Lowering her backside to the floor, she sighed. "I don't want to let go of what I'm feeling, right now." She lightly tapped between her breasts. "At this very peculiar moment in my life, I swear my heart is beating only for you."

Holding out his hand to her, he rasped, "Come here."

After a moment's hesitation, she rose to her feet. Seconds ticked by. Self-consciousness made her fidgety.

"I won't hurt you," he vowed, extending his hand out further.

Lifting hers, she closed her eyes for a moment when his warm fingers enclosed hers. He gave a gentle tug, then another firmer tug urging her to step closer, urging her to stand with her feet planted to each side of his outer thighs. Then he released her hand and, for a long moment, stared up at her through an unreadable expression.

"Wha' are you afraid o', Laura?" he asked thickly.

Swallowing hard, her chin quivering, she achingly replied, "You, and how you make me feel."

His hands gently lit on the back of her knees. With a low groan, he leaned to and nestled his face against the soft mound crowning her groin. Laura clenched her teeth and dipped her head back. Her fingers threaded the hair at the back of his head, kneading, flexing, coaxing him to further explore. For a tormenting time, his palms massaged the back length of her legs, until, hesitantly, he cupped her buttocks, then held her firmly in place. With deliberate slow strokes, he smoothed his face across her abdomen. Now and then, his teeth nipped her through the fabric of her nightgown.

Laura trembled in anticipation, agonizingly sweet anticipation which threatened to consume her in the fires of need. She couldn't ignore the absolute rightness she felt at his touch. Ageless rightness, as though she'd been created for this one man, and no other.

His fingers hooked onto the waistline of her panties, and drew the flimsy material down over her hips. She gulped, trembling, barely in control of the raw passion rapidly building and building within her fevered body. His first tug ravaged her panties, and he tossed them aside. The realization that her womanhood was now bared to him intensified her excitement until she was sure she would perish beneath its power. He gripped her hips and coaxed her back a step. Her breathing became ragged, labored. She pulled the nightgown over her head and mindlessly swung it away. When she felt his lips touch her intimately, ecstasy, akin to a climax, rocketed through her system, tingling to the tips of her fingers, the tips of her toes, nearly causing her knees to buckle when he began to nurse in a manner previously unknown to her. Spasms impaled her reasoning, jolted her wave upon wave.

Crossing his legs Indian style, he gripped her hips and

tugged downward. She straddled his lap, facing him, her gaze never wavering from the passion glazing his eyes. His hands smoothing over her outer thighs, he kissed her, at first lightly, then in a demanding, masterful way that prompted her to thread her fingers through his hair and draw him closer. Lightheaded, weakening with desire, she tightened her fingers within the soft, thick strands.

"God," he breathed against her lips, then nuzzled his brow to one side of her face. "Yer're incredible! Sa soft. I *canna* wait. *Sair ta dae.*" Hard to do. "Sa . . . *sair ta dae.*"

He kissed her hungrily. His arms encircled her, crushing her small, rounded breasts against his chest. Laura's arms folded around his neck, and with the fire's warmth licking along her spine, she melted into the sheer masculinity of his embrace.

She thought his kiss enough to appease her until his hands crept up between their bodies and cupped her breasts. A gasp spilled past her lips. She arched away from him, her hands anchored on the muscular contours of his shoulders. Her eyes closed to the bliss of his kneading her breasts, of his thumbs gently massaging the dark, rigid peaks of her nipples. His tongue caressed the graceful lines of her throat, evoking incendiary pulses to again detonate along her skin. The provocative trail descended to her right nipple, where his mouth encompassed the taut bud.

"Oh God," she moaned, her fingers burying themselves into the hair at her temples.

Roan's hands moved to her back, supporting her as he suckled the nub of her firm breast. Every muscle in his body ached for her. The fire within his groin painfully hardened him, but he was determined not to end, too soon, the maddening ecstasy of his anticipation.

His mouth sought and enclosed her left nipple. His

tongue repeatedly circled it, eliciting a groan from her that rocked him with a shudder of desire. Unable to withstand the conflagration of his needs, he gripped her upper arms, drew her head up, and stared into her eyes with a look that betrayed his impatience to possess her.

Breathless, Laura managed a weak, "Yes."

"Lang syne," he chanted breathlessly, their gazes remaining locked.

His hands cupped her buttocks and eased her onto her knees, then, reaching between her thighs, he positioned himself. His other hand gripped her hip, and he deeply kissed her while coaxing her to lower herself onto his taut member. Her arms went around his neck. Her body trembled as the moist cavity of her loins touched him. A look of uncertainty flashed in her eyes, spearing him with alarm until she reached between her thighs, wrapped her fingers beneath the soft, smooth head of his member, and began to lower herself onto it.

Roan clenched his teeth. His eyes were riveted on her expressions of agony and pleasure when she slowly filled herself with all he had to give. He was dimly aware of losing himself, feeling oddly displaced. Undeniably, he loved this woman. He cherished her very existence, although he vaguely questioned the possibility of feeling so strongly for someone he'd known for so short a time. Ripples upon ripples of pleasure vied to sway him from dwelling on anything but the lovely woman making love with him. Mindlessness was to be expected. Absolute, instinctual need to quell his drive for a climax, normal. But looking at her, perspiration glistening on her expression of bliss, he had to wonder what had doused the friction between them. Her body moved up and down in perfect, tormenting rhythm, stroking him within the wondrous cavity of her perfect body. His muscles grew tauter by the second in response to her. The haze of passion thickened over his brain.

Groaning, shuddering violently, he planted his hands at her waistline to slow her strokes.

"Laura," he growled thickly.

Despite his grip, she increased her movements, grinding his shaft deep within her.

Roan was forced to utilize the extent of his willpower to keep from exploding inside her. Veins rose and mapped his broad neck as he strained to hold back. A pulse throbbed at his temples. He clenched and bared his teeth. The skin across his face grew tauter by the second. She watched him through glazed, bright eyes, studied his face in a manner that betrayed her delight in his readiness.

A cold sliver lanced his brain, startling him. From deep within his subconscious, a voice hissed that she was controlling him again. The idea sickened him, until she released a guttural groan, and her muscles, surrounding his shaft, began to pulsate. Instantaneously, he climaxed, caught up in the most powerful throes he'd ever experienced. At that moment Laura was his world, his universe, the bestower of the most exquisite pleasure life offered.

At the height of their soaring, he kissed her almost fiercely, clutching her against him within the band of his muscular arms. When the last shudder began to wane in their bodies, he wondered if he would ever feel so alive again.

And then—

Nuzzling a cheek to the side of his broad neck, Laura whispered, "Lachlan, I love you."

Liquid ice passed beneath his skin. Rage swelled within his skull. Immobile with shock, he questioned the validity of what he'd heard. Denials stormed the barriers of his reasoning. Laura Bennett had been under the illusion that she'd been making love with Lachlan . . . ?

The idea nauseated him. Barely able to contain his contempt for what he believed to be a master manipulation, he gripped Laura's upper arms and held her away from him. The soft, sensual afterglow in her eyes yanked on his heartstrings. He wanted her again. He wanted to touch and kiss every inch of her, taste her, inhale her, lose himself in the dark, moist cavity between her thighs. Lose himself to utter passion . . . and oblivion.

Unexpected pain gripped every part of him.

He should have known she never would have fallen for *him*.

Laura smiled tiredly. Although dimly aware that something was troubling him, she was uncharacteristically absorbed in her contentment. She languidly traced a finger along his lower lip, staring into his eyes, yet not grasping their betrayal of his withdrawal.

"Wha am I?"

His solemn tone elicited a laugh from her. "Who are you? *You,* silly."

"Ma name."

"Roan . . ." She frowned and smiled at the same time. "Roan."

"Last name?"

"Roan—"

"Ma *last* name!"

His anger took her aback.

"Baird! What's wrong with you?"

His chest rising and falling on labored breaths, Roan clamped down on his outrage. He urged her off his lap. Springing to his feet, he stared down at her as though she'd sprouted horns and had used them to rip him open from heart to groin.

"Get ou'," he growled, pointing toward the door.

Laura couldn't move for several seconds. Then, her movements sluggish, she went to where her nightgown lay in a heap on the floor, and slipped it on. Despite the tears threatening to spill down her cheeks, she squared her shoulders and forced herself to look him in the eye. She refused to try to second-guess his mood change. Their lovemaking had been incredible, and yet he was acting as though she'd hurt him in some way.

"Get ou', Laura," he said, his tone thickly laced with a threat to physically remove her, if necessary.

"What's wrong?" she choked.

"Us!"

The heat of her skin threatened to consume her. Anger-filled words crescendoed in her head, but she couldn't bring herself to voice them. Instead, she softly told him, "Try not to lose any sleep over this. I know I won't." Then, with as much dignity as she could muster, she left his room, almost silently closing the door behind her.

Roan clenched his hands by his sides. Tears he fought back seemed to fill his throat. The room felt colder than ever before, turning his skin to ice.

After several minutes, he lifted his eyes heavenward and allowed a choked sound to escape his control. "Damn you, Lannie," he rasped, shutting his eyes tightly. "Did we amuse you, you swine!"

His movements savage, he stalked to the bed and began to tear away the covers, dumping them onto the floor. Guttural sounds passed his clenched teeth. He wanted to shout his outrage at someone—*anyone*—before it split him in two. And in part, he wanted to blame Laura, but he was rational enough to realize that she'd also been a pawn.

"Roan."

He whirled in the direction of the voice. Reflexly, he balled his hands at his sides. Breathing heavily through his nostrils, he furiously glared at the mistress of the house.

Beth Staples took three steps closer. Her demeanor stayed calm, although her expression betrayed her trepidation. She wore the long-sleeved gown Lachlan hated, the one she'd found in the attic in an old trunk. "I'm responsible, Roan."

"Na."

"I am." She took another step in his direction. "I thought I was helping—"

A tortured laugh burst from him.

"Lachlan's not aware that I interfered." She gave a feeble shrug. "It got out of hand. I'm sorry."

"Sarry?" He quickly closed the distance, planting himself intimidatingly in front of her. "Sarry for wha'?"

"Please put something on."

Her request baffled him, until he looked down and realized his state of undress. Snatching up the sheet from the floor, he impatiently wrapped it around his hips and returned to her. "Now, lass, suppose you explain ta me wha' the bloody hell you thought you were doin'?"

It took Beth several attempts to speak before the words finally came out. "I thought if I just lowered your barriers a little . . . you would find each other."

"Lowered oor barriers?" he muttered. His clenched fists rested warringly on his hips. "Messed wi' oor minds, you mean!"

"No. Roan . . ." Beth deeply sighed and ran a hand through her shoulder-length riotous hair. "It was a whim.

I wasn't even sure I could pull it off, but I felt strongly enough about it to give it a try."

"Abou' wha'?" he shouted, veins mapping his temples and neck.

"You and Laura."

"Wha' abou' us?"

She searched the anguish deeply carved in his face. A strong sense of betrayal emanated from him, washing through her with the effect of a bitter-cold wind. "The two of you aren't meant to be ships passing in the night. Haven't you wondered . . . even a little bit . . . what brought her here, to this house, to us—to *you*."

A scoffing laugh was his first response. "Yer're daft."

"Think about it."

"I don't need ta bloody think abou' i'! It was an *accident!*"

She shook her head. "Everything happens for a reason."

"Ah." He bobbed his head mockingly. "The hereafter blessed you wi' omniscience, eh?"

"No."

"Na?" His eyes grew hard and fierce again. "Did Laura an' I perform adequately for you?" He slapped a palm to his chest. "Were we entertainin'?"

"Dammit, Roan, I wasn't watching or listening!"

"Na? Yer're here, aren't you?"

"Because I . . . *sensed* . . . you blaming Lachlan."

To hide his burgeoning emotions, he turned his back to her. "We mak love an', 'Lachlan, I love you,' she says. I ask her ma name. Roan *Baird,* she tells me."

"I can't offer you a technical explanation for what happened, but when I touched her in the hall, I must have unknowingly left her with a part of myself. Her memory retained my love for Lachlan."

Roan's head came around, his eyes condemningly dissecting her. "You touched me in the hall, tae, didn't you?"

"Yes. A little bit."

"A little bit?" His mouth compressed in a scornful line. "Miraculously, I pulled ou' o' a drunk. Then, lo an' behold, I'm all o'er Laura Bennett like a mon in heat. *A little bit,* Beth? Don't insult ma intelligence!"

"I didn't brainwash either of—"

"Haud yer gab!" he hissed, turning to face her. "Dinna fash yersel wi' a lie claimin' yer're atweel na responsible for Laura an' me gettin' gey thick thegither!"

Beth's expression went blank, then, "I can't defend myself when you lash out in a foreign language," she clipped, folding her arms against her chest.

In frustration, Roan gave a yank at the hair atop his head. Then slower, in as near to English as he could at the moment, he reiterated, "I said, shut yer mouth, an' don't trouble yerself wi' a lie claimin' yer're by na means responsible for Laura an' me gettin' verra friendly wi' each ither."

"Thank you. That's a little clearer . . . I think."

"I wad expect this kind o' betrayal from Lannie, but no' *you!*"

His words caused her to wince. "The attraction was there, Roan. I only . . . gave it a little nudge."

Leaning to, Roan leered into her face, "Stay ou' o' ma personal business! I don't need a bloody *ghost* managin' ma love-life!"

Beth haughtily arched a brow. "What you need is a kick in the ass, my friend."

Rearing back, Roan also crossed his arms over his chest, letting the sheet fall to the floor.

A scolding look flashed in her eyes. "I know all about loneliness, Roan. And I've also experienced the same social withdrawal you've been going through since the death of your son and wife."

"You don't know a *bloody* thin' abou' me, lady."

"I know you go through each day like a zombie." Her eyebrow arched again. "You're a good man, Roan. If someone needs help, you're there, but you never let anyone reciprocate."

"Tis *ma* life."

"Such as it is . . . eh?" she drawled, meeting his heated gaze with steeled determination. "When my mother took ill, Roan, I panicked. I felt trapped. And when she died, I thought the guilt of wishing her dead would crush me. Ironically, I didn't begin to live until I came to this house; until I met Lachlan."

"Spare me."

"Listen to some damn good advice."

Her calm yet authoritative voice wilted his defensiveness.

"For some people, Roan, there simply isn't a significant other. I thought I belonged in that category until I met Lachlan. Granted, our life together isn't remotely normal—being *dead* probably has a lot to do with that—but we love each other.

"Love is precious. Too precious to ignore. I see before me a man capable of unlimited compassion; a man with so much love in his heart, it hurts him to keep it bottled up. So why does he, Roan? Are you afraid of failing in a relationship again? Is that it?"

Testily retrieving the sheet and tucking it around his hips, he walked to a window across the room. He stared into the snow-packed night, blind to the wonderland scene. Weariness weighted his heart. He'd always been a private person, a man who found his own company preferable to that of others. Alone, he didn't have to play a role. He didn't have to pretend that he was content with his lot in life.

"Ask yourself what greater force delivered Laura and the boys into your hands, Roan," said Beth, from close behind him.

He focused on her reflection in the windowpane.

"Ask yourself what a man of your heart and passion has to offer them."

"No' a thin'."

"Who are you trying to convince?" she chuckled softly, resting a hand between his shoulder blades. She ignored the twitch of his skin to shun her touch, and went on, "Laura reminds me a lot of myself—the alive version, I mean. She's strong-willed and determined to make a place for herself in this world. Her family was never close—I grew up like that. We were fixtures as children. I suppose . . . fixtures as adults, too. She doesn't even realize that she's been searching to find herself.

"And the boys . . . they desperately need someone to guide them. I know they don't show it, but they're needy, Roan. Needy for love and kindness. Needy for security.

"Nothing can bring your son back, but there are three boys who can fill that void inside you. Deny yourself, and you deny them. I don't know which is the greater tragedy."

Drawing in a breath, he turned to face her. "Return ta Lannie, Beth. Don't interfere in wha' you can't possibly understand."

"I *do* understand." A mist of tears sprang to her eyes. "That's what hurts so much."

Suddenly needy himself, needy to hold and be held, Roan placed an arm about her shoulders and drew her against him. The warmth of her body took him aback, and banished the chill from his exposed skin.

"This is sa strange," he murmured, staring unseeingly across the room. "A bloody ghost has turned me ta moosh."

The door to his room opened. His sight zoomed into focus on Laura's pale face when she crossed the threshold. As if in slow motion, he felt Beth turn in his arms, saw Laura look in his direction and freeze in midstride.

Her name left his dry throat in a barely audible whisper. A stricken look further paling her, filled his vision.

After a moment, she opened her mouth to speak. Nothing came out but a croak. She turned and fled the room, leaving the door and Roan's heart ajar.

"Don't let her leave believing she was at fault tonight. Tell her the truth, Roan. Everything."

His gaze dropping to Beth's lifted face, he swallowed hard. "She'd spit i' in ma face. She already thinks I'm a madmon."

A sad smile appeared on Beth's lips as she turned completely to face him. "Just think about what I've said. Okay?"

"I'm oop ta ma ears in promises, now."

"I've got to return to Lachlan. He's not going to be too happy when he awakens with a hangover."

A wry expression seized Roan's features. "The mon's dead!"

Beth began to fade before his eyes. "Yes, but not his memories. It'll be very real to him. Take heart, Roan."

She vanished, but *take heart* eerily echoed in the cold shadowed confines of the room.

Five

The warmth of the teacup did little to alleviate the cold in Laura's hands. She paced in front of the staircase, only dimly aware of the boys watching her from their sitting positions on the first three steps. They'd eaten breakfast and were dressed to leave—

If only she could convince someone to drive her to a telephone!

She'd barely slept a wink. Anger continued to pump adrenaline through her veins. With the advent of dawn, snow flurries had begun anew. Unless she left soon, she was sure she would be trapped within the walls of Baird house for the duration of the winter. All things considered, it was a frightening prospect. If the boys didn't drive her insane, Roan Ingliss undoubtedly would.

Several hours earlier, he'd made a poor attempt to justify his actions of last night.

What a crock!

According to him, the ghost of Beth Staples had prompted their lovemaking. At least he was original. Not many men could come up with such a creative lie. She'd gone outside to put distance between them, but he'd followed her, more determined than ever to persuade her of his sincerity. When it became apparent that he would not back off, she'd called him a few choice names, and had even resorted to slapping him across the face. It wasn't until she'd accused him of being a womanizing tyrant that he'd retaliated. He'd kissed her. Passionately. So passionately, she'd forgotten they were standing in calf-deep snow, exposed to the elements. At least, she'd forgotten for a few moments. The instant her reasoning had returned, she kneed him hard in the groin, and left him folded in half on the ground.

He'd think twice before pulling that stunt again.

"We're bored," Kahl grumbled, his chin propped up onto his fists.

"That's good," she murmured absently, staring at the closed doors of the library.

It was already proving to be a harrowing day.

She glanced at her watch. 10:32 A.M.

Sitting next to Kevin, who was positioned on the lowest step, she frowned into the dark remains of her lukewarm tea.

Someone had arrived earlier. By the time she'd gotten halfway through the secondary hall, she'd caught but a glimpse of Roan ushering the visitor into the library. She was in the hall, intending to confront Roan on the matter of her and the boys leaving without further delay, when the woman she'd seen in his arms the previous night, came running down the staircase.

The woman whose portrait hung above the mantel in the parlor. Only now she wore nothing but a man's shirt.

Roan's?

The thought sickened her.

A further blow to her pride came when the woman brushed her off and also entered the library, closing the door, shutting Laura out and deepening her resentment toward the eccentric members of the household.

Her life in Chicago seemed a figment of her imagination, now. She didn't even care if she was missed, or if her atomizer designs for the new perfume line were overlooked, and the account turned over to someone else. There were countless hopefuls waiting for her to make room for them.

Right now, the driving factor in her life was to leave Scotland. Nothing else mattered until that was accomplished.

"What's wrong?" Kahl queried, poking his aunt in the back.

She looked up at him. "I'm waiting to talk to Mr. Ingliss."

"We gonna leave?" Kevin asked, his thin brows drew down in a frown.

"Yes."

"When?" asked Alby.

"I'll know once I talk to Mr. Ingliss."

"When you gonna talk to him, huh?"

"As soon as he comes out of the library, Kevin."

Getting to his feet, Kevin peeked down the hall. "I'll bet the ghost is in there, too."

Laura sighed. "There is no such thing—"

Kevin shot her an impatient look. "I seen him."

"You saw him."

"That's what I said!"

Sighing again, Laura stared into her teacup.

"Laura?"

Kahl's trembling tone drew her gaze to him.

"There's another ghost."

"Honey—"

"He comes in the room at night." Kahl shuddered. "I seen him a coupla times."

"Kahl, you were dreaming," Laura said softly. She

reached out and affectionately ruffled the boy's red-gold mop of hair.

"He's shriveled up," Kevin added, his grave tone causing a chill of alarm to pass through her. "I seen him, too. He stands at the end of the bed, looking at us when he thinks we're asleep."

"Kevin, you're frightening your brothers."

His small shoulders drew in. "I told him to go back through the wall, last night."

"The wall?"

"Yeah. The big thing where we put our clothes . . . ? It kinda swings out, like the shelf-thing in the library. He comes through there."

Although Laura's blood felt as cold as ice, she forced a smile for the boys' benefit. "You're letting your imagination get the better of you."

"Uh-uh." Alby snuggled close to her left side. "He told us ta leave. He sca-wed me."

Instinctively placing her arm about the youngest boy's shoulders, she assessed Kahl and Kevin for several long moments.

"You and Mr. Ingliss were in the hall talking lovey-dovey," Kevin grimaced. "Make love to me, Roan," he mimicked, then gave a theatrical roll of his eyes. "Barf talk. He got *lucky,* huh?"

"Kevin!"

"What? We used ta hear Carrie bonk her boyfriend all the time. No big deal."

Crimson rushed into Laura's cheeks. "Carrie better hope I never run across her again," she muttered.

"She was okay," Kevin said with a shrug. "She had this cool thing she'd tell Yanks she'd meet." Affecting a parody of her voice and accent, he went on, "In York, a road is a gate, a gate is a bar, and a bar is a pub."

Alby and Kahl laughed. Laura couldn't help but grin.

"Where is York?" she asked the boy.

"England, I think. My dad said he'd take us there to the museums, but he never did."

"You must miss him."

Kevin, his face devoid of expression, shrugged. "Not really."

"He didn't like us," Kahl informed with equal aloofness.

"I'm sure your father loved all three of you."

"Naw." Kahl swiped a hand beneath his nose. "He thought we were too noisy."

"And too wound up," Kevin added.

"But—"

Laura bit back her question when she heard a door slide open. Gasping, she passed Kevin her teacup and jumped to her feet.

Four people emerged from the library. Forcing her suddenly heavy legs to move, she approached them. Roan was the first to notice her. Of the four, he alone appeared rattled by something. She somehow knew it had nothing to do with her or her nephews. The other man was laughing as he spoke to an elderly woman. His arm was draped possessively about the shoulders of the woman from the portrait. Several feet away from them, Laura came to a halt. Roan came toward her. It was all she could do not to turn and run, to avoid the humiliation his presence rekindled. His movements slower than usual, he positioned himself alongside her, and lightly placed a hand on her arm. Clenching her teeth against a retort, she peered up at him. His soft brown eyes looked into her own. Despite the hurt and anger gnawing at her nerves, her heart skipped a beat.

Her throat tightened. Submitting to the powerful chemistry his proximity evoked, she lowered her gaze.

So as not to draw attention to herself, she attempted to ease her arm from beneath his touch. His fingers tightened. She looked up at him again with every intention of sending him a visual warning to back off, but again the sight of him staring into her eyes disarmed her.

For a moment, she thought he was about to say something to her. Not another false apology, she hoped in the deepest recesses of her heart. Her temper would flare, and a scene would ensue. Instead, Roan's gaze swung to the trio a few feet away.

"Lannie."

At his beckoning, Lachlan Baird's dark gaze targeted Laura. A secretive smile curved up the chiseled mouth. He winked to the woman within his hold, then dipped his head and whispered something to the elderly woman.

Laura painfully swallowed past the lump in her throat. Who were these people? She was at their mercy, and she didn't like it one bit. Never before had she been so aware of her sheltered existence prior to this trip. With the loss of her daily routine in the States, she was utterly at odds with herself. Put her in an office and she could tackle anything that came her way. Within the sterile, meticulous confines of her apartment, she excelled in utilizing her time among her various hobbies. Art. Music. Reading. Needlework. Here, she was nobody. She had no more identity than her nephews. One Yank among many who'd come to this land.

She reflexly stiffened when the three came toward her. The dark eyes studying her, although friendly on the surface, seemed to penetrate to her core. Unwittingly, she pressed closer to Roan, her hands clutching his arm.

"Guid morn, Miss Bennett," the laird said charmingly.

"Yer're lookin' much better than whan I first laid ma eyes on you."

"He was the first ta arrive efter yer accident," Roan explained.

Laura's fingers kneaded the muscular arm within her hold. "I need to locate a phone."

"Aye, but as Roan has explained, lass, the lines are doon."

"Surely, not everywhere!"

Beth leaned to and asked the older woman, "Miss Cooke, is your phone working, yet?"

"No, I'm afraid not." Her pale gaze shifted to the stranger, then beyond, to where the boys were watching from the bottom of the staircase.

"Perhaps, Miss Cooke, you wad be kind eneuch ta call the American Consulate whan the lines come on?" Lachlan asked her.

"Of course." Her bemused expression melted to one of deep compassion for Laura. "You poor dear. I'll let you know as soon as the lines are in working order."

"Damn me," Roan muttered, then, "Laura, this is Lachlan Baird, Beth Staples, an' Viola Cooke."

Laura offered them a stilted nod of her head.

"The lads," Roan went on, glancing over his shoulder, "are Kevin, Kahl, an' Alby."

Viola beamed them a grandmotherly smile. "Such handsome boys," she crooned.

"Little deils," Roan murmured. Clearing his throat, he asked Viola, "Could you also call ma Aunt Aggie an' let her know I'm all right?"

"Of course, Mr. Ingliss." Viola's bright eyes peered up at the laird. "Could I stay a spell and play with the boys?" She looked at Laura. "There are all sorts of toys in the attic." Her gaze shifted to the boys. "We could pick out a few and bring them down to the library. Would you like that?"

Kevin, followed by his brothers, eagerly came forward. "Toys, huh?"

"Lots of toys."

"Goofy stuff, I bet," Kahl grumbled.

"Let's find out, shall we?"

When Lachlan and Laura nodded their approval, Viola merrily urged the boys toward the staircase. "Now we must stay together," she said, heading up the stairs with them. "You wouldn't want me to get lost in this big old house, would you?"

"Relax, Laura," Beth said kindly, drawing the woman's troubled gaze to her. "This will give us a chance to talk. Have you had breakfast?"

"Yes, thank you."

"Lannie—" Roan scowled at the couple across from him. "Now wad be a bloody guid time ta show Laura yer stuff—if you get ma drift."

"Not now," Beth chided.

"I agree," sighed Lachlan, and smiled at his guest. "Tis true, though, the roads are tae bad ta travel, Miss Bennett. We'll get you ta Edinburgh as soon as possible."

"Lannie," Roan growled.

"But . . ." Laura gestured toward the staircase. "*She* managed to get *here*. The roads can't be *that* bad."

"Miss Cooke doesna live far," Lachlan explained. "Edinburgh's a fair travel, even in a motor caur." A twinkle flashed in his eyes, when he glanced at Roan. "Has no' the new master of Baird house made yer stay comfortable?"

New master?

Her stomach knotting, she spared Roan a scowl. "He's been most . . . generous."

"Generous," Roan parroted, an edge to his tone. "For pity sake, mon, tell her!" His eyes sent a mute plea to Lachlan. "She no' only thinks me a liar, but a *womonizer!*"

"If the shoe fits," Laura clipped.

Clicking his tongue, Lachlan shook his head. "Ingliss, ma friend, I think you need ta wark on yer approach."

"You swine—"

"No' in the company o' the ladies," Lachlan grinned. "Beth, darlin', try ta put Miss Bennett's mind ta ease. Roan . . . A walk in the morn's chill will do you guid."

Glaring down at Laura, Roan retorted, "I've had all the fresh air a mon can tak in one day."

"Come along, Laura," Beth said lightly. "I'll fix us something hot to drink."

Trailing behind her hostess, Laura stopped long enough to retrieve her teacup from the bottom step. She didn't know what to think about the foursome. Part of her wanted to believe that the roads were truly hazardous, but another part, conditioned from watching too many movies, held their motives suspect. She and the boys could . . . *disappear* . . . and who would know? Would Allen Treddock, her boss, think to question her extended absence, or would he simply replace her with one of the "hopefuls"?

Withdrawing from her grim thoughts, she seated herself at the kitchen table and took a long look at the woman refilling a teapot at the sink.

Was Roan having an affair with this woman?

The thought pained her more than she cared to admit.

The other woman was striking. Taller and shapelier than Laura. Her movements were carefree, graceful. Confident.

A pang of jealousy stabbed at Laura. Something else that was normally alien to her character.

"We're not lovers," Beth said, lighting a burner beneath the pot.

A chill erupted within Laura's chest and swiftly coursed through her. Her fingers curled against her palms, the manicured fingernails digging into her flesh.

Was the woman a mindreader, or responding to Laura's inauspicious return to Roan's room last night?

Turning to face the blonde, Beth folded her arms against her chest. "I love Lachlan, Laura. There'll never be anyone else for me."

"I saw you—"

"In Roan's arms?" With a low laugh, Beth crossed the kitchen and seated herself across from Laura. "I was upset, and he was simply consoling me."

Laura couldn't bring herself to meet the other woman's gaze. "It's really none of my business."

"May I ask you a personal question?"

The green eyes cast a furtive look at Beth.

"You're attracted to Roan."

Deep color spread across Laura's cheeks. "I thought you were going to ask me a question, not make a statement."

"Forgive me. Are you attracted to him?"

"I don't know you." Laura forced herself to meet the blue eyes watching her. "And I don't care to know you. I just want to return to the States with my nephews."

An understanding smile softened Beth's mouth. "There was a time, not long ago, I wanted to run away from this house, too. I'm glad I didn't."

"Well, I'm not you, am I?" Laura closed her eyes for a moment, then sighed. "I just want to go home."

"Roan and I were discussing fate, last night."

"Whose?"

Beth again laughed, drawing Laura's despondent gaze to her. "His and yours, mostly. Do you believe in magic?"

The question struck Laura as humorous. "No. Magic is for dreamers."

A glow of enigmatic wistfulness appeared on Beth's face. "Magic is mostly for disbelievers, Laura. I should know.

"You and I may walk different paths, but we're a lot alike." Planting an elbow on the table, Beth rested her chin in the upturned palm. "Sometimes fate deals us a left-field-hand. You have to learn to trust the dictates of your heart, Laura. It may tell you that you *are* already home."

It was on the tip of Laura's tongue to tell the woman that she was insane, but she bit the words back.

Until the weather cleared, she was stuck within these walls.

What would Beth Staples say if Laura told her that Roan had said she was a ghost?

"Miss Staples—"

"Please . . . call me Beth."

A strained smile came and went from Laura's mouth. "Beth, I can't help but feel helpless in this . . . situation."

"You're not helpless. Laura, I don't blame you for feeling out of place and trapped. The truth is, you couldn't have stumbled across a safer haven. Put your fears to rest. When the roads are safe to travel, we'll see to it that you and the boys make it to Edinburgh."

The doubt in the green eyes prompted Beth to add, "Just trust your instincts."

The kettle began to whistle. Beth left her chair. When she reached for a potholder on a hook to the left of the stove, her hand passed through it. The whistling grew louder. Quelling a stab of alarm, she forced a smile and turned to her guest.

"Laura, I have to run. Help yourself to whatever you need." She ran toward the parlor door. "Sorry about this."

Several seconds later, Laura rose to her feet. Cloaked in blessed numbness, she turned off the burner, then stared for a time at the door the woman had passed through.

Was it her imagination, or were the members of this household completely unpredictable?

"My instincts tell me to run and never look back," she murmured. "What do you think of that, Beth Staples?"

Roan tired of biding his time out in the snow-covered east gardens. Brushing aside the downy substance on the wide lower lip of the two-tier fountain, he seated himself and stared off across the landscape. Despite his thermals, Lachlan's clothing, and his lined coat, the morning coldness permeated the marrow of his bones.

He was the master of Baird house?

How was it possible that he could feel so . . . frightened . . . of such a magnanimous gift?

"Yer're losin' yerself, mon," he said sadly, staring into nothingness. "The events o' late have forced you ta experience the pains o' the heart again. Tis no' like I *breenge*. I've ne'er been a rash mon."

Sighing deeply, he rubbed his icy hands up and down his face. "Trouble wi' people is," he sighed again, lowering his hands to his lap, "they can't understand tha' an aiken heart bends ta na hurt, na matter the force o' the deliverance."

"Aye, but a heart o' oak can splinter."

Roan looked up and frowned at Lachlan, who stood an arm's length away. Coatless, his full sleeves flapping in the flurry-ridden breeze, he grinned before sitting alongside Roan.

"Tak i' from me, ma friend, self-counsel can drive you oop a wall."

Despite himself, Roan smiled. "You know tha' for a fact, do you?"

Releasing a woebegone sigh, Lachlan nodded. "Aye. Self-counsel an' women. Brrr. Yer're bloody damned if you do, an' bloody damned if you dinna."

Roan laughed.

A sly gleam stole into the dark eyes. "Course, now, we're better off than ma friend Braussaw there."

His gaze following the direction in which Lachlan pointed, Roan searched until he focused on what he was sure was the object of Lachlan's statement. Perched in front of a barren azalea bush was a partially snow-blanketed peacock.

Roan gulped.

"Earlier, I came ou' ta check on him." Lachlan lazily scratched beneath his chin. "I thought a' first he'd frozen ta death, then i' hit me. Ma bloody bird's full o' sawdust. Imagine tha', eh?"

Drawing in a fortifying breath, Roan forced himself to look Lachlan in the eye. "He got under the wheel o' ma van."

A dark eyebrow lifted.

"At the time, auld mon, you an' I weren't on the friendliest o' terms."

"Sa you had ma bird stuffed?"

Roan shrugged. "He's a bloody sight quieter than the ithers."

"Aye." A grin cracked through Lachlan's soberness. "Aye, he is. Howe'er, Roan, try ta spare the ithers, eh? The birds have been here for mair generations than I can count."

Roan nodded.

"Now, suppose you talk ta me abou' yer troubles."

"Naught ta say, really."

Lachlan grimaced. "Tis me yer're talkin' ta. By the way, she *is* pretty." He grinned broadly. *"An'* stubborn."

"Laura?" Straightening back his shoulders, Roan frowned. "Can't say as I blame her. It must be scary ta find yerself dependent on strangers."

"Fond o' her, are you?"

The gentleness in Lachlan's tone further unsettled Roan.

"I'd have ta be dead no' ta notice such a fine-lookin' lass."

"Fegs, mon!" Lachlan laughed, clapping Roan solidly on the back. "What's *dead* got ta do wi' anythin'?"

Roan blushed, a smile twitching on his lips. "I keep forgettin'. Sarry."

"I dinna mind. Truth be, I sometimes forget, maself." Suddenly serious, he went on, "Alive or dead, a mon must face his fears, Roan. You'll be a fit master o' ma home, I've na doubts in tha' respect."

"But . . . ?"

Lachlan looked deep within the soft brown eyes. "Yer personal life is anither matter."

"Tis none o' yer business."

"You've made i' so."

"Na. You like ta stick yer nose where i' doesn't belong."

"Perhaps, but I ne'er interfere unless tis somethin' tha' affects me personally. Roan, ma lad, I ne'er faithered a child, sa I can only imagine the loss you've suffered. But I do know somethin' o' pain, an' how i' embitters the soul. You've got yer whole life ahead o' you. Start anew. If you keep ignorin' the opportunities passin' you by, you'll wake one morn an' wonder wha be the auld mon starin' back a' you in the mirror."

"I've lived alone tae long."

"'Tis ne'er tae late ta embrace life."

"Na?" Resting his elbows atop his knees, Roan shook his head. "I don't know how."

Lachlan released a long, impatient sigh. "Yer're an ass, mon."

Straightening, Roan narrowed his eyes on Lachlan. "At least I'm an honest one."

"Dinna get yer breeks in an ooproar. I'm only tryin' ta offer you—"

"Advice?" Standing, Roan placed his hands on his hips and scowled at the laird. "Yer bloody advice got me kneed in the groin!"

Lachlan grinned. "Aye, an' you teuk i' like a *real* mon."

"Na. I hit the ground like a mon in excruciating pain! Ach, damn me." He sliced a hand through the air, then trenched his fingers through his damp hair. "I shouldn't listen ta you. I don't know wha' women in yer time were like, but the *modern* womon does *no'* appreciate bein' cornered."

"I ne'er said ta corner her."

"Laura deserves a mon capable o' tenderness, no' some horny fool ou' for a quick fix."

Lachlan shot to his feet, a savage expression darkening his face. "Listen ta me, Ingliss. You've got yerself mired sa deeply in self-pity, yer're slowly suffocatin'!

"Fine. Throw i' all away! The house, anither chance ta love, an' the opportunity ta be a faither, again! Throw i' all away, but mark ma words, *laddie,* it'll return ta haunt you one day."

In the blink of an eye, Lachlan vanished, but his heated

words continued on. "The past is exactly tha'. Gone! Irretrievable! I'm ashamed ta call you a kinsmon!"

Roan closed his eyes until several minutes passed in silence. When he opened them, desolation shadowed their depths. Were he not prone to rejecting genuine friendship, he might have welcomed the laird's support. But Roan Ingliss had distanced himself too long to easily seek counsel. Besides, for whatever reason, Lachlan was determined to match Roan and Laura, and Roan was known by family and acquaintances to defy anyone who dared to pressure him into something he felt he was not ready for.

Shuddering with cold, he drew up the coat collar around his reddened ears and headed toward the house.

His house.

Stopping short of the front doors, he gazed over the facade of the Victorian structure. His heartbeat quickened, and a rush of liquid warmth passed beneath his skin. A smile curved up the corners of his mouth. Brightened his eyes.

Pride filled his chest.

In awe of what he was experiencing, he heaved a wavering breath.

Despite its dark history, Baird House was an undeniable accomplishment. Every stone and inch of mortar remained as a trophy to the man who'd built it, a testament to a century-and-a-half old dream. Lachlan Baird's trophy and dream, now passed down to a member of the bloodline responsible for cutting short his life.

It struck Roan, at this most peculiar moment, that Baird House was more than just walls enclosing three stories. It represented hope.

Turning in place, he marveled at the grounds and the view of Loch Ken.

For generations his clan had endeavored to banish the stigma of Tessa and Robert's sin against Lachlan Baird. Why was he, a direct descendant of Robert Ingliss, offered such a magnanimous gift?

Beth had brought up the possibility of a "greater force" at work in his life. It was becoming more difficult for him to credit the present series of events as mere coincidences.

He'd been a loner prior to the double tragedy three years ago, a man always quietly searching for something he could never define. Adaina had more than once accused him of being distant, unwilling to work on their marital relationship. She'd left him for a fast-talking con artist. A man, she claimed, capable of satisfying her sexual drives.

Burying his hands in the pockets of his coat, Roan's lazily gazed across the landscape.

He'd let his wife leave him without a fight, without so much as a word to change her mind. She'd been a good mother to their son. He hadn't even thought to try to save his marriage for the sake of the boy. His father hadn't fought for him. It seemed natural to step back and accept the meager visitations that Adaina had granted him with Jamey. At the time, it had made his life less complicated.

"It's hard to forgive yourself," said a whisperlike voice.

Cutting his gaze to the right, Roan stared at Beth's diaphanous form hovering just above the ground. The sight of her like this caused him to fill his lungs with cold air. He coughed, coughed again, then inhaled sparingly through his nostrils.

"I didn't get to spend much time with Laura," she said, her image wavering.

"She's oopset wi' me."

Beth smiled. "That's an understatement. How did you manage to put Lachlan in such a foul mood, too?"

Broad shoulders feebly shrugged beneath the lambswool coat. "I lost ma temper."

"He's fond of you, Roan."

"Why? Why me, Beth? I don't understand."

"He admires your inner strength."

His troubled gaze drifted to the loch. "I've lived maist o' ma life in a comfortable dream. Comin' here . . ." He looked at Beth, a wry grin twitching on his mouth. "You don't leave much for a mon ta hide behind, do you?"

The phantom faded until she was barely visible. "I was wrong to interfere last night, but I don't regret it. Roan . . . free yourself. Please." Although she vanished completely from his sight, her voice remained clear and strong. "Your so-called 'comfortable dream' has only served to isolate you from life.

"That *unknown* you've been searching for . . . ? You've found it. Open your eyes.

"Roan . . . stop . . . hiding . . . from . . . yourself."

To Roan's disbelief, he *sensed* Beth's retreat. For several seconds, he stared in wonder at where she'd been, then shivered and drew in his shoulders. He turned again to the front doors. A frown deepened the grooves across his wide brow. Impulsively, he withdrew a hand from his pocket and placed the palm against one of the brown rocks comprising the wall. The surface was surprisingly warm.

A tickling sensation shot down his arm, moved across his chest, and swirled around his heart. Smiling, he looked up at the iron plaque above the doors which read: 1843. A mystical force surrounded the place, but he was beginning to realize that Lachlan and Beth were only a small part of it.

The house itself was a gateway for the lost. The lost. The lonely. The introverted.

A plan burst within his brain, accelerating his pulse and

filling him with such elation, he found it impossible to breathe. He ran through the greenhouse and into the hall, and was about to shout for Laura when Viola Cooke emerged from the library. The electrical aura of his excitement took her aback. Recovering, she hobbled up to him and brandished a sweet smile.

"So, it's finally hit you that you're soon to be the master of the house," she beamed, affectionately squeezing his hand. "I envy you, Mr. Ingliss. I've loved this place a long time."

"You'll always be welcomed here."

"Thank you." Sighing deeply, she glanced back at the front doors. "I should be heading home."

"Are the roads safe enough?"

She beamed him another smile. "I drive like a snail, Mr. Ingliss. I'll be fine. However . . ." She regarded him for a long moment. "Laura's edgy. Perhaps you should give her a little space. I don't mean to stick my two cents in where it's not wanted, but she has a lot on her mind."

"Where is she, now?"

"She took the boys upstairs. Such darling boys."

A secretive grin curved up one corner of Roan's mouth. Viola walked to the umbrella stand by the doors. Helping her into her three-quarter-length coat, he walked outside with her.

"I guess there'll be changes at Baird House now," she said almost sadly, leaning heavily on Roan's arm. "Nothing wrong with change, I guess."

"Depends on wha' i' is."

Viola didn't respond until she'd opened the driver's door to her blue and white Simca. Her pale blue eyes somberly searched his face, as if trying to glean a clue as to his plans for the estate. "Do you plan to reside here, Mr. Ingliss?"

"I think sa."

"Good. Good." The corners of her mouth turned down in a halfhearted smile. She climbed in behind the steering wheel.

Roan stepped back and watched until the car disappeared down the road around the far side of the snow-laden rhododendrons. He reentered the house, inexplicable gloom threading the periphery of his awareness. It had been a strange day all around, and it wasn't even noon.

His stomach growled. Removing his coat and hanging it on a brass hook on the umbrella stand, he headed toward the kitchen.

Nightfall arrived with surprising swiftness. Not once had he crossed Laura's or the boys' paths. The jewels and money Lachlan had offered him were removed from their hiding places and, placed in an embroidered pillowcase, tucked into the bottom of the lowest drawer of his dresser. He'd puttered around the house, fine-tuning his plans for what to do with it. Before he did anything, though, he'd first clear it with Lachlan and Beth.

He ate dinner alone at the dining table, taking his time, in hopes of Laura showing up. When she didn't, frustration prodded his temper. He cleaned up the dishes, strolled through the first-floor rooms again, then headed up the staircase.

The house was unnervingly quiet. Bursting with silence. Extinguishing most of the gas lamps along his way, he went to his room and closed the door.

Several hours later, he lay naked beneath the bed covers, his arms folded beneath his head, his gaze absently watching the shifting patterns the firelight made on the ceiling.

Unbidden, Laura entered his thoughts. Tightness invaded his groin. His eyebrows drew down in a frown, as he looked to the hearth.

A sensation of warmth coursed through him, yet he shivered. Too vividly, he recalled the image of her face in the firelight while they were making love, and the lightly perfumed scent of her skin. His palms tingled, giving him the impression that he was stroking her incredible body again.

With a grunt, he testily yanked one of the pillows from beneath his head and clamped it over his face.

It was all he could do not to go to her room and pull her into his arms.

Desire tortured him; mocked his restraint.

A voice in his head asked him why he was so damned afraid to approach her.

Throwing the pillow across the room, he shot up into a sitting position. "Because yer're leavin', dammi'!"

The sound of his own voice saying the words stunned him. It was true he didn't want her to leave. For that matter, he'd also grown attached to the boys.

Now *that* was truly a shocker.

His anger lessening, he glanced forlornly about the room.

"Wha' could I possibly offer you ta get you ta stay . . . ta stay just long enough ta see if we have a chance?"

A low bitter laugh escaped him. "No' love, eh, Roan? Yer're a bloody coward in tha' respect, an' I'm gettin' bloody tired o' livin' like this!"

Reclining, he rubbed his hands up and down his face, then slapped his arms to the mattress. "Aye, I'm tired o' livin' an' sleepin' alone.

"Come morn, lass—"

A blood-curdling woman's scream bolted him from the bed.

Six

An ache in the lower part of her back woke Laura from a sound sleep. She peered into the pale grayness of the room, wondering for several seconds where she was. Gentle shifting movement cleared her mind. Smiling contentedly, she slipped a hand from beneath the bed quilts and touched the fingertips to Alby's cool brow. He squirmed again in his sleep, nestling closer to her. On the opposite end of the massive mattress, Kevin turned onto his right side, placing his back to his siblings and aunt.

Laura contemplated the three enigmas for a time. She'd known her nephews for about a week, and yet, despite her apprehension about her newfound responsibility, she daily grew closer to them. Until now, she'd been afraid to face what the future held for them. It was mind-boggling how much there was to consider. Changing her residence—there wasn't enough room in her apartment for one child, let alone three. Daycare. Mentally adjusting her precious "spare time" to accommodate *their* needs, Drastic changes in her grocery shopping. Clothing. Readying Kevin and Kahl for school. Finding a reputable pediatrician. . . .

Silently moaning, she eased out of bed.

She made her way to the bathroom, rubbing her upper arms to ward off the chill caressing her exposed skin. A dull glow of embers was all that remained in the fireplace.

After relieving herself and washing her hands, she went to the hearth and moved back the chair supporting Roan's shirt and pants, and boxer shorts. She took in hand the box of matches on the mantel. Kneeling, she placed twigs, balled paper, and two logs within the hearth. She removed a wooden match. And frowned.

Was Roan sleeping?

She'd avoided him all day, but he'd never left her thoughts.

The voice of reason hadn't yet banished him from her heart, nor had they offered her a modicum of insight as to how she'd fallen so hard for him in so short a time. Attraction was one thing. What woman wouldn't appreciate his raw masculinity? But what she was suffering was far more than a fleeting interest. Despite her efforts to the contrary, she wondered about his past, his family, his likes and dislikes. She found herself listening to hear him even so much as mutter to himself. The timbre of his voice, his bearing, his mere presence, were all locked into her awareness. He had a way of watching her that always caused fluttering in the pit of her stomach. Even when she was frustrated and angry with him, mental images of his soft brown irises had a tendency to weaken her. They were expressive eyes, often exposing his gruffness as nothing more than a defense mechanism.

She'd known her share of men who couldn't show open affection. Her father and brother had been like that. It was . . . *unmanly* . . . to expose their emotions.

Men. They had to be a genetic screw-up. Emotions were a vital part of a human being, and yet the masculine half of the species was determined to hide their feelings. What was so difficult about out-and-out honesty? A man could say "I want you," and mean, "I want *sex*." With few exceptions, when a woman said those same words, she meant she wanted the whole commitment. A woman could smile at a man, signaling that she was interested in getting to know him. A man deciphered that communication as, "this woman wants sex." It always boiled down to *sex*. And yet, Roan had seemed embarrassed after their lovemaking. He'd even become angry and ordered her out of the room.

Now, unless she had totally misread the situation . . .

He was a complex man, that was for sure. More complex than most, and she was falling in love with him. That was the real zinger! Not only had she inherited three boys to raise, but she was now caught up in a hopeless relationship with a man she literally knew nothing about.

That wasn't exactly true. She knew he'd had a son. But how he had died, and what had happened to his ex-wife, remained a mystery.

Casting a bleak look in the direction of the bed, she sighed.

Perhaps she alone was not the cause of his turnabout last night. It had to have crossed his mind that his involvement with her also had three small considerations. Ready-made fatherhood was not something a lot of men could accept. The responsibility of the boys scared the hell out of her, and she was their aunt. It was very possible that Roan was not prepared to take on a *family*.

Her heart grew heavy with despair, but anger simmered within her blood.

Men.

A woman could go stark raving mad trying to second-guess their reasoning. She had to get Roan out of her head, out of her heart. With any luck, she would leave Scotland soon. She'd say good-bye, and never look back. She'd forget Roan, and he'd forget her. Her future belonged to the boys.

Resolutely, she struck the match against the strip on the side of the box. The sulfur tip flared. The flame flickered, danced at the insistence of a draft. Shuddering, she stared absently into the light.

Who was she kidding? She would never again be able to look at a fire and not recall the pleasure Roan had given her. That hands so large could be so gentle and soft . . .

Stop it!

She was about to lower the match to the kindling when she saw something move to the left of her. Her awareness noted an alarming stirring of cold air against her skin. Her head swung around. She unwittingly dropped the match as two factors slammed home.

She'd closed the drapes before going to bed.

Now, something swiftly passed the moonlit window.

A scream ripped from her throat. She jumped to her feet. Instinctively, she ran to the foot of the bed to guard the boys against the intruder. Her heart slammed against her chest with each beat. Suddenly, the shadowy recesses of the room multiplied, and darkened to an impenetrable depth.

The boys began to cry and call out to her, but she couldn't force herself to move. Then something else demanded her attention. Her fear-ridden gaze cut to the hearth, where a small fire was bleeding across the Persian carpet.

In the next instant, the chair and Roan's clothing were engulfed in flames.

She screamed again when the door burst open with such force that it slammed the perpendicular wall. One of the boys released an ear-splitting wail. Flopping over the foot of the bed, she blindly scrambled to gather her nephews into her arms.

An expletive rent the air. Laura became aware of someone dashing across the room, but the haze of smoke rising up from the floor, prevented her from seeing clearly.

"Boys!" she cried, frantically coaxing them to leave the bed. They wouldn't budge. Her fear deepening to hysteria, she jumped off the edge of the mattress and made a feeble attempt to pull her nephews toward her. Huddled together, clinging to one another, they resisted.

"Kevin, help me!"

Alby screamed.

Movement again shot her head around. In the distorted light of the elevating fire, she saw a large figure throw something on the flames. Smoke stung her eyes. The boys coughed. She coughed. Amid the frantic movements of the figure came a deeper, harsher hacking.

"Roan?"

A grunt followed her weak call. Then the large figure crossed to the front of the left-side window, and opened it. Icy air rushed into the room, riling the smoke into a swirling mass.

Laura's nerves sparked when something nudged her aside.

"Hurry," came a feminine voice to her left.

Fingers cinched Laura's arm and gave her a nudge toward the door. She resisted until she dimly saw Lachlan Baird swing two of the boys up into his arms. The instant he crossed the threshold, Beth Staples drew Alby up onto her hip.

"Laura," Beth said sternly, pausing a moment before entering the hall. "Follow us to the parlor." Then she hastened into the hall.

When the boys were safe, Laura turned to see where Roan was. Panic knifed her until she saw him kneeling in front of the hearth.

Coughing and placing a hand over her mouth, she crouched alongside him. Resisting a powerful urge to touch him, she linked her arms across her shins, and stared down at the wet towel he'd used to smother the fire.

"I-I dropped the match."

A raspy breath escaped him. His head turned. Diffused moonlight bathed his face, accentuating the warm cast of his eyes.

"Are you all right?"

She weakly nodded. "I-I'll pay for the damage."

Placing a hand on her arm, Roan stood, drawing her up as well. "Don't worry abou' the rug. Lannie'll tak care o' i'." He halfheartedly gazed around him, his nostrils flaring. "You can't sleep in here, tonight, though."

"Roan—"

"Damn me," he grumbled, sparing her a scowling look.

Laura was confused until he abruptly walked to the bed, then a smile turned up the corners of her mouth. Now here was a sight she wouldn't soon forget. Moonlight kissed his naked skin, illuminating his firm backside in stark relief. Heat rose into her cheeks. Her pulse quickened. He wrapped the top quilt around his middle, but it didn't help to lessen her appreciation of his physique. Facing her, he scowled again. Momentarily forgotten was the intruder that had frightened her, and the fire.

"Perhaps you should start wearing pajamas," she suggested, in a tone laced with mirth.

Her humor fled when he brusquely closed the distance. His eyebrows drew down in stormy impatience. He regarded her for several seconds. "If yer're cauld, lass, ask *me* ta light you a fire."

Pride slammed against the interior of Laura's heart. "What?"

"Leave the matches be."

A breath painfully squeezed past the tightening in her throat. "It was an accident!"

"Aye. Damn near a fatal one."

"Ro—*oan!*" She threw her hands up in mounting exasperation. "Don't you think you're overreacting?"

Alarm stabbed at her when one of his hands clamped on the back of her neck and jerked her against the hard wall of his body. The massive breadth of his chest and shoulders completely occupied her vision, until she looked up to peer into the turbulent depths of his eyes.

"Have you e'er smelled burnt flesh?" His fierce gaze lowered to her lips. His fingers flexed against her nape. "Fire destroys e'rythin' i' touches." He stared into her eyes, his own radiating heart-wrenching despair. "Don't mock ma respect o' i'. I know its power."

Tears swelled within her throat. "Your son?"

Swiftly moving away and turning his back to her, he combed the fingers of one hand through his thick hair. "This stunt has taken ten years off ma life."

Willing back her tears, Laura squared her shoulders. "It wasn't a damn stunt, Roan." Pointing, she went on, "I was about to light the kindling when I saw someone run past that window."

Roan walked up to her. "Are you sure?"

"Yes!" Lowering her arm, she stared at the window for a long moment. "I know I closed the drapes before I went to bed. And I'm . . . pretty sure . . . I saw someone."

Looking over his shoulder, he said, "It was probably a peacock."

A bitter laugh escaped her. "It didn't look like a bird to me!"

Sighing, Roan searched her features through a frown. "You probably *thought* you'd closed the drapes."

"Dammit—"

She sucked in a breath when his hand gently lit upon the side of her face.

"You've been under a lot o' stress, Laura. The peacocks prowl the rooftops, tryin' ta stay warm. They've given *me* a start, more'n once."

"I guess," she murmured, forlornly glancing at the window.

"Laura."

His breathy, husky tone sent a chill through her. Meeting his gaze, her heart skipped a beat at the simmering passion his eyes betrayed. His head dipped. Weakening with anticipation of his kiss, she leaned into him.

"Fegs, mon, 'tis no' the time for tha'!"

Roan looked up to deliver the laird a dirty look. Laura shyly stepped back and averted her gaze from the approaching figure.

"Put these on," Lachlan said, his tone laced with mirth. He shoved a bundle into Roan's arms. "The lads are wi' Beth in the parlor," he said to Laura. "They're na worse for their fright."

"Thank you. When I return to the States, I'll reimburse you for the carpet—and anything else that's been damaged."

Roan, who'd been staring at the clothing in his hands during the brief exchange, wanly looked at Lachlan. "Yer trousers cut off ma circulation."

" 'Tis better than yer birthday suit," Lachlan grinned. Humorously arching an eyebrow, he glanced at the charred remains of the chair and Roan's belongings. "You have the worst luck wi' yer claes, eh?"

"Only the past few days," Roan grumbled, narrowing a look at Laura.

With a low laugh, Lachlan headed for the door. "Come doon ta the parlor whan yer're through here." He paused at the threshhold and regarded the couple. "Laura, I regret yer stay has been sa stressful. Tak heart, lass. An' Roan . . ." A wry grin turned up one corner of his mouth. "Be nice."

When Lachlan went into the hall, Roan buried his face in the attire and released an expletive.

"I'm sorry."

Laura's wavering tone prompted him to contritely look at her. "Na, *I'm* sarry for losin' ma temper." Leaning to, he kissed her lightly on the lips, then drew her into his arms and languidly explored her mouth with his own. He lifted his head after a time and searched her face. "I don't know wha' I'd do if anythin' happened ta you or the boys."

"You're not responsible for us."

The cool undertone of her words made him frown. "I *am* responsible, for as long as yer're under this roof."

Withdrawing from his arms, Laura headed out of the room. "I'll be downstairs."

After she'd left, Roan stood for a long time staring off into space. He was beginning to believe he would never understand women, never fathom their hot and cold mood swings. There was only so much a man could tolerate, or ignore.

Perhaps she was still hurt that he'd told her to leave after their lovemaking. And perhaps she'd only allowed him to kiss her because she'd been a wee shocky from fright.

A muffled sound gave him a start. Slivers of ice seemed to form in his blood. He furtively glanced about him. He waited for an indefinite time, his hearing alert, every muscle in his body taut. Although he was sure the sound had to have a reasonable explanation behind it, the hair on his arms seemed to twitch against his chilled skin. His heart raced as adrenaline fed his probing inner sense.

Finally, he decided the fire had left him edgier than he'd thought. Donning the black, snug trousers, then the long-sleeved, saffron-colored shirt, he cast his burned clothing a look of longing before leaving the room. He felt ridiculous in Lachlan's trousers. Jogging down the staircase, he resisted a strong compulsion to tug on the front. His undershorts would have made a world of difference, but he was out of luck in that department, too. Only something short of a miracle would see him through the next few hours without the seams of the trousers splitting, or the tiny ceramic buttons popping off of Lachlan's tautly stretched shirt.

Some of his belongings were at Aggie's. It was a long walk, but if the weather cooperated, it would be worth the hike to get back into his own clothing. He would also be able to assure his aunt that everything was fine at Baird House. Considering her hatred of its owner, she had to be frantic with worry.

He paused at the first landing and, bewildered, ran a hand through his hair.

What was his aunt going to say when he told her that Lachlan Baird had offered him the house, and all that went with it?

Feeling a bit numbed, he entered the parlor. The room was bathed in soft orange firelight. Beth, Lachlan, and the boys were nowhere in sight, but Laura, enfolded in a wool, blue and purple plaid blanket, sat to the left side of the hearth. Nested in her hands was a steaming cup of dark liquid. The sight of her forlornly staring into the flames, pulled on his heartstrings.

He padded across the cold wood floor, stopping within arm's reach of her. Still, she remained unaware of his presence. Mindful of the snugness of his trousers, he gingerly crouched to her right, and cleared his throat.

Wide green eyes turned to him.

"Did I startle you?"

She shook her head, but he knew that he had.

"Where are the laddies?"

"Beth and Lachlan took them into the kitchen."

"Are they all right?"

Staring down into the cup, she nodded.

"Wha' abou' Laura, eh?" he asked kindly, lowering his buttocks to the floor. "How is *she* holdin' oop?"

A tremulous smile appeared on her mouth. *"Oop.* I love your accent."

Roan grinned. *"You* have the accent, here, lass."

"That's true." She sighed and lightly frowned into the fire. "I'm definitely the outsider."

"Is tha' self-pity I'm hearin'?"

Laura's heart-shaped face turned to him, her expression guarded. "No. A reality check." She took a sip of her tea, then offered the cup to Roan. Taking it, he held it to his lips, his gaze studying her facial bruises over the brim.

"I was just thinking," she sighed, lifting her knees and wrapping her arms about her shins, "how deceptive time can be. I've been here for four days, but it feels like months have gone by."

Roan took a generous swig of the tea, then passed the cup back to her. "A lot has happened."

"I haven't been very appreciative of your help, have I?"

A laugh caressed his throat. "I know i' can't be easy for you, Laura. You inherit a family. Wreck yer caur. Find yerself a' the mercy o' strangers. No' ta mention how defensive I've been wi' you. All considered, I think you've proven yer stuff."

"My stuff?"

The smile in her beguiling eyes caused a burst of heat to ignite within Roan's chest. Bruises and all, he'd never encountered a lovelier woman. "Aye, yer stuff. You've a fine temper, an' a constitution ta equal i'. Yer're definitely no' fluff, Laura Bennett. I think you could tackle abou' anythin' tha' came yer way."

Averting her gaze to the fire, she softly asked, "Does that include you?"

"I don't understand."

She frowned for a time before she could bring herself to look him in the eye. "Roan . . . Please don't take this the wrong way, but I need you to . . . to stay away from me."

His shocked expression prompted her to rush on, "I have a life in the States, and my nephews to worry about."

"Laura—"

"Let me finish," she choked, placing the cup behind her. "I used to mock romance books. Brooding heroes; heroines in jeopardy; the sinister Victorian manor . . ." A pathetic laugh caught in her throat. "Well, I won't mock them again, will I?"

"I'm a wee confused abou' the 'broodin' hero' part."

For a long moment, Laura searched the devastating features in front of her. She could no longer deny that she was already in love with him, but she vowed he would never find out. It was impossible for her, now, to abandon all else for the sake of a man. For the sake of love. Prior to Scotland, she'd been too selfish with her time, her independence, to take any relationship seriously. She'd never been in love, though. It was a miserable condition. One, she hoped, the symptoms of which would vanish, given distance and time.

"Laura?"

"I'm sorry. What?"

"I'm just a mon."

Right. "I know."

"I don't think sa." Sliding closer, he captured her chin between a thumb and forefinger. "Wha' *are* you afraid o'?"

She swallowed hard.

"Love?"

"Of course not."

"Tha' quiver in yer tone says itherwise."

"I'm tired."

Roan slowly shook his head, his piercing eyes never breaking contact with her own. "We made love."

Heat surged into her cheeks. But for his firm hold on her chin, she would have averted her face from his scrutiny. "On a whim. It certainly didn't commit us to—"

"Stop lyin' ta yerself," he interjected gruffly. Releasing her, he raised his right knee and rested his right forearm upon it. "An' stop pretendin' there's naught between us."

Resisting an urge to lean away from him, Laura stiffened her spine. "I don't lie, and I don't pretend. I'm merely trying to explain to you that I don't need any more complications in my life."

Quirking up an eyebrow, Roan grinned almost sardonically. "Sa I'm a broodin' complication, am I?"

"Sometimes," she began through clenched teeth, "you're a royal pain in the ass!"

"It won't wark, lass."

"What won't work?"

"Wieldin' tha' verbal shield."

Panic lancing her heart, Laura determinedly forged on.

"Look, I understand where you're coming from. Okay? I'm not stupid."

Roan jiggled his head in confusion.

"The days and nights are pretty cold in this house. It's nice to . . . to have a warm body to snuggle up to. And of c-course, sex is a nice way to pass the time." His eyes grew stormier, stoking her unease. "I owe you a lot, and I pay my debts."

"Laura," he growled.

"However, I'm not comfortable having sex with you, knowing that I'm going to be leaving, soon. So if you would give me chores—"

Like lightning, Roan's left arm shot out and circled her back. His fingers hooked onto her left upper arm. He pulled her down and against his chest, while his mouth was capturing hers in a punishing kiss. After a moment's shock, Laura made a bid to push away from him. His right leg swung over her, boxing her hips between his groin and heel. His free arm wrapped around her, pinning her within an unyielding embrace.

His anger overcame his tenderness. He plundered her mouth, forcing her lips to part beneath the pressure. She moaned in protest. Her fingernails stabbed him through his shirt, his chest and midriff. The tip of his tongue came up against a wall of enamel. Switching tactics, he targeted the soft skin below her left earlobe. His teeth nipped; his lips caressed. A fierce groan of sexual awakening emanated from deep inside her.

"Don't fight me," he rasped, briefly looking into her tear-glazed eyes before lowering his mouth over her lips again.

She shuddered within his hold, then began to relax. He kissed her deeply, his tongue stroking hers, coaxing her into a state of sensual oblivion. His hold loosened, cradling rather than imprisoning her.

"Hey!"

The youthful shout quickly separated the couple. Roan slid back. Laura twisted around.

"Whatcha doing?" Kahl asked jubilantly, skipping toward them.

Laura and Roan exchanged a guilt-ridden glance before she forced a smile. "Feeling better?"

Plopping to the floor alongside his aunt, Kahl swiped a hand beneath his nose. "Beth makes the best hot chocolate. And the ghost made us a sandwich."

"The—"

Roan interjected, "Where's yer brithers?"

Kahl wrinkled his nose at the man. *"Bro . . . thers."*

"Aye, lad. Where are they?"

"In there," the boy replied, jabbing a thumb in the direction of the dining room. His blue eyes shrewdly narrowed on Roan. "You gonna marry my aunt?"

"Kahl!" Laura gasped.

Roan chuckled. "Why do you want ta know?"

Kahl shrugged. "I like it here."

"You do, eh?" Roan's soft gaze swung to Laura. "Perhaps you could help me convince yer aunt ta stay. Tis a big house." He again looked at the boy. "I wadn't mind some help fillin' these rooms."

"You just wanna go ta bed with her," Kahl grinned, looking from one adult to the other.

A dark blush stole across Roan's face. "Weel, lad, that's a wee personal now, don't you think?"

"I ain't dumb, ya know."

"Kahl, please . . . change the subject. Mr. Ingliss is just funning with you."

"Are ya, mister?"

The boy's penetrating eyes took Roan aback for a moment. "I've been tryin' ta convince yer aunt, I'm dead serious."

"Roan, please."

"Now, Laura," Roan chided, a sparkle in his eyes. "The lad caught us lip-locked. Na sense pretendin' he didn't see wha' he saw."

"Roan," Laura rasped, sending him a visual plea to defuse the subject.

A booming laugh entered the room, dousing the rising tension. Getting to his feet, Roan helped Laura up. Kahl jumped to his feet and beelined for Lachlan, clutching the thigh of the trousered leg and wiping his nose across the material. Another laugh came from Lachlan, who, holding Alby on his hip, reached down and ruffled Kahl's shaggy, red-gold head. Beth, holding Kevin's hand, came around Lachlan's tall frame.

"I'm afraid the hot chocolate has wound them up." She smiled at Laura.

Laura offered a sickly smile. Drawing the blanket snug about her, she tried to rise above the pounding of her heart and the weakness in her legs. She felt as though everyone in the room was staring at her, seeing into her soul and dissecting the very essence of her personality. Her lips tingled. Psychological waves of heat moved across every inch of her skin.

Chemistry between people was one thing, her attraction to Roan, another. She couldn't shake the notion to lean into him, completely melt into every atom of his being.

Stop this, she scolded herself. The smile froze on her.

Lachlan lowered Alby to the floor.

Laura watched the laird through a thickening haze of

mental retreat. She was vaguely aware of voices; dimly aware of movement.

What was wrong with her?

Her stomach churned.

Love?

She mentally groaned.

She wasn't falling in love with Roan Ingliss, the man, bod extraordinaire, master of this towering house. She *was* in love with him!

She closed her eyes against the threat of her stomach's contents rising into her throat.

Not again.

Her vision slowly focused on the circular display of swords on the wall to her right. The orange firelight gleamed on the highly polished metal of the blades. She drifted deeper into the comfort zone of her temporary escape, wondering if any of the swords had ever been used in battle. It was possible. Although she hadn't shown outward interest in the antiques sheltered within this house, she had been aware of them—in awe of their *newness*.

As she drifted deeper within herself, an image of her apartment formed in front of her mind's eye.

What did her sterile, meticulous "home" tell others about her? Did anything she'd ever collected, ever crafted, offer true insight into her love of nature? Her love of history?

A translucent, wavering haze manifested in front of her. Somnolently, she watched as the parlor came back into focus, luminescent green framing the scene. The room was cozily warm. The gaslight fixtures on the walls were all lit. A fire roared in the hearth behind her.

The door to the hall closed.

Lightheadedness caused Laura to sway on her feet as

she stared unblinkingly at a couple across from her. A woman of undeniable beauty sat primly on the settee, her vibrant blue eyes staring up at a well-built man to her left. Mud stained the hemline of her long, full-skirted, black and green plaid muslin gown. A short cape of the same material covered her shoulders, and was clasped at the base of her throat with a rose-jeweled brooch. The woman's costume perfectly suited the room, Laura thought, right down to the banana curls fashioned at the sides of the woman's head.

"I canna bear the thought o' him touchin' you," the man said poignantly.

He, too, blended into the ambiance of the room. Short sideburns. His dark hair swept back from his high brow. The black longcoat accented his broad shoulders.

A slow, evil smile spread across the woman's mouth as she reached out with a gloved hand and boldly cupped his crotch. She gave a tug, urging him closer. Then she leaned to and pressed her lips to his lower abdomen.

Laura wanted to look away, but could not.

"Tessa," he groaned, dipping his head back, his profile revealing to Laura his painful need.

"The poor sod will ne'er have me, Robert."

Robert Robert Roberrrrt.

Running a hand over the rigid erection concealed beneath his fawn-colored trousers, the woman peered up through thick, pale lashes. "Tis you I love. *His* paughty hands will ne'er touch ma skin, I promise."

Someone cried out Laura's name, shattering her stupor.

In a matter of seconds, she saw Roan rushing toward her, his countenance ravaged with a look of sheer horror. Something compelled her to look down. As if watching in slow motion, she saw Alby back away from the hearth, a poker in his hands, the curved end scraping across the field-stone. A fire-enveloped log rolled toward him, one end making contact with the bottom of the blanket enshrouding her. Terror squeezed her vocal cords, paralyzed her. Roan swung the boy behind him, abruptly dropped him to the floor, then harshly yanked the blanket from about her. Lachlan snatched it from him, threw it on the floor, and stomped out the flames with a booted foot.

"Are you burned?" Laura heard Beth ask, but to Laura, the voice came from very far away.

She could not pull her gaze from Roan's deathly pale face, the wild fury in his eyes. He trembled violently, his fists clenched at his sides.

After a quick inspection of Laura's person, Lachlan announced, "She's unharmed."

"Thank God," Beth wheezed, lifting a sobbing Alby into her arms.

Kahl and Kevin remained quiet, their fear-induced shock making them look like manikins.

Roan couldn't breathe. Every nerve in his body was as taut as a spring. Although the incident had passed without injury to anyone, fear and anger continued to coil through him, building and building until he could no longer confine them.

Glaring at Laura, he bellowed, "Wha' the hell's wrong wi' you? He could have pitched headlong inta tha' bloody fire!"

"Let i' go," Lachlan warned, placing a hand on Roan's arm.

Viciously, Roan wrenched away, his burning, accusing look riveted on Laura. "Come the morn, I want them ou' o' here, Lannie! 'Tis na place for children!" His gaze targeted the laird. "Na mair, mon! She's na mither!"

"Calm yerself," Lachlan warned in an authoritative tone, his dark, penetrating eyes boring into Roan's.

"Calm maself?" Roan's voice quivered with emotion. "I'll no' stand by an' watch anither child die! Damn you, Lannie! I wash ma bloody hands o' this bunch!"

"Roan, you're understandably upset, but you're scaring the children."

Beth's softly spoken statement caused something to further snap in Roan. Turning toward her, the firelight awarding his features an evil glint, he charged, "The little buggers are obsessed wi' fire!"

"They're just children."

"Wha' have you an' auld Lannie to lose, eh?" he sneered. "Baird House could appreciate three little spirits wanderin' its halls—"

Roan sucked in a sharp breath when a stinging blow was dealt to his face. Stunned, he stared with widened eyes at Laura's poised weapon-hand. In the seconds to follow, the silence in the room held substance. Then a log crumbled on the grate. Red embers crackled, snapped.

"Laura, Lachlan and I will stay up with the boys, tonight. We'll have them sleep in our room, okay?"

Tears brimming her eyes, Laura gave a feeble nod.

Roan stalked across the room to the middle window, and stood in the shadows staring out into the night. Laura remained perfectly still until the other couple had ushered the boys from the room, then she walked to Roan, stopping just out of reach of him.

"Talk to me."

Shivering, Roan crossed his arms against his chest and rubbed his upper arms for warmth.

"What happened to your son?"

"You can't turn yer back on children," he said hatefully,

refusing to look at her. "An' you can't afford ta daydream whan they're around!"

"I was wrong—"

He turned on her so swiftly, she experienced a rush of fear. *"Wrong?* Sayin' yer're wrong doesn't excuse yer stupidity!"

Tears fell in abandon down her cheeks. "Stop it."

"Yer're no' fit ta raise those lads!"

"Roan . . . please!"

Quaking, compelled to rid himself of the demons riding his shoulders, he went on, "Wha' gives you the right ta think tha', because yer're a *womon,* you've got a parental bone in yer body?"

Laura's hand sailed upward, but before it could reach his face, Roan harshly caught the wrist in midair. He jerked her against his steely body, and twisted the arm to her back, imprisoning her in a viselike hold.

"You really don't want them, do you, Laura?" he hissed into her face, oblivious to her sobs, her uncontrollable trembling. "What's one less little bugger ta worry abou', eh?"

"Who are you talking to, Roan?" she wept, looking up at him, her eyes pleading with him to help her understand the reason behind his brutality.

It took a second before her question penetrated his rage. Puzzlement masked his shadowed face, then a contrite form of horror that offered her hope. His hands dropped to his sides. He leaned back, staring at her as if expecting her to strike out at him again.

Comforting herself within her own arms, she gave a toss of her blond head. "What happened to your son?" she repeated.

Roan looked away, then stepped around her to leave.

Laura's fingers clutched the front of his shirt, forcing him to remain unless he pried her free.

"What happened?"

Tears rose in his throat and swiftly filled his eyes. Looking upward, he gave a feeble shake of his head.

"All right. I won't pressure you." Laura cleared her throat in an attempt to alleviate the quiver in her tone. "But you listen to me, Roan Ingliss. I would never wish harm to *anyone,* let alone a child.

"Roan, I never had an irresponsible moment in my *life* until I set foot in this country!"

"I'm sorry—"

"I made a *mistake,* but it will never happen again."

His gaze reluctantly lowered to her face.

Laura swallowed past the tightness in her throat, and stepped back. "I'm going to check in on the boys, then I'm going to bed. Just . . . stay away from us. I'll make *sure* they don't get into any more trouble."

With as much dignity as she could muster, she headed for the door to the hall. When she was halfway to her destination, Roan called her name, prompting her to stop.

"Sleep in ma room, tonight. I'll . . . sleep on the couch in the library."

For a moment, Laura thought to argue. She didn't want to curl up beneath covers that had touched him, or lie atop a mattress that had supported him. But she was too weary and emotionally exhausted to demand another room, or take the time to make a bed.

With a single nod, she left.

For a long time afterward, Roan stared out the window. Self-disgust left him chilled to the marrow of his bones. He wondered if he'd ever shake the past, ever come to terms with the guilt he suffered over his son's death.

Regardless, what he'd said and done to Laura was nothing less than cruel. And the boys . . .

Like it or not, tomorrow, he owed it to them to explain his behavior.

Nightmares haunted Laura's sleep.

The blonde with the bright blue eyes stormed through room after room, wailing and shouting a name Laura couldn't quite grasp. Everywhere this woman went, the walls buckled in and out as if breathing. A bright light followed close behind her, humming with static electricity. Humming with life.

The dream shifted. A boy of about eight, crying so hard the sound could barely pass through his raw throat, pounded small fists against a door. Loud, raspy breathing filled the room he was in, a room Laura recognized as one of the servants' quarters in the tower. As the breathing grew louder and louder, the boy shrank in size, until he'd become so small, a breath of air blew him beneath the door.

Again—

A thousand candles were burning throughout a massive bedroom. Atop a large bed, the blonde hastily straddled a faceless man's legs, and feverishly tore open the front of his shirt. The sound of his groan echoed eerily within the chamber. She unfastened the tiny buttons on the front of his trousers, yanked them past his hips, then screamed. In lieu of his genitals, a gleaming jeweled-handled dagger stood erect.

The blonde again was shouting from the top of the tower. Lightning caged her; thunder drowned out her cries for help.

Back to the tower, where a wall of rock begins to breathe.

A hand that Laura knows is her own, reaches out to touch it. The rocks explode outward, showering her unseen self. A hand shoots out, the fingers cinch her neck. Gasps follow. Laura can't breathe. Amid the airborne dust, a skull emerges, amber eyes glowing within the white sockets—

Laura bolted upright in the bed. Her hand began pounding her chest to force air into her lungs. Cold perspiration coated her skin, matted strands of her hair to her face. Her eyes fearfully searched the darkness, fathomless darkness like she'd never before seen.

The attic, whispered a voice.

A freezing gust of air moved across the bed.

Terror paralyzed her.

Look in the attic, the same voice, sweet and beckoning, said.

"Who are you?" Laura choked, shivering uncontrollably.

In the attic.

Laura adamantly shook her head. She was afraid to close her eyes. Afraid not to. Air eddied around her, caressing her oversensitized skin.

In the attic! the voice said belligerently.

Jumping from the bed, Laura pulled off the top quilt and wrapped it around her trembling, chilled body. Companioned only by the stillness, the darkness, and the coldness of the night, she left the room.

Seven

One moment, Laura was stepping into the hall outside Roan's bedroom, the next, she felt herself awakening with a start. Disbelief robbed her of breath. She stood in the center of the attic, which was illuminated by a soft green glow. Her feet were numb with cold. She clutched the quilt about her more tightly, fearfully surveying her eerie surroundings.

A feminine zephyrous voice filled the room, causing Laura to shrivel within. *"Put them in the attic. I ne'er want ta see them again."*

A male voice, deep, reverberating, intruded.

"Both should be destroyed, love."

"Na, Robert!"

"Tessa, love, if they're e'er found . . ."

"They'll remind tha' deil tha' I bested him. Curse his soul! Curse his soul an' his wealth for corruptin' us!"

An icy breath passed through Laura. She nearly cried out, instead, bit down on her lower lip, drawing blood.

She turned to face the only exit. The staircase seemed miles away. Labored breaths roared in her ears. Her heart thundered painfully behind her breast. A threat of tears stung her eyes, but she refused to succumb to the compelling need to weep.

Again, the male voice eddied around her.

"Tessa, you canna go on like this. Yer're makin' yerself ill."

A woman's sob lanced Laura in the heart.

"He'll ne'er leave us be, Robbie. He'll punish us oor whole lives."

"We sinned, Tessa."

"Sinned? Tis poverty the sin!"

"We sinned against him, love."

"Damn him, Robbie! I hope he wanders aimlessly for all time!"

"Fegs! Dinna curse him na mair, Tessa! Tis oor souls'll be damned for all time!"

"Curse him, Robbie. If you truly love me, curse him!"

"Don't do it, Robbie," Laura whimpered.

"I . . . I curse you, Lannie Baird." His voice rose a full octave. *"I curse yer black soul!"*

Laura's legs buckled beneath her. She dropped to her knees. Tears ran streaming down her pale cheeks.

A void yawned within her. A dark, fathomless void. All sense of existence was denied her. She became trapped within infinite grayness. Cold, desolate grayness. Eternity.

A sudden sense of falling seized her. Then, total absence of movement. Between her breasts, a green glow appeared and pulsated in time with the beat of her heart. She felt herself moving swiftly through nothingness. Coldness invaded her every molecule.

A scream rose in her throat, but became lost within the void.

Then a strong, loud heartbeat filled her ears. It was not her own, but of something behind her.

To move proved almost impossible. After what seemed like hours, she turned on her knees to face a bright, pulsing green glow on the far side of the room.

As if in slow motion, she fought against the leadenness in her limbs and got to her feet. She crossed the room, leaning into the windlike timelessness rushing at her. The glow blinded her, but she went on until her bare toes struck something solid.

Again she went down on her knees. Her eyes closed. She felt the object until she perceived that it was a large trunk. She cracked open her eyelids. The glow was now soft. Pulsating and soft. In cadence with her heartbeat.

Hypnotic.

If the faded and cracked wood was any indication, the trunk was old. A brass plate on the front bore the engraved letters AIKEN. Laura's hands paused short of removing an oval lace covering from the lid when her gaze lifted and spied a tall object, draped with a dark green blanket, standing behind the trunk.

Excitement quivered through her. Getting to her feet, she pulled the heavy object from its niche, propped it against the wall by the small round window, and hastily pulled off the blanket.

A gasp of sheer awe escaped her. She knelt to one knee, a trembling hand reaching out toward the surface of the portrait. Two faces stared back at her: the blonde in her dreams; someone resembling Lachlan Baird. The couple, depicted from the laps up, were dressed in Victorian attire and sitting in front of the fireplace in the parlor, his arm draped over her bared shoulders. While his eyes possessed a sparkle of mischief, the woman's lacked luster. Her pouty full mouth held a hint of grimness.

Laura lowered her arm and folded her hands in her lap. They were a strikingly handsome couple, but somehow ill-suited. The artist had taken great care to portray them as he saw them and, in that, Laura suspected he hadn't cared for the mistress of the house. The present owner bore an uncanny resemblance to his ancestor, although his skin was far paler than the man's in the portrait.

Something compelled her to look at the trunk. Crawling back to it she removed the lace cloth, folded and set it aside, then lifted the lid. Various garments vied for her attention. She languidly fished through the contents, no thoughts going through her mind. The soft green glow remained the only light within the attic.

A soft hum prompted her to look over her shoulder. Dressed in a full-length lace gown, Beth Staples danced across the open floor. Laura wistfully watched her for a time. It never crossed her mind to question the ghostly image.

Somewhere in the house, a woman wailed in the throes of labor.

Laura returned her attention to the trunk.

She withdrew a black satin nightgown, trimmed with purple bobbin lace. Despite the coldness of the attic, she dropped the quilt, stripped out of her cotton nightgown, and slipped on the sensual garment. Empire style with thin straps, it fitted her perfectly except in length. The owner had been taller than Laura by several inches.

Moaning in ecstasy, Laura ran her hands down her satin-covered hips. Cotton would never feel the same. She felt sensuous and powerful. Her hands passed over her breasts. Her hardened nipples tickled her palms.

"I'm back, Robbie," she said in a guttural whisper, her eyes glazed with raw passion. "I've been waitin', love. Tarry na longer in the ither world. Come home, Robbie. Come back ta me."

Stooping in front of the trunk, Laura pushed aside the clothing and exposed the right inner side. A compartment opened. She palmed the cold implement it concealed, and stood.

Eyes devoid of expression inspected the jeweled dagger, which felt hot against her skin. Her gaze cut to the portrait, and riveted on a red glow pulsating on Lachlan Baird's broad chest.

Heat washed through her. A pulse of fury awakened in her heart. Gripping the ornate handle of the dagger, she carried it in a threatening manner to the portrait.

"Curse you, Lannie!" she hissed. "I'll no' rest till I rid ma house o' you!"

Her face a hideous mask of hatred, she plunged the dagger again and again into the breast of the man in the portrait. The magnified sound of the canvas ripping threatened to burst her eardrums. But still she slashed away, shredding every part of his image.

"Fegs!" a voice boomed.

Whirling about, she blindly lurched her dagger-hand forward. Dark eyes widened in surprise and horror combined, then lowered to view imaginary blood seeping through the left breast of his white shirt.

Again and again, Laura plunged the knife into Lachlan, the frenzy burning within her brain supplanting her reasoning. The force of her attack drove Lachlan backward, his staggering steps closing his distance to the staircase. Remembered pain disoriented him. Intermittently his blearing vision saw images of Tessa superimposed upon his houseguest.

Tessa back?

Outrage began to restore his strength. The blade cut into him, just below the left side of his rib cage. With a growl of rage, he shot out a hand to snatch the dagger, but at the instant he would have grasped it, a large figure stepped between him and the crazed woman.

"Laura!" Roan barked, his hands cinching her wrists and holding her arms above her head. "Drop i'! Laura, *drop the dagger!*"

Lachlan stepped aside, a hand covering the wound over his phantom heart. Translucent blood gushed between his spread fingers. He couldn't take his eyes off Roan, whose struggles with Laura were becoming more fierce. Despite his size, she was driving him back . . . back toward the narrow, steep staircase, driving him back with inhuman strength.

"Tak tent!" Roan wheezed. Take care. Using all of his strength to stop his momentum, he growled, "Laura, tak tent no' ta kill me!"

She wrenched from his hold and slashed outward with the dagger. Roan jumped aside, the tip of the blade grazing him just below his left pectoral. Blood trickled down his bare torso, but he hadn't the time to pay it heed, for she swung at him again. This time, he grabbed her right wrist with both hands, twisted the arm, and forced her to release the dagger. The same instant it hit the floor, she collapsed. Roan softened her fall, going down on his knees as he scrambled to get his arms around her. Then, mentally and physically drained, he sat on the floor and placed her head on his lap. His eyes dulled with pain, he looked up at Lachlan, the light from the lantern he'd carried and placed to one side at the top of the stairs, casting the laird's features in unsettling shadows.

"Wha' happened?"

Staring down at the fading blood covering his hand, Lachlan gave a bewildered shake of his head. "She's back."

"Wha?" Roan asked testily, cradling Laura's head in his arms.

"Tessa."

Lachlan's piercing eyes riveted on Roan's face. Roan glimpsed something evil in the laird's expression before the ghost visibly donned a guarded mask.

"Tessa is back," Lachlan said sardonically. His gaze dropped to impale Laura's delicate features. "Get her ou' o' this house, Ingliss!"

Gulping past the raw tightness in his throat, Roan searched Laura's peaceful face for several moments. When he again looked up, Lachlan was nowhere to be seen.

"Wha' is goin' on?" he whispered, caressing Laura's cheek with the back of a hand. He didn't like her ashen color, or the coldness of her skin.

"I've got ta get you ta bed, lass," he grunted, lifting her into his arms and getting to his feet. He looked down at the lantern. The flame within the glass flared up, then quieted. He didn't want to touch the damn thing. What if the flame somehow escaped the glass and ignited her nightgown?

"Damn me," he choked, rolling up his eyes, then closing them with a mute prayer for stamina.

He was bone tired. The cut she'd dealt him was hurting like hell. A dull ache throbbed at his temples.

Fire.

The cursed element possessed the power to reduce him to a quivering coward.

"Roan?"

Beth materialized, nearly causing him to drop his burden.

"What happened?" she asked, dazedly taking in the sight of him holding Laura in his arms. "Lachlan came back to the room looking like death warmed over."

Roan grimaced. "Don't mak me laugh," he groaned,

shifting his burden to a more comfortable position. "Could you bring the lamp along, please? Ma hands . . . they're a *wee* full."

"Of course." She immediately palmed the lantern's looped handle. "What on earth were you two doing up here?"

"I went ta check on her—" He grunted and shifted her again in his arms. "—an' found her gone. Then I heard a noise oop here . . ." A sickly pallor washed over him. "Damn me, Beth, she was stabbin' Lannie whan I arrived. It turned ma blood ta ice. An' she fought *me*. For a wee time, I thought she'd plunged the dagger inta *ma* heart!"

"Dag—"

Beth's troubled gaze lowered to the floor and found the dagger. Taking it into her left hand, she closely inspected the jeweled handle. "Is this the same one Tessa used to murder Lachlan?"

"I don't know. Possibly."

Beth turned her head sharply and stared at the opened trunk. After a moment, she walked to it, dropped the weapon inside, and closed the lid. "No wonder he was in a state," she murmured, then she spied the portrait. Icy invisible talons squeezed her phantom heart. Stepping up to the painting, she bit into her lower lip. Tessa's image remained untouched, while Lachlan's picture was obliterated.

"Ma God," Roan breathed behind her, his horrified gaze glued to the destruction. "Laura must have done tha'. But why, Beth? An' why is she wearin' this . . . this black thin'?"

"It was probably Tessa's." Beth turned and searched Roan's taut face. "Have you sensed anything . . . *weird* in the house?"

"Fegs! Wha' isn't *weird* abou' this place?"

Beth shivered and cast a furtive glance about the attic. "Something's going on, Roan. I've been aware of . . . *something,* but I can't put my finger on what it is."

"Beth . . ." Roan swayed on his feet. "I don't feel tae weel."

"Don't faint!"

"A mon *faint?*" he gasped indignantly. Then, "Aye. Aye, I guess I could."

"Follow me."

A hand on his shoulder, Beth urgently coaxed him across the attic.

Laura awakened alone in Roan's bedroom. The fire in the hearth wrapped her surroundings in a soft orange glow. She made two attempts to sit up. Dizziness felled her each time. Tears sprang to her eyes and slipped from the outer corners. She stared up at shadows dancing on the ceiling, and tried to shake off the willies the nightmare had given her.

It had all been far too real. She could even remember the feel of impact each time she'd driven the dagger into the laird's chest. And his eyes. She'd never forget the look of raw devastation she'd seen in them. Although it'd been just a dream, she couldn't believe her dream-self had been capable of taking a life, especially the life of a man who'd shown her nothing but kindness. He'd opened his home to her and the boys. She'd eaten *his* food. Kept warm beneath *his* blankets.

Forcing herself into a sitting position, she whipped back the covers. A cry lodged in her throat. Dream? How could she be wearing the black and purple nightgown?

What have I done? she silently lamented. Grief was threatening to crush the life out of her.

She'd been in the attic. She'd put on the nightgown. If that much was real, had she found a dagger, and turned it on the laird?

And Roan? He'd been there. She'd fought him.

She'd wanted to kill him, too!

An abrupt sound of something striking wood sent fierce chills through her. Another sound followed. It took her a moment to define what it was she was hearing.

Someone was moving between the walls.

A scream began building in her throat. She flung herself from the bed. Holding up the nightgown so as not to trip on the hem, she ran across the room. She was nearly to the open door when she blindly collided with a solid form. Her scream emerged with a strangled sob. She began to fall backward. Strong hands gripped her shoulders, steadying her, then giving her a firm shake.

"What's wrong wi' you?" Roan snapped.

Looking into his livid expression, Laura shakily asked, "Where are the boys?"

Releasing her, he raked a hand through his unruly hair. "Wi' Beth an' Lannie."

"I was in the attic—"

"Aye, an' damn near lost me ma wits, I can tell you." Placing his hands on his hips, he ran an appreciative glance over her nightgown, and sighed. "Wha' are you doin' in tha'?"

Suddenly self-conscious, Laura folded her arms across her breasts. "I-I found it in a trunk. I must have b-been sleepwalking."

Roan eyed her skeptically, then his stern look melted to one of compassion. Gently drawing her into the security of his arms, he kissed the crown of her head. "Yer're beyond jaggy, lass."

Turning her head, she stared forlornly at the far wall. "I heard something moving between the walls."

"Na."

"I *did*, dammit!"

Sighing with impatience, he held her out to search her pale features. "Laura, yer nerves are on edge—"

"Don't placate me! There's a passageway behind the bookcase in the library, remember?"

"Aye—"

"Well there's probably secret passageways throughout the house! Why won't you believe me?"

"I believe *you* believe," he said with a hint of a smile. He clipped her affectionately beneath the chin with a crooked finger. "I asked Lannie abou' the one behind the bookcase. 'Tis no' a *secret* anythin', Laura. When Lannie designed the house, he had two-foot warkways made between maist o' the exterior an' interior walls."

"Workways . . . for what?" she asked testily.

"Pipework, maistly. You see, Laura, he ne'er wanted the walls ta be altered ta accommodate renovations."

"All the rooms have this . . . this two-foot space?"

Roan nodded.

"Then why can't you admit that there's a possibility that *someone* has been lurking between the walls!" Furious, she stormed to the foot of the bed, keeping her back to him. "The boys swear someone has been going into their room. And I *know* what I heard a little while ago." She turned, glaring at him. "Wait a minute." Her posture stiffened. "You said *Lannie* designed this house, right?"

"Aye," he sighed.

"The same Lannie—Lachlan Baird, who's with my nephews right now?"

Scowling, Roan closed the distance, stopping within arm's reach of her. "I've been tryin' ta tell you—"

"He's a ghost," she flung, her eyes further brightening.

"He was murdered in the master suite, a century an' a half ago. Beth died here, last summer."

His words, although calmly spoken, raised gooseflesh on Laura's exposed skin.

"Where were you before conveniently coming through that door?" she asked, pointing to the door in question.

He glanced over his shoulder, then leveled a darkening scowl on her.

"It's been *you,* hasn't it?" She shivered uncontrollably. "You've been trying to scare us away from here."

"Laura," he growled.

"Just spare us the scare tactics," she sneered, a catch in her voice. "Come morning, I'm taking my nephews and leaving this damn house! Leaving *you!* We've been nothing but an inconvenience, but I assure you, *Mr.* Ingliss, I'll send you compensation for your valuable time once I return to the States!"

"Are you bloody quite through?" he asked through clenched teeth.

"Aye," she said scornfully.

"Ma turn. Lannie an' Beth *are* ghosts, although, granted, tis hard ta fathom since they're sa . . . lively, sa ta say."

"You're warped."

He leaned forward in a threatening manner. The look in his eyes warned her to be silent. "An' I would ne'er stoop ta frightenin' *anyone,* you stubborn, unreasonable womon!

"An' last but no' least, I don't relish the idea o' you an' the laddies leavin'. For some reason I can't bloody well understand a' the moment, I *love* you."

Laura jerked as though he'd struck her. Her eyes seemed

too wide amid her pale face. She leaned against the foot of the bed for support.

"Cat got yer tongue, eh?" he quipped, with a flush to his cheeks. Suddenly intimidated by his revelation, he shifted from one foot to the other. His gaze went wandering to avoid her own.

"You're insane," she said finally, her voice little more than a hoarse whisper.

He forced himself to look into her eyes. "Is tha' all you have ta say?"

Laura swallowed hard and averted her gaze. "Just leave me alone."

A slow transformation settled over Roan. Cold, deadly anger hardened his eyes, made taut the skin across his features, and stiffened his posture. His nostrils flared. A chill passed through Laura. As if compelled, she looked at him. The sight of him looming over her, his rage glaringly clear, overwhelmed her with the worst terror she'd ever known. Ice replaced the blood in her veins. Her feet became rooted to the floor. She wanted to flee the room, the house, *him,* but she couldn't bring herself to even whimper.

"Tis always been *yer* way!" he snarled, his breath fanning her face. *"Gang yer ain gait, you dochter o' the deil! I wash ma bloody hands o' you!"*

Laura's temper flared, dousing her fear. "Get out! I never want to see you again! If you truly loved me—"

His hand shot out and cinched her throat, cutting off her air. The fingers tightened. threatening to crush her windpipe. Her eyes wide with fear, she stared into the maniacal pools of his eyes. He meant to kill her, and she didn't possess the strength to stop him.

"Ne'er again," he hissed, then released her as if sickened by the touch of her, and stormed from the room. He was halfway down the staircase when a wash of weakness swept through him. His legs grew rubbery. Sitting on one of the steps, he lowered his face into his hands. When he looked up, he stared at his surroundings through a bewildered look.

"I've got ta lay off the scotch," he murmured, giving himself a shake. A chill settled in his bones. His stomach churned. He looked over his shoulder and, deciding he was closer to the second-floor landing than the first, he gingerly rose and made it to the top of the stairs. A hand against his middle, his face the color of light gray chalk, he staggered down the hall to the right of the staircase. He entered the last bedroom and closed the door behind him. In the semi-dark, he found an unmade bed and collapsed across it.

His eyes burned. His lungs ached unbearably. He coughed, then again, and made a feeble attempt to get back up.

He collapsed. His fevered brain was trying to warn him that something was wrong.

Within seconds, a long moan was followed by his slipping into unconsciousness.

Meanwhile, Laura paced the floor to the left of the bed, a hand massaging her reddened neck. She was no longer afraid. She was angry and hurt, vexed by his harsh words.

After all they'd been through, how dare he tell her to go her own way. And how *dare* he call her the daughter of the devil!

A strong sense of a presence whirled her to face the door. Standing at the threshold, looking dejected and exhausted, Alby rocked on his feet waiting for her to speak.

"Alby!" she gasped. Crossing the room, she knelt in front of him and lovingly touched the fingertips of a hand to his cool cheek. "Why are you wandering around this big old house?"

"Sumpin' woke me up," he pouted.

"Were you having a nightmare?"

He shook his head.

Laura glanced at the bed. "Do you want to sleep with me tonight?"

He nodded, then abruptly threw his arms about her neck and hugged her. As quickly, he drew away, clasping his hands in front of him.

"Do you need to go to the bathroom?"

He shook his head. "I'm thirsty."

Laura laughed low. "How about a warm glass of milk?"

He wrinkled his nose.

"It'll bring the Sandman with his magical sleeping dust."

"No sa."

"I guess you're too big for that one," she smiled. Standing, she took him by the hand and led him to the bed. She tucked him beneath the covers, then leaned over and planted a kiss on his brow. "I'll warm up some milk and be back in a jiff. Stay in this bed, Alby, okay?"

"Okay."

Laura fingered a soft dark curl on his brow. "You promise?"

He eagerly nodded, then his expression crumpled to one of sadness. "What if the ghost comes for me?"

Straightening up, she sighed. "He won't. I'll hurry."

Alby sat up and watched her leave the room. A frown drew down the dark slashes of his eyebrows. "What about the scawy man?" he asked in a small voice.

"Al, you in here?" someone whispered. Kahl's head popped around the door frame. Seeing his younger brother, he ran across the room and jumped onto the bed with a high-pitched squeal. Alby fell back on the pillows and scowled at him.

"Go away."

"No way, man," Kahl grinned wickedly. He glanced about him. "Where's Kevin?"

"I dunno."

"Where's the big guy?"

"Dunno."

Kahl rolled his eyes. "Okay, where's Aunt Laura?"

"Making me some milk."

"Why?"

Alby snorted and kicked the top covers. "Cause I can't sleep!"

"Okay. Okay! Chee. Ya know . . ." The mischievous gleam in his eyes deepened. "The ghosts are gone. We can go to the tower if we want to."

"Nope."

"How come?"

" 'Cause I promised ta stay here, that's why."

Kahl grimaced. "You're such a baby."

"Am not!" Alby shouted, sitting up and taking a swing at his brother. Missing, he petulantly folded his arms across his small chest. "I'm tellin'."

"I don't care. Hey." Kahl wiggled his pale eyebrows, then inched closer to his brother. "I'm hungry."

Alby, refusing to respond, stubbornly jutted out his lower lip.

"Maybe there's cookies or something in the kitchen. Wanna check it out?"

"I'm s'ppose ta stay here."

"Aunt Laura won't mind. She's in the kitchen, right?"

After a moment, Alby nodded.

Kahl shrugged. "So . . . what's the problem? Kevin's

probably already there. He's probably eatin' all the cookies!"

"Yeah?"

"Yeah."

Taking his brother's hand, Kahl pulled him from the bed and led him toward the door. "The ghosts won't be gone long, you know," he whispered as they walked into the hall.

"Why was Lannie mad?" Alby stopped in his tracks and peered up at Kahl. "Did he find out Kevin tooked his boots and threw 'em out the window?"

Kahl shrugged, his fingers tightening on his brother's hand. "I dunno. Who cares?"

"I like Beth." Alby's voice quivered as his brother jerked him toward the staircase. "She's nice."

"She's *dead.*"

"And nice," Alby said defensively.

A soft sound captured Kahl's attention. Pausing at the top of the steps, he looked to his right, in the direction of the curtain covering the entrance to the tower. The heavy fabric swayed. He squinted to see more clearly in the dim gaslit area. His curiosity was hooked.

Alby, also looking in that direction, tried to pull his hand from his brother's grip.

"C'mon," Kahl whispered. He dragged the younger boy to the curtain, but before he could further investigate, a sound behind the closed door to his left, gave him a start.

Alby began to cry.

"Shh!" His hand trembling, Kahl gripped the knob and slowly opened the door. Beyond lay inky darkness.

"Alby, there's stairs here, remember?"

"Don't wanna go," he whimpered.

"Quit being such a baby. If we go this way, we can sneak up on Aunt Laura. Wouldn't that be fun?"

"Yeah."

"Then come on."

Gulping, Alby held tightly to his brother's hand, and followed closely at his heels. He didn't like the dark. He didn't like the stale smell in the stairwell, either. But he did like the idea of scaring the wits out of his aunt.

Four cautious steps down, the door at the top closed. Terror gripped both boys. Then another sound, a soft *swish,* filled the narrow passageway.

Both boys released a cry. Then something lifted Alby and painfully gripped Kahl's arm, and led them away into the darkness, away from the stone stairs. Kahl's quick mind soon determined that they were being hauled between the walls. While Alby wept, he inwardly struggled to clamp down on his fears. Lachlan had told them never to fear the unknown, but Kahl would have felt better if Kevin had been with them. It was upon him to protect Alby.

The coldness of the fingers pulling him along could be felt through his pajamas. The grip hurt, and he was sure it was meant to.

Another *swish* was heard. He was harshly jerked forward, then shoved. A cry escaped him when he hit the floor. Another shriller cry was released when he realized that he'd been left in one of the bedrooms, and that the intruder had continued on in the passage with Alby. Jumping to his feet, he pounded his fists on a wall, and screamed Alby's name over and over.

Alby was beyond crying. Fear paralyzed him, paralyzed his vocal cords. His teeth remained clenched against the jarring stride of his abductor.

Another wall opened. The three-year-old felt himself being abruptly lowered. His abductor hissed, a sound that conjured up monstrous images in the boy's mind. He was roughly thrust away, struck the floor, and rolled into depthless blackness.

On the third floor, in a closet in one of the bedrooms, Kevin's fists frantically drummed at the locked door.

It seemed to take forever for the milk to warm. Rubbing her arms to ward off the chill in the kitchen, Laura impatiently paced in front of the stove. Her temples throbbed with pain. Her eyes burned. Queasiness churned in her stomach.

She wondered if she would ever feel warm again, safe again, *normal* again. Come morning, she and the boys were leaving this house. She was determined to put this nightmare behind her and get on with her life. Once she was settled back into her previous mundane existence, she would then try to sort through everything that had happened in this house. She would sort through the imaginary and the real, neatly categorize it all in her mind, then relegate it all to a lesser plane of importance in her memory.

With a start, she remembered the milk. A groan escaped her at the sight of the liquid bubbling over the brim of the pan.

"Damn," she muttered, testily turning off the gas burner. Tears filled her throat, adding to her frustration. "To hell with—"

Her muscles tensed at a faint sound. Focusing her hearing, she remained perfectly still for several seconds.

Nothing.

She was releasing a sigh when another sound, of scurrying, alarmed her.

Her gaze riveted on a closed door to the left of the stove. She went to it, hesitating for several seconds before she could bring herself to turn the knob. The door opened inward. The soft light in the kitchen permitted her to see two stone steps. The rest of the stairwell was pitch dark.

"Boys?" she croaked.

She gulped and lifted a hand to the base of her throat. A cold stirring draft swept against her skin. She shivered.

"Boys?"

A soft *swooshing* sound could be heard moving in the close darkness somewhere above her.

A frown of impatience creased her brow.

Alby wouldn't attempt to frighten her on his own. It could only mean that one or two of his brothers had also gotten up.

"Come down here," she said firmly.

No response.

Muttering beneath her breath, she returned to the kitchen, lit the wide candle centered on the table, and returned to the foot of the steps. The flickering light gave her partial visibility of the lower half of the passageway, but it also cast long eerie shadows on the rough rock walls.

"Alby? Kahl? Kevin?" She paused in hopes one of them would respond. "I'm warning you. I'm in no mood for games. Come down here this instant!"

Silence.

Determinedly, she started up the steps, the stones beneath her bare feet shockingly cold. She held a hand in front of the flame to prevent the draft from extinguishing her light source, but it also lessened its luminance.

"Alby, you promised to stay in—"

An odor teased her sense of smell. She inhaled deeply. Recognition gave way to sheer terror within the very core of her.

Gas!

"Alby!" she wailed, then a scream ripped from her throat

when a dark mass unfolded and rose from the steps a short distance ahead, looming like a giant bat, its massive wings lowering toward her. Before she could release another scream, pain exploded in her left shoulder. The candle fell from her grasp as she pitched backward. She hit the stairs, tumbled in a complete turn, then crumpled in a heap on the landing.

Agony radiated through every atom of her being. Blinding lights danced in front of her eyes, preventing her from seeing the advance of her attacker. A thud struck her at the base of her skull. Unconsciousness made a fierce bid to claim her, but she fought to remain alert.

Cold washed across her prone body. Dimly, she realized she was being dragged across the floor, then hoisted up, and cast off. As if in slow motion, she felt herself landing amid an undulating sea of burning ice.

Darkness closed in. The blinding lights faded.

Boys, she silently lamented, then slipped into blessed oblivion.

The cloaked figure returned to the stove and switched on all the top burners, and the oven, then fled past the threshold into the night, barely avoiding Laura's head with the heels of the thick-soled black boots.

On the third floor, Kevin curled up in the corner, hacking coughs weakening him.

Below, Kahl used his pocket knife to unlock the bedroom door. His eyes burning, he was disoriented by the fumes eddying around him. He blindly made his way to the staircase. He wept within. He didn't know where his brothers were, or his aunt. Or Roan. Or the ghosts. He had to find help. His aunt had gone to the kitchen.

Stumbling through the darkness on the first floor, he made his way to the kitchen. Tears stung his eyes. He could barely breathe. Something smelled horrible, but he couldn't place it. He groped for the door, desperate to reach the outside. Ignoring the hiss of the gas pouring from the vents on the stove, he staggered down the three steps to the snow-covered ground.

And tripped over his aunt's sprawled motionless form.

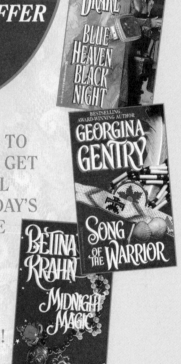

Eight

Laura didn't want to keep rising through the layers of pain, but something urgent was forcing her toward consciousness. From far, far away, she could hear someone calling her name. She became aware of her body jerking, although she was sure she was not moving of her own volition.

"Aunt Laura!" Kahl wept, his tugs on her arm growing weaker. "Laura, I'm scared! Wake up!"

Scared. One of the boys is scared.

Her lids fluttered open.

White. Painful . . . cold . . . *whiteness.*

Lowering his head to the small of her back, Kahl bitterly wept. Its sound penetrated the dullness in her head and awakened primal instincts. Despite the pain and her stiffness, she lifted a hand and gently squeezed the boy's leg. His head shot up. His red swollen eyes searched hers with disbelief.

"Kahl," she hoarsely murmured.

"Get up, Aunt Laura!"

An explosion rocked the ground. Amid a shower of shattered glass, Kahl screamed. Laura curled into a fetal position, then cranked herself up into a sitting position. She couldn't think straight. Pain radiated through her shoulders and back. An invisible vise tightened and tightened on the back of her skull and neck.

"Kevin, Alby!" Kahl cried wretchedly, tears streaming down his face, his arm raised in a pointing gesture toward the house.

Through the swirling haze of her dizziness, Laura focused on flames shooting out from the kitchen and tower windows.

"My . . . God," she rasped, floundering to her feet.

Her eyes widened in horror. Summoning almost inhuman strength, she snatched Kahl up into her arms, turned and fled. She didn't feel pain, or the cold, or anything but overwhelming terror. Another explosion jettisoned the kitchen door out into the sideyard. A *whoosh* of flames extended outward as if coughed from the throat of a ferocious dragon. A blast of air plowed into the back of Laura, lifting her and the boy, and sending them flying. She somehow managed to twist around and land on her back, sparing Kahl the brunt of her weight.

Kahl was screaming a raw sound of anguish. Laura's instincts took over. Her eyes riveted on the burgeoning flames. She got to her feet and hastened the boy to his. She took him by the arm and led him to the front of the house, staying back what she hoped was a safe distance of sixty-plus feet.

Flames were visible on all the floors. Laura's gaze swept the front of the structure, again and again. A scream came bubbling up from the pit of her stomach, into her throat.

"Roan! The boys!"

Half of her delirious mind wanted to chance running into the house to search for the occupants. A saner half warned her to remain with Kahl.

Her world began to spin, faster and faster until she fell to her knees. Anger and fear helped her to retain a tenuous hold on consciousness.

Kahl repeatedly whimpered her name.

She'd failed them all.

What was wrong with her?

The milk!

No, God, please don't let it be I left the stove on!

Had the pilot gone out?

No . . . no, it wasn't the time to find a safe little niche to place the blame.

If she didn't know better, she would swear she was dying. Her energy was draining away. She was slipping into the darkness. The *damn* pain! It made her want to die!

Voices invaded her ears, stampeded through her head. She groaned silently when she felt herself being jarred and lifted, jarred and carried—

"Roan?" she rasped, straining to open her eyes.

He was safe. And he would have saved the boys.

Her knight in tarnished armor.

She attempted to laugh. Searing pain in her lungs forced her to cough. The cough seized her muscles with raw agony.

"She's near fruze ta daith!" cried a feminine voice.

Laura felt herself sinking downward until a hard surface formed across the back length of her. A semblance of warmth enfolded her.

"Roan . . . The boys . . ."

"Lie quiet, lass," a matronly voice crooned above her. "Fetch me ma bag. Hurry, Tommy!"

Tommy? Where am I?

> *Let these delight the throng.*
> *For her o' duskier lustre*
> *Whose favour still I wear,*
> *The snow be in her kirtle,*
> *The rose be in her hair. . . .*

The words humming through her mind brought warmth to the marrow of her bones.

"You remembered, Robbie," she said feverishly. "You still love me, dinna you?"

A wistful smile appeared on the chubby-faced woman leaning over Laura. "Take a whiff o' this, lass."

Ammonia fumes seared the insides of Laura's nostrils. She fully came to, gasping for air. Her wild gaze riveted on the stranger staring down at her.

"You'll be okay," the woman smiled, then cast the house a furtive look.

Laura focused on the engulfed structure. Her heart rose into her throat, but she managed, "Kahl? Where's Kahl?"

"Wi' Farley Campbell, miss."

Shouts rained around her. Despite the woman's hand trying to anchor her down, Laura sat up, clutching the wool blanket she'd been laid on.

Everywhere she looked, there were people. People silently watching the house, their expressions ranging from horror to indifference. People running about, shouting orders. People and more people covering the landscape.

Then Kahl moved into her line of view. The next moment, he flung himself into her arms and wept against her bruised shoulder.

Her vision zoomed in on a figure precariously balanced on a windowsill on the second floor.

Roan!

Getting to her feet and clutching Kahl's hand, she inched her way through the thickening horde of spectators. She stopped a few yards from six men holding taut a blanket to catch him.

"Jump!" one of the men shouted. "Hurry, mon! We've a catch!"

Laura wanted to scream. Behind Roan, she could see a wall of fire moving toward him. She wanted to turn back the hands of time and go back to that first night of the accident.

With all the strength she possessed, she called out, "Roan! Don't be afraid! Jump!"

She waited a moment, then, "Roan, please! The men down here will catch you in the blanket."

He cast off, sailing into the air. Laura's heart swelled, then became a weighty inanimate object behind her breasts until he bounced off the blanket and hit the ground.

Wood creaked from every part of the house. Fire roared, reaching for the heavens.

Trying to suppress coughs, she led Kahl along, following closely behind the three men dragging Roan away from the house. Behind her, small explosions went off. Windowpanes exploded outward from every side of the house.

"Laura!"

Tearing her gaze from the men placing Roan upon a blanket and covering him with coats, Laura looked to her left to see Alby pull free of a woman's hold on his hand. He ran to Laura, with his arms wide open. Despite her pain, her weakness, she lifted him into her arms and hugged him tightly.

"Laura, Laura," he chanted, as he wrapped his little arms about her neck.

"It's okay, hon. It's okay," she wept. "Kevin—" She looked into the boy's eyes and felt her blood plummet to her feet. "No. No . . ."

Whirling to face the house, she released a tortured cry. "Kevin!" Her gaze searched the sea of faces around her, but not one remotely looked liked her oldest nephew.

"Kevin!" She cried out to the crowd, "There's still a boy in there!"

Placing Alby on his feet, she knelt beside Roan's semi-unconscious form. "Roan! Roan, did you see Kevin? I couldn't find him! Roan!"

Roan opened his eyes. After several moments, he was able to focus somewhat on Laura's features.

"Kevin?" he rasped.

Laura burst into tears and drew the boys in her arms closer against her. "I couldn't find him. And I couldn't reach you."

"Stand clear!" a rough-voiced man ordered.

The people standing shoulder-to-shoulder on Roan's other side, moved out of the way for a large man. He went down on a knee, with one beefy balled hand resting on his hip. "Roan, laddie. 'Tis Ben. Yer pub mate. Can you hear me?"

"Aye," Roan wheezed. "I'm no' deaf."

Resisting the hands trying to keep him down, he sat up. Coughs seized him. Ben's hand roughly clapped him on the back several times.

"Take i' easy, mate. You swallowed some smoke, by the looks o' i'."

"Jamey . . . Ma son—"

Reality cruelly returned home to Roan. He stared into the rounded face of his old friend, and felt a swell of tears lodge in his throat.

"Jamey's gone, mate. But you saved the lad here."

Roan squinted at Laura, then at the back of the boys' heads she kept pressed against the hollows of her shoulders.

"Kevin," he said. He was about to push up to get on his knees when excruciating pain razored through his left arm.

"My airm's broken!" he gasped, then doubled over during a coughing fit.

"Lucky tis no' yer back," Ben said gravely. He looked at Laura, then again at Roan. "She claims one o' the lads didna make i'," he said thickly. Then he glanced up and scowled, and bellowed to the crowd pressing closer for a look at Roan, "Get back! If you canna lend a hand, gae home, the lot o' you!"

Roan. "Roan."

In front of the curious spectators, Beth materialized and immediately knelt to one knee in front of the new laird of Baird House. "Are you all right?"

Roan nodded. With Beth and Ben's help, he got up onto his feet. Neither he nor Beth noticed the sickly look of shock on Ben's face, or the awed expressions of the strangers filling the driveway.

"I've got ta get Kevin," Roan insisted, finally beginning to feel like himself again, despite the pain racking his body.

"Lachlan's searching for him."

Blinking hard, Roan looked deeply into Beth's troubled eyes. "Can he help him?"

"If it's within his power, he will," Beth said, her voice cracking with emotion.

"Kevin," Laura whimpered, rising to her feet with a boy sitting on each of her hips.

With his right arm, Roan reached out and urged Alby to come to him. Surprisingly, the boy clung to Roan's broad neck.

Laura, who had not realized Beth had actually materialized from thin air, turned in the direction of the house and uttered, "Please, God. Give me a second chance to do right by them."

Roan stepped to her side. "Lannie will find him. Have faith, Laura. We must have faith."

Sobbing, she laid one side of her face to Roan's chest. "It all happened so fast!"

"Aye, lass. I know," Roan soothed, absently planting a kiss on the crown of her head. "Thank God you two made i' ou' okay. Kahl? Yer're no' hurt, are you?"

"Where's Kevin?" the five-year-old bitterly demanded.

Roan cast a fearful look in the direction of the house. "Comin', laddie. Lannie will save him. I feel i' in ma bones." *Dear God, mak i' true. For us all, mak i' true!*

Tongues of fire lapped at the night through the desolate portals of what had been the windows. A chimney on the west side of the house began to crumble. Flames reached high into the midnight sky from several of the rooftops.

"Lannie," Roan said in a prayerlike whisper. "I'll promise you anythin' if you just bring Kevin ta us, alive an' unharmed."

Fed by the broken gas lines, the flames grew until the manor's stonework exterior could barely be seen. Not a murmur stirred among the spectators. All eyes were riveted on the destructive element consuming the region's most famous house.

Laura's legs weakened, forcing her to lower Kahl to the ground. She wanted to lean completely into Roan's powerful body, and weep herself into forgetfulness. She'd never been a dreamer, nor a believer in the powers of prayer. She didn't even know where to begin, and self-loathing ate away at her stomach.

She closed her eyes for a moment, opening them when murmurs began to circulate around her. She glanced absently at the faces, then in the direction their attention was focused.

The fire. The destruction of flesh and bone, history, and dreams.

Then, amidst the blaze, an image was spied slowly emerging.

"Lachlan!" Beth cried joyously. Her diaphanous form moved toward him as he lumbered toward Roan and Laura. They, as well as everyone else, remained frozen in shock when Lachlan and Beth came to stand in front of the anxious couple. In Lachlan's arms was a wide-eyed Kevin, who, for the first time in his life, was absolutely speechless.

"The saints be with us," Ben muttered, hastily blessing himself as he stared wondrously into Lachlan's taut face.

Joy was overcoming Roan when he released a sob and sank to his knees. He hugged Alby tightly with his good arm, then with a kiss to the boy's cheek, set him on his feet. Lachlan placed Kevin down, without letting his gaze waver from Roan's ravaged features. Kevin endured hugs and kisses from his aunt, then turned to stare for a long moment into Roan's tear-filled eyes.

Although Roan suspected that Kevin had started the fire, he reached out with his right arm and drew the boy against him. "Thank God," he repeated, over and over, until Kevin stepped back and pointed up to Lachlan.

The crowd inched closer. No longer was the manor the center of their attention. It was the man who'd walked through the flames, unscathed, carrying a boy in his arms who also appeared untouched by the wrath of the blazing inferno.

Beth proudly peered at Lachlan's profile. She could feel the pull of the grayness tugging on her, but she clung to this world, relishing the rise of emotions emanating from Lachlan.

Laura rose to her feet. Her wide eyes drank in the strange

couple. Behind her breast, her heart thundered, drummed in her ears, her throat, the center of her brain.

A portly woman came through the crowd and beelined for the children, gathering them into her arms and holding them to her sagging bosom. "The bairns are cauld. I'll tak them ta ma caur ta warm them oop."

Laura was too rattled to object. She'd seen the master of Baird House walk through the flames with Kevin, but her mind refused to accept it as reality. In an absent gesture, she helped Roan to his feet, and stood close to his side as he and the laird stared intensely into each other's faces.

"Thank you," Roan said in a barely audible voice to Lachlan, and made a helpless gesture with his good arm. In the next second, Lachlan was embracing him.

Another hush fell over the crowd.

Lachlan held Roan out at arm's length and searched his face, a question in his dark eyes. The laird was beginning to lose his physical integrity, fluctuating between the two worlds.

"Dusk 'fore dawn, laddie," he said with a crooked smile. Then stepping back, he drew Beth's fading form into his arms, and together they vanished into the night.

Mixed emotions pummelled Laura. Awe. Wonder. Utter joy. Disbelief that the boys' *ghost* had been real all along.

No . . . *ghosts*.

Beth Staples, too.

And Laura had thought Roan insane.

Her world began to ebb away from her.

Laura fainted.

For several seconds, Roan stared down at her as if disbelieving she had fainted. Then his own experience, and his own pain, caught up with him. He collapsed alongside her, unaware of what a romantically poetic image the two of them presented to the crowd.

He had convinced himself that he would always feel as numb as he felt now. Numb inside. Numb outside. Four days had passed since the fire. It seemed like a lifetime. Two lifetimes.

The rocker gently swayed to and fro beneath him, in front of a warm, cozy fire in his Aunt Aggie's red-brick fireplace. The skin beneath the cast on his left arm itched. At least the break had been clean. Considering what could have been, he should be feeling damn lucky, but he wasn't. He was grateful that Laura and the boys had survived, although to look at the bruises and cuts on her face and body, reminded him how close she'd come to death. But he wasn't at all grateful for his own life. Countless times he'd questioned his reasons for jumping out the window. Cowardice. He'd been afraid to die. Worse, he'd been terrified to experience the agony of the flames, as his wife and son had.

"Roan, ma dear, have some tea ta warm yer insides."

His gaze swerved at the sound of Agnes's soft tone. He studied her wrinkled visage for a moment, then shook his head and again stared into the flames.

"You've got ta pull yerself from this depression." Her eyes were filling with despair as she sighed and perched herself atop a faded oak stool to the left of the rocker. "She's leavin' this day."

His dull gaze swung to her face.

"Borgie an' Ben are goin' ta tak them ta Edinburgh."

A slow frown materialized on his brow.

"Borgie?"

"Aye. Ben's got tha' big German truck that'll tak the

rough roads. You might want ta say yer guidbyes ta them, Roan."

"The lads are afraid o' him."

"Borgie?" Agnes smiled. "Na. They're still jaggy, is all."

Roan's frown darkened to a scowl. "I don't trust Borgie wi' Laura."

"Fegs, why no'?" Agnes gasped.

"He tried ta rape Beth."

"Wha said such a thin'?"

"Beth," he replied dully. " 'Tis why Lannie attacked him. 'Tis why his hair is white, Aunt Aggie."

"How can you sit in ma home an' defend tha' deil?" she snorted, rising to her feet.

"He's no' so bad." Roan cut his gaze back to the fire. "In maist ways, he's just a mon."

"He's touched yer brain!"

"Na, Aggie. He gave me the house." His pained gaze lifted to search the incredulity brightening her eyes. "His precious house an' his worth."

"Tis all gone, now!"

"Tis no' *his* fault."

"Na?" Her coy tone caused him a chill. "Perhaps, Roan, he made the offer, then brought i' doon ta spite you."

"He wouldn't do tha'."

"Yer're bewitched!"

Roan groaned deep within his chest. "Na, dammi'! Leave him be, Aggie. Ta be fair, he's lost mair than all o' us put thegither."

"He's a monster—"

"He saved Kevin," said Laura coldly from the kitchen door.

Roan stared at her, inwardly wincing at the pathetic sight she presented. She was dressed in one of Agnes's old wool dresses, which hung badly on her slender form. Her hair was disheveled. Dark purple and yellow bruises appeared on every part of her exposed skin.

Agnes passed a contrary look at the woman as she stepped further into the room. "For tha', I, tae, am grateful, lass. But you dinna know Lannie like *I* do!"

"I know enough," Laura said wearily, lowering her stiff body into a comfortable chair on the opposite side of the hearth. "How are you feeling, Roan?"

"I'm no'," he grumbled.

"Can I get you somethin' from the kitchen?" Agnes asked Laura.

"No, thank you."

"Then I'll leave the two o' you be. I'll check on the laddies."

Laura nodded absently, her gaze riveted on Roan's taut profile. When Agnes had left the room, she asked, "Did she tell you?"

"About you leavin' this efternoon?" His brooding gaze impaled her. "Aye. Yer're in na shape ta travel."

"I have no choice. The phone lines are still down."

"There's always tomorrow."

Laura sadly shook her head. "Agnes gave me her address. I'll write as soon as I get settled in the States."

"Don't bother," he said, his monotone response sparking her temper. "Tis better we cut all ties."

"Is that what you really want?"

He nodded.

"Sometimes, Roan, you're a real sonofabitch."

His gaze swept to study her for a time. "It wouldn't have warked between us."

"I agree, but I don't see why we can't remain friends. Keep in touch."

A low bitter laugh vibrated in his chest. "Keep in touch?"

"Stop it."

Her sharp tone prompted him to arrogantly arch an eyebrow.

"I've been wrong about a lot of things, Roan, but so have you." She looked down at her hands which were clasped atop her lap. "I asked Aggie about your son. She told me I should ask you." She looked up, her gaze scanning his handsome features. "Tell me what happened. Please."

For a long moment, he scowled at the flames. Then he sighed a woeful sound, and began his story.

"I realize now tha' I ne'er loved Adaina. We enjoyed sex thegither, but little else. She thought me cauld an' insensitive. An' . . . aye, I guess I am tha' sort.

"Whan Jamey was born, we got closer for a time. Sa I thought, till two years later whan I learned she was havin' an affair wi' a mon I thought a friend. Gus Mackerby. Guid . . . . auld . . . reliable . . . Gus."

He fell quiet for a time, unaware that the fingers of his right hand were roughly kneading the arm of his chair.

"Adaina expected me ta tak on Gus, but truth was, I didn't care enough ta cause a scene. We na sooner separated, Gus moved in. I didn't care much abou' tha', either. In some ways, I was relieved ta be ou' o' the marriage.

"At first, there wasn't a problem wi' me seein' ma son whane'er i' suited me. He was all I cared abou', all I e'er wanted.

"I'd heard rumors abou' Gus bein' tae strict wi' ma boy. I told Adaina I'd tak him away from her if she wasn't careful. She laughed, an' said I wad ne'er tak the lad, for i' wad require me ta mak a commitment ta him, an' a commitin' mon I wad ne'er be."

He sighed again, and worked the stiff muscles in the back of his neck.

"Anither year slipped by. Ma visits ta Jamey grew fewer, though, for the life o' me, I don't know why. I loved tha' boy. His laughter always brought sunshine inta ma life. . . .

"I was supposed ta tak Jamey for a three-day weekend. Adaina an' Gus had made plans ta tak a short holiday ta London.

"Damn me, I don't know wha' got inta me, but I resented them plannin' ta gae off thegither. I deliberately went on a drunk the night before, me an' ma sa-called buddies. I stayed a' one o' their houses, knowin' Adaina wad be frantic whan I didn't show tha' morn.

"By late efternoon, ma conscience got the better o' me, an' I drove ta the house. . . ."

Pain ravaged Roan's face. Squeezing his eyes shut, he tried to block out the memories of the rest of that day.

"Go on," Laura said in a gentle, understanding tone.

"The place was on fire. Great flames were loomin' above the back o' the house. By Jamey's room!

"At first, I could do nothin' but stare. Then I saw Gus comin' toward me. He said Adaina had rushed back in ta get Jamey. Sirens were closin' in. Those bloody, deafenin' sirens. But above them, I heard Adaina scream. It went on an' on, growin' higher in pitch till I was sure i' wad shatter ma brain.

"I tried ta run ta the front door. Two men tackled me doon. No' Gus. He stood watchin'. Watchin' ma wife, ma son, ma home, become swallowed oop in those horrible flames. I fought ta ma feet, an' i' was then I saw Adaina pressed against the parlor window. I could see wha' remained o' Jamey in her arms. Her hair . . . Gone.

"I was prevented from goin' ta her. Prevented from tryin' ta smash through tha' bloody window ta pull them ou'.

"An' then I could see only flames lickin' oop the window. A wall o' flames . . ."

A sob caught in his throat. He lowered his head, but he could not stop the tears from escaping his closed eyelids.

Moving as quickly as her battered body allowed, Laura knelt to his side and rested her hands upon his right hand, which fiercely gripped the arm of the rocker.

"There was nothing you could have done to save them, Roan," she wept, her heart breaking in two for him.

His chin quivered. He stiffened with the strain to hold his emotions at bay. "Jamey wad have been wi' me, an' Adaina on her holiday if no' for me!"

"You don't know that for sure. Roan . . . things happen. We can't try to rationalize every disaster. We'd go insane. Things just . . . *happen*. It's . . . part of life."

"Ask me wha' started the fire," he demanded harshly.

"What, Roan?"

His pain-ridden eyes swung to look into hers. "One o' Gus' cigars, smolderin' in the couch."

"That has nothing to do with you."

"Na? If I'd picked oop Jamey on time, *na one* would have been in tha' house!"

"Roan, *please* . . . let go of the past."

"'Tis the past wha' holds on, Laura." He stared into the flames, his powerful shoulders sagging beneath the burden of his remorse. "I damn near failed Alby."

"But you didn't! Look at me. Dammit, Roan, *look at me!*"

His tear-filled eyes swung to her face. Laura wanted to kiss away his pain at that moment, kiss away his tormenting memories. "Stop punishing yourself. You're a good man,

Roan. A kind . . . gentle man. I know. And I thank God for delivering me into your care these past few days."

"Don't, Laura."

"I *will* write, and you'd better write back!"

"Don 't leave. No' yet."

She gulped past the tightness forming in her throat. "I have to go."

A mask of hardness slid down over his face. "Aye, sa you say."

Borgie Ingliss walked into the room, his white hair standing on end, an open bottle of beer in his hand. "Can you be ready in a couple o' hoors?" he asked Laura.

"Yes."

"Ben's gone ta fill the truck. He'll be by abou' two."

"Thank you."

Laura looked at Roan. The distance she read in his eyes caused a chill to squirm along her spine. Standing, she kissed him lightly on the cheek. "I've got to emotionally prepare the boys to leave. I'll be back in a while."

"I won't be here," he rasped.

"Roan, don't be like this."

"Like wha', eh? Maself?" He raked a contemptuous look over her wan face. "I ne'er cared for guidbyes. Tak care o' yerself an' the lads."

Laura wanted to shout at him, but instead, briskly walked from the room. Borgie watched her leave, then sat in the chair she'd occupied, and released a nasal chuckle.

"She's a fine-lookin' womon, she is," he chortled.

Roan leveled a deadly look on the man. "I know wha' you tried ta do ta Beth Staples."

"Me?" Borgie feigned a look of innocence. "I offered the womon a ride—"

"Save yer breath, you— But I'm warnin' you, cousin,

if you sa much as look a' Laura in a way I don't like, I'll do mair n' turn yer bloody hair white!'"

A sneer formed on Borgie's thin lips. "I'd watch ma threats if I were you, *cousin.* Yer're in na shape ta threaten a child, let alone *me.*"

Although it pained him to do so, Roan rose from the chair. His powerful chest rose and fell with his every deep breath. His eyes possessed the fires of hell. "You've been warned, you swine."

From the corner of his eye, Borgie watched his cousin leave. A wicked smile played across his mouth, then he tipped the bottle and gulped down its contents.

A sound of satisfaction gurgled from his throat, and he swiped an arm across his mouth. He belched. Glanced over his shoulder. Then smiled a smile of pure malice.

"Tae bad abou' Kist House, eh?" he chuckled low.

Nine

Laura refused to dwell on Roan's callous disposition. Her head ached. Every bone and muscle in her body painfully protested her slightest movement. She tried to focus on the fact that she was getting closer to returning home. Whatever happened after she arrived in Chicago, would prove a cinch compared to her Scotland ordeal.

He had every right to feel bitter. The house, and all its magnificent belongings, were gone. The fact that it had been a *fire* that had caused the destruction, was undoubtedly a weighty factor to his withdrawal. He'd lost everything he'd loved to that single element.

Damn, why did he push her away? She *did* understand what he was feeling, although she'd never personally lost anyone or anything of value to fire. But she ached for his losses along with him. She wept within for his suffering. If she sincerely believed remaining in Scotland for a time longer would help him get back on his feet, she would! But she was convinced that he didn't need further complications in his life right now. He needed time and space to heal his emotional and physical wounds. She had every intention of returning to Scotland in the near future. Next year if her finances permitted. Contrary to what she'd *told* him that last night in Baird House, they hadn't had sex, but had *made love.* It had been no fling. She'd lost her heart to him, and he had admitted to being in love with her.

How or why she didn't know. They hardly knew one another. But then, they'd lived what seemed a lifetime in a matter of days.

She liked Agnes, and all the strangers who had offered their help, their kindness, and who had collected articles of clothing for her and the boys. She liked them all.

Except Borgie.

Roan needn't have warned her. The instant she had laid eyes on him, something in his manner, the way his gaze had boldly looked her over, had left her with a strong wariness of him. She didn't relish sharing a vehicle with him, but he was going along to keep Ben company on the return trip from Edinburgh.

Zippering the oversized worn piece of luggage that Agnes had given her, Laura leaned over to appease a wave of dizziness. She wanted nothing more at that moment than to lie down, close her eyes, and escape the pain, emotional aches, and exhaustion for a time. Although Agnes had made her and the boys a large breakfast, her stomach felt empty. Queasy.

And in knots.

She couldn't shake the ridiculous notion that she was afraid to leave Scotland. Afraid to leave Roan. Afraid to allow time to widen the gap between . . . *unfinished business?*

What business?

Their relationship?

Ha. That needed work, and neither of them was in an emotional position to seriously plan for a future together.

He was in love with her, but didn't want to be. Now that made more sense. It also explained his gruffness, his shutting her out. It wasn't that he needed time to work through his ordeal, he *wanted* to end what he considered to be a threat to his chosen way of life!

He was admittedly a loner. Falling in love had not been in his plans for *his* future. It wasn't that he was struggling with his losses, but struggling with indecision. That last night in Baird House, he'd told Kevin that he was trying to convince her to stay. She hadn't taken him seriously and, now that she thought about it, rightly so. He'd adamantly stated more than once that he didn't want responsibility—especially not the responsibility of her and the boys! He'd lost his wife and son. Now he was torn between accepting a ready-made family, and turning away from the pressures that presented.

"Yer're in na shape ta travel," said a gruff voice.

Slightly turning her head, she saw Roan standing in the open doorway. Paleness accentuated his gaunt features. Despite the defensive thrust of his shoulders, the rigidity of his bearing, and the grim set of his mouth, his eyes betrayed deep sadness.

Are you hoping I'll make up your mind for you? she thought achingly.

Gingerly straightening, she allowed her gaze to linger on the cast covering his left arm from the wrist to the elbow. He refused to use the sling. He refused to take the pain pills the clinic had given him.

"I'm in better shape than you are," she said finally, softly. Unable to bear looking at him any longer, she lowered her gaze to the luggage. "Have you gotten any sleep?"

Roan paused a few seconds longer, then, as if reluctant to do so, walked to the foot of the bed.

"You don't have ta go, Laura," he said huskily.

Turning her back to him, she placed a hand over her

abdomen and heaved a fortifying breath. *No, I don't have to do anything, Roan. But you haven't convinced me . . . seriously tried to convince me that you really want me to stay.* "I'm sorry about the house, and everything you lost."

"I'm no' a material mon!"

His bitter tone cruelly lanced her control. Tears swiftly welled in her eyes and spilled down her ashen face. "Will the fire be investigated?"

He nodded, then murmured, "Aye."

"I . . . I think I might have—" Her voice caught. "—have left the gas on."

"Wha' are you talkin' abou'?"

"In the kitchen." She lightly sank her teeth into her sore lower lip. "I vaguely remember something about the stove. I—umm, think I left one of the burners on."

"The first explosion was on the third floor."

"No, I'm sure—"

A scowl of impatience darkened his face. "Laura . . . i' started on the third floor!"

"Oh . . . no," she choked, turning to face him. "Oh, God, please tell me the boys were in no way responsible!"

Roan's demeanor softened. "It doesn't matter how i' started, Laura. Wha' does matter is tha' we all made i' ou' safely."

Tears spilling from her eyes, she gave a stilted shake of her head. Her drawn-in shoulders quivered. "It matters to me."

"Weel, I don't know how i' started, sa let i' go."

Again she shook her head. "Promise me you'll let me know what the investigation reveals."

"Dammi', Laura, quit harpin' on the bloody fire!"

Although her face was piteously wet with tears, her posture was undeniably hostile. "If I'm responsible—or my nephews—I have a right to know. I pay my debts, Roan! I-I'll make arrangements to pay you back every cent!"

A mantle of warring stubbornness enfolded Roan. "I don't want yer money, or yer bloody pity!"

"Tough! I'll inquire about the investigation, myself!"

Roan clenched his teeth, unlocking them when he heaved a fortifying breath to quiet his temper. "Ben's in the parlor. Tis no' polite ta keep him waitin'."

Turning on a heel, he briskly left her staring after him. He entered the front room, where Agnes sat on an overstuffed couch with the boys, and Ben and Borgie were talking by the front door. All eyes turned on him. Ignoring their questioning looks, he sat in the rocker by the hearth and tersely stated, "She'll be ready shortly."

Alby scrambled from the couch and ran to Roan. He climbed onto Roan's lap and, pouting, his chin quivering, wrapped his arms about Roan's broad neck. "Don't wanna go," he sobbed.

Roan's heart painfully constricted. He looked at the others in the room before circling the boy's back with his uninjured arm. "I'll miss you tae, you little bugger," he said huskily, a forced smile turning up a corner of his mouth. Alby's arms held tightly, the back of his head pressed against Roan's jaw. Despite his inward struggle to deny himself the slightest emotional release, tears misted Roan's eyes. "Can you promise me somethin', lad?"

Alby nodded.

His hand massaged the boy's back. He said, "Tak care o' yer aunt. An' help yer brithers ta settle inta yer new home."

Drawing back, Alby's dark blue eyes somberly searched Roan's face. "Where's Lachlan and Beth? Can't we say good-bye ta them?"

Roan heaved a ragged sigh. "Weel, Alby, 'tis hard ta say where they are. I know they'll miss you."

"Really?"

A genuine grin brightened Roan's features. "Aye, really."

"Do ya think it hurts ta be dead?"

Roan blinked in bewilderment. "Wha' a thin' ta ask."

"I want ta know."

Roan's comical gaze swept to the others before meeting the boy's again. "Weel, Alby, I think 'tis safe ta say they don't feel pain."

"But Lachlan made a bad face when I kicked him."

Roan chuckled. "Could be, he didn't like you kickin' him."

The small shoulders moved noncommittally.

"We didn't start the fire," Kevin said adamantly, his hard gaze riveted on Roan.

"No one's accusin' anyone, laddie."

Kevin left the couch and went to stand a short distance from the rocker. "*You* think one of us did it. Don't you?"

"Miss, I'll tak tha'," Ben said, breaking the spell of tension in the room when he hurriedly rushed to Laura and took the luggage from her grasp. He cast Roan a look of warning as he headed out the front door, to load the case into his truck.

Roan searched Laura's guarded expression for a time before returning his attention to Kevin. "I'm no' accusin' anyone, Kevin. I told yer aunt, i' doesn't matter how i' started. I'm just grateful na one was seriously hurt."

"You're glad we're going," Kevin said.

Quickly reaching out with his right hand, Roan cupped the back of Kevin's head and drew him toward him. "Listen ta me verra carefully, Kevin. I care a lot for you boys, an' I'm no' happy yer're leavin'."

"Yeah, sure. That's why you're always nagging at us, right?"

A stab of guilt prompted Roan to lower his gaze for a brief time. When he next looked into the boy's beguiling eyes, he read in them a desperate need for the boy to be convinced otherwise.

"Whan yer're right, yer're right, lad. I've been a grump, an' I apologize. Trouble is, I was o' the mind we'd have some time ta really get ta know one anither. But fate kinda threw us a curve, eh? Had I known we wad be partin' company sa soon, I wad have been mair patient."

He went on when Kahl came to stand alongside his brother. His gaze swept over the boys' drawn faces. "You've a new life waitin' for you in the States. A new adventure ahead o' you. I'm envious, laddies."

"Come with us," Kahl said, a quiver in his tone.

A sad smile played across Roan's mouth. "Truth be, I wish I could, but I've tae much ta do here."

"Like what?" Kevin asked.

"Weel, like healin', an' checkin' on the house."

"Is the house all gone?"

"Maistly, Alby. Some things might have survived. I don't know."

"Will you write to us?"

Kahl's question further aggravated Kevin. "Course he won't. He's just being nice cause we're getting outta his hair."

Roan's gaze kindly lingered on Kevin's flushed face. "I ne'er say wha' I don't mean. Aye, I'll write, an' I'll be lookin' forward ta hearin' from the three o' you."

"You promise?" Alby asked in a soft voice.

In response, Roan planted a lingering kiss on the boy's brow.

"It's time," Laura said abruptly, tightening the loaned wool coat about her. If she didn't leave now, she knew she never would. "Say good-bye to Agnes, and thank her for all her kindness."

Roan's gaze impaled her while the boys hugged and thanked the older woman. Her insides were coiling into knots. She forced an outer calm. Next year, she vowed. If they were meant to be together, then the separation wouldn't prove a mistake. He'd have time to think. Time to consider all the ramifications that went with the responsibility of taking on a woman and three boys. He'd have the time to forgive and cleanse himself of the past.

Laura headed for the front door, which Borgie held open. The boys dashed ahead of her, waiting on the stoop. Agnes rushed into the kitchen, returning with a small sack. Handing it to Laura, she tearfully explained, "Some snacks ta get you by on the trip."

Reaching for the sack, Laura realized her hand was trembling.

"Yer're no' goin'," Roan said angrily.

Suddenly aware that he was standing behind her, Laura turned to face him. Her heart sang out with joy. He was telling her that she was going to stay. He wasn't going to let her slip away—

Crimson stole into her cheeks when she realized that he had spoken to Borgie. Her insides shriveling, she made a half turn toward the door.

"I spoke ta Ben," Roan went on. His hard gaze riveted on Borgie's face.

"Tha' sa?" The white-haired man smirked. "Na one said shi' ta me."

Roan's posture became instantly hostile. "Weel, *I'm* sayin' i' now. Besides, I'll be needin' yer help a' the house."

"Kist House?" A scoffing laugh burst from him. "O'er ma dead body will I e'er go near tha' place again!"

"Suit yerself, but yer're no' goin' ta Edinburgh wi' Ben."

An evil sneer marred Borgie's already unpleasant face. "Wha died an' left you boss?"

Ben showed up at the door. His gaze scanned the two men. "Ah, Borgie, ma truck will be crowded as i' is. I appreciate yer offer, though."

Glaring at Ben, Borgie then turned and took a threatening step in Roan's direction. Agnes's hand flew over her heart. Responding to the suffocating tension in the room, Laura placed a hand to Roan's chest, and hurriedly suggested to Ben, "Please, take the boys to the truck. I'll be along in a minute." She looked up at Roan. His fierce gaze continued to bore into his cousin. "Roan, may I speak to you *alone* in the kitchen?"

Agnes took hold of her son's arm and gave it a tug. "Come along, Borgie."

"I'm no' movin', mum," he gritted out.

"The hell you say," she fumed, giving his arm a slap. "Come ta the kitchen!"

Glaring at Roan, he permitted his mother to lead him out of the room.

Alone with Roan, Laura gave his chest a rap with her knuckles. "What's wrong with you? Are you trying to start a brawl in your aunt's house?"

Tearing his gaze from the direction of the kitchen, his unsettling eyes stared deeply into hers.

"I've na love for the mon."

"I would have never guessed," she said flippantly. Her anger made her eyes bright. "The trouble with you is, you always want everything *your* way. Grow up, Roan! This *poor me* attitude of yours stinks."

"I don't have an *attitude.*"

A disparaging sound rattled in her throat. "I don't have the time to waste standing here arguing with you."

She turned to leave. A hand on her arm stayed her.

Her heart was painfully drumming. She disparagingly looked up at him.

And it struck her at that moment, how much she loved his face!

"You've got tha' look again," he said sourly.

"Beg your pardon?"

"Yer're beggin' ta be pree'd."

Again, crimson stole into her cheeks, accentuating the greenness of her eyes. "You arrogant—"

He quickly placed the fingertips of his right hand against her lips. His glowing look faded to one of regret and such sadness, Laura felt her blood rush to her head. She trembled, staring up at him, praying for him to take her into his arms and kiss away the remains of her faltering determination to leave.

To her profound disappointment, he lowered his hand to his side and stiffened.

"Tak care, Laura."

Gulping back the tears building in her throat, she dejectedly walked out the front door, closing it behind her without sparing him a last glance.

The instant she was out of sight, Roan lifted his misting eyes heavenward. He clenched his hands, ignoring the pain shooting up his broken arm.

For four days, he'd struggled with the notion to convince her to stay with him, but the uncertainty of his future had won out. He was without a job. Without a home. Without hope of turning his life around. He refused to lean on her through the trying months to come. It was a man's duty to support a wife and children!

"Damn me," he choked.

He'd never expected anyone like Laura or the boys to come waltzing into his life.

"Damn me!" he repeated belligerently, and returned to the rocker in front of the hearth.

It was three days later before Roan returned to the remains of the manor. The seven days which had passed since Laura and the boys had left, were a blur to him. His casted arm rested in a sling about his neck. He'd lost weight. His rugged features bespoke the trials he'd endured that terrible night of the fire. He'd grown quiet and remote, a man existing under a perpetual cloud of hopelessness.

He stood at the front of the cottage, staring at the blackened exterior of the main house. Very little life was visible in his usually expressive eyes.

"Lannie? Beth?"

He didn't expect them to answer. Since the night of the fire, he hadn't seen or heard from them. The manor was destroyed, and its lord and mistress had completely vanished. Not too long ago, he'd plotted to rid his clan of the laird. And yet, the idea now of never seeing Lachlan or Beth again left in him a void that was almost unbearable.

"Laura an' the boys have returned ta the States." He sighed, ignoring the ache that remained in his lungs. "Tha' promise has been carried through, you auld swine."

Emotional pain became deeply etched in his features. "It shouldn't have ended like this. Yer home, mon." Tears brimmed his eyes. "Aggie says guid riddance. She doesn't understand. You an' yer grandfaither's scotch, eh? We bonded all right. You teuk a piece o' me wi' you, you bloody pain in the ass."

Jabbing at the air with his right index finger, he went on bitterly, "It was simpler whan I hated you, Lannie. Damn you, mon, you filled ma head wi' dreams na mon like me has a right ta haud dear ta his heart!"

Picking up a rock, he walked to within five yards of the front of the house. Angrily, he flung it at the wall, and from his effort to release his anguish, his feet slid out from under him. He slammed onto the icy, graveled yard, and released a stream of Scottish invectives.

"Breakin' yer arse winna accomplish a thin'," said a grave voice, as hands hooked beneath Roan's coated armpits and hauled him up onto his feet.

Astonished, Roan turned to find himself staring into Lachlan's brooding eyes. Just beyond the laird's shoulder, Beth tipped her head and smiled in greeting.

"Where the bloody hell have you two been?" Roan said in an inordinately high-pitched tone.

"Gatherin' oop oor energy," the laird said matter-of-factly.

Beth stepped to Lachlan's side. "How's your arm?"

"Fine," Roan grumbled.

"Laura an' the laddies have left, eh?"

"Aye." Roan gave a negligent shrug. "She couldn't get away fast enough."

"I'm sorry," Beth said gently.

"For me?" Roan released a scoffing laugh. "She was an impossible womon. I'll miss the lads."

Lachlan and Beth exchanged a dubious glance.

"You'll miss *her*, tae," the laird said gruffly. "Yer're a fool ta have let her go."

"Don't stick yer nose inta ma love life, Baird."

"I wad if you had one," Lachlan grinned, then his gaze shifted and he soberly scanned what remained of his house. "Tis sa bleak."

Roan couldn't bring himself to look upon it again. "Aye. I'm sarry. I know how much this place means ta you."

"Aye," Lachlan sighed.

Roan shifted self-consciously. "Anither thin'. The peafowls are gone. I thought I saw a peahen in the east pasture, but i' turned ou' ta be a wee dog."

"They'll come home," Lachlan assured, his gaze traveling the front of the property. He couldn't remember a time when the peacocks and hens hadn't been around.

"I hope sa," Roan murmured.

Beth silently observed the two men. She arched a slim eyebrow. Lachlan had surprisingly accepted the destruction of his treasures, his home, although Beth had been aware of a void within him that he did his best to camouflage. And Roan. He was so easy to read. He was lost and bewildered. Miserable. For too short a time, Laura and the boys, and the responsibility of becoming laird to the manor, had given him renewed purpose. He believed it all lost to him now, as it had been when he'd lost his son.

These two men, whom she loved so very dearly in different ways, seemed incapable at the moment of realizing just what the future held for them. So it was upon her, she felt, to enlighten them. But to succeed, she knew she was going to have to resort to something stronger than a mere suggestion.

"You promised Lachlan anything if he saved Kevin, didn't you?" she reminded Roan, who raised a questioning brow at her.

"Aye, but—"

"You're a man who keeps his promises," she added in an airy, cheerful manner, ignoring Lachlan's frown at her.

"Aye, but—"

"Roan, you're wasting valuable time wallowing in self-pity," she sighed.

"Wha's goin' through yer mind, darlin'?" Lachlan asked suspiciously.

Beth's sparkling eyes scanned Roan's features. "You're a carpenter. Right?"

Aghast, Roan shot a look at the house behind him. When he again looked at the couple, a high-pitched laugh ejected from his throat. "I'm no' a miracle warker!"

Dawning lit upon Lachlan's face. "Ah." He smiled broadly, then kissed Beth briefly on the lips. "Wha' a deilish mind you have, lass."

"You can't be serious," Roan laughed unsteadily, his eyes nearly rounded with disbelief. "Restore Baird House? I'd need mair lives than a cat!"

Cockily crossing his arms against his chest, Lachlan quipped, "Tha' could be arranged." He winked at Beth, then narrowed his eyes on the stunned man across from him. "O' course, you'd be one o' the dead," he grinned.

Roan grimaced. "I'll pass, thank you."

Sounds drew their gazes to the private road. Shortly, four cars and two large trucks parked on the graveled area in front of the carriage house. As people began to emerge from the vehicles, Roan recognized Ben and several other men from the pub. Then to his amazement, Agnes stepped from one of the cars and led the small group to the waiting trio.

To Roan's further astonishment, his aunt beamed a smile at the laird, and gave a bob of her head in greeting to Beth.

"Sa, you didna high-tail off," she cackled to Lachlan.

Her high spirits were taking years off her age. "Ma worst luck!"

Lachlan smiled, then bowed graciously to her. "Guid ta see you tae, you auld corbie."

"Nice way ta talk ta the lady plannin' ta see yer grand house restored," she huffed humorously.

"Aunt Aggie, what's goin' on?"

Ben, his gaze remaining riveted on Lachlan, spoke up. "Aggie's come oop wi' a plan. Crossmichael an' Castle Douglas are joinin' thegither ta rebuild this place."

Color returned to Roan's face, and he laughed unsteadily. "You serious?"

"Ne'er mair serious," Agnes sniffed.

"The power of the people," Beth murmured, her eyes misting with tears. When Lachlan's arm went about her shoulders, she pressed closer to him. "Thank you, Agnes."

The old woman proudly thrust back her shoulders. "Merchants are willin' ta supply everythin' we need. Baird House is a landmark. An' we Scots are no' 'fraid o' hard wark, are we, Roan?"

"Aye," Roan grinned. "We're strong o' back an' spirit."

"Tis a debt I'll ne'er forget," Lachlan said to Agnes, his tone thick with emotion.

"Tis one I winna let you forget!" she exclaimed.

Roan unexpectedly walked away. When he stopped, his back was to the group. With a gesture for the others to remain where they were, Beth went to him and placed a hand on his shoulder.

"The dress *does* mak you look like a spook," he said unsteadily, avoiding directly looking at her.

"She'll be back."

"Wha?"

Beth slapped him on his uninjured arm, then stepped

directly in front of him. This time he looked into her eyes, although it took all of his willpower to do so.

"You may be able to fool everyone else, but Lachlan and I know you're in love with Laura Bennett. She will return, Roan. And with the boys."

"Yer're sure o' tha', are you?"

"As sure as I know I was always meant to be here," she replied softly. "Don't ever forsake love, Roan."

"She ne'er said guidbye."

"Maybe because she knows she's going to return."

Roan digested her words, then looked up at the charred ruins with an enigmatic light in his eyes. Drawing in a fortifying breath through his nostrils, he searched Beth's lovely face.

"I owe you ma life."

"Then live it to its fullest." Placing an arm about his middle, she urged him to walk alongside her toward those waiting patiently for their return. She retained her hold when they stopped, and smiled at Lachlan when he stepped to Roan's other side and draped an arm over the man's shoulders. The scene depicted the trio's strong bond of friendship, and a single tear escaped down Agnes's weathered cheek.

Suddenly it occurred to Roan what Lachlan had meant the night of the fire when he'd said, "Dusk 'fore dawn, laddie."

One phase of life had to end, before another began anew.

Roan wasn't sure if Laura and the boys would return, but if they did, Baird House, restored in all its glory, would be waiting for them.

In the meantime, he once again had a dream, and family and friends to take the edge off his loneliness.

One thing he *was* sure about: Beth and Lachlan would remain for a very long time. For as long as he needed them.

Which, in his heart, would be until the dusk of his corporeal life.

His heart swelled with joy, while he searched the faces around him. "C'mon, you motley bunch!" he laughed boomingly, gesturing widely with his good arm. "We've a house ta restore!"

Ben surveyed the building, then comically rolled his eyes. "Aye. Tha' we do."

Lachlan sobered unobserved. He walked around to the east side of the house, to the frozen fountain, and seated himself on the rounded lip of the lower basin. All around him, snow glistened. It was a sun-bright day, the air crisp and clean and, despite the charred remains behind him, smelling of newness.

He'd thought of visiting Roan at Agnes's. He'd thought over a lot of things since the fire. In part, he was glad Laura was gone. After the incident in the attic, when she'd taken the dagger to him, he'd been forced to open his eyes to Tessa's presence. Robert was one thing, but—

"You're a chauvinist."

Beth's soft tone gave him a start. Looking guiltily over his shoulder, he watched her amble to his side, her hands clasped behind her.

"Yer're readin' ma mind again," he accused with a frown. His dark-eyed gaze surveyed the contours of her beautiful face.

"There is something that has always bothered me," she sighed, sitting cozily close next to him.

"Wha' is tha', love?" he asked suspiciously.

"Why is most of your anger directed toward Tessa?"

He winced and looked down at his hands, which rested atop his knees. *"She* was ma wife."

"But *he* walled you up, knowing that you were still alive."

For a time, he pondered her logic, then looked into her eyes. "He was weak, Beth. Wha' *he* did, he did ou' o' love for her."

"But what *she* did, she did out of love for him."

Lachlan scowled. "Tis no' the same."

"No?" Heaving a sigh of impatience, she arched an eyebrow. "How long have you known?"

"Tae long. Tae long, lass."

"Lachlan, you know I love you."

"Aye."

"You also know I draw the line when it comes to you going off half-cocked."

"Tis a bloody—"

"Neyer mind. Back off. Let them find their own way."

"Tis no' tha' easy."

Taking his chin between her fingers, Beth eased his head around and planted a kiss on his mouth. "Lachlan, *back off*. I will not allow you to hurt Roan and Laura because of a century-old vendetta."

"Tessa an' Robert owe me—"

"*Roan* and *Laura* owe you nothing! Now promise me that you'll let everything run its natural course. Lachlan . . . ?"

"Aye."

"Aye, what?

"I . . . winna interfere."

Leaning back, Beth frowned. "Why don't I believe you?"

Lachlan's eyebrows shot upward. "Fegs, lass! Should I write in blood?"

"No. No . . . but you better not be planning anything."

Getting to his feet, he threw his hands up in a futile gesture. "You've ne'er trusted ma judgment!"

"Not when it comes to the past." Beth stood and planted her hands on her hips. "You're a stubborn man, Lachlan, and you have a tendency to react before thinking."

Ruddy color appeared in his face, and his near-black eyes snapped with vexation. "Beth ma-lass, yer're no' bein' fair."

"Fairness has nothing to do with it."

A burst of Gaelic sprang from him. "There are some things we'll ne'er see eye ta eye on!"

"What's goin' on here?" asked Roan, cautiously walking toward the couple. A scowl darkened his face. "Why are the two o' you arguin'? Abou' the house?"

Lachlan visibly shook off his temper and forced a lop-sided grin. "Na. Beth's lecturin' me."

Roan was quick to note the dirty look Beth dealt her mate. He looked at the laird, with suspicion shadowing his eyes. "Lecturin' you abou' wha'?"

The taller man squirmed. "Ma conduct around yer family."

Although Roan nodded, the suspicion remained in his measuring gaze on the laird. "Tell me, Lannie, do you have a problem wi' me restorin' yer house?"

A look of genuine surprise masked Lachlan's face. "Na, mon. Tis fittin'—"

"Fittin'?" Roan asked harshly. "I see. Sa you *do* haud me responsible for the fire."

"No' for the fire."

Roan missed the enigmatic undertone in the laird's voice. "Tell me, Lannie, where were you an' Beth whan you were supposed ta be watchin' the boys?" Angrily, he went on, "You don't leave lads their age, alone!"

"I'm to blame," Beth said in a barely audible voice.

"Be damned if we explain oorselves ta an Ingliss!" Lachlan hissed.

A breath lodged in Roan's throat. "Yer're guid, auld mon. Bloody guid."

"Wha' are you talkin' abou'?"

"*You,* you swine! I seriously thought we'd become mates." Roan sucked in a breath through his nostrils. "You've been bloody usin' me, haven't you?"

"It's not like that—"

"Tis between *us,*" Roan snapped at Beth, gesturing to Lachlan and himself. "Hear me weel, you auld fool," he went on, glaring at Lachlan. "I'll restore *yer* bloody house, an' break ma back warkin' till I replace e'ery possession o' yers. Then ta hell wi' you! Straight ta bloody hell wi' you!"

Roan stormed off. Beth waited until he was out of sight before drawing back her shoulders and leveling a heated look on Lachlan.

"Nice going."

"He misunderstood."

"Misunderstood? Dammit, Lachlan, sometimes I just want to give you a good, swift kick in the—"

The laird began to fade. "Later, Beth."

He vanished, leaving her alone in the company of her temper.

For a long minute, she heatedly tapped a bare foot on the ground. Then she sighed. Sighed again, and threw her arms up in exasperation.

"Later, huh? *Right.* There's nothing worse than a man with too much time on his hands."

Muttering beneath her breath, she faded into the daylight.

* * *

He'll ne'er let go. You failed in the attic, but then, you dinna know he was already dead.

Go back. Tis yer destiny. Unfinished business—

Laura bolted into a sitting position, gasping for breath. Trembling violently, she stared into the semidarkness, lost and bewildered, terrified of what, she didn't know.

Scrambling off the edge of the bed, she reflexly reached out and turned on a lamp. Light flooded the room. After a moment, her fears began to wane. Her wits returned, and she wearily sank onto the edge of the bed.

She glanced about the room, then stared for a long time at the open door to the adjoining room where the boys slept. It was her own indecision that had made her suffer through sleepless nights since her arrival in Edinburgh six days ago. Six of the longest days of her life.

Although her luck had changed, she was hard-pressed to appreciate it. When she'd arrived at the embassy, it was to discover that her purse had been turned over to the police, and they, in turn, had messengered it to the American Consulate. Her credit cards and money were all there.

Anthony Walker, of the embassy, had been enormously helpful in getting her the two rooms at the Prescott Inn, two blocks away from his office. He'd also put a rush on furnishing copies of her nephews' birth certificates, and processing their passports, although the latter wouldn't be ready for several days yet.

One more day cooped up in this room, and Laura was sure she would crack. She was grateful for all the help she'd received while in this country, but the longer she remained, the less she wanted to leave.

Unfinished business.

She could never remember what the nightmares entailed, but for the fourth night, she'd awakened in a cold sweat and unable to breathe. Hour after hour, day after day since leaving Roan, she found herself trembling uncontrollably and always on the verge of tears. A hollow ache seemed a permanent fixture in the core of her heart.

She'd never felt so miserable!

The boys, too, had been uncharacteristically sullen. And although she was grateful for their docile behavior, it also worried her.

Lifting a half-emptied glass from the nightstand, she sipped tepid water.

Was Roan missing her half as much as she missed him?

Choking on a little swallow of water, she replaced the glass alongside the lamp with a shaky hand. She hugged herself, tears filling her eyes, and gently rocked to and fro.

She *would* return.

Unfinished business.

She winced when pain lanced her temples.

A cold purposeful breeze passed through the room, sweeping through her. She gasped, freezing in place, her eyes widening fearfully.

Unfinished business.

Forcing herself to shake off the fearful gloom mantling her, she rose to her feet and walked to the adjoining room door. Leaning against the framework, she recrossed her arms and sadly regarded her nephews. The nightlight of the lamp awarded her a soft view of them. They were huddled together in the center of the queen-sized bed, their small forms lost beneath multiple blankets.

For the first time, she wondered what their life had been like with their father. Had her brother ignored them, as Kevin had implied? Or had Jack been so caught up in grief over the loss of his first wife, that he'd simply withdrawn into himself? Whatever the reason, he had to have known he'd fathered three wonderful sons.

"I promise to do my best by you," she whispered, with a catch in her voice.

An unbidden memory of Lachlan Baird flared up in front of her mind's eye. The picture fell back, revealing the attic in the mansion.

Laura found she could not release the breath building inside her lungs. Rooted by terror, she watched her own hand, clutching the handle of a dagger, thrust the gleaming blade again and again into his chest. She experienced his pain, the agony of each slice, the warmth of his blood seeping onto the front of her flannel nightgown. His horror-filled eyes glowed in his incredulous countenance. She could feel his breath on her face. She could feel his energy waning . . . feel him slowly fading . . . feel his *rage*.

Wrenching herself from the spell, she staggered to the bed and weakly climbed onto the mattress. Breaths roared from her lungs. Trembling seized her hands.

Then she spied what was lying on the unused pillow.

A jewel-handled dagger. Dark red blood was pulsing from its razor-sharp edge and staining the blank whiteness of the pillowcase.

A scream manifested in the pit of her stomach and swiftly rose into her throat. But at the instant it would have escaped, a cry detonated within her skull.

Unfinished business!

Suddenly the room was stiflingly still. She felt as though hundreds of invisible eyes were watching her.

Squeezing her eyes shut, she outwaited the violent quaking in her body, outwaited the fear which had nearly claimed her sanity.

Then, just when she'd finally convinced herself that it had all been nothing but her imagination, and her pulse rate was slowing to normal, Roan's voice invaded her mind.

"Gang yer ain gait, you dochter o' the deil."

She opened her eyes, once again trembling, and once again in the company of sickening fear.

"How did I know what you were saying?" she asked herself in a whimper, her face deathly pale. "I don't know Gaelic!"

A soft feminine laugh caressed the inside of her skull.

Clamping her hands over her ears, she tightly closed her eyes.

Leave me alone!

An icy breath passed through her.

Gasping, she lowered her hands and opened her eyes.

She looked down to find the dagger resting atop the pillow.

There was no blood.

No stain on the case.

Only the *dagger.*

After a moment to work up her nerve, she lifted the implement. At first it felt like ice, then it grew uncomfortably warm against her palm.

The blade grew brightly crimson, pulsing with the rhythm of a strong heartbeat.

All expression left her eyes.

Clutching the dagger to her breast, she stared off into space and murmured, "Unfinished business."

Ten

The pristine north field stretched out before him, and gave him a sense of smallness. It was incredibly beautiful. Moonlight was reflecting on blankets of snow beneath a black velvet, star-speckled sky. Serene. A world unto itself.

Wistfully sighing, he turned to regard the scaffolds constructed around the house. He would never underestimate the force behind human nature again. The volunteers had worked from dawn to dusk for the past four days, clearing out rubble, building scaffolding inside and out, and preparing the house for the renovations.

During that time, Roan had refused to dwell on Lachlan's betrayal. He'd been a fool to even think there could be any kind of earnest friendship between them, but he'd come to terms with that. Restoring the house offered him purpose, and he'd also come to realize that, without purpose, he might as well dig himself a deep hole and bury himself alive.

Christmas was only two weeks away. He'd scoffed at Harry Douglas when the man had vowed the construction part of the renovations would be done in time to celebrate Christmas Eve in the manor. But now, reflecting on how much had been accomplished in so short a time, he was beginning to believe in the possibility himself.

Beth had made several appearances, talked with the

workers, and chatted with the wives who kept up a camp on the south lawns. She'd helped them cook and pass out blankets. She'd worked alongside Agnes to haul some of the charred things from the house. And watching her, he'd been reminded of how *alive* she was, and of the love and concern and compassion her ghostly being harbored. He admired her. He always would.

Lachlan was another matter.

The old laird had blessed all with his absence, although there had been times when Roan was sure he could feel those dark eyes watching him, boring into the back of his head.

Making his way through the rest of the wooded area at the back of the house, he climbed the white fence and headed across the field, in the direction of the massive oak.

He took a long moment to read the inscriptions on the four headstones beneath the snow-laden branches, then heaved a sigh and said, "Beth, could I have a talk wi' you?"

A second later, a green luminous mist rose up from the ground in front of her headstone. Beth materialized. Her hand was smoothing back her hair. "You rang?" she smiled.

Roan grinned and prodded the frozen snow-packed ground with the toe of one boot. "You do make a grand entrance," he said, winking at her. The moonlight enhanced her lovely features. A gentle breeze played through her curly locks. Unbidden, Laura popped into his thoughts, her green eyes flashing at him, her full lips pursed in a pout. Damn! He missed her temper, her chiding . . . her smile. It was as if a part of him was missing. An important part.

Finally, dispelling her image, he said, "Perhaps you could explain somethin' ta me."

Beth arched an eyebrow. The smile remained on her lips and in her eyes.

Lifting his left arm, he casually bent it to and fro at the elbow, then twisted and turned it at the wrist. "The maist peculiar thin' happened this morn, lass. I woke oop wi' a terrible burnin' beneath the cast. It buggered me so, I went ta the clinic this efternoon ta have i' checked." Airily, his gaze never leaving Beth's face, he jerked up his coat sleeve as far as it would go. "Notice, Beth, there's *na* cast."

"My my," Beth murmured, regarding his extended appendage. "You're a fast healer."

"Aye, sa i' seems."

She lifted her hands in a gesture of surrender. "Okay, so I prompted the healing along."

A frown creased his wide brow. "Sa . . . you can do tha' sort o' thin'."

"It was another experiment."

Roan grinned. "I'm no' complainin', mind you, but I had a helluva time convincin' the doctor tha' he hadn't gone bonkers."

Beth's laugh echoed across the field. "I can imagine."

"Can you, now?" Slipping his hands into his deep coat pockets, he rocked on his feet. *"Five* x-rays, mind you. An' whan he removed the bloody cast, he still had trouble believin' the bones had knitted thegither."

"I'm sorry," she chuckled with an airy shrug of her slender shoulders, "but it didn't make sense to have you laboring so hard on the house, and suffering with a broken arm."

"Ma thanks, Beth."

"Any time."

Her gaze flitted toward something in the direction of the house. *At last!* Guarding her excitement, she looked Roan in the eye. "The house is already beginning to shape up."

He nodded. "We're hopin' ta have the construction wark done by Christmas Eve—which reminds me . . . Do you think His Nibs will mind us havin' a wee celebration in the house if we succeed?"

"His Nibs?" Beth frowned and gave a chiding shake of her head. "You're still upset with him, aren't you?"

"No' really. Disappointed, maistly, but I guess he has his ways, me, mine." Looking down, he poked at the ground again. "Actually, once ma temper cooled doon, I realized he'd come a long way in a short time. At least—" He searched Beth's face for a long moment. "—we can be civil ta one anither, which is mair than we could manage in the beginnin'."

"You're okay, Roan Ingliss."

He grinned sheepishly. "It helps ta have a guardian spirit lookin' o'er ma shoulder."

"Mmm. Guardian spirit. It does have a nice ring to it, doesn't it? But tell me, how's everything else going in your life?"

He lifted a questioning eyebrow.

"Don't be obtuse," she sighed, crossing her arms against her chest.

"Obtuse, eh?" He smiled ruefully. "Could be any number o' things yer're referrin' ta."

"Right. Okay, I'll play along. Roan Ingliss, do you miss Laura and the boys?" He frowned, prompting her to rush on, "The truth. I promise you won't melt into the snow if you should fess up to what you're actually feeling."

"Aye, I miss them." In an abrupt gesture of vexation, he shrugged deeper into his lamb's wool coat. "I *do* miss them, an' I can't get *her* ou' o' ma mind.

"Beth, i' all happened sa fast. I was sa . . . sa frustrated wi' her an' the laddies, an' the whole situation, then next I knew, I couldn't be around them enough." He sighed, and raked his fingers through the hair at his temple. "I don't know wha' ta think anymair. The days come an' go in a blur. Is i' possible ta lose yer mind wi'ou' knowin' i'?"

Beth released a deep, throaty laugh. "Yes, but I think your problem is called *love*. An affliction, I know, but it has its moments."

Roan's grin warmed his features. "Yer're a blunt womon, Beth Staples, an' . . . an' I'm bloody grateful for oor friendship."

Without hesitation, Beth reached out and clasped one of his hands' between her cool palms. "So am I."

He glanced down at their grasp, and grimaced. "His Nibs will be poppin' oop, accusin' me o' handlin' his womon," he said nervously. Beth dropped her hands away, and he returned his to his pocket. "Speakin' o' *him,* where has he been hidin' since the fire?"

"Sulking in the grayness."

Roan rolled his eyes.

"Whenever we argue, it takes him a while to store up his energy."

"The mon has a temper."

"Not unlike someone else I know," she quipped, a mischievous gleam in her eyes.

"Guilty as charged. Difference is, though, I can't poof away."

"No, but you do withdraw. You have a tendency, Roan, to try to shut out what hurts you. One day, you'll realize that emotional pain is a healing factor."

"Tha' sa, Dr. Beth? Mmmm. I'll have ta remember this next time I'm in misery oop ta ma ears."

"Just face a few truths. It's as simple as that."

"Truths? Wha' truths are we talkin' abou', now?"

"Laura. Your future together."

"It doesn't seem we have a future. No' wi' her thousands o' miles away, an' me here."

Beth gave an exasperated shake of her head. "Whose fault is that?"

"Yer're wantin' me ta place the blame on ma shoulders?"

"They're mighty big shoulders, Roan. You allowed your pride to stand in the way of asking her to stay."

Roan scowled. "I *did* ask." He sighed. "In a way, I did ask, but she wasn't listenin'."

"I'm listening now," came a husky voice from behind him.

His heart shooting into his throat, he whirled about.

"This is where I say good-night," Beth grinned, fading into the landscape.

Tightness formed within Roan's chest as he raked his gaze up and down Laura's small form. His hands balled within the coat pockets. He couldn't speak. He was afraid if he said anything, her image would dissolve, and he would once again find himself stuck with his own dubious company.

"You're scowling at me," she said finally, in a small voice, watching him as if expecting to have to flee at any moment.

He made every effort to clear his expression, but the scowl remained deeply etched.

"My purse was recovered and sent to the consulate." Looking down, she gestured to the three-quarter-length, smart blue coat she was wearing. "The boys and I went on a shopping spree. I rented a car, and here I am." When he remained silent, she sighed raggedly, nervously. "I know it doesn't make sense, but I love you, Roan. I don't want to leave Scotland, or you, or the life we could build here together."

Impatience lending an edge to her tone, she went on, "I'm fresh out of inhibitions. I'm not expecting you to marry me. I don't care if we live together, so long as we're *together*. If the responsibility of the boys worries you, I'll do whatever it takes to make all of our lives easier. I'm not a weak woman, and I *am* capable of pulling more than my share when it comes to finances and the comforts of the men in my life. Which are now four. And I'm ready to take on the role of mother, aunt . . . and your lover, for as long as the boys need me, and you want me.

"Now that I've gotten all of this off my chest, would you *please* say something!"

"You rented a caur?"

Bewildered, Laura blinked at him.

"You *drove* here from Edinburgh?" he asked in a voice two octaves higher than his normal.

"Yes. I rented an automatic. The roads were pretty good, and I didn't even get lost. Not once. Not bad for a Yank . . . *eh?* "

Too rattled to appreciate her humor, he gasped, "You *drove* from Edinburgh?"

"Roan—"

"Dammi', womon, are you *crazy?* "

A spark of anger went off inside her. Without thought, she drew back her right hand, reached down for a handful of snow, packed it carefully, then sailed it through the air. Roan jerked back when the snowball caught him on the cheek.

"You needed that," she said airily, shaking her smarting hand, her eyes seeming eerily bright in the moonlight.

Stunned, he touched his throbbing cheek, and peered at her beneath his drawn-down, thick eyebrows.

"Has the investigation been completed on the house?"

He nodded.

"And . . . ?"

He shrugged.

A frown briefly touched Laura's face, then cleared when she walked up to him, leaving little space between them. Gripping the front of his coat, she rose up on tiptoe, and stared deeply into his eyes. "It isn't wise to provoke a woman who has spent the better part of the day traveling foreign roads, in the company of three very lively, talkative boys. I'm on the edge, Roan Ingliss, and your silence is pushing me over the brink!"

At that moment, her arrival struck him as humorous. He released a brief, booming laugh before winding his arms about her and holding her against him.

"It's about time," she grinned, snuggling closer to his powerful body. An invitation danced in her eyes, her sensuously parted lips.

"Damn me," he chuckled nervously. "I can't believe yer're actually here!"

"That makes two of us. Roan?" Her voice deepened to a husky, sensual tone. "I was hoping for a different kind of greeting."

Without wasting another second, he lowered his head and captured her mouth in a searing kiss.

He would never be able to describe the rightness he felt at that moment, the rightness of holding her, kissing her deeply, the two of them once again on Baird territory. And he could not imagine ever feeling happier than he was right now. His blood sang out in joy, in perfect harmony with his every nerve, muscle, flesh and brain. She'd not only returned of her own free will, but had admitted to being in love with him. It was more than he would have ever dared to pray for. A small voice in the back of his head told him it was more than he deserved.

She shuddered out of sheer contentment, broke the kiss,

and nuzzled her brow against the contours of his face. "I couldn't stay away. I missed you so much. The sight of you. The touch of you." Looking into his eyes, she inhaled deeply through her nose, then smiled a smile that warded off the chill of the night. "The musky scent of you. I'm afraid I'm hooked on you, Roan. Away from you, I start experiencing withdrawal."

"Is ma lass becomin' a poet?" he asked almost shyly. Breathing sparingly, he studied her face, as if to further enhance his mental image of her. "Or am I dreamin'?"

"Want me to pinch you?"

"The snowball was enough, thank you."

She strained on tiptoe once again, and was about to kiss his beckoning mouth when he looked up and stiffened. Turning her head to look in the direction of the house, she asked, "What's wrong?"

Releasing her, he stepped to her side. "Where are the boys?" he asked gruffly, his narrowed gaze riveted on the house.

"At your aunt's. Why?"

"You came here alone?"

Shivering, she turned, linked an arm through his, and pressed closer to his side. "You're scaring me."

"I saw a light movin' around the second floor. I asked you, lass, did you come *alone?*"

"No." A chill blossomed in the pit of her stomach. "No, Borgie came along to show me—"

Roan released a gurgle of a cry, then lit into a run. Laura followed as best she could, her boots not equipped with skid-free soles as his were.

Before they'd gone but ten yards, a sound of rumbling began back at the oak, deep in the ground, seemingly beneath the headstones. Unsteadily sliding to a stop, Laura stared in that direction, while her heartbeat was hammering at her temples. Fear built within the pit of her stomach.

The sound grew louder. Unaware that Roan had gone on quite a ways, then had turned and was running back in her direction, she stared in disbelief as the headstones keeled over one at a time, in an eerie domino effect. She couldn't move her feet, not even when Roan was suddenly beside her and tugging on her arm. By the time he realized the thundering was not from the heavens, the ground began to yawn apart in a rapid pathway toward them.

"Run!" he cried, taking her by the hand.

Laura slid most of the way to the fence. Roan dragged her along as if she were a sled. He helped her over the fence, barely getting over himself before the planks burst into the air. The chasm chased them through the trees, around the house, and mysteriously came to a halt the instant it came to the stone steps of the greenhouse which served as a front entry to the manor. Huddled together on the small stoop, Roan stared down at the dark cleft. Fear boiled in his blood, yet left his skin like ice.

"Stay close to ma side," he warned, in a tone sharper than he'd intended.

Opening the greenhouse door, he ushered her ahead of him. She tried to open the great double doors, but found them locked. Roan fumbled with a set of keys he'd kept in his back trouser pocket, hurriedly unlocked the door, then pushed her into the hall.

He slammed the door shut behind them. "Borgie!" he called, panic in his raw tone. "Borgie, come doon!"

He took the lead in the semidarkness. The staircase was dimly lit by moonlight filtering through a massive hole in the wall. Laura followed, her stomach queasy and threatening to reject her supper. She was too afraid to remain on the ground floor alone, and too afraid to let Roan venture upstairs on his own.

On the second floor, he waited for her to catch up, then went into the doorless bedroom he'd used until the night of the fire. A dark figure moved by the window. The thin beam of a flashlight cut out.

"Borgie! If you know what's guid for you, you'll get ou', *now!* Lannie knows yer're here!"

A sound of fumbling was heard. A moment later, a match was lit across the room, illuminating the white-haired man while he hastily lit the kerosene lamp he'd been carrying.

"You *bloody* fool!" Roan hissed, advancing across the room. "Have you a death wish, mon?"

Borgie held the lamp up shoulder-high. The glow cast off from it lent sinister shadowing to his angular features. "I've found some o' the jewels," he grinned, patting his left coat pocket. "I knew they'd survive!"

Roan felt suddenly lightheaded. "How did you know I'd brought them ta this room?"

A brief look of panic masked the man's face. Then he grinned, his countenance becoming skeletal-like in the flickering lantern light. "I have ma ways, cousin. A finder's fee is due me. I'll tak a few o' the stones—the rubies, I think. I love the color o' rubies. Dark red. Red as blood."

Roan quaked with anger, his fists balled at his sides. Stepping alongside him, Laura linked an arm through his, in hopes it would be enough to sway him from lunging at his cousin.

"They belong ta Lannie!"

Borgie spat to one side. "He passed 'em doon ta you, you said."

"They *belong* to him!"

"Na! He did this—" He gestured to his white hair. "—ta me. He *owes* me, Roan! An' I intend ta collect ma dues!"

"I'll give you yer dues, you bastard!" came a guttural hiss. Thunder rolled across the ceiling, vibrated through the flooring.

Laura clung tightly to Roan. Her horrified gaze riveted on Borgie, who cast his wild gaze about him.

"I'll handle this, Lannie," Roan barked, his gaze never wavering from his cousin. "Yer jewels will remain. You have ma word!"

A freezing wind whipped through the room, circled and circled until Lachlan appeared, standing between the two men, his murderous look fixed on Borgie. "I'll break yer neck wi' ma bare hands!" he threatened, shaking a fist at the white-haired man. "I warned you ta ne'er come near ma property again!"

Borgie cast his cousin an imploring look.

Roan shivered in fear of the ghost's rage. "Lannie, go an' let me handle this. He'll ne'er return!"

Lachlan's lips drew back, baring gleaming white teeth. "How *did* the fire start, Borgie, lad?" he asked scathingly.

Roan met Laura's gaze for an electric moment, then regarded his cousin with deepening horror. "Borgie, tell me tis no' sa." An excruciating second passed in silence. *"Borgie!* Ma God, tell me tis no' true!"

The white-haired man grew sickly pale. "No' me, I swear!"

"Lyin' Ingliss swine," Lachlan growled.

The words were like a severe blow to Roan. He stared at the ghost's profile, visibly wounded by the words spoken against his bloodline. "I'm an Ingliss, tae."

Lachlan's flame-tinged eyes swung to Roan for but a moment. "I warned him ta stay away."

"We share the same blood, he an' I!" Roan bellowed. "Ingliss an' Aiken blood!"

A fierce breeze swept into the room. The next instant, Beth appeared, standing across from Lachlan and between Borgie and Roan and Laura. "Let it go, Lachlan," she warned, her anger matching his own.

"No' whan this—" Lachlan flung out a hand in Borgie's direction. "—rodent o' the deil dares ta trespass in *ma* home!"

"This is Roan's house now," Beth reminded him, trembling, her shoulders tautly held back. *"You* leave!"

Beth released a choked sound when Lachlan's eyes became glowing red embers. She'd never known him to be so out of control. The fury radiating from him, robbed her of warmth, and left such a void inside her, she expected to implode into its core.

Oblivion.

But for the innocent in the room, she would have welcomed oblivion.

Gone was any remnant of the man she loved. She was aware of suffocating evil, so powerful a presence, she nearly abandoned her present existence to escape it.

Lachlan's dark side. She'd known about it for some time. She'd not only witnessed it unleashed, but had unwittingly linked with it on several occasions. Rage had never been a part of her makeup. Nothing near as dark and sinister as what lay at the core of her mate's character. She'd sensed the monster of his rage, seen it in her mind's eye more times than she cared to count. It had nearly driven her away, nearly taken over all that was good in Lachlan.

And it was free once again, its host, Lachlan, not even aware of its deadly potential. It fed off his past, hibernating in the sea of betrayal that had become the energy force of his soul.

"Lachlan, I'm warning you!" she cried, desperate to touch upon his compassion before it was too late. "I won't stand by and watch you assault an unarmed man!"

The red eyes cut to her briefly. Beth gasped. His look robbed her of energy, plunging her life force into a well of frigid hopelessness. She no longer possessed the power to help herself, let alone the others. The monster reigned over them both. He reigned over anyone unfortunate enough to be within its range.

A silent scream spilled past her lips.

An invisible hand slapped up against her front, and pushed her into the hall.

Roan, dazed by her swift retreat, was about to shout at Lachlan when he, too, was slammed by something unseen and shoved out of the room. Laura cried out, her hands outstretched to Roan. She cried out again when she felt herself sliding across the floor toward the couple in the hall.

Their legs felt paralyzed. The threesome turned their heads in Borgie's direction. His face was gaunt with terror, his eyes ludicrously large in his deathly pale face. His hand trembled so, the lantern swayed beneath the handle bridging his upturned palm. Shadows danced across the room, ominous dark etchings mingled with silver blue moonlight.

Beth felt herself slipping from awareness. Summoning what little strength she had left, she released a broken wail of anguish.

Absolute darkness and soundlessness fell like a curtain around the threesome, entombing them, coiling invisible restraints about their physical beings and their wills.

Beth wept in silence, uncaring that it was depleting what little energy was left in her.

Laura stood frozen in shock and terror. She tried to counsel herself to worry about Borgie's plight, but the darkness and silence had swallowed her completely. She couldn't see, feel, touch, or smell Roan. She couldn't sense another presence. It was as if she were utterly alone. In the darkness. In the silence.

Buried alive.

Unfinished business.

Roan also believed he'd been entombed alone. He pounded his fists against solid nothingness, enraged with fear for Laura and Beth—and in the back of his mind, for Borgie.

His cousin had brought down the laird's wrath.

Damn Borgie's greed!

Roan'd seen the look on Beth's face. Never had he witnessed such torment, such devastation. And Laura. He'd sensed her fear as if it'd been his own. Where was she? Was she still terrified? It maddened him to think of her needing him, and he couldn't reach her. He couldn't even *see* her.

"Laaaaaannie!" he stormed, driving his fists relentlessly against the darkness.

Panic overpowered Beth. She became aware of an unfathomable *something* trying to merge with her life force—to rob her of her existence.

"Lachlan!" she wailed, pushing outward with what little power she could summon. "Lachlan, *stop!*"

"Lannie!" Roan barked, his fists hammering the air. "Release me! Let me *ou'!*"

The inky blackness winked, then began to wane to shades of gray.

The voice of an unseen Lachlan rang out, "I'll see you dead, you blastie!"

A cry of sheer terror pierced the air. Roan, Beth, and Laura looked into the bedroom in time to see Borgie rise into the air by invisible means, dangle a moment, then fly through the paneless window.

"Oh ma God!" Roan wailed, running to the orifice. He leaned over the sill. Below, in the snow, Borgie's twisted body lay in a heap.

Disbelief rooted Beth. She was only vaguely conscious of Roan and Laura running down the staircase. An image of glowing red eyes burned in her mind. Her phantom heart felt agonizingly branded by Lachlan's betrayal.

She loved a man incapable of controlling his rage. At least, she *had* loved him. At the moment, she felt nothing but contempt for him. He'd betrayed her trust in him, and her belief and her devotion to his gentler side. He'd become that monster right in front of her eyes, and that monster had lashed out at a man incapable of defending himself.

A low, gut-birthed groan swelled into a cry of desolation, reverberating throughout the house. Her quasi-life seemed utterly futile, without purpose.

No. Not entirely without purpose.

She couldn't pass on to the next plane of existence and leave Lachlan loosed on an unsuspecting world. She'd drag him with her. She'd end his vengeance against the Inglisses once and for all.

Snow flurries swirled around her when she next materialized. Her chest moved with pseudo-breaths. For a time, she stared down at Laura, who knelt alongside Roan at Borgie's side.

The house creaked in a chilling lament, shattering what little serenity the night had left to offer.

"His pulse is verra weak," Roan said breathlessly.

"We don't dare move him. Roan, you have to find a phone and call for an ambulance."

His stricken gaze peered into Laura's eyes. "A phone . . . ? Aye . . . aye, a phone." He stood, but remained rooted, visibly confused.

"I left the keys in the car." Unconsciously, Laura stroked Borgie's cheek. "Hurry, Roan!"

Roan turned, and gave a start when he saw the translucent form an arm's length away. The haunted depths of Beth's eyes hit him in the gut, drawing him from his stupor. "Stay wi' Laura, Beth."

She nodded. Her gaze riveted on the unconscious man. She was unaware of Laura staring at her, of the questioning fear the green eyes betrayed.

"I think he's . . . going to die," Laura said unsteadily.

Beth's gaze lifted to search the other woman's face. She shook her head, then shook it again more adamantly. "He can't die. Not here. Not because of—" Her voice caught on a sob. "Not because of . . . Lachlan."

Laura's fear of her presence finally penetrated Beth's awareness. Going down on her knees, then sitting on her folded legs, she tearfully regarded the blonde.

"Hatred is so evil, Laura," she said tightly, her head tipped to one side. "Hate and rage . . . I don't possess the strength to stand up against Lachlan's—"

"Need of vengeance," Laura completed, with such detachment, Beth shivered.

"Laura, this has to end."

"Unfinished business."

Beth slowly nodded, translucent tears spilling down her face. She further slipped into the grayness, fading before

Laura's dulled eyes. "Help us, Laura. Help us before it's too late."

"What could I possibly do?"

"Search your heart for the answer."

When Beth was gone, Laura murmured, "Too late." With slow, mechanical movements, she opened her shoulder purse, fished through the contents, and removed the dagger.

The jewels glistened brightly in the moonlight, winking up at her. With every movement of her hand, the gleam reflecting off the blade rendered slashes of light across her face.

"Tae late," she whispered, her face devoid of expression. "Na heart. Na search. Na answers. Tae . . . late."

Somewhere in the night, a dog howled mournfully at the moon. The bleak sound caressed Laura's soul, once again stirring the presence sheltered deep within her subconscious.

Her gaze lifted unseeing to the house.

Unfinished business.

What did it mean?

She'd thought it had been Roan. Their relationship.

Now she wasn't sure about anything.

Without lowering her gaze, she leveled the sharp edge of the blade against her left palm, and lacerated the tender skin. Nothing indicated that she'd felt the slightest pain. Blood spilled from the wound. Dark red, black-red blood fell against the light medium blue of Borgie's coat.

Behind her, a dark shape moved among the trees.

Watching.

Listening.

Waiting.

A cloud passed in front of the moon. A cacophony of howls serenaded the night. Behind her, the orange glow of the fallen lantern made a bid to embrace the surrounding darkness.

Mindlessly, Laura replaced the dagger in her purse. Her hands dropped to her sides, palms upright. Within seconds, her left palm pooled with blood. It trickled between her fingers, unnoticed, tinting the blanket of white beneath the hand.

She wanted to weep, but she didn't know why. She only knew that something was very wrong, and she was somehow responsible.

When Roan returned some time later, it was to find her lying unconscious beside his cousin.

Movement beside her roused Laura from her deep sleep. She didn't need to open her eyes and, with the dawn's light filtering into the room, verify that Roan had climbed into bed with her. His musky, wintry scent filled her nostrils. His arm draped across her middle as he spooned against her, snuggling close.

Her eyelids cracked open to reveal bloodshot whites surrounding her green irises. Dark shadows underscored the puffiness beneath her eyes.

She'd only lain down an hour ago.

"How's Agnes holding up?" she asked hoarsely.

"She's refusin' ta leave his side. God, Laura, he's gone inta a coma. It doesn't look guid."

No. None of it was real. She was going to really wake up at any minute. What scared her the most was that she would awaken in her apartment, to the realization that she'd only dreamed about having found her significant other.

"Is yer hand still buggerin' you?"

Dully, her gaze focused on her bandaged left hand. Some

dreams could be *so* real. She could even feel pain. "I still can't remember how I cut it."

"I'm sa sarry you came back ta all this," he said thickly, the cool fingers of his left hand stroking the hair at her exposed temple. "You've had ta deal wi' tae much stress."

"I'm a survivor." *Am I?*

A sad smile touched his mouth before he kissed her sweatered shoulder. "Aye, you are, thank God." Lowering the side of his face to the pillow again, he stared absently at the back of her head. "Aggie's sa quiet, Laura. Whan I left, she was just starin' doon a' Borgie, showin' na emotion a' all. 'Tis all *ma* fault."

The meaning behind some dreams was also elusive, as now. "How are you responsible?"

"I let Lannie sway me from ma original plan. I'd first gone ta Baird House ta find a way ta banish him."

"Only he can banish himself. Don't you know that by now?"

Her cold, distant tone sent a chill through Roan. Bracing himself up on his right elbow, he placed an anchoring left hand on her shoulder and turned her onto her back. Her gaze swung around to meet his. Sadness washed through him. His poor Laura. Her face still bore bruises and small scars from the night of the fire. She seemed more fragile than he'd ever seen her. Small and fragile and lost beneath the covers on the bed.

"What's Agnes going to do if Borgie dies?"

Roan closed his eyes for a moment. "I don't know. He's her only child. She's ne'er denied his faults, but she's ne'er denied her love for him, either.

"She's goin' ta need me for some time now, Laura. I can't abandon her, especially if he . . . dies."

"I wouldn't expect you to."

His gaze lovingly swept over her features. "It means *us* will be on haud for a time."

A smile gave life to her eyes once again. "I'm not worried about us." *Unless this is a dream.* "Just don't shut me out, Roan. I want to help in any way I can. The boys, too. They really took to Agnes. They may help her to get through the trying times to come."

Roan grinned and shook his head. "Have I tauld you lately how much I love you?"

"Last night, at the hospital."

A blush crept into his cheeks. "Where I turned somewha' green while they were stitchin' yer hand."

Lifting her uninjured hand, she lovingly stroked his jawline. "You look terribly tired."

"Aye. I've a wicked headache, but I've got ta get back an' check on Aggie."

"Rest for a while.

His gaze lingered on her lips. "Wi' you?"

A mischievous gleam came and left her eyes. She turned back onto her right side, and plumped her pillow before laying her head atop it. "Sleep. We have the rest of our lives to make love."

A low moan rattled within his chest as he snuggled against her.

"Close your eyes and get some rest."

"Aye. For a wee time."

A soft, tenuous smile graced her lips. Her eyelids closed. "Aye. For . . . a . . . wee . . . time."

Within seconds, they both were fast asleep.

The cottage was bathed in quiet. A neighbor had taken the boys the previous night.

In the parlor, standing in front of the cold hearth, Lachlan despondently stared at a framed picture on the mantel. A much younger Agnes smiled back at him, her arm about the shoulders of a sulky twelve-year-old boy.

Borgie.

Lachlan lowered his face into his hands for a time. He'd given a lot of thought as to what had happened last night, but he couldn't make sense out of most of it.

Yes, he'd lost control, but he didn't feel any more so than usual where Borgie was concerned. He'd left the house abruptly upon realizing that pushing Beth into the hall had been his biggest mistake to date. He dreaded another confrontation with her, especially since she had every right to be angry with him.

Roan and Agnes were another matter. Damn him, but he liked the man! And the old woman . . . She didn't deserve to lose her only child—even if that child *was* such a useless corbie!

It would take more than smooth talk to straighten out this mess. It would probably require more of him than he believed he had to offer.

Unfinished business.

He'd focused too long on Tessa. He'd let down his guard and had abandoned his self-restraint.

There had to be a way to make it all right, but he was at a loss as to where to begin.

A soft rap came at the front door. He stared at it, wondering if he should answer. On the fourth knock, he crossed to the door and swung it open. Surprise, then gratitude beamed on his face at the sight of Viola Cooke standing demurely on the stoop.

"Mr. Baird," she said, in a voice trilling with her own surprise to find him there. A second passed. Clearing her throat, she asked, "May I come in?"

Lachlan stepped aside and gestured for her to enter. He

closed the door, lifted an isolated finger to his lips to hush her, and led her the short distance to the couch. He remained standing while she unbuttoned her navy blue, full-length wool cape, and seated herself.

"Yer're an answer ta ma prayers," he crooned, bowing to her.

"I just got the news about Borgie Ingliss. I thought maybe I could offer to watch the boys."

"They're no' here, right now." Lachlan furtively glanced in the direction of the bedroom that secreted Roan and Laura. "I need yer help, dear lady."

"Whatever I can do," she said kindly.

Lachlan moistened his lower lip with the tip of his tongue. "I'm responsible for the mon's fall."

"Oh, dear."

He bobbed his head. "Aye, oh dear, oh . . . dear. I'm oop ta ma ears in trouble, an' I havena a clue as to how to explain wha' happened. No' tha' *I* understand wha' happened."

"Word is, Mr. Ingliss was *thrown* from a window on the second floor of Baird House."

Lachlan gave an exasperated roll of his eyes. "I didna throw the mon *anywhere.*"

"Then how did he fall?"

He shrugged his broad shoulders, then scowled. "I'm no' sure. 'Tis all so muddled in ma mind. Tae much happenin' a' once."

"You've been under a lot of stress—"

His laugh cut off her sentence.

"Stress? Dear lady, I'm *dead!*"

Viola's eyes mistily regarded his strong features. "We all have our crosses to bear, Mr. Baird."

A frown darkened the laird's visage. "What's wrong?"

A tear slipped down one wrinkled cheek. "I loved that

house." Withdrawing a lace-edged handkerchief from her cape pocket, she daintily dabbed at her moist nostrils. "It breaks my heart to see it so . . . ravaged."

Lachlan went down on a knee, and took her hands into his own. "In the great scheme o' things, i' was but a house. Ma concern lies wi' the livin'. Will you help me?"

From the depths of her heart, she replied, "I would give my life for you."

"Nothin' so drastic, dear lady," he sighed with relief.

Eleven

His head lowered, Roan elbowed his way through the
dart players and observers at Shortby's. The place was
packed. No one seemed to notice his arrival until he'd
reached the bar and ordered his usual from the young bartender, Jimmy MacDormick. Too numb to pay much heed
to what was going on around him, he settled on the only
vacant stool, oblivious to the hush that had fallen over the
room. Oblivious to Jimmy's scowl. No sooner was his mug
of bitter placed in front of him, than he tipped the rim to
his lips and drank down a third of the brew. He wiped the
back of a hand across his mouth. His stomach was so empty,
he could almost swear he heard the tepid liquid bottoming
out. A moment's light-headedness plagued him. His gaze
became lost within the dark color of his ale, his mind a
million miles away.

Laura hadn't been happy about him going out for a brew.
Hell, she didn't understand that a man sometimes had to
get away, get rowdy, let off a little steam. Not that he
planned to do anything but enjoy one simple pint. Mostly,
he just wanted a little space to think.

During the past week, he'd either been with Laura or his
aunt. At the hospital or home. The days had blurred together. He hadn't even been aware that it was Friday, or he

might have stayed at home to avoid having to be friendly with his dart mates.

Sighing, he downed another good portion of the bitter, closing his eyes while he reveled in the feel of the liquid sliding down his throat. His skin tingled. A comfortable dullness cushioned his brain against his attempts to think too deeply.

"How's Borgie these days?" asked a nasal, raspy voice.

Opening one eye, Roan set his glass down and turned slightly to regard Arnald Markey. The probing quality in the older man's dark eyes didn't settle well with Roan. He was tired of answering the same questions, day after day. . . .

"Or have you seem him lately?" Arnald queried with a mocking grin.

"Wha' makes you think I wouldn't be visitin' ma cousin?"

"I ne'er said such a thin', mate. A wee defensive aren't we? Is yer conscience botherin' you, or wha'?"

My conscience?

Roan turned to face the man completely, hardness creeping into his pale brown eyes. "If you've somethin' ta say, mon, spit i' ou'."

Arnald Markey spat on the front of Roan's coat.

One of the men, sitting at a table in the front right corner of the pub, guffawed. Someone else scolded him. Everyone kept their eyes on the two men at the bar. It'd been a while since a brawl had blessed the establishment, and Silas had instigated that one when one of his regulars had stiffed him on a long-running, sizeable tab.

One eyebrow arched, Roan casually eyed the offensive matter.

"Matter-o'-fact, Roan, we don't want you aroond here anymair."

"Speak for yerself," Silas said to Arnald, walking behind the bar from the direction of the water closet. "Roan, let me buy you a pint. Turn around an' chat wi' me."

Roan remained motionless, but for a muscle ticking at his jawline. He glowered into Arnald's beefy face, waiting, just waiting for the man to make the wrong move.

"You side wi' the deil, you bed the deil. Na friend o' Borgie's will have anythin' ta do wi' you."

The bloody hypocrites. "I didn't know Borgie *had* any friends," Roan quipped, his gaze sweeping the room, daring anyone to contradict him. Then he looked Arnald straight in the eye, and offered a lopsided grin. "Yer're in yer cups, Arnie, but because I'm a mon o' principles, I'm goin' ta deck you anyway."

Arnald guffawed in Roan's face. As calm as could be, Roan drove his right fist upward, catching the bigger man beneath the chin. A sharp clack of teeth rang out. Arnald's eyes rolled into his head as he keeled over backward and hit the floor in a dead faint.

Pandemonium ensued.

Weeks of frustration found an outlet through Roan's swinging fists. Faceless bodies converged on him. His ears were deaf to the expletives detonating around him, deaf to the several patrons goading the brawlers to draw blood.

From behind the counter, Silas scratched his balding pate. Glass mugs were being broken. Chairs and tables were upended. The floor was slick with ale. But he enjoyed a good fight, and he'd known for a long time that Roan was operating on a full head of steam.

Tempers had been building since Borgie's accident, although very few spoke to the man, let alone cared what happened to him. The outrage stemmed from the fact that it had occurred at Baird House. Folks in Crossmichael were a wee touchy when it came to that place.

Two men dragged Roan across the center of a table, punching him as he dropped to the floor and attempted to roll away.

Silas frowned deeply, then shook his head when Roan jumped to his feet, both fists flying and nailing fleshy targets. In the far left corner, Remmy O'Hallary danced an Irish jig on the center of a round table, his mug held shoulder-high, ale sloshing over the rim.

A fist rammed Roan in the midriff, prompting a grunt that the onlookers cheered.

It was Roan against four now, and Silas wasn't sure who was getting the worst end of the deal. Roan possessed a high tolerance to pain.

One of the four, Willy Canabra, released a high-pitched howl when Roan ducked, and James McKenna's fist popped the wrong man in the nose. Blood spurted from Canabra's nostrils and through his fingers as he tried to stop the flow. With a triumphant laugh, Roan elbowed Canabra in the gut. Canabra fell hard on his butt. Swinging up with the same arm, Roan rammed his fist up under McKenna's chin.

McKenna hit the floor with the grace of a sack of potatoes.

Silas winced as the last two men grabbed Roan from behind by his coat, lifted him off the floor, and sent him sailing over one of the few standing oblong tables. Then Silas's own temper flared when three more men hauled Roan to his feet, and another drove his fist into Roan's midriff.

"Haud i', now lads!" he boomed, hurrying around the counter.

"Just gettin' started," one large man snarled, then turned to have a shot at Roan.

"I said *haud i'!*"

The pub became quiet but for the heavy panting of the participants. Closing in, Silas shoved his way to Roan, his fierce look prompting the men who were confining Roan's arms, to release him.

Roan fell to his knees. The back of his trembling hand swiped across his bloodied mouth.

"Hollan, Arnald—an' you two by the window," Silas began heatedly, with one balled fist resting on a hip, "lend a hand in cleanin' oop the place." He targeted the man who'd been about to punch Roan. "Jack, fetch me the mop. C'mon you pack o' hooligans! You had yer fun, now's the time ta pay wi' a bit o' sweat!"

"I'll take care o' i'," Roan rasped, unsteadily getting on his feet. He cast those around him a scornful look, then met Silas's gaze. "An' I'll pay for the damages."

"Get yerself home, lad," Silas said kindly, clapping Roan on his upper arm.

"Kist House," one middle-aged woman sneered, pointing an accusing finger at Roan. "That's where *you* belong!"

"Auld Lannie went tae far this time," Arnald spat from his slouched position on one of the stools.

"Borgie better pull through," the elderly man who had been dancing the jig, piped up. "Orwise, we plan ta raze tha' bloody house, once an' for all."

Roan numbly regarded the hostile faces around him. "If you all know what's guid for you, you'll stay away from tha' place," he warned.

"Wha you worried abou', eh?" another woman asked,

contempt marring her wrinkled face. "Lannie . . . or yer cousin?"

Roan swayed on his feet. Who *was* he trying to protect? He didn't know any more.

Releasing a sound of disgust, he staggered through the gawkers, to the door, and stepped out into the cold, bitter night. He slammed the door shut, dislodging soft snow from a small overhang above him. The stuff plopped on top of his head, working its way down the back of his coat. In a taunting ballet, snow flurries swirled around him.

Ignoring the sting of the open wounds on his hands and face, he limped across the parking lot to his van, and climbed in behind the wheel.

Pain thundered in his head. His vision was blurry. He briefly contemplated walking to his aunt's rather than risking driving, but the idea of forcing his stiff leg muscles to carry him, prompted him to start the engine and pull out onto the narrow road.

He couldn't think. The headlights' glare off the snow smarted his eyes.

Who *was* he protecting?

Borgie's greed had brought about the confrontation, but Lachlan could have backed off.

Viola Cooke had told him of Lachlan's visit to his aunt's house. *Damn the mon's audacity!* To his knowledge, Aggie didn't know of the laird's intrusion into her home. That was all she needed. She'd aged ten years in one week. He was sure her heart wouldn't take much more stress.

So Lachlan couldn't remember exactly what had happened that night?

Convenient.

Roan cursed himself. Why couldn't he focus his anger at the laird?

His world was again falling to pieces, and he couldn't do a thing to stop it.

He slammed on the brakes. The blood was rushing from his head. He dazedly gaped at the desolate building looming off to his left.

Reflexly, he switched off the ignition.

It wasn't possible, he tried to rationalize.

Baird House?

Aggie lived in the opposite direction. What was he doing in the parking area by the carriage house?

Anger energized his protesting muscles. Climbing out of the van, he took a long look at the mansion, then swung his gaze to the dwelling he'd used when he'd first come to work for the laird. Soft light could be seen through the window. Someone was inside. How he was sure it was Lachlan, he didn't know.

The door was unlocked. Breathing heavily, he entered the carriage house, immediately spying Lachlan, who was sitting on the cot across the room. Roan slowly approached. Several candles were lit atop a crate by the pillowed end of the cot. The laird looked up not once. His attention was on the piece of wood he was whittling.

"You bring me here?" Roan asked testily, stopping a few feet away.

Lachlan gave a low shake of his head. On his palm he turned over the nearly-completed lion he'd been working on, and frowned.

"Stay away from Aggie's."

Now the laird's gaze rolled up to look at Roan. "How's yer cousin farin'?"

"Wha' do you care?"

Lachlan's eyebrows peaked above his dark eyes. "I care tha' I canna remember wha' happened."

Despite his raw, bloodied knuckles, Roan clenched his hands at his sides. "No," he sneered. "You only care tha' you lost yer temper in front o' Beth!"

"Tha', tae. But *you* have also had yer doubts tha' I tossed him ou' the window."

Roan quaked with anger. "I know I didn't do i', an' I'm *bloody* damn sure Laura an' Beth didn't, either!"

Diligently adding the finishing touches to the wooden piece, Lachlan shrugged his broad shoulders. "I know how i' looks. An', granted, whan I think back, i' seems verra possible tha' I . . ." His brooding gaze nailed Roan for a moment before lowering to the lion. ". . . *unwittingly* sent yer cousin through the window."

"You were ou' o' control!"

"Aye." Setting his carving tool by the candles, he reached down for a burlap sack and lifted it onto his lap. He was about to place the wooden lion inside when he became pensively quiet, his gaze locked onto the finished piece.

"Ma brither Ian was a fine whittler. He used ta mak the maist wonderful puppets for the tent shows whan they came ta town. 'Lan', he'd say, 'Tis a thinkin' mon's skill. The hands keep busy, but yer mind is free ta ponder the ways o' the world.' I miss ma brithers this time o' year."

Placing the lion into the sack, he stood and held it out to Roan, who remained motionless, glaring at it.

"For the laddies," Lachlan explained. "Christmas is nearly here. I wanted ta give them somethin'."

Roan's anger plummeted. Torn with indecision once again, he went to the window and buried his face in his hands.

Lowering the sack to his side, Lachlan closed half the distance. "Roan, what's troublin' you?"

A bitter laugh burst from Roan as he whirled to face his

family's tormentor. "Wha' could possibly be wrong, eh?" he laughed theatrically, his hands gesturing wide. "Borgie's in a coma. Aggie's no' sleepin' or eatin' worth a bloody damn. Now I'm ta bear *anither* burden on these shoulders o' mine?"

Lachlan silently waited for him to continue.

"Wha' you ask?" Roan flung snidely. "I'll tell you *wha'!* Wha will be yer next victim? You see, *auld mon,* some o' the same folks who were here helpin' ta wark on yer house, are now talkin' o' levelin' the place ta the ground."

Lachlan's face remained expressionless.

"How many o' them will you vent yer rage on?"

In lieu of a response, the laird shoved the sack into Roan's hands. Roan stared down at it for a long time. When he again met the near-black eyes, his expression was one of bewilderment.

"I don't understand you."

"You ne'er did," Lachlan said sadly.

He faded from sight, leaving Roan to stare dazedly into space.

The homey sound of a rocking chair moving to and fro greeted Roan when he entered his aunt's house. A weary smile tugged at his sore lips when he saw Laura sitting in front of the hearth, her head bent, her hands nimbly working a set of knitting needles. He softly closed the door, and placed the sack of wooden toys on the couch. An arm pressed to his aching middle, he walked to the rocker, bent over, and planted a kiss on her cheek.

She smiled.

"Wha' are you making?"

"Scarves an' hats for the boys."

A flicker of puzzlement creased Roan's brow. Had he only imagined she'd spoken with a Scottish burr?

"Aggie knits a storm e'er winter," he said absently, while his gaze fell on the sack of toys. "Ah, I saw Lannie a' the carriage house. He's carved some toys for the lads. Maistly animals."

"How nice."

Nice?

"Any coffee on?"

Laura looked up. She blinked, then whitened when she noticed his face. "What happened?" she cried, dropping the ball of yarn and needles to the floor, and jumping to her feet.

"Don't touch," he grimaced, staying her outstretched hand in midair.

"Roan!"

"I was in a wee fight a' the pub."

"A *wee* fight?"

He smiled ruefully. "You should see the ither men."

"You were fighting with more than one?"

He opened his arms. With a groan, she stepped into his embrace and laid her head against his shoulder.

"You've got to get a grip on your temper," she chided in a small voice.

"Aye. Where are the lads?"

"Lisa took them again." She inspected his face. "She claims the boys are absolute angels at her house."

Roan chuckled. "Her ain can be a handful." He glanced down at the yarn on the floor. "Maybe *I* should take oop knittin'."

Glancing down over her shoulder, Laura said, "My grandmother used to make the most beautiful afghans." She sighed. "I definitely don't take after her."

"Oh, I don't know." Drawing her closer, he brushed the tip of his cold nose against her brow. "You were workin' a mean stitch when I came in."

Leaning back, she frowned at him. "A mean what?"

"You were knittin'—"

"Roan, I don't even know how to hold the needles." With a scoffing laugh, she gingerly touched his lower lip with the tip of an isolated finger. "I tell you what. Go fix yourself some coffee, and I'll draw you a hot bath."

For a moment, he thought to argue with her about what he'd seen when he'd come in, but an image of her joining him in a foaming hot bath easily swayed him.

"Are you goin' ta scrub ma back?"

Her eyes sparkled. "Only if you scrub mine."

He glanced across the room in the direction of the kitchen. "Aggie home?"

"She was for a little while, then left with Ben for the hospital."

"Na change in Borgie?"

Laura shook her head. "She didn't say very much, except that she was planning on staying the night at the hospital. Ben mentioned that Dr. Waikens has been monitoring her when she's there. It was his suggestion that she sleep over."

Rolling his eyes in relief, he deeply sighed. "He's been her doctor for years."

"He'll take good care of her. Now . . . we need to worry about you." She stepped out of his hold and ran a sympathetic gaze over his battered face. "You look terrible."

"I love you, tae," he grinned. Heading for the kitchen, he asked, "Can I fix you a cup o' coffee or tea?"

"No, thanks."

He disappeared into the kitchen. As if compelled, she lowered her gaze to the yarn and needles. A chill shuddered through her. Hugging herself with her arms, she went into the small hall off the parlor, and into the sole bathroom. On the far wall of the blue and gold room sat a deep claw-foot tub. Corking the drain, and sprinkling some bubble bath on the plug, she turned the taps to a desired temperature. The soothing sound of cascading water awakened her fatigue. She sat on the floor, with her arms braced along the rim of the tub, and laid one side of her head upon her forearm.

Knitting, of all things.

Roan must be punchy. By the looks of his face, he'd taken quite a beating.

"Laura!"

Startled, she turned her head to see Roan standing inside the doorway. Then she snapped her head around, released a gasp at the sight of bubbles rising up in front of her, and hastily turned off the faucets.

"Did you fall asleep?" he asked, placing his cup of coffee on the toilet tank.

"I must have." Rolling up the sleeve of her baggy sweater, she dipped her hand into the water and pulled the cork, then watched until the iridescent foam had lowered several inches. She replaced the plug, and ruefully smiled up at Roan. "Oops."

"Oops," he parroted, grinning. He'd removed his coat and boots in the living room. His red plaid shirt was only half buttoned, revealing a thermal T-shirt beneath it. He was about to finish unbuttoning his shirt when she rose to her feet and pushed his hands aside.

"That's my job." Her gaze locking with his, she pried the dark buttons free and helped him out of the shirt. "Hands up, sir," she said lightly, tugging the thermal from the waistband of his pants.

His arms went up, but he winced.

With great care, she drew the thermal top upward. Her gaze ran over the muscular planes of his chest as it came into view. Roan finished the task and tossed the garment to the floor. He unfastened his pants, watching her expression of appreciation for his physique. When several seconds later he stood nude in front of her, he quipped, "Yer're o'erdressed for the occasion, aren't you, lass?"

A delicate blush rushed into her cheeks. Her eyes twinkled with anticipation.

"Are you sure you're up to this?"

He glanced down, and grinned wickedly. "I'm no' salutin' for ma health, darlin'." Releasing a throaty sound, he pulled her into his arms and lowered his head. But at the instant he covered her mouth, he jumped back with a grunt, and his hand dabbed at his split and swollen lower lip.

Laura arched a cocky eyebrow at him. "I can see this is going to be a painful experience for you."

"Painful be damned," he grumbled, cozying up to her. "Na worse agony than a mon denied a little lovin'."

"Spoken like a true stud," she laughed. "Climb in."

He looked disparagingly at the tub. "Alone?"

"Temporarily."

Her seductive tone caused a shudder to course through him. His heart was hammering with excitement as he lowered himself into the blanketing heat of the water. Bubbles oozed over the sides of the tub. He moaned contentedly, his muscles instantly responding to the soothing effect of the bath.

Dipping a clean face cloth beneath the bubbles, Laura then passed it to him. He held the hot, wet cloth to his face, lowering it in time to witness her peel out of her sweater.

Laura was vitally aware of him watching her undress. In part, she reveled in the sensual demonstration, but her shy side prompted a crimson blush to stain her cheeks. When the last vestiges of her underwear were removed, she stepped into the tub, pausing a moment for effect, before sitting, facing him amid her share of the bubbles.

Roan released a low whistle. "I still can't believe you came back."

"It's a sure thing, Roan Ingliss. You're stuck with me."

He nodded wistfully.

"Did you see Lachlan when you were at the carriage house?"

He scowled. "I'd rather no' talk abou' him, right now." He slid toward her. Once she positioned her feet beyond his hips, he glided her onto his lap.

"I love you, Laura. I know I'm no' always attentive, or able ta tell you wha' I'm feelin', but I need you ta always know tha' yer're a part o' me, I can ne'er lose again."

Resting her forearms upon his shoulders, she twirled the tendrils at his nape around her fingertips.

"It's strange, Roan, but I feel as if we've been together for a very long time. My life in Chicago seems so hazy now."

"Are you sure abou' stayin' in Scotland? You know, I was thinkin' . . . maybe the five o' us should gae ta the States. I could get a job—"

"Baird House needs you."

He laughed a bit uncertainly. "The house doesn't *need* anyone."

Unfinished business.

"We can't leave with unfinished business shadowing our lives."

"Laura, I'll no' find a local ta wark on the place."

"Then we'll do it ourselves." She brushed her lips against the side of his broad neck, then nipped the corded flesh with her teeth. A secretive smile graced her mouth when he released a spurt of breath. "As long as we're together . . ." She trailed the tip of her tongue along the left side of his jawline, stopping when she reached his earlobe. ". . . we can do anything." Her lips surrounded the fleshy lobe. Her teeth gently nibbled.

Chills of delight rocketed through his body. His hands came up to cup her breasts, her hardened nipples pressed to his palms.

"Brace yourself," she whispered by his ear. "I'm about to take you on a ride through heaven and hell . . . and everything in between."

Straightening back, she gripped his wrists and guided his arms to each long side of the tub. Braced in this manner, he closed his eyes and dipped back his head. He desperately wanted to feel good. Good about himself, the day, anything that could make sense out of his life.

Her hands moved down his chest. Her fingertips kneaded the muscular planes. She massaged his waist, his hips, his outer thighs then, more slowly, purposefully, his inner thighs. The tension he'd been carrying for weeks mercifully drained away. Her hands worked magic, lulling his weary body and mind to another world.

He didn't realize that he was nearly asleep until he heard a scratchy voice call out, "Roan, lad, are you home?"

"Oh . . . God!" Laura whispered, staring wide-eyed at the open bathroom door.

"Aggie!" Roan gasped. For a man his size, he nimbly scrambled from the tub, threw on the white robe hanging on the back of the door and, tying the belt, closed the door as he left the room.

"Roan!"

"Aggie, wha' are you doin' home?" he asked more

brusquely than he'd intended, entering the parlor to find her wringing her hands in the middle of the room. He stopped in his tracks, suddenly struck by how old she looked. How old and shriveled and . . . frail?

She'd never been frail in her life!

His next words came out in a barely audible croak. "Is i' Borgie?"

Agnes began to crumble. By the time Roan had helped her to sit on the couch, Laura emerged from the bathroom, dressed in the jeans and baggy sweater she'd worn earlier.

"What is it?" she asked anxiously, sitting to Agnes's right. Roan went down on a knee in front of his aunt, his hands cupping one of her own.

"Aggie, is Borgie . . . ?"

A tenuous rein on her sobs, she shook her head. She sniffed, then heaved a fortifying breath. A tear spilled down her pale cheek. "His heart . . . It stopped. They . . . brought him back."

"Is he still in a coma?"

"Aye, lass." She sniffed again, then swiped her sweatered arm beneath her moist nostrils. "I'm so scared for ma boy."

Laura affectionately placed an arm about the woman's hunched shoulders. "Don't give up hope."

The watery, pale blue eyes filled with such despair, Laura felt a chill run up her spine.

"He'll make sure ma boy doesn't mak i'."

Roan scowled. "Wha are you talkin' abou'?"

"Tha' *deil!*" Agnes hissed. "I was tellin' Borgie he had ta get better for Christmas, remindin' him o' last year, whan he made tha' huge snowmon in the front garden. You werena here, Roan. Truly, i' was the finest snowmon I've e'er seen, an' I've seen a few in ma day.

"Anyway, I was talkin' ta him whan suddenly the room

got cauld. No' chilly, mind you, but *cauld*. It teuk ma breath away. Ma bones ached sa, I wanted ta cry.

"Then I . . . I . . . I felt *him* in the room."

"Lannie?"

"Aye, Roan." Tears fell in abandon down her cheeks. "His darkness filled me. I've ne'er felt i' sa strong. Sa . . . o'erpowerin'. I couldna cry ou'. I couldna do anythin'! He wad have done Borgie dead right there, if no' for Dr. Waikens comin' in ta check on me.

"You think Lachlan Baird was at the hospital?"

Agnes's eyes held a wild gleam in them. "I know wha' I know, Laura! He came ta finish ma boy!"

Roan squeezed her hand to draw her attention to him. "Aunt Aggie, I don't think tis wi'in Lannie's power to go tha' far from Baird House."

"He comes here!"

"Aye, darlin', but the hospital is tae far. Besides, I can't believe he'd—"

"He's washed yer brain!"

"Brainwash, Aggie, an' na, he hasn't."

"Tis true wha' I hear." Recoiling from him, she pulled her hand from his grasp. "Tis tha' bastard you defend! Yer ain cousin lies near death, an' tis tha' *bastard* you protect!"

"Roan is concerned about Borgie. We all are."

"It was the vilest evil I felt in ma boy's room," Agnes wept. "He'll tak ma son from me. He'll tak ma Borgie!"

"I won't let him."

"Neither will I," Laura also vowed, exchanging a worried glance with Roan. "You need to rest, Agnes. You won't be much good to Borgie when he comes to, if you've made yourself ill."

"I canna sleep.

"I thought Dr. Waikens was goin' ta have you stay a' the hospital tonight."

"I thought i' wise ta come home. Thought . . . maybe Lannie wad follow me an' leave Borgie ta his rest."

"That's i', Aggie," Roan said sternly as he stood. Taking her hand, he drew her to her feet. "Yer're goin' ta bed, an' yer're goin' ta rest. Na argument! I'll gae an' have a talk wi' Lannie. You have ma word, he'll no' bugger anither member o' this family!"

Hope cleared the aging eyes. "How, Roan?"

"Beth," he said tightly, watching Laura rise to her feet. "She'll help us ta stop him. Laura, will you give Aggie a hand ta bed? I need ta get dressed."

"Roan, promise me you'll be careful around *him*."

He kissed the wizened cheek, grimacing when pain reminded him of his bashed lips. "I know how ta handle Lannie Baird."

Laura wasn't so sure. Dread coiling within the pit of her stomach, she forced herself to smile for Agnes's sake. "You'll feel a lot better in the morning after a good night's sleep," she said, coaxing the older woman toward the hall. Before turning the corner to Agnes's bedroom, Laura cast Roan a worried look. His gaunt features told her that he also wasn't sure about approaching the laird.

By the time she'd helped Agnes to change into a flannel nightgown, gotten her into bed, and had talked the woman to sleep, nearly an hour had passed. Laura returned to the parlor to find Roan fully dressed with his coat and gloves on, pacing the floor.

"Let it wait until the morning."

Roan stopped short at the sound of her voice. His haunted gaze riveted on her. "She restin'?"

"She finally fell asleep." Closing the distance between

them, Laura placed a hand against his chest. "I'm worried about *you*, Roan. If Lachlan turns on you . . ."

With a groan of anguish, Roan capped his skull with his hands. "I canna think straight!"

"What's tearing you up?" she asked in a whisper of a tone. "Roan, I know something's eating away at your gut."

Lowering his hands, he gestured his deepening sense of futility. "Sometimes . . . I swear I know the mon as well as I know maself. Laura, I'm havin' the bloodiest time believin' him crazed enough ta gae ta the hospital."

Laura shivered. "I think he's capable of anything."

"Aye, tis true, but . . ." Releasing an exasperated breath, he walked in a complete circle. "I know i' sounds ludicrous, but I *need* ta believe in him!"

"Roan . . ." Draping her arms about his neck, Laura held him close to her trembling body. "I'm scared, and I'm not even sure why. Don't go near that house tonight. Not in the dark."

"Day or night," he sighed, brushing the back of a gloved hand across her cheek, "doesna mak a difference. I have ta know wha' he's doin'."

"Then I'm going with you."

"Na. Stay wi' Aggie."

"I'm going, dammit!"

He lifted his hands in a placating gesture. "All right, but i' means I'll have you ta worry abou' there, as well."

Hastily donning her boots and coat, she snatched up her shoulder purse from the couch, and followed Roan out the door and to the van. He held the passenger door open for her, shut it, then walked around the front of the vehicle. Laura trembled violently, from the cold and her trepidation of returning to Baird House. She clung to a slim hope that she could somehow keep Roan from losing his temper with the laird.

The laird. Lachlan Baird. A *ghost!*

The driver's door opened. Roan climbed in behind the wheel. Laura was about to ask him once again to reconsider, when searing cold slammed the length of her body. For several seconds, her heart stopped, her brain shut down. Her external senses became trapped in an inexplicable dark void.

A spectral breath spilled from the core of her being. Life returned to her eyes. Life in the guise of rage.

Turning her head from Roan, she opened her door and slid off the seat. "I'll be right back."

Agnes woke with a start. A hoarse gasp came spilling past her dry lips. Pain radiated throughout her chest. She attempted to sit up. It was as if a massive weight had been placed upon her torso. Her arms and legs felt eerily buoyant.

She stared wildly into the darkness, her mind trying to will a scream. Movement stirred the cool air by the right side of her face.

Roan!

The bottom of her two pillows was pulled free.

Roan, help me!

A thought lanced her brain.

Was Borgie in trouble?

Why else would she feel such fear?

Was he slipping away? Leaving her?

What would she do without her only child?

She'd secretly hoped for grandchildren.

If he died, all her dreams would die with him.

Roan . . . what's wrong wi' me?

To lift her head but a few inches off the remaining pillow proved an enormous strain.

A burning sensation began above her heart. She focused

all her concentration on it. Was she losing her mind, or was a phantom hand burrowing into her chest, clutching her heart in an unmerciful grip?

Countless brilliant white stars danced in front of her eyes.

Was her heart failing her?

She wailed within the confines of her skull.

Dr. Waikens had warned her to avoid any more stress.

Was she going to die? Would Borgie come out of the coma to learn that *she* had left *him?*

She managed to release a choked sound.

A guttural laugh echoed within the room, and it was then, she realized that she was not alone.

Laura . . . ?

Every nerve in her became inflamed with awareness. Her brain homed in on an ominous presence. Terror tightened its strangulating fibers around her reasoning, tightening and tightening, making her teeter on the brink of madness.

Lannie! You deil! Get away, you deil!

Something soft fell over her face, but the softness waned beneath tauntingly slow increased pressure. By the time she realized that her other pillow was the object cutting off her air supply, it was too late.

Spasms seized her oxygen-starved body. Her lessening heartbeat hammered against her eardrums.

Lannie was killing her.

She would die and his vaporish presence would forever taint her soul.

He would deny her everlasting peace.

Damn yer . . . black . . . heart. . . .

Twelve

Roan couldn't take his gaze off the chasm as he made his way across the field, toward the headstones beneath the oak. A little voice in his head warned him to flee the laird's land, abandon his plan to elicit Beth's help. Even the night air held an element of foreboding. Whenever his imagination began to get the better of him, he forced himself to remember how close he'd come to making love to Laura in the bathtub.

Unfinished business.

When he arrived at the headstones, he was mildly surprised to find them righted. Had Beth or Lachlan attended to them? It really didn't matter. The chasm was all the reminder he needed.

Had Lannie's temper been as uncontrollable when he'd been alive?

Shuddering, he crammed his hands into his coat pockets and frowned at Beth's headstone.

He didn't understand why he felt guilty at the prospect of asking for her help. She was the only one who could remotely control the laird—except for the night Borgie had been injured.

But Lachlan seemed reasonably calm, now. That could change in the blink of an eye, especially if he came to resent Roan going to Beth for advice.

"Beth, I need ta see you," he whispered, his heart seeming to rise into his throat.

Several seconds passed before she materialized on the far side of her headstone. He stepped back, stunned by her desolate, ragged appearance.

"You look . . . a wee jaggy," he said unsteadily.

Her hand absently smoothed back the hair at the top of her head. She sighed and came around the monument, leaned against it and speculatively eyed him.

Roan gulped past the tightness in his throat. He suddenly wanted to leave, to walk away and leave the poor woman alone. What right did he have to further implicate her in the Baird/Ingliss battle?

"Beth . . ." Withdrawing his left hand from the pocket, he made a feeble gesture. "This isn't right. I shouldn't be here."

"You came about Lachlan," she stated dully, her gaze seeming to stare through Roan to some far-off place.

"Are you all right, lass?"

A weary smile ticked across her lips as she met his worried gaze. "It ain't easy avoiding him," she quipped. "I nearly passed on, Roan."

"I'm surprised you didn't."

"Hmmm. I certainly thought about it." She released a sigh, her breath vaporizing in front of her face. "But I have two very good reasons why I have to remain."

Roan cocked his head inquiringly.

"You and Laura," she explained. "Actually, make that five good reasons."

"The lads?"

She nodded. "I miss them, although it hurts like hell when I'm around them for too long."

"I don't understand."

For but a moment, her chin quivered. "I'll never have a child of my own."

"I'm sarry. I didn't think."

She released a low laugh. "Because, Roan Ingliss, you still have trouble thinking of me as a ghost."

"Aye, tis true. Beth—" Scowling, he looked down at his feet. "Aggie believes Lannie has been ta the hospital." He met her steeled gaze, his brow smoothing. "She's convinced he wants ta finish Borgie off."

"What do *you* think?"

Roan shrugged. "Part o' me believes i' possible."

"And . . . ?"

"Ma heart doesn't buy i'. I know . . . I know . . . we all saw wha' he became in the house tha' night, but . . ."

"But what, Roan?"

"Damn me!" he fumed, running a hand over the top of his head. "I came here ta ask you ta help me banish the mon, but tis no' goin' ta come ou' tha' way!"

"Indecision has always been your worst fault," she said softly, staring off to one side.

"The mair I think abou' tha' night, Beth, the less sense i' all makes!"

Her gaze swung to his face. "What doesn't make sense?"

"E'erythin'! I know he was angry—enraged because Borgie had come inta the house, but *you* were there, tae. I've seen him back doon just ta please *you,* Beth."

Walking a few paces past Roan, Beth glared at the remains of Baird House. "He was too out of control to care what he said or did that night. I'll never forget his eyes—" Her voice caught on a sob and, squeezing her eyes shut, she folded her arms against her middle.

Roan drew in a deep draught of the freezing air. "Sometimes I imagine he's in ma head, Beth, makin' me feel an' say things tha' I wouldn't ordinarily. I can't get somethin' off ma mind." He walked around the statuesque figure, faced her, and placed his hands upon her drawn-in shoulders.

"Whan I found him an' Laura in the attic, he said tha' Tessa had returned."

Pools of despair filled Beth's eyes as she looked up at him.

"I've been toyin' wi' this crazy notion, Beth. Suppose . . ." He glanced over his shoulder, in the direction of the house. ". . . Tessa's spirit *was* here. An' wha' if she was behind Laura tryin' ta stab Lannie, an' Borgie goin' ou' the window."

"Why would—" Beth irritably sighed. "Why would Tessa stay around? I think Lachlan would have sensed her if she had."

"But he said she'd returned. I remember tha' clearly. Lannie has but one thin' left ta lose, Beth. *You!*"

"I'm not sure what you're trying to get at."

Roan lowered his hands, then pensively massaged the underpart of his chin. "Yer're the key, somehow. I may be confused by a lot o' things these days, but I know tha' mon loves you mair than anythin'. So I keep askin' maself, why wad he risk losin' you o'er somethin' as stupid as ma cousin trespassin' in his bloody house? He doesn't remember actually causin' Borgie ta fly ou' the window."

"He has a selective memory," she said bitterly.

"He's ne'er kept his feelin's or faults ta himself in the past, has he?"

Beth testily shrugged.

"Now . . . *if* Tessa was around, Beth, wha' better revenge could she perpetrate on Lannie, than ta destroy yer love for him? Wha' could hurt him mair than ta lose you?"

"There's something you're not aware of, Roan. Tessa *is* back, but it's not for revenge."

The blood drained from his face. "She's *here?*"

"So is Robert."

Roan swore under his breath.

"Roan—"

A blood-curdling scream razored the night.

Roan turned. His horrified gaze riveted in the direction of the house.

"Laura! God, Laura, I left her in the van!"

He lit into a run, unaware that Beth vanished. Twice he fell, further bruising his battered body. His brain was afire with fear.

Laura. She'd insisted on remaining in the van, despite his pleas that she stay close to him.

Damn me!

He was beelining for the van when another scream rang out. This one possessed a feral quality, nearly overpowering his instinct to find her. Changing direction, he burst through the greenhouse door, then the one leading into the hall. Guided by nothing but his honed sixth sense, he stormed up the staircase to the third floor and turned right.

At the end of the hall, light beckoned him from the master bedroom. He charged into the room, oblivious to the dozens of lit candles, oblivious to Beth's translucent form standing by the blackened fireplace. All he could see was Laura struggling with Lachlan, whose hands cinched her raised wrists. Animal sounds emanated from her. Roan felt bewildered and lost. Her face was a contorted mask of hatred. She kicked fiercely at the laird, and ferociously tried to twist from his hold.

Finally, Roan found his voice. "Tak yer bloody hands off her!"

Uncharacteristically calm, Lachlan spared Roan a glance. "Tell her ta stop 'fore she hurts herself."

Roan jerked back in surprise. "The only harm ta her, is *you!*"

Casting Roan a disgruntled look, the laird released her. No sooner was she free, she swooped down, lifted something into her right hand, and lunged upward. Roan's blood turned to ice. For several seconds, he could only gape as she drove the jeweled dagger into Lachlan's chest, again and again, each thrust more purposeful.

Beth's horrified expression zoomed into Roan's focus. Tearing his gaze from her, he blinked at the heinous scene in front of him, then rushed forward. Grabbing Laura's arm, he yanked her toward him, and away from Lachlan. In a lightning move, she turned on him, driving the dagger toward his heart. The gleaming tip was a hair's breadth from piercing his chest, when Lachlan's hand sailed out and caught her wrist. Then as swiftly, from behind her, he swept an arm about her middle, lifted her off her feet, and wrenched the dagger from her grasp with his free hand.

Roan's legs threatened to buckle beneath him. He was dimly aware of Beth at his side, of her fingers digging into his right bicep. His hearing was filled with Laura's hissing and Gaelic curses.

Gaelic curses?

Roan forced himself to stare into the dark eyes intensely watching him.

"Look a' her, Roan," he demanded in a deep, hypnotizing tone. "See beyond the packagin'."

Roan was confused. What was Lachlan talking about? Packaging? This had to be a nightmare—

Time swept past him, moving so fast, light-headedness threatened to keel him over. With every ounce of willpower he possessed, he struggled to maintain his footing and keep his knees locked. The motion slowed. The room, he realized, looked exactly as it had prior to the fire.

No!

There was a difference.

To the left of the fireplace was a vanity, its top covered with feminine toiletries and a gold hairbrush set neatly placed upon a filigreed, mirrored tray. Vases filled with freshly cut roses graced the mantel and bedstands.

More deeply perplexed than he'd ever been in his life, he looked at Lachlan questioningly. It was then he noticed a superimposed visage of another woman on Laura's face. Her hair, too, was different. Parted down the middle. Long banana curls fashioned with ribbons in front of her ears.

As though from far away, he heard Beth cry, "He's not ready for this!"

Not ready for what?

Insanity, was his guess.

"If you love me, Robbie, you'll help me ta kill him!"

Laura's lips—the double-version image of them—had mouthed the words, but it had not been her voice.

Although he had heard her speak in that exact voice before.

"Kill him!"

Suddenly, Roan was back in the fire-ravaged room. Numbness weighted his limbs.

"Robbie!" Laura wailed, tears streaming down her ashen face.

Roan dropped to his knees. He felt as if the life had been drained from him. Images flashed through his mind. He desperately wanted to blame Lachlan for them, to believe the laird was projecting the images, but to deny the truth now would be to deny his very own existence.

Lachlan released Laura as if the touch of her sickened him. She dropped to her knees in front of Roan, her arms winding about his neck and holding onto him for dear life, while her hate-filled gaze dissected the laird.

"I gave you both e'ery chance ta right the wrongs o' the past," he said, his tone laced with contempt and pain combined. He gestured expansively. "Tis all yers once again, but I vow, you'll no' know a day's happiness."

With a wretched cry, Laura sprang to her feet and faced him, her fists clenched in front of her.

"You pathetic excuse for a man!" she cried, the Scottish burr not present. "You came to my village and seduced me with promises of wealth! *You* created the monster in me!"

"Look inta yer ain soul," he said scathingly.

Roan slowly rose to his feet, standing directly behind Laura.

"My *soul?*" she laughed bitterly. "If you dangle a piece of meat in front of a starving man's face, he's going to grab it, whether it's rancid or not. *You* have never known hunger—how it eats away at the lining of your stomach! Or cold that settles into the marrow of your bones, until it's an effort to get out of bed each morning!

"Nine of us girls watched our mother die a slow, agonizing death! *Nine of us!* Then you come along, Mr. *I'm your savior,* and you never once asked if my heart belonged to someone else!"

"You wanted i' all," Lachlan growled.

"Yes," she hissed.

Realization slammed home in Laura's duo-occupied brain. She fell back into Roan's arms, her face devoid of color, horror defining the contours of her eyes.

"No," she whimpered, shaking her head in disbelief. "It's not possible."

Roan could say nothing, only stare at Lachlan and wonder what was going through his mind. At long last, the pieces of the puzzle fit together. The truth was finally out.

"Lachlan," Beth said achingly, her eyes pleading with him to show compassion to the stricken couple.

The laird's hard gaze softened on his woman, softened beneath such a depth of pain, he didn't have to tell her that it would take some time before he could forgive her lack of faith in him. He faded away.

Weeping, Beth melted into the floor. The sound of her misery echoed for seconds later.

"It can't be," Laura wept, turning and flinging herself into Roan's arms.

Roan closed his eyes, murmuring, "Aye, lass, we're back. An' we're na better than we were a century an' a half ago."

Agnes and Borgie Ingliss were buried side by side in a small cemetery in north Crossmichael, where three other family members had been laid to rest.

A dark cloud of gloom hung over the town. Not much had been said aloud about either's death. Borgie had died in his sleep, roughly about the same time it was believed that his mother had suffered a heart attack. Some folks thought it a shame. Agnes had been well-liked, while her son had been only tolerated for her sake. A growing number of others harbored deepening superstitions. The renowned *curse* of Lachlan Baird fed their fears, instilled beliefs that to even think of it, was to possibly bring it upon themselves. Roan, Laura and her nephews, Ben, and Silas, had been the only ones to attend the double funeral. In the four days that followed, three neighbors had come to the cottage to offer their condolences.

In three days, it would be Christmas.

Laura's hand trembled as she held out a red glossy bulb to place on the Douglas fir that Roan had purchased the previous night. Alby and Kahl had strung popcorn and cranberries. Kevin sullenly sat on the couch, not really watching or listening, or caring one way or the other about the pending holiday. A hole existed where his heart had been. He'd been the one to discover Agnes, and now his small shoulders were burdened with a secret. He desperately wanted to tell his aunt—Roan. But they wouldn't believe him.

A strained smile appeared on Laura's lips when Kahl began to hum "Silent Night." However, it vanished the instant her gaze fell upon Kevin. Her heart grew heavier. The boys had been through so much. She couldn't look at her oldest nephew without wanting to pull him into her arms and chant that everything would be all right. If only she could. Not only had he refused to let anyone touch him since finding Agnes, he also steadily grew more withdrawn. Nothing she said seemed to reach him.

"Alby!"

Kahl's sharp, scolding tone brought her gaze to the youngest boy. At the same moment that she saw him trying to insert a plastic candy cane in his left nostril, the front door opened and Roan entered carrying an armload of firewood. She snatched the candy from Alby and, ignoring his wail of protest, pulled aside a carton of decorations that was sitting in front of the wood rack.

"Gimme!" the youngster demanded, stomping a foot.

Kahl grimaced. "You're such a baby."

"Am not!"

"Enough," Laura said wearily, half her attention on Roan as he transferred his burden to the rack. "Would you like some tea?" she asked him, over-sensitized to the detachment he'd shown her since the funeral.

"Na . . . thank you."

He pulled off his gloves, shucked out of his coat, and ambled to the small closet across from the door. Absently, as if it were an afterthought, he closed the front door with a nudge of his boot heel.

"Are you hungry?"

He glanced over his shoulder at her, his dull gaze seeming to stare through her. "Na . . . thanks. There's some soup left. I can heat i' oop for you an'—"

"We had some a little while ago."

"And pancakes," Alby informed, staring at the candy cane clutched in his aunt's hand.

Kahl snorted. "I'm still hungry."

Raking the fingers of a hand through his hair, Roan faced the group. He glanced at his watch. "How abou' if we make a batch o' Christmas cookies."

Kahl wrinkled his nose. Alby released a squeal of glee and dashed to the kitchen.

Roan sadly regarded Kevin for a few seconds. "Kevin, care ta give us a hand?"

For a time, Kevin stared off into space. Then his despondent gaze swung to Roan.

"Kevin?" Laura prompted.

He shook his head.

"Come along, Kahl," said Roan, holding out his hand to the boy.

Kahl militantly stood his ground. "That's sissy stuff."

Roan arched a brow. "I guess tha' means you don't want a cookie whan we're through."

It only took a second for the five-year-old to change his mind. Running ahead of Roan, he disappeared into the kitchen. Roan followed with a leaden gait, leaving Laura with Kevin.

"Want to help me finish decorating the tree?"

Kevin remained silent, staring off into space. Despite the sensation of tears filling her throat, Laura sighed and seated herself next to him. Hesitantly, she placed an arm about his thin shoulders and drew him against her.

"We all miss Agnes, Kevin," she said softly, then kissed the top of his head. "Especially Roan. I know it's hurting him to see you so withdrawn."

"Why do people have ta die?"

His raspy voice painfully yanked on her heartstrings. "It's part of life, hon. We're born, we live, and we die. The world would be awfully crowded if no one died, wouldn't it?"

After a moment, he swung his despondent gaze up to study her face. "I never got to say good-bye to her. Not my dad, either."

Tears welled up in Laura's eyes. "I know it must hurt terribly, Kevin."

He nodded.

"But you know, you and your brothers gave Agnes a lot of happiness during the short time we were here. That counts for a lot."

"It does?"

A wavering smile graced her mouth. "She adored you."

Kevin's dreamy gaze shifted to the Christmas tree in the corner of the room. "She didn't look happy. She scared me."

A chill speared Laura's heart. "When didn't she look happy, hon?"

"Last night."

"Ah . . . you must have been dreaming."

Kevin soberly met her gaze. "Naw. I woke up and she was standing at the foot of the bed. At first I couldn't see her face too clearly. She was kinda green and like fog."

Swallowing painfully past the lump in her throat, Laura prompted, "Go on, Kevin."

"Well, she was trying to say something. I couldn't understand her. She started to cry. Real hard. And she reached out to me, but I was afraid to let her touch me."

"Of course you were."

"Her face got a little clearer, and she looked like she hurt a lot, Aunt Laura. It made me feel awful." He tapped his fist to his chest. "I hurt here real bad, but I didn't cry. I was afraid if I did, she'd try ta hold me."

His chin quivered. Tears misted his eyes. "I should have let her. I shouldn't have been afraid of her."

Laura's arms wrapped about him and held him dearly to her. Tears spilled down her pale cheeks. "Honey, I'm sure she understood. You're just a little boy."

"You believe me, don't you?"

Holding him back, Laura searched his ravaged face for a long moment. "Yes, I do. She was probably trying to say good-bye, Kevin."

"Why couldn't she look normal, like Lachlan and Beth?"

"I don't know. But how about if we concentrate on making this Christmas special for your brothers and Roan?"

"I'll try."

"Oh baby," Laura wept, hugging him again. "You boys have been so brave through all the craziness. I'm so grateful I have you in my life. I'd be lost without you."

"Me, too," he sobbed, hugging her as tightly as he could. "And I promise to be real good from now on. I promise."

Framing his face with her hands, Laura laughed. "Always be yourself, Kevin. Don't change for anyone, or anything."

He thought over her words, then earnestly stated, "If I had one wish, Aunt Laura, I would wish to be magic."

"You are magic, Kevin."

"*Real* magic, Aunt Laura. I would fix Baird House, and make us all happy again."

"As long as we're together, we'll always have magic."

"Enough to fix the house?"

Laura sighed. "You really liked that place, didn't you?"

He nodded, then swiped the back of a hand beneath his moist nose. "I miss it. Even the bad man couldn't make me not want to stay there."

The bad man.

Laura reflexly stiffened. So much had happened since their return from Edinburgh, she'd forgotten the series of events prior to the fire. Someone had loomed up on the servant stairwell. And someone had hit and kicked her and dragged her outside. Now that she thought about it, *why?* Why drag *her* outside and leave Roan and the boys in the house?

Borgie? Had he been the one terrorizing the boys? Had he been the one she'd seen pass by the window in the bedroom?

A knock at the front door gave her a start. Jumping up, she crossed the room and opened the door. Viola Cooke stood primly on the stoop. A smile of greeting appeared on her thin lips at the sight of Laura.

"May I come in?"

"Of course."

The elderly woman passed Laura, who shut the door and offered to take her coat.

"Oh no, dear. I can't stay long." The faded blue eyes lit up as they swung to Kevin. "Well, young man, are you ready for Saint Nick?"

Kevin shrugged.

Roan came from the kitchen. "Good evenin', Miss Cooke."

"Dear Roan, I'm so sorry about your aunt. I planned to attend her funeral, but I was a bit under the weather."

Roan smiled sadly in understanding. "How are the roads?"

"Quite good, actually. I'm sorry I didn't call first, but I was anxious to see the boys." She cast Kevin a grandmotherly look. "The poor dears have been through so much."

Roan's troubled gaze met Laura's briefly, then cut away. "Aye. But they're strong lads. Aren't you, Kevin?"

"Yeah."

A sigh heaved Viola's bosom as she folded her hands against her abdomen. "I have a favor to ask."

"What is it?" Laura asked.

Viola smiled warmly at Kevin. "I would dearly love to take the boys for the night. Some friends and I have put together a pre-Christmas surprise for them. Gifts and sweets."

"You want to take them overnight?"

"Laura dear, you and Roan need some time together— alone—and me, well, I haven't any grandchildren to spoil. I promise to return them tomorrow night."

The doubt in Laura's expression prompted Viola to rush on, "I will keep my eye on them every minute. Besides, Bertha and Katherine will be there, too."

"I-umm, I-I guess it's up to the boys," Laura stammered.

Sliding off the couch, Kevin walked to Viola's side. "Sounds okay. Kahl and Alby will think it's cool."

Laura looked to Roan for his opinion.

"The lads could use an upper," he said brusquely, wiping his floured hands on the half-apron tied at his waist.

"All right. Kevin, go ask your brothers if they want to go."

He went into the kitchen. During the seconds that passed, Laura stared at Roan, waiting for him to say something further. He'd barely spoken to her since that last time at Baird House. No matter how hard she'd tried, he avoided almost all contact with her.

The boys came into the parlor. Alby and Kahl's eyes were wide with excitement. Kevin remained somber.

"You got us presents?" Kahl asked Viola.

"Lots and lots," she laughed.

Alby released a squeal of joy.

"I'll pack them a bag," Laura said to the older woman, and went to the boys' room. When she returned a few minutes later, it was to find Roan squatting in front of them. He zippered the jackets she'd purchased for them in Edinburgh, then gave each a hug.

"You be good for Miss Cooke," he instructed, erecting himself.

"We will," Kevin assured.

Alby eagerly followed Viola to the door.

"Hey," Laura chuckled, placing the brown luggage on the floor, "don't I get a hug?"

She sank down and opened her arms. Grimacing, Alby allowed her to embrace him, then jubilantly clasped Viola's gloved hand. Kahl's hug was as brief, but Kevin lovingly wrapped his arms about her neck, and kissed her on the cheek before stepping out of her hold.

Fresh tears began brimming her eyes, when Laura passed the small luggage to Viola, then stood at the open doorway and waved to the boys as they followed her down the snow-packed pathway. An icy breeze swept into the house. She closed the door and, bracing her back against it, regarded Roan's hostile posture.

"We need to talk."

He hastily untied the apron and tossed it onto the back of the chair to his left. "No' tonight."

"Why not tonight?"

He removed his coat, hat, and gloves from the closet by the door, and began to don them.

"Where are you going?"

"Shortby's for a bit."

"Roan . . . Dammit, we have to talk!"

"No' tonight!" he barked, his face livid, his eyes condemning.

"We're *not* Tessa and Robert."

"Excuse me," he said tightly, indicating that he wanted to leave out the front door.

"Think about it, Roan! For a reason I can't begin to understand, Lachlan has planted their memories in us!"

"Laura . . . *move* ou' o' the way!"

"Have you once considered all the events that brought me to Scotland?" She released a near-hysterical laugh. "Everything that brought my *brother* to England? His first wife dying, his second wife tricking me into coming to visit with the boys! Can you honestly shrug it all off as the hand of fate?

"I'm an *American!* I don't have one iota of Scottish blood in my veins."

With a growl of contempt, Roan grabbed her by the arm and pulled her away from the door. Before she could regain her balance, he'd slammed out of the house, leaving her to gape in stunned incredulity at the closed door. It was seconds later before her temper doused the fiery empty ache in her heart.

"Damn you, Roan Ingliss!"

Reincarnation. It was the most ridiculous concept she'd ever heard, especially since she'd taken the time to reflect on the countless paths involved in bringing her to this particular place and time. She couldn't explain the haunting dreams of the blonde and the man the woman called Robbie. There were a great many things that defied *any* explanation, but that didn't mean she was willing to accept that she was Tessa reborn.

The mansion was somehow the key.

There were times when she'd experienced an inexplicable hatred of Lachlan Baird. She'd been forced to accept the existence of ghosts—*very real ghosts*—and the idea that another *presence* had influenced her, made more sense than reincarnation.

Her mind seemingly afire, she removed her coat and gloves from the closet and put them on.

The answers had to be at the house. Perhaps even the spectral laird was being manipulated by something more powerful than he could perceive. Whatever was behind the series of bizarre events, she was determined to get to the bottom of it.

She exchanged her slippers for knee-high black boots, left the house, and plodded through the calf-high snow to the red Ford Escort she'd rented in Edinburgh.

Fear lingered at the periphery of her mind. She would have preferred to return to Baird House with Roan, but he was beyond emotional reach these days, at least where she was concerned. He openly showed his affection for the boys. However, he became rigid whenever she entered the same room he was in. Sometimes, she caught him watching her from beneath his sandy-blond thick eyelashes, watching her with something akin to sorrow, and other times, something akin to disgust. She fostered the hope that if she unraveled the mystery behind Tessa and Robert, she'd win Roan's heart once again. Too much was at stake for her not to try. At this point in her life, she couldn't imagine a future without him.

"I love you," she murmured, starting the engine.

She backed out of the driveway, inwardly fighting to banish her fears, her trepidations. She didn't relish the idea of summoning Lachlan Baird. His eyes . . . She dreaded confronting their intensity again. He possessed a way of looking through her that left her feeling as though he'd branded her soul.

Heading down the main road to the mansion, she thought of Beth. *She* was an ally. At least Laura felt sure that the woman possessed enormous compassion and understanding.

Woman.

Ghost.

She wondered what the living Beth Staples had been like. And she wondered how such a mild-tempered woman endured a man as stubborn as Lachlan.

Man.

Ghost.

It was hard to differentiate.

And why wonder, anyway? Roan possessed a stubborn streak that was every bit as bad as Lachlan's.

Too soon, she spied the regal silhouette of Baird House to her right. Her hands gripped the steering wheel so tightly, pain shot through her wrists. Her heartbeat accelerated.

Despite her determination to hold back her fears, they rose into her throat and threatened to shut off her oxygen.

She cut the wheel and turned onto the driveway, accelerating steadily to make the incline. The pavement proved icy in patches, but not as slick as it'd been that first night. She crested the top, pulled up to the carriage house, and shut off the engine. Before her courage completely deserted her, she climbed out on the right side of the car, absently slinging the strap of her purse over her shoulder. Her gaze never wavered from the structure. She approached the greenhouse, her gait determined, her shoulders held tautly back.

Her first attempt to call out Lachlan's name, caught in her throat. She'd never felt so cold, so isolated and alone. The house loomed over her, a sentinel of the supernatural. She could feel it watching her, probing her inner awareness.

She shuddered uncontrollably.

Run, her mind cried, but she refused to obey the warning.

"Lachlan! Lachlan Baird, it's Laura!"

Her shaky voice softly echoed in the night. The three-quarter phase moon cast the house and grounds in silver-blue, glimmering soft light.

"Please, I must talk with you!"

Silence.

"Beth . . . Beth are you here?"

Within seconds, the beautiful woman materialized to Laura's left, once again wearing the white gown with the flowing sleeves. Beth's eyes lacked their usual luster. Her cheeks were gaunt, her curly hair in disarray.

"Beth . . . ?"

"He's nowhere to be found," she replied dully, looking off in the direction of the driveway.

"I'm sorry." Laura swallowed past the lump in her throat. "Is there anything I can do?"

The blue eyes swung to search Laura's. "It must be hard for you to . . . accept everything that's been happening."

"Do *you* really believe in reincarnation?" When Beth didn't answer for several seconds, Laura went on, "It's impossible, Beth." She laughed low, nervously. "I'm an American. As far as I know, I don't have any Scottish ancestors."

"I don't think lineage has anything to do with it," Beth said kindly, her expression one of deepening pain.

"I-I could never k-kill anyone, Beth."

A soft smile appeared on the specter's shapely mouth. "Lachlan told me that some souls return and return until they've atoned for their sins. I'm not sure if I believe that or not, but you and Roan *were* once Tessa and Robert."

"How can you be sure?"

"Your aura."

"My what?"

"Your aura. No two are alike."

"I-I don't understand all this hocus-pocus stuff. I'm just an ordinary woman, with ordinary hopes for the future. If . . . *if* I had been someone else in another life, someone as cold and calculating as this Tessa, wouldn't I be the same now?"

"Are you?"

"No!" Laura cried, appalled that Beth would even ask such a question.

Beth morosely regarded the facade of the house. "You were once the mistress of this house. Coming from poverty, I can almost imagine how you must have felt." Her unsettling gaze searched Laura's pale features. *"Almost* imagine, but I'm still having trouble understanding how you could have—"

"I didn't! I couldn't *kill* anyone!" Laura cupped her head with her gloved hands. "How can I convince you of something that bears no evidence!"

"Denial has always been your weakness, Laura. And Roan's, until he finally opened his mind to the truth."

Tears escaped down Laura's cheeks. "This is insane!"

"Is it?" Beth folded her arms against her. "I'm not trying to cause you more pain."

Laura hesitantly made a turn toward her car, then faced the ghost again. "If you find Lachlan, please tell him I must talk to him."

"You've seen what he's like when he's . . . upset."

Laura nodded numbly. "I'm more afraid of not knowing the truth. Beth . . . ? Where were you the night of the fire?"

Beth stiffened defensively. "Why are you asking?"

"Did you know there was someone else in the house? Someone dressed in a dark cloak with a hood?"

Beth frowned. "Are you sure?"

"Absolutely. He was in the servant stairwell, and reared up. I was so startled, I fell down the steps. Then he hit me on the back of the head with something, kicked me, and dragged me outside. When I came to, the house was in flames."

For a long moment, Beth remained thoughtfully quiet. "Lachlan and I were playing with the boys. They wore us out. By the time they'd finally gone to sleep, we were forced to retreat into the grayness. We barely gathered enough energy to return during the fire."

"The boys claim someone grabbed them. I don't know how it could have slipped my mind, but Kahl swears that he was deliberately locked in one of the bedrooms. Kevin mentioned something about being locked in a closet, but I couldn't get him to elaborate. Beth, what's going on? Why would someone drag me out of the house, and try to trap the boys inside during a fire?"

Beth looked in the direction of the main road. "Did you or Roan report this to the police?"

"I didn't. I'm not sure if Roan knows anything about it. Why?"

"Earlier, I materialized in time to see several police cars, and a black van, pulling out of the driveway. It's hard to see in the dark, but there's a section of rhododendrons that have been cordoned off with yellow bands."

Shivering, Laura turned in the direction Beth was pointing.

"Two men were searching the ground. I couldn't catch anything they were saying."

"Roan said the fire investigation had been completed," Laura said tightly, looking at Beth. "Do you know what was determined?"

Beth gave a solemn shake of her head.

Laura shivered again. "Maybe it was arson, and maybe something was found to point the finger at the culprit."

"I don't know. All I could see was a deep depression in the ground."

Laura sighed through her nostrils, and winced. "What's that odor?"

In lieu of answering, Beth snapped her head around and glared in the direction of the rhododendron hedges lining most of the driveway. Laura's gaze rapidly swept the area, detecting nothing unusual. But her inner sense warned that something was about to happen.

"What is it?"

"Trouble," Beth rasped.

Within seconds, a widespread series of lights started up the driveway. A symphony of engine sounds disturbed the peace and stillness of the night.

"Beth?"

"Get out of here, Laura," the specter ordered, pointing to the red car. "Don't try to interfere with these people."

"People? What's going on— Oh, God . . ."

Laura stared at the procession of cars rolling to a stop a hundred feet from where her rental was parked. Car doors opened and slammed shut. Angry voices fell on her ears.

"Oh my God," Laura croaked, backing up until the house supported her back. A crowd of men and women cautiously approached. She tried to focus on their faces, but her gaze was morbidly drawn to the axes, sledgehammers, shovels, and rifles they carried.

"Laura!" Beth hissed, floating to her side. "There's been enough bloodshed on these grounds! Don't try to stop them!"

Laura cried out when Lachlan unexpectedly appeared, standing seven feet away, his back to her. Her gaze cut to Beth's stricken face, who obviously also feared what the laird would do to anyone who dared to threaten his home.

"Return ta yer families an' homes!" Lachlan boomed, his hands curling into fists at his sides.

"We'll send you ta hell, this night," one man bellowed. Many with him cheered his words, boosting his bravado. "We've enough o' this cursed place!"

Beth melted into the rock and mortar of the house.

"An' I've eneuch o' yer bloody superstitions!" Lachlan roared.

Laura's eyes widened. One man in the crowd raised his arm. She couldn't see what he held up, but she sensed what was about to happen. Without forethought, she cried,

"No!" and lunged forward. She could hear an object *whoosh* through the air, saw it gleam but a moment before she dashed in front of the laird, placing herself in the projectile's path.

Something embedded itself in her chest. The impact sent her reeling backward into the ghost's arms. She looked down. Her trembling hand slowly lifted toward the jeweled handle protruding from the front of her coat.

Cries rang out.

Her world grew darker. She felt herself being lowered to the ground, Lachlan's arm supporting the back of her shoulders. Bewilderment filled his dark eyes. Bewilderment and misery.

The deepest darkest recesses of her subconscious opened. She recalled the very same expression on his face the night she'd driven the dagger into his heart—that fateful night in *1844*.

Suddenly, she was terrified of dying before she could cleanse herself of her guilt. But her life was slipping away, seeping out of her body with the steady flow of blood the dagger had undammed.

Where are you, Roan? Take care of my nephews! Love them enough for the both of us. . . .

Roan languidly tipped the third flute of scotch to his lips and gulped down the contents. The liquid burned his throat on its way to his queasy stomach. He was nearly on the verge of the oblivion he craved, the absolute numbness he needed to get through another night.

Only one other patron was in the pub, an old-timer perched on the farthest stool from him. He'd noticed the man glaring his way, with a grimace that puckered his near-toothless mouth. He didn't care. Silas had been uncharacteristically quiet and avoiding Roan, but Roan didn't care about that, either. The roof could fall in on his head right now, and it wouldn't faze him.

Robert Ingliss.

Had his ex-wife and son paid for the sins he'd committed in another life?

The mere notion haunted his sleep and waking hours.

God, how he loved Laura!

No wonder.

A century and a half ago, they'd taken a man's life and had stolen his house and fortune.

He remembered first meeting the laird. He remembered his kindness before and after he and Tessa had arrived at his home. And he remembered, foremost, admiring the man who had been smitten with the only woman Robert had ever loved.

"Damn you, Tessa," he slurred, his head bobbing as he drunkenly peered into the empty flute.

"Mr. Ingliss?"

The authoritative tone came from behind him. Slowly cranking himself around on the stool, he squinted at a man dressed in a gray trench coat. Short black hair, and piercing grey-green eyes were visible beneath the rim of his matching gray hat. Although Roan was drunker than he had been in years, he got the distinct impression that the man was someone of importance. That . . . or a thug.

"Mr. Ingliss," the man repeated, removing a wallet from an inside pocket of his coat. He flipped it open to reveal a gold badge with the engraved lettering, Shields Agency, and the number 116, which Roan had to squint to focus on. "I'm Detective Connery of the Shields Agency."

"How bloody terrific for you," Roan grumbled, facing the counter once again. "Silas! A bitter if you please!"

"Mr. Ingliss, I'm afraid I must ask you a few questions."

Roan grimaced, then grinned lopsidedly at the old man several stools away and lifted his empty flute in a mocking salute.

Behind him, the detective's expression remained deadpan, except for a hardening glint in his eyes. "Mr. Ingliss, a frozen body was found on the Baird Estate this afternoon. What can you tell me about it?"

Roan eyed Silas as the man edged his way back behind the bar, his wary gaze remaining glued on the stranger.

"A body, he says," Roan chuckled, pushing the flute toward Silas. "Don't spare the scotch, ma mon."

The detective locked eyes with Silas and gave an adamant shake of his head.

Silas made a poor attempt to smile at Roan. "Yer're already in yer cups, lad."

"Mr. Ingliss."

Sighing petulantly, Roan swiveled around and leveled an impatient look on the man. "'Tis ma name, but I'm gettin' bloody sick o' hearin' i'."

"Then answer ma question, Mr. Ingliss."

Roan winced. "I forgot the question . . . whoe'er the bloody hell you say you are."

"At three-fifteen this efternoon, Jacob McCoy discovered a body in a shallow grave on the Baird estate. Wha' can you tell me abou' the corpse?"

"Damn me, I can't think," Roan muttered, striking his brow several times with the heel of his hand. "A corpse, eh?" He chuckled, then slowly stiffened atop the stool. "A corpse." His eyes cleared of their dullness. "Jacob McCoy discovered a corpse. Wha' the bloody *hell* was Jacob doin' on Lannie's property!"

"Mr. Ingliss—"

The detective stepped back a pace when Roan unexpectedly slid off the stool and wobblingly straightened.

"Silas," Roan growled, his gaze repeatedly scanning the room, "where is e'eryone? Where the bloody hell are the regulars?"

The detective steeled a questioning look on the nervous man behind the counter.

"Silas!" Roan boomed, turning so quickly in the direction of the man, he nearly lost his balance.

"They went ta Kist House, lad."

All color drained from Roan's face. He swayed. *"Wha'?"*

"I tried ta talk sense inta them, but they were tae fired oop ta tear the place doon."

"Lannie," Roan breathed, bending over to fight back a wave of dizziness.

"I did ma best ta stop them," Silas said anxiously.

"Aye, aye I'm sure you did." Forcing himself to straighten, Roan turned to face the detective. "You've got ta tak me ta the estate. I'm in na shape ta drive."

"It's wi'in ma rights ta haul you ta the nearest station for questionin', Mr. Ingliss."

"You *bloody* fool! Wha' abou' the rights o' those idiots plannin' ta storm the estate?" Roan hissed. "Lannie's ou' o' control! He'll no' hesitate to protect what's his!"

A look of skepticism marred the detective's face. "Yer're referrin' ta the infamous Lachlan Baird?"

Roan's face grew dark with anger. "Don't mock me, you bloody ass!"

"Yer're drunk, Mr. Ingliss."

Roan released a boom of a laugh. "No' drunk enough! Lannie's as real as you or me. An' if you find tha' tae much for yer poor mind ta grasp, listen oop!

"I'm the reincarnation o' Robert Ingliss, the mon who walled oop the poor bastard after his wife plunged his dagger inta his heart!" He staggered toward the exit, flinging over his shoulder, "An' that's why tis *ma* responsibility ta stop ma mates 'fore tis tae late!"

Winston Ian Connery exchanged a harried look with the pub owner, then headed out of the building after Roan.

Thirteen

The scotch and ale Roan had consumed made it almost impossible for him to keep his footing on the slick ground. Fear alone kept him going, kept him scrambling back onto his feet. He was aware of the detective staying close at his side, but his main focus was riveted on the cars and trucks lining the driveway.

The silence terrified him more than anything else.

What would prompt a mob—especially a superstition-driven mob—to be quiet?

Cresting the hill and rounding the rhododendron hedge, he blinked repeatedly at the immobile figures gathered by the carriage house. Bent like an ape to accommodate his aching muscles and poor balance, he forced himself to keep moving, his brain seemingly afire with his efforts to rationalize the scene.

The detective tightly grasped Roan's upper arm, forcing him to halt. Roan gingerly straightened and was about to warn the man to release him when his vision zoomed in on Lachlan. It took another second before the actual scene penetrated his alcohol-induced stupor.

"Laura," he wheezed, violently wrenching his arm free of the cinching fingers. He staggered closer, his eyes widening in sick horror, his jaw slack. The detective remained at his side, his hands nested within the deep pockets of his trench coat. Snow flurries began to fall. Large, virginal and downy flakes. Roan teetered to a stop, the toe of his boots within inches of Laura's still body.

The instant the detective saw the dagger protruding from the woman's chest, he reached into the breast of his coat and removed a slim-line mobile phone. Tersely, he explained the situation, and requested an ambulance. He replaced the instrument, grateful that he'd already called in for backup.

Despair seeped into his awareness, despair emanating from Roan Ingliss.

"Laura," Roan whimpered. Tottering on his feet, he took a step back, then dropped to his knees.

Lachlan's dark eyes, surprisingly misted with tears, searched Roan's ashen face. "She jumped in front o' me," he said, his tone riddled with perplexity.

The detective went down on one knee, reached out, and pressed his fingertips to a spot below her jaw. "She's alive, but her pulse is verra weak. An ambulance is on the way."

"Laura," Roan choked, his trembling hands held out. "Why, Lannie? Is this wha' you've been waitin' for?"

Lannie?

The detective drew back, his penetrating gaze watching the man who held the woman in his arms.

"Na, Roan. The dagger came ou' o' the crowd. She was suddenly in front o' me. I couldna stop i' from happenin'!"

Roan quaked with raw grief. Rage boiled up from the pit of his stomach until he was compelled to throw back his head and release a heart-wrenching wail.

"Roan," Lachlan rasped, "listen ta—"

With the speed of lightning, Roan clutched the front of Lachlan's shirt and shook him. His teeth locked and bared, he cried from the deepest depths of his anguish, "Tak i' from her body an' put i' in *ma* heart!"

Horrified, Lachlan shrank back.

"Do i', mon!" Roan wept, his fists trembling. "You have the power. Send us off thegither!"

"The boys," rasped a weak voice.

Roan leaned back on his folded legs. Tears wet his face, blurred his vision so that he could only hazily make out Laura's pain-racked beautiful eyes staring up at him.

"The boys," she repeated, an edge of desperation in her tone.

"She should lie quiet," the detective advised.

"Roan—" She coughed, and a whimper of pain escaped her.

"Don't talk, Laura-lass."

"Promise me . . . Roan . . . you'll—" She clenched her teeth against the agony radiating through her, then forced herself to complete, "—take care of the boys."

"There's plenty o' time—" Roan desperately met Lachlan's somber gaze before going on. "I promise you, love. I'll tak care o' you all."

Laura eased her head to the right, and stared up into Lachlan's features. "I couldn't let the . . . dagger hurt you . . . again."

"I loved you, Tessa," the laird said huskily.

"I know. *We* . . . know. I'm . . . sor- . . ." She closed her eyes for a moment. "Sor . . . ry. Lachlan . . . forgive us."

Her eyelids closed, and she went limp.

Liquid warmth spread through Lachlan. The rage that had fed the curse, floated out of him, freeing him of its ugly weightiness. At that moment, he felt more alive than he ever had in either of his existences. Alive, and powerful with the grace of forgiveness.

Without thought as to how Roan would react, he pulled the dagger free of Laura's body.

Roan gasped, his horrified gaze riveted on the weapon. "Use i'!" he cried to Lachlan. "Damn you, *you pathetic auld mon,* end i', *now!"*

Simultaneously, Lachlan removed his left arm from beneath Laura, and placed the dagger on the ground with his right hand. "I've tauld you, laddie, i' buggers me ta na end whan you call me *auld."*

His right hand shot out, cinching Roan's left wrist. His left hand deftly opened the front of Laura's coat. With inhuman strength, he forced Roan's balled hand to press atop the bloodied breast of the woman lying between them.

The detective recoiled, with his hand flattened across his mouth. Nothing in his extensive training had prepared him for this.

In the distance, sirens lanced the night.

Help was at last on its way.

Lachlan smiled. His mischievous eyes swept over Roan's livid countenance. "Do you believe in the magic o' love, laddie?"

"Yer're insane," Roan sobbed, the blood beneath his hand seeming to sear his flesh.

"Do you believe?"

Roan became aware of a strange tingling in his fist. He breathed in hoarse spurts, his heart thundering behind his chest. Desperation and a hint of hope, softened his eyes. "Aye. *Aye,* I *believe!"*

"You've got ta believe you both deserve ta live, Roan."

Roan couldn't tear his gaze from the dark, mesmerizing eyes in front of him. His chin quivering, he shamefully stated, "I buried you alive . . . in the tower."

"A wee part o' you did. But then was then, an' now is

now. It'll tak us both ta give her a spark o' life. Understand, laddie? We *both*."

The sirens cut at the edge of the property. Bobbies stormed through the hedges and made their way to the front of the house. Conscious of their arrival, Winston Connery rose to his feet and, with his identification raised for those approaching to see, he held out his other arm in a warning for them to stay back. All the while he observed the strange scene of the two men and the woman, he was conscious of electricity charging the air.

Something miraculous was about to unfold.

Roan trembled uncontrollably. "How?" he whispered.

"Open oop, mon. Yer're questionin' ma motives."

"Na."

"Yer distrust is keepin' ou' the magic. Roan . . . dinna lie ta yerself."

Squeezing his eyes shut, Roan tried to clear his mind of its burgeoning guilt. Then a thought struck him. Breathlessly, he asked the laird, "Whan did you first know I was Robert?"

A smile of satisfaction softened the lines of Lachlan's mouth. "O'er ma grandfaither's scotch."

Roan bewilderingly searched Laura's peaceful face before meeting Lachlan's gaze. "Tha' long? An' yet you . . ."

"Aye. Now we're cookin', laddie."

The tingling in Roan's hand intensified. Hope swelled within his heart. "You made me yer heir."

"Yer're the closest thin' ta a son I'll e'er know."

"Despite . . . ?"

"The heart speaks louder than the tongue," Lachlan said sagely, his eyes seeming to possess firelight within their enigmatic depths. "An' you know in tha' bloody big heart o' yers, you've purged the weakness tha' companioned you whan you walled me oop."

"Aye. I'm no' tha' mon, Lannie," Roan said in a barely audible voice. "An' Laura's heart is guid, tae. We're no' the same as we were back then.

Liquid warmth gushed through Roan's veins. "We're free."

Lachlan released a thin sigh of relief, and nodded.

"Free," Roan repeated, staring lovingly down at Laura. "Can you hear me, lass? We're *free!*"

A moan of ecstasy rumbled deep within Lachlan's chest. The power of his soul was magnifying and ebbing outward to Roan, seeking to bond them spiritually. Roan, too, experienced the waves of raw electricity crashing through his body, submerging his brain in a boundless plane of awareness. Blindly, he reached out with his right hand. Lachlan eagerly clasped it, soaking in the natural warmth it offered. Both men closed their eyes, breathing sparingly in perfect rhythm with each other.

Unbeknown to them, a luminescent green mist materialized around them, pulsating in rhythm with Roan's heartbeat. The bobbies fanned out. Their billy clubs were held out as a barrier to keep back the awestruck spectators trying to edge closer to the scene.

Detective Connery hesitantly reached out to touch the strange mist. The instant he made contact, he felt every nerve in his body sing. Stunned by the euphoric feeling throbbing through him, he jerked back, keeping his hands tightly pressed against his midriff.

Roan felt exquisite pain rip through him. An electrical spasm rocked him. Then the pain concentrated within his chest, shot down his left arm and flowed through his fist. A shudder coursed through him, a shudder not unlike a fierce orgasm. Despite the wintry night, perspiration beaded his brow and the space between his nose and upper lip. The cords in his broad neck stood out.

A hoarse cry escaped Lachlan as he was propelled back on his butt by a whiplash of electricity. Roan was struck a second later. His back hit the ground.

The mist vaporized.

Murmurs rose among the onlookers.

Fighting against the tides of weakness washing through him, Roan rolled over and got onto his hands and knees. He crawled the short way back to Laura's side. Breathing heavily, he looked up to see that Lachlan was wavering between solidity and translucence.

"Lannie."

The laird's head slowly lifted. A lopsided grin broke though his strained, gaunt features.

Roan looked down at Laura's face. At first he couldn't see any difference in her, then he saw her eyelids flutter.

"My God," he murmured repeatedly, nervously drawing her into his arms as he sat atop his folded legs. "Laura? Laura-lass, yer're back!"

Her eyelids lifted. Bewildered green eyes peered up at him.

With a burst of laughter, Roan rocked her against him, then lowered his head and kissed her deeply until he felt her hands push at his chest. He lifted his head. His sparkling, tear-filled eyes began hungrily taking in every contour of her face.

"I remember . . ." She reached beneath her sweater, to where the dagger had been. Smooth skin met her probing fingertips. "Roan . . . I don't—" Her gaze swerved to Lachlan. "—understand."

"We're free, Laura," Roan laughed unsteadily, his gratitude radiating from the look he passed to the laird.

"Why would you do this, Lachlan, after everything we did to you?"

Leaning over his legs, Lachlan wearily gave a shake of his head. "Weel, lass, I guess you caught me in a moment o' weakness. Speakin' o' which . . ." He grimaced as he stared through his fading, raised arm. "The grayness is beckonin'."

Sitting upright, Laura held out a hand to the laird. "Don't go yet, Lachlan. There's so much I want to say."

"It has all *been* said," he grinned.

"Detective!" one of the bobbies called.

Winston Connery frowned at a man standing on the wrong side of the barricade. He impatiently gestured for one of the bobbies to bring the man to him.

William Finney kept his head lowered, even when he was urged to stop within arm's reach of the detective.

"He claims to have thrown the dagger," the bobby announced, his narrowed gaze riveted on the man's profile.

Lachlan, Roan, and Laura got to their feet. Roan's arm swung protectively around her shoulders.

"What's yer name?"

The man's head came up. Large dark eyes stared at the detective from a sickly pallor. "Bill Finney."

"Mr. Finney, you claim ta have thrown tha' dagger a' this womon?"

Bill's despondent gaze cut briefly to Laura. "No' a' her, sir. I'd na intention o' throwin' i' at all, I swear!"

"It simply flew from yer hands, is tha' i'?"

Bill looked back at his mates, then at the detective. "This womon crowds next ta me, sir, an' puts the bloody thin' in ma hand. An' next I knew, I was throwin' i', but I swear, i' was against ma will!"

"Wha' did the womon look like?" Roan asked.

"An auld womon." Bill strained to search the faces in the crowd. "Auld, an' wearin' a long, dark, hooded cape." He turned to address the detective. It was then he spied the woman standing on the stoop. "There! She's right there!"

All eyes turned in her direction. Standing demurely, her hands clasped in front of her, Viola Cooke calmly regarded the faces of her peers.

"Miss Cooke?" Lachlan glided into a half turn. "Why wad *you* hand this mon tha' weapon?"

"To spend you of energy, of course." She walked toward Lachlan, leaving several feet between them.

"It was *you* I saw on the stairwell just before the fire," Laura cried out in accusation.

"You and Roan Ingliss have been a thorn in my side for far too long." Her hardened gaze targeted Lachlan. "My whole life has been spent preparing to join you. How *dare* you accept that Staples woman as your mate! I saved myself for you! All these long years. These cursed lonely, long years. And what did I get for my devotion, my loyalty? *Old and shriveled!*"

"I didna know," Lachlan murmured.

"It's all been for *you,* Master Baird. Borgie . . . Agnes. These two *murderers*—" She glared at Roan and Laura. "—had you not interfered! They all hurt you." Her gaze softened on Lachlan. "I alone have loved you. I *died* for you, Lachlan Baird."

"Mother o' God," the detective gasped, recognizing her as the corpse that had been found that afternoon.

Mindless of him, she went on, "I dug my own grave, set the house on fire, then covered myself in snow and waited for death. It took so very long, my dear Lachlan. So very long. I nearly lost my courage. I had to keep reminding myself that I *had* to die here in order to remain with you. It's all been . . . for you."

"The boys!" Laura cried, remembering that Viola had taken them for the night.

The faded blue eyes cast Laura a hateful look, then once again softened on the laird. "I can give you something that whore can never give you, Lachlan. Can Beth give you sons? Three magnificent sons?"

Realization staggered the laird's reasoning.

"We'll be a family," Viola sang out, her arms opened to the night.

"Where are the lads?" Lachlan asked in a strangled voice.

Tipping her head to one side, Viola sighed, "Preparing, my love. You can't stop me. You haven't the power left. Be patient. All will soon be right."

No sooner had she finished, than a series of explosions detonated within the house. Screams razored the air. Bodies scurried to find shelter from flying rock, mortar, and wood. Roan, clutching Laura's hand, pulled her into a run out of the blast area.

The explosions continued for what seemed an eternity. Lachlan and Viola stood their ground, staring at one another, his expression one of stark desolation, hers one of utter triumph.

Hunkered by the rhododendrons alongside Roan and Laura, the detective stared at the flames billowing out from the window portals as if observing fire for the first time in his life. The element seemed to possess infinite rage, lapping furiously at the night, reaching out far beyond what remained of the exterior walls.

Laura wept hard, her face buried against Roan's chest, who refused to believe that the boys had been caught in the inferno. Long minutes passed. The sirens of the fire brigade closed in.

All the while, Lachlan stood numbly amid chunks of fallen wall, staring at the woman across from him. It all made sense now. She'd been the one who had flung Borgie from the window. She'd been the one to provoke Laura's memories, to deliver the dagger to Edinburgh.

Yes, he'd known about that, but only from Laura's thoughts after her return.

He'd been blinded to Viola's purpose all these years.

She was indeed powerful. He could sense it, feel its pulsing force. But it was an evil power, one born to destroy and breed misery.

The flames quieted within the structure. Tunnels of black smoke rose into the air. The explosions were done. Morbid peace blanketed the grounds.

"Come boys," she joyously called out, her arms held out toward the house. "We're a family now."

Rage filled Laura. Shoving herself away from Roan, she jumped to her feet and ran toward Viola. But before she reached her, the woman whirled about. The fiery malignant look in the blue eyes stopped Laura in her tracks.

Roan came up behind Laura, and anchored his hands on her shoulders. "You'll no' get away wi' this!" he swore to Viola, trembling with frustration and anger combined. "They were innocent children!"

"What is innocence, but a condition by which to be led?" she flung scathingly. "You had the audacity to think *you* could take over this house—become master of it!" She laughed, but the sound held no mirth. "I am the mistress of Baird House, and no one shall ever claim it from me!"

"Tis Baird/Ingliss land, an' will be for as long as this earth exists," came a strong voice from out of the night.

"Aggie!" Roan cried, his gaze searching for her.

Winston Connery edged closer to Roan and Laura. His incredulous gaze was also sweeping his surroundings. He was beginning to wonder if this was ghosts' "old home" week, although he still couldn't accept that this Aggie was the same Agnes Ingliss who had died a few days ago.

"Aggie!" Roan cried out again.

From around the west end of the house, Agnes urged the boys toward the awaiting group. Half the distance away, the boys took off in a run, flinging themselves into Laura and Roan's waiting arms. Agnes, her stride slow yet purposeful, brought herself to stand between the reunited family and Viola's deepening wrath.

"The lads remain wi' the livin'," she said regally, her cold blue eyes boring into Viola's livid face. "I removed them from the house before the gizmos you left behind went off. An' I plan ta protect them inta their auld age, you sarry *bitch!*"

"You don't belong here!" Viola hissed.

"Tis because I've been connected ta this place sa long, is why I'm here." Her gaze cut to Lachlan, who stood in the distance. "Ma apologies for thinkin' i' was *you* who done me in. Least i' gave me the strength ta remain till I learned the truth."

Arching a path around Viola, Lachlan came to Agnes's side. On impulse, he swept up her wrinkled hand and pressed his lips to its cool back. When he straightened, his expression was one of sheer gratitude. "Yer death saddened me," he said, with a telltale crack in his voice.

"Aye, I'm sure i' did. You thought you'd lost yer sparrin' partner."

Again on impulse, Lachlan wrapped his translucent arms about the thin figure and hugged her. Tears filled Agnes's eyes. After a moment, she returned the embrace, although it was difficult for her to fully grasp his semi-solidity.

"Have you forgotten about me?" Viola shrieked.

Everyone's attention riveted on her hostile stance.

"I am here to stay!"

In the blink of an eye, Beth materialized behind the woman. Her arms swiftly wrapped about the cloaked form and, to insure her hold, she cocooned the woman in a psychic mesh.

Viola raged. Calmly, Beth took a moment to observe the boys and the couple coddling them, then she looked at Lachlan and offered a sad smile.

"I love you."

Her words stabbed him in his pseudo-heart.

"Beth, you canna—"

"There's no other way," she said, her voice cracking with emotion.

Her eyes closed briefly. When she opened them, a single tear spilled down her cheek. A strong breeze came from out of nowhere and swept around her and her violently squirming captive. "I love you," she repeated to Lachlan. Then she soared upward, carrying Viola into the sky, higher and higher, until she'd become but a speck among the grayness.

Lachlan alone saw a light appear in the heavens. He felt its attraction, but resisted with all the willpower he had left. Despite the vast distance, he saw Beth soar into the light with Viola, until the mysterious opening closed its door.

A sob escaped him. He sank to his knees, his face lifted

to the sky. The greatest emptiness he'd ever known was threatening to overpower him.

"Lannie, wha' happened?" asked Roan, crouching in front of the laird.

"She's passed on," Lachlan rasped.

"She'll come ba—"

Lachlan shook his head. "There's na comin' back from tha' place. She did i' ta assure Viola couldna return. Ma Beth. Ma sweet Beth . . ."

Roan looked up to find his aunt staring at the laird with deep sympathy. A mixture of warming emotions filled him. It had been a night he would never forget. Glancing at the spectators trying to inch past the wall of bobbies, he knew Baird House had given birth to new stories which would roll off the tongues of Scotsmen for generations to come.

A small hand rested on his shoulder. "Roan, tis time you an' Laura teuk the lads home. They've had a tryin' night."

Rising to his feet, Roan timidly touched his fingertips to his aunt's cool, wrinkled cheek. "We'd thought yer heart had failed, Aggie."

"A pillow o'er ma face did the trick," she said airily. "Dinna grieve. I've ne'er felt better in ma—oops, ne'er mind."

Lachlan rose, but his usual exuberance was missing from his bearing. "Aggie, may I a word wi' you?"

She walked several feet away, Lachlan following.

Roan grinned down at Laura, whose eyes smiled adoringly at him from her kneeling position with the boys.

"Mr. Ingliss."

Winston Connery stopped Roan from returning to Laura. Facing the man, he arched a challenging eyebrow.

The detective released a controlled breath, and shrugged

his broad shoulders. "I wonder if you have a suggestion on how I should write this report?"

A brief laugh escaped Roan before he could curb it. "I'm afraid I can't help you there." He glanced behind him at the house. "'Tis a magical place, this Baird House. Put tha' in yer report, detective."

"Roan?"

Agnes returned to his side and linked her arm through his. Lachlan stood behind her, an enigmatic gleam in his eyes.

"I'll be stayin' on here. For a time."

"Can't you come home?"

She nodded happily. "I could, but I've things ta do here, Roan. You'll understand, in time. Go home now."

Roan looked at Lachlan, a wavering sigh passing his lips. "Is there anythin' I can do for you?"

"Na. Aggie an' I . . . weel, we have a lot ta talk abou'."

Laura prompted her nephews to walk to the foursome. Kevin, his eyes bright with wonder, smiled up at Agnes.

"You look pretty good for bein' dead," he quipped.

"Someone was kind enough ta dress me in ma favorite Sunday frock," she said brightly, her hands smoothing the front of the navy blue dress with its lace bib. "But enough abou' me, ma lads. You sleep tonight, an' dream guid dreams. There's naught ta fear na mair. You have ma word on tha'."

"Vi was the bad man," Kahl said dully.

"Aye." Bending over, Agnes placed a kiss on each boy's brow. "I love you, lads." Straightening, she sighed wistfully. "An' I'm countin' on you three ta help ma Roan an' yer aunt ta mak you all a fine family."

"We'll be good," Alby promised sleepily.

"Not too good," Laura said with a soft laugh. "I've gotten used to a little excitement in my life."

"A little?" Roan shook his head, then held out his hand to Laura. His strong fingers clasped her hand. He tugged her to him and deeply, although briefly, kissed her. "I see I've ma wark cut ou' for me."

"You have no idea," she grinned mischievously.

"I'd like ta mak an announcement 'fore I completely fade," Lachlan said, his voice carrying in all directions of his property. "Christmas Eve, abou' ten, yer're all invited ta gather here wi' yer families. I've a few words ta say 'fore I leave this warld, an' I promise a gift yer sarry eyes will no' soon forget."

He disappeared.

A hush fell over the people. Snow fell more rapidly now. Wet, large flakes were clinging to everything they touched. Little by little, the crowd dispersed. Cars and trucks slowly left the driveway. The bobbies remained until the last spectator had left, then they joined the firemen, who had been unable to get close enough to the house to use their equipment. But it didn't matter. The flames were nearly gone. There was nothing left within the structure except charred mortar, stone, glass, and metal.

The detective eyed the house for some time after everyone else had left. He'd heard tales of the house and laird since his boyhood, and had thought them just that . . . tales. A practical man trained to respond to reason and not matters of the heart or imagination, he wondered how he would feel about his experience this night, come the cold daylight of morning.

He was scheduled to fly to Paris, early in the morning on the twenty-fourth. He was half-tempted to cancel that flight.

"*A gift yer sarry eyes will no' soon forget,*" the laird had promised.

It was tempting to stay and witness such a gift, but the detective had things to do and people to see.

What kind of *magic* would Lachlan Baird perform on Christmas Eve?

It certainly couldn't be anything more miraculous than bringing a woman back to life!

Shrugging deeper into his coat and turning up the collar, he turned away from the house and headed in the direction of his car.

Fatigue was slowing her movements by the time Laura quietly closed the boys' bedroom door and padded into Roan's bedroom. She regarded him sadly. He sat on the edge of the bed, his head lowered into his hands. Although the room was chilly, he wore nothing but white boxer shorts.

"Can I fix you some tea?"

He looked up and smiled tiredly, then patted the mattress beside him. Laura sat and cuddled close to him, her right hand rubbing his hairy chest. She sighed contentedly. For the first time in her life, she felt lighthearted. Unburdened. She drew up and folded her semi-bare legs atop the mattress, and nestled her temple against the bulging bicep of his right arm.

"I guess the reporters have finally given up. It's quiet in the neighborhood."

"Two days o' dodgin' the bloody lot is mair than enough. But we're part o' the miracle, aren't we?" He sighed. "They'll hound us till they get their interviews."

"How are you holding up?"

"Me?" He chuckled softly, draping an arm across her back. "God, lass, *you* died. I can hardly believe yer here wi' me now."

"You can't get rid of me that easily."

"Tis no' funny, Laura," he rasped. Propping up her chin with a bent finger, he stared forlornly into her emerald eyes. "I was ne'er so frightened in ma life."

Laura straightened back, then playfully nipped his shoulder. But when she spoke, her words and tone were undeniably serious. "In the eighteen-hundreds, I loved you more than anything in that world. I love you even more now, Roan. This time, no one will be sacrificed. Our love will remain pure and strong, and it will bond our family like no other.

"I promise you my loyalty and devotion; my love until the end of time. And I promise you happiness and peace."

Tears threatened to fill his eyes. "I love you. I've been such a bastard."

"No, Roan. You were only standing up to the Tessa flashbacks I was experiencing. But it's all in the past. We've been given a second chance. And Roan . . . I don't intend to screw it up.

"Let the reporters have their *bloody* story. We've nothing to hide anymore. I don't care if the whole world knows what it took to bring us back together. Isn't magic something we should share?"

With a groan, he turned and wrapped his other arm about her, holding her tightly against him.

"I love you so much, i' scares the hell ou' o' me."

"Tis a womon's way ta keep her mon," she said teasingly.

Her hands dipped beneath his arms and glided up his bare muscular back until her fingers hooked onto his broad shoulders.

"Is it my imagination, or has it been forever since we made love?" she whispered by his ear.

Grinning, he rubbed his chin along her jawline. "Are you tryin' ta seduce me, *Miss* Bennett?"

"Are all Scotsmen so slow to catch on?" she chuckled, closing her eyes to the bliss of him caressing her skin.

"Slow, eh?"

His hands slipped beneath her long pullover sweater. She gasped in surprise when the coldness of his skin brushed against her midriff. Her nipples became rigid buds against his massaging palms. Shivers coursed through her body, rapidly followed by searing ignitions of delight. She moaned deep in her throat. Her breasts swelled within his cupped hands.

He robbed her of breath when he gently fastened his teeth on the side of her neck. His tongue sensuously stroked her soft skin, provoking a flame of desire to awaken in the heart of her groin.

Laura wanted to melt into him. She clung to him, relishing his firm, powerful body, inhaling his musky scent. Her eyes rolled behind her closed lids. She remembered their years of lovemaking in their former life. He'd been a wonderful lover then, undeniably superior now. He owned the ability to bare her soul with his mere glance, his mere touch. A liberated modern woman might mock the idea of *belonging* to any man, but she did belong to Roan, heart, mind, and spirit.

His mouth covered hers, at first kissing her in a teasing, tentative manner. She played along, although secretly wanting him to kiss her senseless. His kiss finally deepened. But it didn't last long. With a husky groan, he pulled her onto his lap, then rolled over until she was stretched beneath him. His mouth sought hers again, awarding her such pleasure she thought her heart would explode behind her aching breasts. His erection pressed against the side of her outer thigh. When he began to gently rub himself against her, an almost painful tightening gripped her low in her abdomen.

Breathing heavily, he trailed his mouth along her cheek, down her neck, all the while, his hands slipping her sweater up to expose her breasts. Her muscles grew taut with desire when his lips encircled her left nipple and began to suckle in a slow, taunting manner. She arched her back, compelled to urge him to suck harder. Her chest ached with each hoarse breath she drew.

"Oh, God," she wheezed, her eyes closing amid an expression of blissful torment. Perspiration broke out on her smooth, flushed brow. Her teeth locked, and she arched higher while her left hand cupped his nape and drew him closer. His teeth nipped. She jerked with a spasm of pleasure. When his tongue began to slowly adore her, incendiary pulses coursed through her veins, burst within her brain.

Cocooned in mounting, mindless ecstasy, she stretched her arms above her head and squirmed beneath his ministrations.

Her fingers were clutching and unclutching the quilt beneath her, when Laura parted her legs in invitation. His caresses gradually worked their way to the moist cavity of her womanhood. Pleasure rippled along her flesh, sang within her heart, and cushioned her brain in a boundless haze. His mouth left her breast, his tongue went sweeping down her belly. An orgasm caught her unaware. The force of it made her cry out. Her body quaked. She tried to turn away from his wondrous strokes, but he wouldn't permit her to deny him this pleasure.

She opened her eyes and stared pleadingly at him. He

watched her expression with glowing satisfaction, and when he was sure she'd reached her maximum tolerance, he removed his hand and hastened out of his shorts.

Laura decided it was time *she* took control. Sitting up, she took him by the shoulders and shoved him onto his back. Then she straddled his lower torso, seductively slipped her sweater over her head, and flung it aside.

"You play dirty, *Mr.* Ingliss."

"I do, eh? Am I ta be tortured?" he grinned.

Placing her hands on his shoulders, she lowered herself and kissed him passionately. When she sensed he was beginning to lose himself to it, she straightened. She stared into his passion-glazed eyes for a long moment. Then she raked her fingernails gently down his chest just hard enough to awaken every nerve in his body. When she reached the plateau of his rib cage, he attempted to snare her wrists. Instead, she cinched his arms and, smiling wickedly, coaxed his hands above his head. Anchoring his wrists, she bent low and nipped at his left earlobe. He squirmed beneath her. She nibbled and stroked with her tongue, delighting when his body tensed with desire. She was forced to release his wrists when she slid down his body, exploring as she went.

She tested his tolerance for what seemed a month of forevers. Stroking his chest, his thighs, his hips, and teasingly, his manhood. A sheen of perspiration covered his face, neck, and chest. His body temperature rose higher and higher. His heart hammered against the inside wall of his chest.

"Laura-lass," he said through clenched teeth. "I'm sufficiently primed, thank you."

She arched an eyebrow, devilishly questioning his statement.

In a voice husky and raw with sensuality, she said, "Tell me what you want, Roan Ingliss."

His hands readily gripped her hips and urged her up from his lap. He stopped there, his eyes relaying what more he desired of her. A soft glow bathed her features. What he wanted, she wanted to give him. She reached for him. He quivered. Exquisite, rapturelike torment masked his face. Her fingers curled around his erection, holding it in place while she eased herself down onto it.

The instant he entered her, a moan rattled within his chest. She enveloped him slowly, lowering herself a little bit at a time, torturing him with anticipation. His strong fingers kneaded her thighs. His hips thrust upward. Bliss impaled her, sweeping her into its promising embrace. They were alone in the world. Two lost souls who had found each other. Two reborn souls capable of offering their partner a plane of ecstasy few could even imagine, let alone experience.

Their awareness became one. Their search for gratification, one. In perfect rhythm, their minds and bodies in perfect synchrony, they strove toward their united goal. Gradually, they climbed the craggy face of the mountain of rapture, their psyches locked onto the memories of their other life in each other's arms.

The spell was temporarily broken when Roan sat up, and lowered her onto her back. Her arms circled his neck. He kissed her hungrily then, pinning her wrists to the mattress above her head, he began full, controlled thrusts into her body, all the while staring deeply into her eyes.

The first ignition of a climax took control of them. Thrusting to meet its force, they tensed in anticipation. Laura first, then Roan a moment later, they gave themselves over to the sheer pleasure of it. Roan collapsed atop her, his face buried at the side of her neck, in a damp nest of her blond hair.

Wallowing in the aftermath of the experience, Laura stared unseeingly up at the ceiling. She was completely exhausted, but never more content than she was now. Her arms weakly folded across his back. Her breaths came in short spurts between her parted lips.

"Damn me, tha' was a quicky," he grunted, easing some of his weight off her.

Laura rolled her eyes, then released a short laugh. "I don't think I could survive a *prolonged* version of this."

Propping himself up on his elbows, Roan blinked down at her. "Anythin' short o' two hoors is unmonly."

She glanced at the digital clock on the nightstand. "We began this shortly after eight." She grinned up at him. "It's nearly ten-thirty, my lustful Scot."

Roan eyed the clock for several seconds before muttering, "Damn me, I'm guid."

"You're *something*," she chuckled, stroking his jawline with the back of her fingers. "Since you seem to be so full of yourself, how about fixing us something to eat? I'm about starved."

Groaning, he buried his face to the side of her head again.

"A little energy goes a long way," she cooed suggestively.

With that incentive, he sprang from the bed, and ran out of the room.

Laura languidly drew the quilt around her cooling body, and curled into a fetal position. She watched the doorway, waiting for him, knowing that when he returned, he would be wearing nothing but a disarming, utterly charming grin.

True to character, he appeared in the doorway, the grin

in place, his arms laden with plates and bowls of food and snacks.

A wistful sigh passed her lips.

It was going to be a very long night.

But a night, she knew, of countless pleasures.

Nudging the door closed with a heel, Roan approached the bed. "There's enough calories here ta spark a new record for us, Laura-lass."

Laura dubiously arched her eyebrows. Exactly what did he mean by a *new* record?

"At least three hours," he boasted, easing his armload onto the bed. "Maybe four," he added jubilantly.

In response, Laura pulled the quilt over her head.

Fourteen

Laura didn't want to wake up. The bed was warm and cozy, compliments of the homemade quilts, and Roan's body spooned behind her. She reluctantly cracked open her eyelids to find the room bathed in bright grey light. Morning had come too soon, but she could hear the boys giggling somewhere in the house, and knew she had to get up.

Roan's arm was draped across her middle, the hand cupping her right breast. A lazy smile spread across her pouty lips. He had to be exhausted. She certainly was!

Easing his arm off her, she did her best to slip from beneath the covers without waking him. But before she could lower her feet to the floor, his eyes shot open.

"What's wrong?"

"It's morning. The boys are awake."

Groaning, he rolled onto his back and rubbed his closed eyelids with his balled hands. Laura watched him dreamily. Reddish-gold stubble blanketed his lower face. He yawned and stretched his arms, linked the fingers of his hands, turned his palms upward, and cracked and popped his joints. Then he scratched his hair-covered chest while working his mouth to alleviate its dryness.

"You're not a pretty sight in the morning," she said, straining not to laugh.

His bloodshot eyes swung to her, and he grinned sleepily. "You wore me ou', womon."

Leaving the bed, she went to the chair in the corner and picked up her robe. She put it on. Her good-natured glance narrowed on him. "Go back to sleep."

Roan's gaze lazily swept the length of her. "I've a better idea," he grinned mischievously. He patted the mattress where she'd been lying. "Come ta bed, darlin'."

A shiver of delight passed beneath her skin. "You're insatiable."

"Aye, an' bloody ready ta start the day off right."

"The boys—"

"Can haud their ain for a wee longer."

A squeal of glee came from the parlor. With a glance at Roan, she headed for the door. "On second thought, Mr. Horny Toad, I think you should get up and fix breakfast."

Sitting up, Roan ran his hand up and down his scruffy face. "You do, do you?"

"Aye, lover," she chuckled, and opened the door.

She closed it behind her, frowning at the gleeful, shrill sounds the boys were making. Her hands smoothed down her hair, and then tightened the belt of her robe as she crossed the small hall into the parlor. She expected to find the tree toppled over and the colorful wrapping paper on the gifts shredded and strewn across the room. What she did find caused her to stop in midstride and place a hand over her heart.

In the middle of the room, Lachlan Baird sat bent over his crossed legs, his arms covering his head to protect him from the boys, who were excitedly jumping atop and over him. Alby dropped to his knees, snorted like a bull, and rammed his head into the laird's side. Then he squealed when Lachlan's long arm shot out and captured him, and hauled him across his lap.

Kahl released a long-winded grunt, folded his hands over his chest, and pretended to fall dead against Lachlan's back.

"You little buggers!" he laughed, straightening his spine and making a feeble attempt to capture all three within his arms. Kevin foiled the plan. He flipped himself over Lachlan's broad shoulder, forcing the ghost to catch him lest he fall on top of his youngest brother. Lachlan's revenge was to cradle the boy in his arms, and vibrate his lips against Kevin's exposed midriff. Kevin's laugh nearly pierced Laura's eardrums, prompting her to end the rough play.

"Okay, boys! That's enough!"

Four pairs of eyes turned in her direction. A laugh escaped her before she could suppress it. What a sight! Lachlan—his hair in wild disarray, his white, poofy-sleeved shirt torn in strips at his shoulder— peered up at her amidst a sea of pajama-clad, spindly legs and arms, draped all over him.

"Alby, Kevin, Kahl," she said, forcing her tone to sound stern. "Get up off of Mr. Baird. *Now.*"

Grumbling beneath his breath, Kevin got to his feet and helped his brothers up. "I told you she was a poop sometimes," he said to Lachlan.

Releasing a breath through pursed lips, Lachlan rose and haphazardly attempted to straighten his shirt. "Now, lad, you show yer aunt her due respect."

Kevin grimaced, then poutingly offered, "I'm sorry, Aunt Laura."

"It's not our fault if Lannie's more fun than you are," Kahl said in earnest.

A grin strained to form on Laura's lips. "No . . . no, I guess it isn't. Have you three brushed your teeth?"

"Aw, nuts!" Kevin fumed. "My teeth ain't gritty yet!"

Lachlan spared Laura a bemused look before turning his attention to the oldest boy. "Weel, now, Kevin, you just put a nasty taste in ma mouth. Yer're no' settin' a guid example for yer brithers. Now run along an' help them tend ta their wee mouths."

Kevin eyed the towering man, then leveled a comical look on his aunt. "I love the way he says *brithers*. Yo, *brithers,* follow me to the can. Hep hep hep hep . . ."

The three of them, single file, marched past Laura to the bathroom.

Her gaze was sparkling with laughter, as she faced the laird. "You're very good with children."

Suddenly self-conscious, the tall, strapping laird made a bid to comb his fingers through his shoulder-length, snarled hair. A moment later, he lowered his hands to his sides and offered a halfhearted grin. "I hope you dinna mind me droppin' in sa unexpected."

Laura shook her head. "No. As a matter of fact, I'm glad for the chance to thank you again, you know . . . for bringing me back."

A sobering shadow crossed Lachlan's face. He clasped his hands behind him then, after several seconds of deep thought, he casually crossed the room, leaving what he believed to be a comfortable arm's length of distance between them, for her peace of mind. "Na thanks are needed, Tes—" He scowled, then tried to vanish it with a lopsided grin. "Laura," he amended almost shyly. "Yer return unburdened ma rage. I'm as grateful for wha' you've given me."

Laura studied his rugged, handsome face. A sliver of memory began surfacing from her former life. "You were a kind and overly generous husband, Lachlan. I wish . . . I wish I had been a different person back then."

"More like the womon 'fore me, now, eh?" he grinned in earnest. "I did a lot o' thinkin' between last night an' this morn. If things had been different back then, I wadna have ma Beth now, wad I?"

"Probably not. Are you really . . . leaving tonight?"

"Aye. I'm no' complete wi'ou' her. I'm sure you an' Roan feel the same abou' one anither."

Laura smiled sadly. "We do."

"Wha' is i' like, havin' the memory o' anither life?"

She sighed deeply and took a moment to think about her reply. "At first it was scary and . . . unbelievable. Now it feels kind of . . . normal." She smiled. "Not bad for someone who didn't even believe in ghosts before coming to Scotland."

Lachlan's gaze caressed her features. "I wish all the best for you an' Roan. An' those lads. They're fine lads, Laura. Real fine."

"They are. They're going to miss you."

"They'll have Aggie—ooh, by the way, lass, I hope yer're no' opposed to her grannyin' the lads. She'll be a fine nanny, I can promise you."

His revelation took her aback, but she quickly recovered. "Will she be able to . . . be like you and Beth?"

"Appear *real,* you mean? Aye. She's already taught herself the way."

A fluttering sensation passed through her stomach. "I like Agnes. The boys adore her. And of course Roan . . ." She sighed again. "We'd love to have her with us."

"As i' should be," he murmured, an enigmatic gleam in his eyes.

Roan came waltzing in from the bedroom, with a heavy

blue robe carelessly tied about his middle. Mindless of his guest, he pirouetted toward Laura. His eyes were closed, his lips pursed for a kiss. Laura clamped a hand over her mouth to prevent herself from laughing out loud. He turned one last time, then leaned in her direction and smacked his lips.

"Give us a pree, lover."

A squeak of mirth escaped from her. Roan lifted his eyelids, spied a tall figure standing to his left, and released a startled gasp. Wide-eyed with embarrassment, he faced the laird.

Lachlan airily raked a glance over Roan. "Yer're a sight for dead eyes," he dryly quipped, although amusement glowed in his eyes.

"I'll leave you two alone," Laura chuckled, and headed for the bathroom.

Roan watched until she disappeared from sight then, absently ruffling the hair covering the top of his head, turned a sheepish grin on Lachlan. "Guid morn ta you, tae."

"Can you mak a decent cup o' tea, laddie?"

Roan grimaced. "I hate bein' called *laddie*, abou' as much as you hate me callin' you *auld*."

Lachlan laughed. Clapping Roan on the shoulder, he turned him around and led him toward the kitchen. "I wanted a few words wi' you 'fore tonight."

They crossed into the kitchen. Roan gestured for the laird to sit at the medium-sized, old oak table, while he went to the stove and took the kettle in hand. At the sink, half-filling the copper-bottomed vessel, he said over his shoulder, "I expected Aggie ta show oop."

"She's a' the house."

Shutting off the tap, Roan arched a questioning brow. "Is she comin' home?"

"I'm no' sure."

While Roan placed the kettle on the stove and turned on the gas beneath it, Lachlan inspected an antique salt and pepper set.

"Do you remember those?" Roan asked, seating himself across from the laird.

"Aye." A wistful expression softened his features. "Mary brought them for her mither—Christmas 1860, wasna i'?"

"Sometime aroond then."

"I was fond o' Mary. She looked like her mither, but she hadna Tessa's temper."

"One o' the stories passed down, was tha' you wad watch her play wi' her dolls in the attic. Tha' true?"

Nodding sadly, Lachlan returned the silver set to the center of the table. "Ma only regret . . . no' havin' wee ones ta carry on ma name." He grinned crookedly and met Roan's gaze. "Which is why I'm here."

Roan scratched the top of his head. "Ah, an' here I thought i' was because you missed me."

"Yer're feelin' verra guid this morn, eh?" Lachlan asked coyly.

"Aye."

"Beat yer record, did you?"

Crimson flooded Roan's face. "Wha'?"

"Dinna ruffle yer feathers, laddie," he laughed. "I popped in last night, hopin' we could have a wee visit. Soon as I heard you mention yer goal for the eve, weel . . . I left."

"Appreciate i'," Roan muttered.

"Weel?"

Roan regarded Lachlan's devilishly arched eyebrows, and scowled.

"I'm a wee curious," the laird grinned.

"Na. No' quite."

"You've years ta practice."

The fading blush darkened once again. "You came ta speak ta me abou' somethin' *specific,* didn't you?"

"Aye. Lovely shade, yer face," Lachlan chuckled, then visibly sobered. "Tis abou' ma home an' fortune. It remains yers."

Wryly, Roan nodded.

"I've recovered the jewels an' maist o' the money, Roan. I put them in a trunk in the cellar. Which reminds me—" He grinned. "—the scotch survived. Hardy stuff."

"Lannie . . ."

The kettle began to whistle. Jumping up from his chair, Roan remained thoughtfully quiet while he fixed two cups of tea. He returned to the table, placing one cup in front of Lachlan, and seated himself, avoiding the dark, probing gaze.

"Lannie, I'm no' tae keen on takin' yer money or home."

"Wha else is there for me ta leave ma treasures? Roan, lad, tis right you should have i' all. You've a family ta tak care o' now. Besides . . ." He took a long sip of his tea, wrinkled his nose, and went on, "I liked yer idea o' turnin' the place inta a retreat."

"I ne'er said—"

"It was on yer mind 'fore the first fire."

"Speakin' o' which . . ." Frowning, Roan despondently pushed his cup away. His gaze unseeingly leveled on the handle. After a moment, he placed his elbows on the table, and buried his face in his hands for several seconds longer. "Na one in these parts will lend a hand or back to help rebuild the house. This last . . . the floors are gone. I-I know you performed a miracle in front of a few . . . bringin'

Laura back ta me, but I talked ta a mate o' mine a' the pub yesterday, an' he said na one wants ta see the place restored.

"Lannie, they're just ordinary people. You an' the house represent their darkest fears. Wha' one person might consider a miracle, anither sees as somethin' evil."

"No' efter tonight," Lachlan said mysteriously.

Roan leaned back in his chair and warily eyed the man. "Wha' have you got planned?"

"If I tauld you, i' wadna be a surprise, wad i'?" he grinned. He sobered, locking gazes with his host. "One last promise, Roan Ingliss."

Sighing, Roan nodded.

"Accept ma gift."

"If i' means tha' much to you."

"It means the warld ta me."

"All right, then. Lannie, are you really goin' on tonight? You could stay—"

"No' wi'ou' Beth." Lachlan rose from his chair. "I've one last thin' ta get off ma chest."

Roan slowly cranked himself up onto his feet. "Sometimes, yer're a regular pain in the ass."

"Yer're playin' faither ta those lads now. Bahookie's a kinder word ta use around wee ones, laddie."

Roan laughed.

Despair shadowed the taller man's face. He looked away, then brought his dark eyes to meet Roan's. "There winna be time tonight for a proper guidbye," he said huskily, his expression trying to tell something to Roan that he couldn't grasp. "Despite oor history, I'll miss you."

Roan briefly looked off to one side. It was all he could do to hold back the emotions rising up inside him. "I'll miss you, tae. It'll be bloody quiet wi'ou' you poppin' in an' ou' o' ma life."

"Will you remember me kindly through the years?"

Despite his mental effort, a fine mist of tears sprang to Roan's eyes. He again looked away, but couldn't bring himself to say good-bye in this way. Meeting the laird's probing gaze, he managed a wavering smile.

"I'll make you anither promise, *auld* mon: I'll always carry you in ma heart."

A tense moment passed. Then, as if unable to contain himself, Lachlan whisked Roan into his arms and hugged him. A hoarse breath ejected from his phantom lungs. He drew back, exposing a tear escaping down his cheek before he began to fade.

"Thank you, laddie," he whispered, and vanished completely from sight.

Roan wasn't given the chance to recover his emotions. Laura entered the kitchen. He abruptly turned his back to her, and struggled to hold back the tears pressing at the back of his eyes.

"Roan, are you all right?"

"Right as rain," he tried to say cheerily, but his voice cracked.

"Where's Lachlan?"

"Gone." Heaving a fortifying breath, he walked to the sink, turned on the cold water tap, and brusquely cupped the liquid to his face. When the tap was turned off, he peered upward to see Laura's hand on the white porcelain handle.

"He upset you," she stated, running her fingers through the back of his hair.

Straightening, he braced his hands on the edge of the sink, and lowered his head. "No' the way you think. Damn me, Laura, I hate ta see him gae sa soon."

"I know," she said in a whisper.

Lifting his head, Roan gazed deeply into her eyes, compassionate eyes that told him she truly understood what he was feeling.

She rubbed his back between his shoulder blades, soothing his tensed muscles, his melancholy. "Did he happen to mention what he planned to do tonight?"

Roan shook his head.

"You're concerned, aren't you?"

"Ma gut's in knots. I don't know why."

"Does he still want you to rebuild the mansion?"

"Aye." Turning, he drew her into his arms. "You feel sa guid." He tightened his embrace, snuggling, molding her against him. Her face turned up, the pools of her emerald eyes capturing his attention. "Have I told you lately, yer're the maist beautiful womon e'er born?"

She wrinkled her nose at him. "I don't recall you ever saying anything like that."

"Hmmm. It must have slipped yer mind."

"I don't think so," she smiled. She glanced over at the stove. "I was expecting a four-course breakfast. How disappointing."

He playfully jiggled his sandy-blond eyebrows. "I'll make you a seven-course masterpiece if you promise ta sneak back ta bed wi' me whan the boys go doon for their nap."

Laura released a theatrical sigh. "If I must."

With a burst of laughter, Roan swooped her up into his arms. "You minx!"

"I told you," came a smug little voice, "they do it in the kitchen, too."

Roan's expression went deadpan as he lowered Laura to her feet, his gaze on the three boys standing by the doorway.

They looked like angels, their hair combed, their hands folded in front of them, smiles exposing their teeth.

"We do *wha'* in the kitchen?" he asked with a scowl.

"Bumpity bump bump bump," Kevin replied in a singsong manner. "Kahl owes me two pence."

"For what?" Laura asked, although dreading the answer.

Kevin pointed to Roan. "It was a sure bet you couldn't last *three* hours."

Laura and Roan rolled their eyes in unison, then looked at one another.

"We need a bigger house—wi' *solid* walls."

Laura regarded her nephews with an arched eyebrow. "Or earplugs for the little darlings."

"Perhaps a verra large spankin' stick," Roan added, gleefully eyeing the now-squirming boys. *"Verra* large, indeed."

"You wouldn't dare," Kevin challenged, backing through the doorway.

"I wouldn't, eh?"

Roan lunged for them, snatching Kahl and Alby in his arms in his pursuit of the oldest boy. By the time Laura walked to the parlor, Roan and her nephews were embroiled in a wrestling match on the couch, and Roan was trapped beneath the energetic trio piled on top of him.

Laura braced a shoulder to the wall and watched them for a time. A wistful, faraway smile graced her lips.

A daughter would be nice, she thought. *A little girl with Roan's eyes.*

A little blond daughter with Mary's sweet disposition.

Breath-robbing sorrow welled up in her from the ancient memory.

Mary Blossom Ingliss.

Tessa's first and most cherished daughter.

One spring rainy morning, Mary had left the house, and had never returned. The sixteen-year-old had vanished from the face of the earth and had never been heard from again.

The pain in Laura's heart felt very real, and very new. Tessa—Laura, herself, in some respect—had never recovered from the loss of her daughter. Her heart had sustained an open wound of unrelenting grief, until Tessa's body had at long last given out.

It occurred to Laura that she could search through the records—providing there were any—and try to unravel the mystery behind the young woman's disappearance.

Greater miracles had been accomplished since her arrival in Scotland.

No one could simply vanish without a trace. . . .

Winston Connery passed over the psychic beacon for the third time before coming to a stop. His hands in the pockets of his trench coat, he coldly stared down at a depression behind a group of large rocks. Although it was daylight, he could see the shimmering psychic energy print that had been left behind. He looked up. A strong image manifested in front of his mind's eye.

It was night. Late at night. A man lay on the ground by the house. A woman—the Bennett woman—was sitting beside the man. She held something in her hand—

Reaching out with his psychic sense, he zoomed his mind's eye on what she held.

The dagger he'd seen imbedded in her chest three days ago.

He watched in trained detachment as she sliced open her

palm with the edge of the weapon. Her expression, vacant yet deadly, sent a chill through him.

Why was she looking like that?

Had she been aware that she was being watched?

He sank to his knees at the very spot where a killer had knelt. His nostrils flared.

Focus, he counseled himself. He couldn't afford to assimilate the killer for too long. It had proven too costly in the past.

A killer had watched her. Winston experienced the killer's madness, his lust to overpower the woman.

Fear?

The killer known as the Phantom had experienced a rush of fear?

Fear of what?

Bolting upright, he clenched his fists within his pockets.

The images were gone. His reluctance to cling too tightly to the prints had caused him to fail once again.

Gazing across the massive remains of the building, he felt his heart rise into his throat.

Baird House held the answers. He didn't know why he was so sure.

If he hadn't thought to probe the back of the building the morning after the fire, he *would have* been on the plane to Paris.

He would have discovered that the lead had been false.

The Phantom was *here!*

Pulling up his collar over his red-rimmed ears, he walked back through the woods to where his car was parked on the street.

When he was out of sight, Agnes stepped in front of the second floor window, in the room Roan had used. Her frown deepened the crevices on her wrinkled brow, but deepening interest in the young stranger snapped in her eyes.

A psychic, she mused. No wonder she was having such a hard time reading his mind.

His personality was also a challenge. On the surface, he appeared controlled, but she had managed to decipher a fragment of his aura, and in that, had touched upon the thin shield which barely held back his darker side. Of course, she was just learning to use these mental powers. She could have misread him.

But she didn't think so.

He possessed a conflicting mixture of personalities and passions. Whether he realized it or not, he was in desperate need of help—exactly the kind of troubled soul that a place like Baird House could put on the mend.

A little love. A little hocus-pocus.

"You'll be back," she whispered through a knowing smile.

She vaporized and returned to the grayness to collect enough energy to see her through the "gift" Lachlan planned to offer that night. If he accomplished even half of what he'd sworn to her, it would be a night like no other in the world.

Fifteen

The greenish, luminescent mist surrounding Lachlan was all that lit the remains of the parlor. Agnes found him floating above the partially fire-gutted floor, in front of the barren fireplace, staring up at where Beth's portrait had been. She paused at the blackened door to observe him for a time. It still amazed her how *human* and *alive* he was. Too bad she'd had to die to completely banish the blinders she'd worn most of her life.

His sadness permeated the room. She sensed it as if she herself were experiencing it. She also felt his anxiety with leaving his home. Only his love for Beth Staples was giving him the strength to pass on into the unknown. She understood his doubts. What if there wasn't an actual state of existence beyond the light? He would not only lose his home, his Beth, but even his memories of her.

She couldn't imagine an existence without the companionship of memories. For that matter, she couldn't imagine a *non*existence at all!

Voices carried into the room from outside. Hours earlier, she'd stood in the tower and watched cars slowly passing by, and wondered just how many of the locals would find the courage to come to the estate.

"Are you aware o' the gatherin' ou' there?" she asked

Lachlan, pointing to the gaping holes where the windows had been.

It was several seconds before he turned his gaze to her. He nodded solemnly. "They're quiet eneuch."

Agnes folded her hands in front of her, her gaze flitting over his strong features. "You could always remain here. Yer're part o' this family, Lannie."

"Aye." A despondent smile tugged at his chiseled mouth as he looked up to where the portrait had been. "As much as I wad love ta watch the lads grow oop, I canna stay wi'ou' ma Beth. There's a fierce ache o' emptiness inside me. Fierce an' infinite, Aggie."

Agnes lowered her head. She understood what he was feeling. There was also emptiness yawning within her, an emptiness left since the loss of her son.

"Forgive me, Aggie," Lachlan said kindly. Her head came up, and he regarded her for a time. "I ne'er liked yer son, but he didna deserve ta die sa young."

Emotions threatened to close off her throat, but she none-theless managed, "He wasna always sa . . . difficult."

Lachlan gave a desolate shake of his head. "None o' us were perfect, were we?"

"Speak for yerself," she said airily, then sobered. "If you see him . . . ? Wad you tell him his mum is thinkin' o' him? Tell him . . . I love him?"

"Gladly, I will."

Sighing deeply, Agnes looked toward the south wall. Unseen waves' rippled across the room, signaling her awareness. "They're growin' restless."

Lachlan turned to face the direction. "Aye, but I'm waitin' for *him*."

Her eyebrows drew down in a frown. "He's a curious one, this Mr. Connery."

"Aye. Aye, he is. An' he's a troubled mon."

"Weel, he came ta the right place."

Lachlan smiled.

A ponderous expression accentuated the lines in Agnes's face. She tapped the first two fingers of her right hand to her chin for a time, then said distractedly, "I keep wonderin' how they're goin' ta react ta yer gift."

An enigmatic gleam manifested in Lachlan's dark eyes. "Maist will tak i' to heart."

Agnes arched a white eyebrow. "Wha' abou' the ithers? We're talkin' abou' some o' the same who were prepared ta level this place ta the ground."

After a second of silence, he shrugged. "Tis useless ta haud a grudge." He winked at her, grinning. "As weel as we now know, eh? They thought me responsible for Borgie's fall. Canna blame them. I was beginnin' ta wonder maself."

"But wha' if they construe the 'gift' as the deil's play?"

Again Lachlan fell silent. Then he frowned and replied, "Anyone wha can find darkness in a winter's rose, is beyond hope."

His inner sense locked onto a new arrival on the grounds, and he straightened with an air of exuberance. *"He's here. Fegs! The mon's aura is strong!"*

"I can feel i', tae!" she gasped, a hand over her phantom heart. "This is weird, Lannie, this *knowin'* business."

"You'll get used ta i'."

She chuckled. "Mind you, I'm no' complainin'!"

"Tis guid ta hear, you auld corbie."

Warmth spread through the woman's spectral being. A smile rejuvenated her visage, and she held out a crooked arm. "There was a time whan I fumed ta hear you call me such! Sa much has changed. Now . . . I wad be honored, Master Baird, sir, if you wad kindly escort me ta the gala."

"Ma pleasure," he said. Then he kissed her hand and linked his arm through hers.

Gliding across the floor, they passed into the hall, and headed in the direction of the front doors.

"Wha' the bloody . . ."

Winston Connery had been stunned to find a wall of people blocking the streets bordering the south and west property of the Baird estate. Never had he witnessed such a gathering, and hoped he never would again. Forced to back up and park two blocks away, he left his car, locked it, then sank his gloved hands deep within the pockets of his trench coat, and began his walk through the large, wet flakes beating down from the heavens. The bitter night air permeated his clothing, compounding his chill of trepidation. He'd nearly convinced himself to remain at the inn. Nearly. Something powerful had compelled him to return. Something he couldn't quite define.

His doubt intensified when he unwittingly began to pick up on the emotions and thoughts of the people he approached. It usually wasn't so easy, so overwhelmingly received. He raised his mental shields, blocking out what he could as he inched his way through the packed bodies. The going was slow, ridden with apologies and false smiles to the disgruntled people he pushed past.

Murmurs of *"the deil"* fell on his ears, inducing a perpetual scowl to darken his features.

The devil? Lachlan Baird?

The bloody hypocrites! They called him the deil, and yet they had packed themselves in like sardines in hopes of witnessing a spectacle.

When at last he'd made his way through the throng, he

was again stunned to discover the driveway lined with reporters from newspapers and television stations. Bright lights were trained on the ravaged facade of the house. Cameras were at ready. Men and women alike were jotting down notes, talking into microphones.

He ambled across the ice-crusted snow covering the south property. Ironically, only five people had ventured more than halfway across the front lawn. The rest kept back, afraid to venture too close to the *dreaded* grim manor.

Several yards away, he recognized the five as Roan Ingliss, Laura Bennett, and her three nephews, who were fidgeting beneath the blanket the couple had secured around them. Winston closed the distance. His expression was guarded when Roan turned to look at him. When he stopped at the man's side, he gave a brief nod of greeting. Roan's eyes, he noted with deepening unease, possessed an element of mistrust.

"Are you here on official business?" Roan asked.

Winston glanced down at the boys' upturned faces. Immediately he sensed their eagerness to cut loose, and he grinned despite his attempt to appear aloof. Then he met the woman's gaze. He liked her eyes. Friendly, yet dissecting. She was mentally questioning his reasons for coming. Roan, on the other hand, projected a curious aura of smugness. Winston couldn't shake the notion that—although it was impossible—Roan had been expecting him. Now how could the man know, when Winston hadn't decided until the last minute? Roan wasn't psychic.

Cursed place.

Winston received the thought, but didn't know from which of the spectators it had originated.

The crowd grew more restless with each passing second.

He didn't have to read their minds. Their nervous tension rippled through him, intensified his own case of the jitters.

He gratefully focused his attention on Laura and Roan as they protectively stepped in front of the boys when several of the reporters came toward them.

Winston stiffened. Roan was on the defensive. The man had a short temper. He didn't relax until the vibes emanating from the man lessened in strength. So Roan had a temper, but also steel-like control when necessary.

A barrage of questions pummeled the couple. Roan instinctively placed a protective arm around Laura's shoulders. For every question, he replied, "Na comment," but the undaunted reporters kept hammering at them.

Admiration for the man flooded Winston. He couldn't have projected a calmer front himself.

Kevin kicked one television newsman in the shins. Kahl and Alby were satisfied to throw snowballs. Their aim was somewhat off, but the activity was appeasing their mischievous personalities.

Winston further relaxed his guard. He opened his mind a little more, imbibing a small portion of Roan's emotions. The man was admirably protective of his new family. His love for the woman and the boys was so strong, Winston couldn't help but envy him. His gifts had never permitted him to openly love anyone. Not his family. Certainly not a woman. His job was his life.

His job didn't fear his abilities, it relied on them. He couldn't snuggle up to it, and it didn't wear a tantalizing scent, but then, it was incapable of shrinking away from him.

"Get tha' bloody thin' back!" Roan warned, an arm lifted to shield his eyes from the glare of a camera spotlight.

"You're frightening the children," Laura scolded the man whose shoulder bore the weight of the camcorder.

A cacophony of alarming sounds rose up from the crowd. The light of the camcorder swung away from the couple to the front of the house, mingling with the others trained on the mystical pair who emerged from the greenhouse.

Reflexly, Roan placed his hands on Kahl and Kevin's shoulders, anchoring them. Before Laura could grab Alby, he took off into a run, and didn't stop until Lachlan had caught him up into his arms. The sight of the ghost holding the child, quieted the onlookers. Winston found the scene oddly disquieting. Kevin and Kahl wrenched free, and ran to join their brother. Roan and Laura stayed rooted. His arm circled about her waist and held her close.

Winston mentally noted everything.

He'd never thought highly of human nature. He considered mankind the cruelest animal of all. Perhaps viewing countless corpses had hardened him. Perhaps he'd always been emotionally removed from his species.

But for the squeals of the boys, silence prevailed. The snow fell faster, glistening like jewels within the harsh lights flooding the focus area. Curiously, the media refrained from intruding while Agnes and Lachlan hugged and spoke with the children.

He'd never known a reporter to respect a private moment.

But this wasn't exactly private, was it? Lachlan was saying his good-byes to the children. Winston could feel the ghost's sadness. And Agnes . . .

The scowl returned to his face.

This latest ghost was nearly on the verge of tears.

Ghosts sobbed piteously haunting sounds. They rattled

chains. But he'd not once heard of one actually shedding a tear.

He found himself wishing to see one spill down her cheek.

Much to his disappointment, she held them back.

Lachlan urged the boys to join their guardians. When they were back with Laura and Roan, the laird heaved a breath and took a long hard look at the spectators. One cameraman started toward him, immediately backing up when the specter lifted a hand in warning.

A grin tugged at one corner of Winston's mouth. Lachlan's bearing alone demanded admiration. Regal. Confident. Lord of his kingdom.

Again, Lachlan swept a measuring gaze over the mass.

"He's waitin' for somethin'," Roan whispered to Laura, who nodded in agreement.

Winston agreed. Then the laird looked directly at him, and his insides knotted. Realization burst within his brain.

Yes, he'd been expected. The laird had *summoned* him. He wasn't sure if that pleased or unnerved him, but he couldn't stop himself from feeling awed by the ghost's incredible range of influence.

But why had he been summoned? Had everyone here—

No.

He'd been singled out.

Was it possible the laird knew of Winston's desperate need to believe in miracles? At this point in his life, a miracle was exactly what he needed to direct him away from the abysmal sense of helplessness that had been slowly suffocating him since his tracking of the Phantom had begun.

Even a small miracle would be welcomed. Anything that

would lighten his heart and restore his logic, without which, he was lost.

"Welcome ta ma home," Lachlan said, his voice carrying to the boundaries of his property. "I depart this night ta join ma Beth, but I couldna leave wi'ou' offerin' a gift ta those both for an' against ma existence."

Winston's heartbeat quickened. Damn if the laird wasn't reaching out, even to those who still marked him a devil.

"Tae many o' you fear me an' ma home," Lachlan went on. "You fear the unknown. But Roan Ingliss is now the master o' this grand place—" He cast a comical look over his shoulder, and amended, "—this *once* grand place, an' I ask you all ta respect him an' his plans for this land. An' I implore you ta open yer hearts ta wha' yer're abou' ta experience."

Anxious murmurs passed among the crowd.

Roan turned his head, and offered a mysterious smile to Winston. A shiver worked its way up Winston's spine.

Lachlan paused then, with a solemn shake of his head, he went on, "Baird House belongs ta lovers an' dreamers." His dark gaze settled on Roan's face, and a smile turned up the corners of his mouth. "Dusk 'fore dawn, laddie. Tis how i' should be."

He heaved another breath, one wavering with emotion. "It was once said tha' a mon shouldna love wha' canna love him back. Obviously, tha' person ne'er came ta ma home, for I have loved this place, an' i' *has* loved me in return. As i' will ma heirs, for as long as there is earth upon which it can stand."

His arms slowly lifted out from his sides, his palms facing the spectators.

"I'll no' be long, Beth," he murmured poignantly.

A second passed. Two. Three. The silence of the people

was thick, oppressive. No one moved. Anticipation crackled in the air.

A cramp in his hands made Winston realize that he had his fingers tightly crossed. Grateful that his pockets concealed what he considered a childish superstition, he breathed deeply through his nostrils and watched the two ghosts with deepening curiosity.

Then it began.

The artificial media lights inexplicably went dark.

Gasps and murmurs rose up among the crowd.

From the spot where Lachlan and Agnes stood, a ground-hugging mist, embedded with countless pulses of light, slowly began to sweep out in all directions. Cries rang out, but still no one moved.

The mist swept beneath the boys' feet, prompting them to jump up and down and revel in its uncanny warmth. Lovingly embracing one another, Roan and Laura stared down at it, their faces beaming with sheer delight. Then the mist rolled past Winston, throwing his psychic awareness into consternation. A thousand angelic voices sang within his skull. He felt as if his person and his soul were being caressed by caring hands, soothing away his fears, his secreted darkness, his *helplessness*. He turned to watch the mist roll toward the rhododendron hedge. Everyone the substance touched, became enraptured. The crowd moved closer across the lawn, while the collective media stood frozen in awe.

When every part of Baird land was covered with the mist, the substance brightened. Its soft yet brilliant glow bathed the property in ethereal light.

The snow and ice melted, then rapidly seeped into the ground. Almost immediately, buds formed on the various plants throughout the property. Leaves opened on the trees. Flowers blossomed.

Spring awakened in full glory.

Winston watched the spectators remove their winter gear, most draping their coats over their shoulders or arms, others dropping them to the ground. The people divided again and again, some migrating to the east gardens, some toward the back of the house, and others hovering by the hedges and the south gardens.

Winston's attention became riveted on the rose garden, where the vibrantly colored petals were beckoning him. His feet seemed to possess a mind of their own. He ambled to the spectacular display.

He found it impossible to breathe as he plucked a purple rose from its stem and placed it upon a leveled palm. A crystalline substance coated the edge of the petals. The sparkle mesmerized him. He felt as if he were soaring in the heavens, completely unburdened in mind and spirit.

A "gift" the laird had promised. The word was utterly unworthy of such a *ferlie,* a wonderment.

Tearing his gaze from the mysterious winter rose, he observed the others around him. Such joy permeated the air, he had to strongly resist a compulsion to tap into every nuance of it. Others came to the rose beds and plucked the blooms. He found it curious that the men and boys seemed content to merely stare at the petals in their hands, while the women and girls held them to their breasts and cheeks. Needing to set himself aside from those of his gender, he lifted the rose and brushed the soft petals against his lips.

An image swept across his mindscreen.

Rose laughing and dancing amid the flower beds, her light brown hair shining beneath a sunlit sky.

Rose. Named after Montrose, where she'd been found near-dead, in a deep grave.

Here was her salvation, and his one true hope of capturing the phantom. *Here* was the gateway to the future, a gateway promising an end to his relentless pursuit of the killer.

Blanketed in euphoria, he turned and made his way back toward the house. Roan, Laura and the boys were with Agnes and Lachlan, exchanging good-byes. For a moment, Winston thought himself an intruder. He glanced down at the rose, then looked up to find the laird's dark eyes seemingly staring into his soul.

"Bring her here," Lachlan said softly, reaching behind him and resting a palm to the glass of the greenhouse.

Winston couldn't respond. Dumbfounded, he could only stare at the laird. He was vaguely conscious of Laura and Roan watching him, vaguely conscious of the questions in their minds trying to invade his awareness.

"Tis time," Lachlan said to Roan.

Seconds passed. Somewhere in the night, church bells chimed the midnight hour.

Roan swallowed hard past the lump in his throat. He took a step back, then abruptly lunged forward and embraced the laird. It was brief. Lachlan was gripping Roan's arms and giving him a push away. But Roan reached out for Agnes, and hugged her dearly before he could bring himself to release her.

Tears welled in Winston's eyes. He couldn't remember the last time he'd even come close to having a good weep. It took all of his willpower now not to succumb. He backed away along with the boys, Roan, and Laura, his gaze never wavering from the laird's peaceful expression.

Something more was coming, but for the life of him, he

couldn't imagine anything more breathtaking than what had already occurred.

"Bring her here."

The laird *knew* about Rose! Perhaps he even knew the identity of the killer—

Unexpectedly, the image of Lachlan Baird became lost within a wide shaft of light—light so brilliant it should have blinded an onlooker, but didn't.

The phenomena remained poised for an indefinite time. Agnes faded into the house. Gradually, the visitors began to gather on the lawns. Watching. Waiting. Floral mementos were clutched in their hands.

"Guidbye you . . ." Roan's voice cracked. A tear escaped his control and trickled down his face. ". . . you *auld* fool," he completed through a smile laced with piercing sadness.

Sobbing, Laura buried her face against Roan's shoulder. The boys clung to their guardians' legs, their tear-filled eyes watching what had been the laird.

"For you, Roan an' Laura," came Lachlan's voice in a loud whisper. "Yer dawn has a' last come."

The shaft of light broadened in width and height, expanding until nothing could be seen of the house. Seconds passed, then the light began to pulse. A bright white heartbeat. Too soon for the spectators, the effulgence swept into the original shaft, and sailed upward, soared upward until, high in the night sky, it burst into a tiny star and vanished.

Winston fell to his knees. The euphoria had too suddenly deserted him, leaving him feeling unbearably empty. Lachlan Baird was gone. Vanished. He'd sensed a brief opening of something beyond the heavens and, for a split second, had sensed Beth Staples appearing in the portal.

Lachlan Baird had returned to her. Winston knew he should feel immense happiness for the spirits, but he couldn't deliver himself out of the depths of his own sense of loss.

"Are you all right, mon?"

He bewilderingly peered up into Roan's eyes. The concern in them snapped him from his stupor. He unsteadily got to his feet. After a moment to compose himself, he offered the couple a stilted nod of his head.

"Bring *who* here?"

Winston was spared answering Roan's question when a cry of glee razored the air.

"Aunt Laura!" Kevin gasped, pointing to the house.

Compliments of the glowing mist, everyone was able to view Baird House, restored in all its former glory, just as it had been prior to the fires. One by one, interior lights came on in all the rooms. Seconds after the attic was lit, Agnes stepped through the greenhouse door. Elation beamed on her face as she gestured widely for everyone to enter.

Roan took the lead. Laura, the boys, and Winston followed closely behind. Gradually, the others began to file in, their fears and superstitions temporarily relegated to a plane of lesser importance.

The mist remained during the tours into the wee hours of the morning. Every room was visited. Cameras flashed. Videotapes were filled. Agnes remained out of sight the entire time, patiently waiting until only Roan, Laura, and the boys remained. They found her in the parlor, sitting primly on one of the settees, her hands folded in her lap. A fire roared in the hearth, casting the room in golden-orange light.

Roan walked up to the coffee table and ran his fingers through his unruly hair. "Tis all here," he said incredu-

Mickee Madden

lously. "E'erythin'! E'erythin' Lannie owned has been restored!"

"Did you really believe he'd leave the place ravaged as i' was?" Agnes grinned. "The mon had class, ma lad. *Real* class."

Alby scampered onto the settee next to Agnes. A dreamy smile glowed on his face as he laid his head upon her lap. Agnes stroked his temple with her fingertips, looked up at Laura, and sighed contentedly.

"The lads must be exhausted. I believe their room is waitin' on them. Mind if I tuck them in?"

Kahl wound his arms around his aunt's leg. "I'm not tired," he pouted, then spoiled the declaration by yawning.

Kevin yawned and stretched out his arms. "I am. I'm pooped. C'mon, Kahl. Alby."

Sitting up, Alby tilted his head and searched Agnes's face for a long moment. "Are you gonna stay with us?"

"For a verra long time," she smiled.

"Are you our grandma now?"

"If you wish."

Alby grinned tiredly. "I wish . . . an' wish . . . an' wish."

Before her emotions could get the better of her, Agnes stood and held out her hand. Alby wasted no time. He slid off the settee, and eagerly clasped her fingers.

"I love you, Grandma Aggie," he murmured sleepily.

Agnes lifted him into her arms and lovingly kissed him on the cheek. "An' I love you." She looked at the other boys, her eyes misted with tears of happiness. "I love all ma laddies, wi' all ma heart."

"You still got one of those?" Kevin asked in earnest.

Roan laughed outright. Laura smiled and shook her head.

"Aye," Agnes chirped. "Now come along." Collecting

the older brothers, she herded them toward the hall. "In a few days, when all has settled doon, we'll have ta decide which rooms you'll want."

"You mean our *own* rooms?" Kahl asked through a yawn.

"Yer verra, verra own."

Laura stepped to Roan's side, and snuggled against him when his arm draped across her shoulders. They watched Agnes and the boys ascend the staircase. No sooner were they out of sight, than Laura turned into Roan's arms and laid her brow against his collarbone.

"If this is a dream, I don't want to wake up."

Smiling wearily, Roan tightened his embrace, molding her against his warm, rock-hard body. "Tis scary ta feel this guid."

"I know what you mean." Her fingers kneaded his back, and she languidly rubbed her brow against the blue plaid flannel of his shirt. "My brain and body can't tell whether they're exhausted or exhilarated."

Roan chuckled, then kissed the crown of her blond head.

"I just thought of something." Grinning crookedly, she looked up to stare deeply into his eyes. One of his eyebrows arched in anticipation of her next words. "The boys totally forgot that it's Christmas morning."

"Ah." Lifting a hand, Roan lazily brushed the back of his fingers across her cheek. "Sa did I.

"Wha' say you an' I gae back ta Aggie's for the tree, fixin's, an' the presents? It shouldn't tak but a couple o' hoors ta set e'erthin' oop here."

Resting her forearms atop his shoulders, she linked her fingers at his nape. "I'm ready for *anything,"* she grinned wickedly.

A gleam of mischief instantly danced in his eyes. "Anythin', eh?"

"Ab-so-lutely *anything.*"

Roan released a thready breath. "Ookay. Wha' abou' helpin' me ta turn this place inta a sanctuary—a refuge— for people tryin' ta find themselves?"

Laura whacked him on the chest. "I love the idea, but that's not what I—"

With a low laugh, he swept her into his arms and captured her mouth in a spine-melting kiss. He kissed her with the all the passion they'd shared in the past and in the present, kissed her like a man possessed to become one with his chosen and destined mate.

The past would never again rise up to haunt them. They were spiritually free to live and love, as no other couple had within the walls of Baird House.

Their time had at long last come full circle.

Reluctantly ending the kiss, Roan regarded the slightly swollen lips angled up at him. His heart skipped a beat. He stared into the emerald pools of her eyes and swallowed past the emotional lump rising in his throat.

"I love you, Laura-lass. Till ma dyin' breath, I swear I'll move heaven an' earth ta mak you happy."

"It's impossible for me to be any happier than I am right now. Roan . . . welcome home."

With a laugh, he lifted her into the air and spun around, then lowered her to her feet and kissed her deeply once again. As abruptly, he jumped back, took her by the hand, and pulled her toward the door to the hall.

"The faster we get back, the sooner we can settle inta oor bed!" He stopped short in the hall, spun her around again, and kissed her on the brow the instant he placed her on her feet. "The *master* bedroom!"

A mask of seriousness slipped over her face when Laura lifted a hand to quiet him. "Actually, Roan, maybe I should save myself until we're married."

His look of shock rapidly melted to one of devilishness. "O'er ma dead body," he chuckled. Ignoring her gasp, he swung her over his shoulder and marched toward the door.

Laughing, she managed, "Our coats!"

"Ha! All you need is *me* ta keep you warm."

The instant he carried her into the cold morning air, she gasped again. "Roan!"

"Yes, dear?" he crooned.

"Put me down."

He didn't stop until he'd reached the rental car parked by the carriage house.

Laughingly, she cried, "Did you hear me?"

Silence and his immobility followed.

"Ro—oan!"

He lowered her, a grin splitting his handsome face. "I was only practicin' ma soon-ta-be husbandly duty o' ignorin' ma womon."

"Oh . . . really?"

"Aye."

Reaching up, Laura pinched his earlobe. "Now listen up, wise guy. If you ignore me, *ever*, I promise I'll get even."

Roan feigned a fierce shudder, then laughed and pulled her into his arms.

Somewhere in the distance, multiple cries lanced the early morning peace.

"What the—!" Laura gasped, releasing Roan's earlobe and clinging tightly to him.

Roan dipped back his head and laughed. "Tis the return

o' the bloody peafowls!" His bright eyes searched Laura's flushed features. "Lannie said they'd come home."

A devilish gleam crept into Laura's eyes. "Maybe we can convince them to leave again."

Roan laughed low, and kissed the tip of her nose. "I don't think so. Do you still want yer coat, love?"

She regarded him for a long pensive moment. "I don't know." Standing on tiptoe, she linked her arms around his broad neck, and inched her mouth toward his. "Ask me again after you kiss my socks off."

"I had somethin' a wee mair personal in mind," he said huskily, then swept her into a kiss that promised to heat the marrow of their bones.

At the moment, their lives were consumed with their love for each other and the boys, and the wondrous gift of a second chance that Lachlan had bestowed on them. They had no way of knowing that in a few months, just when the media was winding down from the "Miracle of Baird House" hype, the manor would begin a new chapter of its own.

Indeed, the walls would become a sanctuary for the living who were lost and desperate, and also for the restless spirits searching for a gateway through which to reenter this world.

In time, the new master and mistress would come to realize that the manor, itself, was alive, and that it longed to possess a soul.

A seemingly impossible undertaking by human standards.

But any house worth its space, knows . . .

. . . *everything comes to those who wait.*

Be sure to watch for Mickee Madden's next book:

Written in the Stars

Coming soon from Pinnacle Books!